# Blind Chance

## Meryl Sawyer

A DELL BOOK

Published by
Dell Publishing
a division of
Bantam Doubleday Dell Publishing Group, Inc.
666 Fifth Avenue
New York, New York 10103

ISBN: 0-440-20446-1

Printed in the United States of America
Published simultaneously in Canada

August 1989

10 9 8 7 6 5 4 3 2

KRI

*For Jeffrey*

*The way to love anything is to
realize that it might be lost.*

G. K. CHESTERTON

# ON LOCATION:
## *The Sea of Cortéz*

# Chapter 1

"You may as well waltz into the director's trailer naked."

Alexa exhaled sharply and glanced down at her bikini — three triangles of red fabric held together by a snare of thin straps. She couldn't have had less on if she'd been in her underwear. "I've got a top in here somewhere." She dumped the notebooks and pens from her well-worn Louis Vuitton tote and retrieved a sheer cover-up from the bottom of the bag.

"That can't be all you have," Linda insisted in her well-modulated English accent.

"I've never needed anything more. I spend all day on the beach." She waved her hand at the stretch of white sand and the wind-ruffled water beyond. "I'll run over to the wardrobe trailer and get—"

"No." Linda shook her head, tossing her long, dark hair, her blue eyes incredulous. "We don't have time. It took me twenty minutes to find you. Everyone's waiting."

"I'll have to go into the meeting in this cover-up." Alexa flicked her foot at a small lizard skittering by. "These guys have seen women in a lot less," she added with a flippancy she didn't feel.

"They're in there," Linda said, indicating the director's spe-

cially equipped production trailer. "Let me take your bag."
She lifted the overloaded tote off the sand and slung it over
her shoulder, again wondering why the director had sent for
Alexa. Linda didn't have a clue, but she didn't like it. Ever
since they'd arrived in Mexico, things had gone wrong. Little
things at first, things that could easily be attributed to the
usual complications of setting up to film on location in an
isolated part of a foreign country. Lately, though, Linda had
begun to suspect the project was jinxed. Things went that
way sometimes. In the two years she'd been assisting on
Hunter films, she'd never seen it happen, but she'd heard
enough superstitious industry gossip to know that when
things got off to a bad start, they frequently didn't recover.
Was that happening now? For Alexa's sake, she hoped not.

"Catch you later," Alexa tossed over her shoulder.

Linda watched her friend walk away, thinking the men inside the trailer would have trouble focusing on the problem
once the scantily clad blonde joined them.

Stopping in front of the trailer, Alexa could hear men's
voices, raised and angry. She tapped on the trailer door, but
the voices continued their heated exchange. After taking a
deep breath she rapped on the door. This time the talking
ceased and the door swung open. A gust of arctic air greeted
Alexa as she entered the air-conditioned room. Their startled
expressions flustered her. Why hadn't she brought something
else to wear? She felt her neck and ears grow warm and knew
a dull red was creeping up beneath her tan. She scanned their
solemn faces and sought the director, Giles Acton, the only
one in the room she knew.

His elfin form slumped in the leather swivel chair, Giles
looked up from his desk and gave her a wry smile. With an
impatient gesture he ran his fingers through the corona of
tight gray ringlets covering his head. Thick black eyebrows
furrowed, accentuating his sharp brown eyes.

"Alexa, this is Steven Hunter from Hunter Films," Giles
said, introducing a man in his late thirties with a face that was
a sculptor's dream—blue eyes and ash-blond hair brushed
flawlessly across his forehead.

*Drop-dead good-looking,* she thought, reaching for his extended
hand.

His eyes swept over her in a calculated appraisal of what

the flimsy cover-up revealed. "Hello, luv. I've overlooked my duties as producer by not meeting you earlier. Your book's fabulous, luv. It's certain to make an Academy Award–winning picture."

Steven smiled at her with a grin guaranteed to shame the Cheshire cat's. Alexa realized fate had perfectly cast Steven Hunter, impeccable in his cream-colored Armani suit, as a movie producer. Until he'd spoken and she heard his accent as he punctuated every sentence with the word "luv," she'd never have guessed he was British. "Hello," Alexa replied, pulling the cover-up closer to her body.

"And Mark Kimbrough from Triad Investments. He's provided the financing for the film."

Alexa looked across the room to where Mark Kimbrough stood with his back braced against the wall. Their eyes met and his response to the introduction was an almost imperceptible nod. Mark's wintry gray eyes and hard, blunt features suggested an uncompromising nature. Unruly black hair and above-average height gave him a truly masculine appearance without being what Alexa would call handsome. She waited for him to speak. When he did not, she gave him a perfunctory smile.

"We're in a bloody mess here, Alexa." Weary lines had formed around Giles's eyes, intensifying his perpetually worried expression. "Melanie is having a bit of difficulty doing the seduction scene."

Alexa recognized the classic British understatement but wondered how she could help the director. She knew the production had been held up because Melanie Tarenholt's acting had been unable to satisfy Giles. But why had he sent for her?

"A fine English actor like Colin Avery should, with proper directing"—Steven paused and looked at Giles—"be able to carry someone less talented in such a short scene."

Giles's laugh was stilted. "Poppycock! Melanie can't act. Even Colin can't help her. She should stick to that silly soap opera on the telly." Under bushy, grizzled brows, his amber eyes rolled heavenward.

Alexa wound and unwound a strand of hair around her index finger. While they argued, apparently forgetting her, she remained silent, her thoughts racing. Mentally she reviewed the months she'd spent as story consultant. She'd

worked with the art director who'd meticulously constructed
the village and the costume designer who had painstakingly
re-created hundreds of period costumes. But the preproduction phase had long been over, and Alexa wouldn't be needed
unless someone wanted to verify some historical point. Why
had Giles sent for her now when they were embroiled in a
directing dispute? A tight knot in her chest, she sank into the
nearest chair.

Steven gave Mark a wary look. Everyone seemed to be
waiting for him to say something. His long legs were apart in
a slightly challenging stance. One arm held his sports coat
open; his hand was thrust into his trouser pocket. Even without speaking he had a certain brusqueness that intimidated
her.

"The point is"—Mark's cool voice was clipped with a British accent—"we have to work with this cast. I've put up over
eight million pounds re-creating this . . ." He paused and
waved his hand in disdain at the set. ". . . this nineteenth-
century Mexican village, not to mention the additional cost of
bringing the cast and crew to this Mexican backwater to film."

"This scene is essential to the story—" Alexa hesitated. She
silently reminded herself that she'd sold the film rights to her
book. She had no business interfering now. She was here as a
story consultant. Nothing more. "I don't want my novel
ruined," she finished weakly.

"Why all the fuss for such a small part?" Steven smiled at
her while his gaze slid from her eyes to her shoulders to her
breasts. "What will this scene be? A bit more than a walk-on
performance—less than five minutes' film time." He tossed his
blond head and shrugged. "Let's use some of the footage that
has already been shot."

Shocked, Alexa realized Steven Hunter couldn't possibly
have read her book or he'd know why this scene was vital. If
the producer didn't know, the way things were going *The Last
Chance* would be a terrible adaptation of her best-selling novel.
And she couldn't do a damn thing about it.

Giles drew his small frame up and addressed them. "My
reputation means too much to me to use what footage we
have now. I'd rather leave this scene out, but I know how
important it is. Before I let you cut it, I want Alexa to work
with Melanie."

This was so unexpected it took Alexa a minute to comprehend what he meant. "Me?"

"Perhaps a woman's perspective will help, particularly since you're the author." Giles came over to Alexa. "God knows nothing else has. We're so far behind schedule now that I'm going to cut this scene if she can't perform it properly."

"Ha-have you tried rewriting it? Perhaps Melanie doesn't—"

"Seven times. And we've shot around her as long as we can. We have to make our decision now."

"Jesus Christ!" Mark interrupted. "Do you expect her to do your job?" In two angry strides he was across the room and standing in front of the window overlooking the beach where the idle crew members were sunning themselves. "I want this settled. I haven't the time to let some twit who hasn't a thing better to do than to sunbathe the day away try her hand at directing. I have to leave in a few days."

Twit? Alexa swallowed hard, trying not to reveal her outrage. It took all her self-control not to tell him what an arrogant prick he was. Hadn't someone told him her job was over? "On call" for technical questions, she wasn't merely sunbathing. She spent the day on the beach writing.

"Mark," Steven said, his voice low, "I think we owe it to Giles to give this a try. Will it take long?"

"No," Giles responded calmly, apparently unscathed by the outburst. "We have Colin Avery standing by to play his part in this scene."

A swift tide of apprehension swept over Alexa. "I don't know if I can be of any help," she mumbled to Giles as he led her out of the trailer. She followed him through the encampment of light trucks, trailers, motor homes, and vans surrounding the newly constructed movie set. Finally they reached the thatched hut where they were set up to film the scene.

"I'll get Melanie," Giles said, leaving Alexa alone amid a tangle of electrical cables, cameras, sound equipment, and lights. She liked Giles and trusted him. He'd consulted her frequently, calling upon her knowledge of the obscure bit of English history that was the basis of the film. He'd tried to include her even though the thorough research of the art director and costume designer left little for her to do but rub-

ber-stamp their efforts. She wanted to help him if she could;
she just didn't see how.

Smiling, Colin Avery strolled into the hut, and Alexa returned his smile. Colin had to be one of the most endearing
men she'd ever met. He wore khaki shorts and a camp shirt
with epaulets and brass buttons. All he needed was a pith
helmet to look like a dashing version of a big-game hunter on
a safari in Africa instead of an actor on location in Mexico.

His flawless British stage voice conveyed disgust as he said,
"This is useless, you know." Colin's bright blue eyes surveyed
her and he shrugged, his chestnut hair shifting slightly. "It
won't do, not at all. Melanie simply cannot act. Soaps—that's
where she belongs. You know, you Americans aren't the only
ones with those tedious programs. We have them too."

"What do you think Steven will do if we can't help Melanie?"

"Nothing. Producer is just his title. He spends all of his time
shuttling the dailies to Los Angeles where his father makes all
the decisions."

"Nigel hasn't been around. Is that usual?" Alexa still wasn't
sure how the motion picture business worked. When she'd
negotiated the sale of her book to Hunter Films, she'd assumed Nigel Hunter would be the producer. He had yet to
appear. Instead there were numerous people, including his
son, Steven, running around with the title producer attached
to their names—line producers, coproducers, assistant producers, associate producers, and executive producers. Where in
hell was Nigel?

"Giles is the type of director who likes lots of freedom. He
and Nigel have had a number of successful motion pictures.
But the fact that Nigel's not been here at all is unusual."

Alexa kept her tone casual. "Do you know Mark Kimbrough, the major investor?" She was certain Colin must. An
English actor with superstar status, Colin seemed to know
everyone in British film circles. One of the few Americans on
the set, Alexa again felt at a disadvantage because she knew
almost no one.

Her question seemed to amuse Colin. "Most of the U.K.
knows Mark Kimbrough. He's what you Americans call a ty-
coon. Comes from a poor family but he's made a fortune in
real estate. Can't think of anyone I respect more."

"But he—" Alexa stopped when Giles returned with the actress.

Melanie Tarenholt wore a sheer white tube dress that looked as if she'd been spooned into it. Her long, platinum-blond hair hung in loose curls around her baby-doll face and, as always, she was enveloped in a cloud of sweet perfume. Alexa noticed Melanie's usual sultry pout was absent and her wide, baby-blue eyes were hostile. She didn't acknowledge Alexa or Colin. She stood off to one side, twirling a long-stemmed pink rose.

Colin arched one fine eyebrow and whispered to Alexa, "Melanie smells like the perfume counter at Harrods."

Alexa giggled but stopped abruptly when she saw Mark and Steven walk into the hut. Melanie's sultry pout returned and ignited into a welcoming smile directed at Mark. "Hello, Mark . . . Steven."

"Melanie." Alexa vied for her attention. "Come sit with me. Let's talk this scene through." Alexa sat in a director's chair and pulled her cover-up down, trying to make it conceal the tops of her thighs. She motioned for Melanie to take the seat beside her.

Flashing a flirtatious look at Mark, the buxom blonde ambled over and bounced down into the canvas chair. Melanie crossed her legs, idly swinging one foot and tapping her knee with the pink rose. A look of adolescent petulance replaced her pout. She refused to look at Alexa, staring beyond her instead at nothing in particular.

"Melanie," Alexa repeated, conscious that everyone was watching. "Your character, Pamela, knows she's lost the man she loves to another woman."

Melanie let out an audible sigh that sounded like a huff of disgust and shifted in her chair so that she no longer faced Alexa at all. Alexa continued, trying to retain her sense of professionalism. "Colin's character, Thomas, no longer wants Pamela." Alexa looked up and Mark's gray eyes unexpectedly met her gaze. She realized how trite and insipid this must sound to him. She rushed on, "Of course, your character is tenacious. She refuses to give up the man she loves. She has tried everything she can think of to get him back. Finally she decides her only chance is to lure him to her bed. In this scene she's filled with pain, not desire. Do you know what I mean?

Have you ever felt that way? . . . I have. I think most women have."

Alexa waited for a response. Still refusing to look at her, Melanie swung her foot faster. The once-perfect rose limply thudded against her knee. Frustrated at Melanie's attitude and her own inability to express herself, Alexa paused to catch her breath. Then a better way to explain the essence of the scene came to her. "The whole time she's seducing him," Alexa continued, "she's on the verge of tears because she knows it's hopeless. It's not a seduction so much as a desperate act." Alexa hesitated, startled at how poignantly she felt this. "Because in the end most women have only themselves with which to bargain."

Seconds passed while Alexa waited for Melanie to respond. Surely she understood it now, Alexa thought. Or was it just that, having been through something very similar, she had a unique empathy for the character?

"That's exactly how I played it," hissed Melanie, throwing a belligerent look at Giles.

Giles's tone was neutral, but his brown eyes snapped fire. "I want to see vulnerability and pain in this scene, not a laughing, cloying sex kitten." He turned to Alexa. "Could you and Colin show Melanie what we mean?"

"Show her?" Alexa repeated inanely. She never expected the stakes to change like this.

"Ridiculous!" huffed Melanie. "She's not an actress. I do seduction scenes all the time on television. I'm the best."

"This is bloody nonsense. Accept one of the takes you already have of this," Mark interjected, "or omit the scene entirely. Why waste time going over it *again?*" He deliberately emphasized the word "again."

Mark Kimbrough obviously disliked having his time wasted. He shook his head. Hopeless, his expression said. A smug look of triumph glowed on Melanie's baby-doll face.

"Alexa, give it a go," Giles asked, his eyes pleading with her.

Alexa knew they were at a stalemate now. If she couldn't help Melanie, Giles would have no choice but to cut the crucial scene. But how did Giles expect her to show Melanie anything? The woman considered herself above advice.

Colin took his position and gestured for Alexa to join him.

A circle of intense light hit them as the set was illuminated. Alexa's mouth went dry. Melanie was right—Alexa wasn't an actress. Suddenly she couldn't recall anything she'd written, much less how the screenwriter had adapted it.

"Relax," whispered Colin, his handsome face filled with concern. "Just improvise and I'll play along with you. It's the emotion they're looking for, not perfect dialogue."

Think of Paul, Alexa told herself. Remember how you felt when he left. You would have done anything to keep him. The suppressed hurt and bitterness from her divorce resurfaced once more. As she thought about Paul, haunting images unfurled, torturing her with a replay of her fight to retain his love. A futile fight.

Colin spoke first, beginning the scene for Alexa. She concentrated on the past—on Paul. She played the belittling scene —a slice of her own life—all over again, but this time she pleaded with an actor she hardly knew, not the man she'd loved for over ten years. She forgot everything as she slipped into the character she'd created. Tentatively Alexa began to seduce him. Like a siren, she taunted him with her body, urging him ever closer. After attempting to ignore her Colin's character responded to emotions too compelling to deny. In a gesture of exasperation mixed with tenderness, he pulled her to him and kissed her. The intimacy between them grew with each kiss. While Colin portrayed the lust his character experienced, Alexa balanced precariously on a razor's edge between passion and tears. As Colin's arms tightened possessively around Alexa, a sob rose in her throat and tears crested in her eyes.

Alexa didn't realize the scene was over until Colin offered her his handkerchief. She glanced up and her surroundings intruded with force. Immediately she became aware of the mechanical whir of the camera. *No one mentioned anything about filming this.* Startled, she realized there was total silence on the set, a deep, echoing silence like the unnatural quiet after a crack of thunder.

Uneasy, she sought the director, but Giles and Steven were hunched behind a camera. Her eyes met Mark's. Leaning nonchalantly against a camera, he was staring intently at her. Alexa spun around to face Colin. He stroked her hand and in his warm, blue eyes she saw astonishment and respect.

"That's what you want?" Melanie screeched at Giles. "Bugger-off!" She threw down the rose and flounced out of the hut.

Colin laughed soundlessly at Melanie's dramatic exit before saying, "You were bang-on."

Alexa looked at the men to gauge their reactions to Melanie's conduct. Off to one side the director and producer were still conferring in low voices. Mark stood transfixed beside the camera, his face expressionless, his gray eyes riveted on her. Alexa felt a deep flush warming her neck when, without warning, the lights clicked off, plunging the set into darkness. She blinked, trying to become accustomed to the lack of light.

Giles's voice sounded remote, disinterested. "Thanks, we have what we want."

# Chapter 2

Mark gazed out the airplane window at the barren land surrounding the Los Cabos Airport. Alexa, he grinned. Christ! What a surprise. He had expected the author of such an intellectual novel to be a frumpy middle-aged woman, not a blonde in her early thirties with vivid green eyes and a voluptuous body. No, he smiled to himself, he'd never expected Alexa. From the moment she'd entered the trailer, he'd had to force himself to look away.

Putting thoughts of Alexa aside, Mark stretched in the lounge-style seat, moving his long legs forward, thankful the Hunter Films private jet was a classic Lockheed Jetstar. Newer jets, like the Falcon 50, might be faster, but they sacrificed the spaciousness and headroom of the Jetstar. He sat on one side of the aisle, facing another seat separated by a drop-leaf table covered with paper work he'd earlier removed from his briefcase. Unable to concentrate, Mark glanced across the aisle at Steven and Giles, seated facing each other discussing the shooting schedule. The other four seats available on the plane were on the unoccupied plush gray sofa opposite the well-stocked bar and galley. In the rear of the plane a discreet door blended into the paneling, concealing the restroom and baggage compartment from the main cabin.

Preparing for takeoff, the plane lurched forward and trundled down the rough runway. Rows of cactus and scrub brush shot past the jet. It gained speed and finally lofted high above the Baja peninsula. As the jet circled around toward Los Angeles, a storm was brewing in the south. Dark clouds sulked in the distance; thin bands of lightning flickered on the horizon. When the plane completed the turn and climbed to its cruising altitude, a cloudless sky beckoned them north.

Another case of lust at first sight, Mark told himself, as thoughts of Alexa again surfaced. He wondered just what his chances were of getting her into bed in the few days remaining before he returned to London. Christ! There ought to be some payback for investing his money in this financial black hole. He silently cursed his own stupidity. No, he corrected himself, not stupidity—greed. Discontented with his considerable financial success, he'd wanted more. He thought he'd discovered a sure thing when he invested in a movie based on an international best seller and produced by a financially responsible film maker like Nigel Hunter. It had proven to be monetary quicksand.

Mark closed his eyes and reviewed his options. There weren't any. He couldn't withdraw from the film now. If he did, he'd be faced with a dead loss of money and reputation. The fact was, once the cameras rolled, independent producers had investors over the proverbial barrel. They had to pour money into the film until completion or have nothing to show for their investment. Losses, he reminded himself, were a necessary part of financial risk taking. Great fortunes were never made by pursuing a wholly conservative course. Yet he'd never suffered a severe financial setback, and he didn't want one now.

"It's going to cost too much to replace Melanie. Don't you agree, Mark?" Steven asked, raking his fingers through his expensively styled blond hair.

With difficulty Mark forced himself to respond to the question he'd already answered several times since they left Alexa and Colin. He glanced across the aisle to where Giles and Steven were seated and shook his head emphatically. "It will be worth it to get it right."

"You didn't think so when we flew down here." Steven's blue eyes narrowed.

"That was before I saw Alexa do the scene. It would cost too much to recast, but when we have someone who satisfies the director right there, it's the practical thing to do. Giles feels Alexa will perform the part better than Melanie, and I agree."

Mark barely suppressed his annoyance at Steven's inability to make a decision. He'd insisted on leaving the production with the secondary unit and dragging Giles back to L.A. to consult with his father, Nigel. Shit! What a waste of time and money. His money. Why the hell had Nigel made Steven producer if he didn't have the balls to make a simple decision like this one? Mark wished he had the authority to make the change, but he didn't. He was merely an investor.

"You thought Alexa was just another writer screaming about artistic integrity, correct?" asked Giles. The late afternoon sun sinking into the Pacific cast a crimson glow across the director's woolly gray head. He looked more relaxed, less worried than when Mark had arrived that morning.

"Something like that," Mark answered. Artistic integrity versus bottom-line reality had nothing to do with what he thought. He was still having difficulty adjusting his mental image of the author of *The Last Chance* with the woman he'd met.

"I knew. I knew. I've been behind a camera for twenty-five years. It loves Alexa. But the most important thing here is chemistry. Colin and Alexa have it. Couldn't you tell?"

"Absolutely," Mark replied. Together they had chemistry, all right. Alone, Alexa had sex appeal.

Steven stood up and walked over to the bar. "I just don't know what my father will say about Melanie's contract." He plinked two ice cubes into a tall tumbler and filled it with vodka. "Those contracts are tricky, you know."

Mark shrugged. What crap! The Hunter Films contract could easily be broken. Nigel Hunter was too savvy to box himself into a contract without a loophole. Steven kicked off his Ferragamo loafers and stretched out across the sofa. He smoothed his blond hair into place and took a long drink.

Mark looked out the window, rudely cutting off the conversation. He had no use for Steven Hunter. He was one of those men who relied on his father's name to magically open doors. If that didn't do the trick, Steven used his good looks to get him what he wanted. Mark had to admit Steven's little-boy smile enhanced his credibility, particularly with women. They looked into Steven's soulful blue eyes and fell for his bullshit.

There'd been a time, in his adolescence, when Mark had envied Steven Hunter. He seemed to have the two things Mark knew he'd never possess: striking good looks and a famous father. Now, looking back across all those years, Mark felt guilty. The fact his father had been a lorry driver rather than a well-known producer had been nothing to be ashamed of. A pang of sadness surged through him. If only his father had lived to share his success with him. But he was gone and there was nothing Mark could do about it, just as there was nothing he could do about his looks. Women never did obvious double takes over him the way Alexa had when introduced to Steven. It no longer mattered to Mark that he was considered merely average looking. He'd learned what counted was success. With money had come power and all the women he could ever want. It gave him immense satisfaction to know he'd done it all on his own.

Looking below, Mark saw the Pacific had claimed the sun, and deep shadows covered the uninhabited land. Melanie, he thought: overblown figure, phony blond hair, and ambition that exceeded her talent. Instantly Alexa's image replaced Melanie's. Alexa wasn't beautiful, but she had that quintessential California-girl appeal. More than that, she had talent and determination. Undoubtedly he'd alienated her, but he'd felt he was being practical and businesslike until he saw her perform. When he returned to Mexico he'd take a page out of Steven Hunter's book and turn on the charm with Alexa.

The perky, redheaded flight attendant emerged from the cockpit, where she'd been seated during takeoff, and asked, "May I bring you a drink?"

She asked them both the question, but Mark noticed she looked directly at him, giving him the same come-hither smile she had when they'd boarded.

"Glenlivet . . . neat," Giles said.

"Brandy and soda for me," Mark added, noting how her form-fitting gray tunic piped in burgundy matched the interior of the jet.

Giles moved across the aisle and took the seat facing Mark.

"I'm quite certain Nigel will approve this change, but I'm not so sure Alexa will agree to it."

Startled, Mark hadn't even considered this possibility. "Why not? Every woman wants to be a star."

Giles took a sip of the drink he'd just been handed before answering. "Not Alexa. I know, because she and my wife, Renata, have become quite close. Alexa's even friendlier with one of my assistants, Linda Carlisle. Do you know her?"

Mark accepted his brandy and soda, ignoring the way the attendant leaned forward, giving him ample opportunity to view her impressive cleavage.

"I've met Linda before . . . years ago." How could he forget her? Statuesque, blue-eyed, silky brown hair. A world-class heartbreaker. And Renata Tremaine—once the brightest star on the English stage. She was lucky now to get any work at all. Why would a successful director like Giles Acton marry an actress obviously bent on self-destruction? And what about Alexa? Overnight success, it seemed, had gone to her head, causing her to divorce her husband. Alexa MacKenzie was undoubtedly smitten with herself, and that thought irked him. He was attracted to her, but if he came to know her, he'd surely be disappointed. All things considered, they were a trio to avoid.

Giles interrupted his thoughts. "Alexa sees herself as a writer, not an actress. And she can be remarkably stubborn when she believes in something."

"Why did she insist on being story consultant? There's really nothing for her to do except watch."

The thought of paying the author of the novel to stand around and "consult" on sets and costumes when they already had entire departments to do just this irritated him. The whole world of film making had to be the most unbusinesslike industry he'd ever encountered. When he extricated himself from this financial quagmire, it would be a cold day in hell before he invested in the arts again.

"Alexa's a bit lost." Giles's amber eyes were mellow in the early evening light filtering through the small windows. He glanced over his shoulder at Steven, who'd consumed his drink and fallen asleep. "Her husband divorced her last year and it still has her rather upset."

Mark digested that information carefully. He'd noticed immediately she wasn't wearing a wedding band, and Steven had told him she was a divorcée. He'd assumed, apparently incorrectly, she'd shed her husband for a new career. From some distant part of his mind unbidden memories rushed back. Caroline—their divorce. He suppressed a sigh as the old sadness flowed through him. It always amazed him how all these years later Caroline could intrude on the present when he least expected.

"I take it Alexa was not the one who wanted the divorce?" Mark said, tentatively testing this new idea.

"No, she didn't even expect it."

Mark shook his head sympathetically. He hadn't expected it either.

"I don't think she wanted to be in Los Angeles after the divorce," Giles added. "But she found out how positively boring making a movie is. Hours of setup, makeup, early calls, hurry up and wait. You've got to be in love with it if you're going to enjoy the months of agony."

Mark nodded, knowing how Alexa felt. He'd been in Los Angeles for the past week trying to find out why there were so many delays in filming. After spending hours watching reels of jumbled daily footage, Mark had given up trying to understand the process. Apparently some witch doctor in the editing phase would perform the ultimate sorcery that would turn the thousands of feet of film into a motion picture.

"Alexa gave up and retreated to that beach of hers to write."

"Her beach?" When he had arrived early that morning, Mark had seen all the bodies strung out on the sand in front of the idle set. At the thought of that multitude lazing in the sun the churning in the pit of his stomach returned. With the movie stalled and runaway production costs, why did scores of people have nothing better to do than improve their tans?

"The steep ridge that runs down from the hills to the beach," Giles said. "Did you notice it?"

"Yes." Mark tried to relax, to forget the financial snarl this movie was in. "Lots of cactus and huge rocks."

"Alexa has made a trail over it to the cove on the other side. It's a bit of a trek. Only a few of us know she did it, so she has lots of privacy over there. Says she needs it to write."

Mark imagined Alexa on a deserted beach, her tanned body enticingly stretched across a towel. Inwardly he smiled.

"Alexa's writing a play for Renata." Giles became more animated. "It'll be her comeback. I know you're thinking that I don't want Alexa to become an actress, and that I want her to stay with the play because of Renata."

No, Mark thought, that wasn't my reaction at all. A play starring Renata would bring Alexa to London. A tremor of excitement ran through him until he remembered Renata's problem. "Well . . ." Mark chose his words carefully. "I was wondering if Renata's up to a play."

"Renata hasn't touched anything in over two years." Giles answered the unspoken question. "But it's impossible to get her work. I wouldn't agree to direct this film unless she was given a small part. I simply must rebuild her reputation."

Mark nodded. So that was how Renata had received her part. How had Melanie managed to land hers?

"Renata belongs on the stage." Giles's enthusiasm was obvious. "She'll be fine in her small role in this movie, but all her training has been in the theater. Her voice is too precise, her timing too dramatic for the best results in front of a camera."

Mark felt the plane descending. They must be nearing Los Angeles. "And Alexa?"

"A natural. The camera gets in close. It sees things in your eyes that aren't even visible in the front row of the theater."

Mark agreed. Her acting ability had taken him by surprise. Recalling what Giles had told him about her divorce, it occurred to him that perhaps it hadn't all been acting.

"I know how concerned you are about the cost overruns," Giles began, "and the impact they'll have on your investment."

Mark again nodded. "Concerned" was a complete understatement. "I knew it would be expensive to film entirely on location but . . ." He deliberately let his voice trail off. He wanted to hear what Giles had to say. So far all Mark's information had come to him from Nigel filtered through Steven. He didn't trust Steven. Never had, never would. When Mark had joint-ventured this film with Nigel Hunter, Steven had been working with Hunter Films' television subsidiary. If Mark had known Steven would be named producer on this film, Mark would never have given Nigel a pound. He'd as-

sumed Nigel, with his usual hands-on approach, would produce this himself. Never assume anything, Mark reminded
himself, never.

"Look, it's not unusual for a picture to experience problems
in the first days of a shoot. The cast and crew came from the
U.K., as you requested, but many of them had never worked
together before." Giles took another sip of his scotch. "Now,
they're functioning as a cohesive unit, the best I've ever
worked with. And this novel's the hottest property Nigel's
ever acquired. All Hollywood tried to talk Alexa MacKenzie
into filming her book, but it took a Brit to convince her."

Mark chuckled. He knew how Nigel had convinced her.
He'd also managed to persuade Mark he should invest in this
movie. So that honest, no-bullshit approach worked with
Alexa. He'd have to remember that.

"We'll be back on schedule as soon as we work out this final
snag. I want to make up the time, too. My profit points are
contingent on having this ready for a December release."

"I'm counting on it," Mark answered. A December release
date would qualify the film for the Academy Awards the following April. One or more awards, or even nominations,
would assure the film's returning the two and one half to
three times cost necessary to break even. It reassured Mark to
know Giles responded to the monetary rewards involved.
That would keep him actively trying to meet the deadlines
and forestall the continual cash drain. In all fairness Mark
knew much of the delay had been beyond the director's control. The production had been beset by bad weather, equipment failures, and problems with the local authorities.

In keeping with industry custom Giles was shooting out of
sequence, filming as rapidly as possible unrelated scenes using
the same sets. Secondary units were filming as well, shooting
scenery and water sequences. The earlier delays could be
overcome if this wrinkle with Melanie could be quickly resolved.

"Gentlemen," the attendant interrupted, "we'll be landing
in ten minutes." She walked toward her seat, turning her head
and flashing Mark another smile before disappearing into the
cockpit.

As they emerged from the jet and walked over to the private hangar where the Hunter Films jet was housed, a rush of

chilly air banished all memories of the warm Mexican sun. Waiting beside the building, an incandescent silver limousine caught the light of the gibbous moon. With a flourish the chauffeur swung the door open, and they climbed in. Gesturing to the sleek car phone, the chauffeur informed Steven he was to call Mexico immediately.

"What now?" asked Steven, waiting to be put through to Cabo San Lucas.

Mark adjusted his position to accommodate his legs. He watched Giles pour three drinks from the tiny bar tucked between the stereo speakers. The chauffeur kept accurate notes, Mark decided, noticing the bar contained Glenlivet scotch for Giles and Hennessy Extra for himself. Apparently Steven was drinking Absolut vodka these days, because a bottle of it sat in a tandem silver bucket alongside a bottle of Dom Perignon.

Steven had reached someone; he was listening intently and shaking his head. More bad news, Mark realized as Giles handed him his brandy and soda.

"The bloody bitch cut me off!" Anger distorted Steven's handsome features. "Operator! Operator! You cut me off in the middle of an important call." Steven covered the mouthpiece with his hand. "The Mexican police are searching the hotel where everyone is staying. . . . Yes, operator? Well, keep trying." He slammed the receiver into the cradle.

Pivoting in his seat, Steven faced Giles. "They have a reliable tip that drugs can be found in one of the rooms." His statement was really an accusation. "Do you realize they can shut down the whole production if they find anything?"

Giles's hand shook, causing the ice cubes to clink against the side of his glass. "I'm certain Renata's not involved."

Alexa scowled at the cockroach marching across the ceiling above her bed. These bugs seemed to be a fact of life in Mexico. The creature found a friend, and they danced an exotic jig. Disgusted, she checked her watch—eight o'clock. It was time to dress for dinner, but she was still exhausted. It had been useless to try to nap after doing that scene with Colin—too many memories. Paul's face came up on the screen in her mind. The still-open wound ached although the divorce had been final for months. She recalled with startling clarity their last night together.

For months their lovemaking had been off. Cold and detached, Paul performed mechanically. Attributing his attitude to the friction over the sale of the movie rights to her book, Alexa decided to smooth things over, to return their relationship to normal. After a protracted dinner at Spago, where Paul insisted they go so all Hollywood would know he negotiated the phenomenal sale of her book to the elite British film maker Nigel Hunter, Paul and Alexa returned to their Benedict Canyon home.

Alexa hung the filmy green Holly Harp gown she'd worn in her closet, noting how quickly Paul had shed his clothes and climbed into bed. "Don't go to sleep," she called across the room decorated in variegated shades of mauve. "Let's do a little private celebrating."

He didn't answer, but she went ahead and slipped into the black nightie he always found so sexy. She raced down the hall into the bar and retrieved the chilled bottle of Tattinger she'd earlier placed in the fridge. She popped the cork and grabbed two champagne flutes before returning to the bedroom and finding he'd turned the lights out.

"Darling," she called softly, but received no response. She placed the bottle and glasses on the nightstand. Placing her hand on his shoulder, she shook him gently.

"I'm tired," Paul mumbled.

Alexa sat there a moment wondering why he'd been so withdrawn all evening. Although he'd been friendly to the people who drifted by their table to say hello, he'd been even shorter with her than usual. Something was wrong—had been wrong for some time now. She refused to let it fester any longer. After she left on the talk show tour tomorrow, she wouldn't be home for weeks. She flicked on the bedside lamp.

"I want to know what's wrong. Why are you treating me like this?" She hated the childlike pleading she heard in her own voice.

Paul opened his brown eyes and scooted into a sitting position. Brushing back his blond hair, he said, "I want out."

"Out? A divorce?" He couldn't mean it. They'd had their disagreements. What couple didn't? But she always had given in to his demands. Even against her better judgment she'd sold the movie rights to her novel. The deal he insisted upon had just been signed two days ago.

"My attorney filed this morning."

"Why? Let's talk things over," she managed to say, still unable to believe what he'd told her.

Paul looked away, that bored, faintly disgusted look she'd seen too often lately on his face. She threw her arms around him, hugging him, begging him to give her another chance. Some primal instinct told her to use the one weapon Paul found irresistible—her body. If only he'd make love to her, they would be close again and he'd explain what she'd done wrong. Then she'd know what she needed to do to keep him.

She had no trouble arousing him, but he took her with such uncaring force that he left her bruised and sobbing. Minutes later she heard his Carrera screeching down the canyon, taking him out of her life forever.

No looking back, she told herself, watching the cockroaches scurry away. Concentrate on the future, on your career. You can't do anything about the past.

A loud banging sounded at her door, and Alexa swung to her feet. Barefoot, she padded across the cool Mexican tile and cautiously opened the door a crack. Outside a storm prepared to release its pent-up fury. The turbulence of the wind whipping through the palm trees made it like looking into a wind tunnel. Linda and Renata rushed past Alexa, slamming the door behind them.

"The police are on their way up here." Linda's words came out in a breathless rush.

"Tell them you're Melanie Tarenholt," Renata commanded, brushing her windblown red hair out of her blue eyes with a ring-spangled hand.

"What?" Alexa was thoroughly confused.

"Do you have any identification with your name and picture on it in here?" Linda asked, an anxious look on her face.

"No, why?" Alexa asked, becoming alarmed. "Remember, you took my tote before the meeting. It had my passport, wallet—everything. Where is it?"

"In my room." Linda raced over to Alexa's bureau and jerked open a drawer. "Pretend you're Melanie."

"Why?" Alexa demanded. Chills crept up the backs of her arms. "What are you looking for?"

"Drugs," Renata yelled from the dressing area and bathroom adjacent to the bedroom. She rifled through Alexa's closet. "The police will be here any minute."

"Stop!" Alexa demanded. "Tell me what's happening."

Linda stood close to Alexa and stared intently at her. "The police have a tip that you have a cache of cocaine in your room."

"Impossible," Alexa gasped. "You know I don't . . . I never—"

"In here," Renata signaled from the bathroom. "This is what they're after." She held up a plastic bag of white powder.

"That isn't mine," Alexa said, her voice barely above a whisper. "It wasn't there this morning!"

Renata dipped a finger into the bag and tasted its contents. She nodded, her spicy red hair bouncing off her shoulders. "Coke."

A loud pounding at the door was followed by shouts in Spanish. The only word Alexa understood was *policía*.

"Say you're Melanie," Linda whispered, heading toward the door. "Trust me. I'll explain later."

Alexa grasped Linda's arm. "Why? I haven't done anything. That bag isn't mine. This is just some crazy mistake. I'll explain it to them."

"Just a minute," Linda called out in an overbright, cheery voice. Unbuttoning her blouse and kicking off her sandals, she turned to Alexa, seeing her friend had no idea the trouble she was in. "For crissakes, this is Mexico. Don't you know what goes on down here?"

Mutely Alexa nodded. An image of a lifetime in a Mexican jail loomed ominously in her mind. Where in hell had that bag come from? How had it gotten in with her cosmetics, which were right on top of the counter where the police would have been certain to find them?

When Linda opened the door, four uniformed Mexican policemen, their guns drawn, bolted into Alexa's room.

"Alexa MacKenzie?" The captain demanded in heavily accented Spanish.

"No, I'm Linda Carlisle. What do you want?" Linda deliberately widened her blue eyes, hoping her face looked innocently concerned. She gave her unbuttoned blouse a nudge so it gaped open, revealing a sizable portion of her lacy bra and a full breast.

They gawked lecherously at Linda for a moment before the captain pivoted to confront Alexa. "Alexa MacKenzie?"

"Mel-Melanie Tarenholt," Alexa stammered. "Is there a problem?" She resisted the urge to clench her hands into tight fists to keep them from trembling.

With the barrel of his gun the captain waved Alexa aside. They marched toward the bathroom jabbering in Spanish. Suddenly Alexa became aware of the shower running. What on earth? Why would Renata choose now, of all times, to shower? Just as they started into the bathroom, someone banged on the front door. Linda jerked it opened. Colin Avery stood there. Above his head the lightning-streaked tops of the palm trees bent sideways in the wind.

"Melanie," Colin said, crossing the room and possessively slipping his arm around Alexa, "is there a bit of difficulty here?"

The captain holstered his gun and walked over to them. *"Señor* Avery." The captain grinned, showing stark white teeth beneath a pencil-thin black moustache. He bowed deferentially and enthusiastically shook Colin's extended hand. The other officers waited while Colin chatted companionably in fluent Spanish with the captain. Apparently Colin's status as an international superstar extended even to this remote part of Mexico.

"Melanie, love." Colin beamed at Alexa and drew her even closer. "The captain has graciously allowed us to keep our dinner engagement in town. They don't want you. They're looking for Alexa MacKenzie."

"But—" She couldn't leave them here like this. The instant the police found that bag, Linda and Renata would be arrested.

"Let's go. We're late." Colin gave the captain a man-to-man look as if to say, "Women."

Alexa retrieved her shoes from beside her bed. The muffled hiss of the shower continued. How could she walk out like this? Sooner or later they'd discover she wasn't Melanie and Colin would be arrested as well as Linda and Renata.

Colin's hand moved up her arm, his fingers clamping down tightly. He firmly guided Alexa to the door Linda held open.

Outside, the wind howled forlornly, and the black sky whirled. A slash of lightning flooded the room with a blinding violet-white glow. The lights flickered momentarily and then a deafening crack of thunder rocked the building.

Alexa turned and saw Renata's reflection in the full-length bathroom mirror. Droplets of water trickled down her magnificent breasts. Standing stock-still, Renata's expressive blue eyes were wide with surprise. She was absolutely naked in front of four leering policemen.

# Chapter 3

Mark attempted to ignore the tension in the car. He turned to Giles, who was staring out the window, apparently lost in thought. Steven's eyes were fixed on some distant object. Since last night's interrupted phone call they had been unable to get through to Mexico. Efforts to reach the hotel this morning had proved futile as well. Finally Mark had insisted they go ahead with their plans, meet with Nigel Hunter, and show him the footage they'd brought with them.

As the limousine serpentined its way up the curves of Coldwater Canyon, Mark looked out the tinted glass window at the pseudo-Tudor mansions with tennis courts in their front yards and gardens so carefully manicured that it appeared beauticians, not gardeners, tended them. At the summit of Mulholland Drive the car made a few lazy turns before it plunged down the other side of the hill into the smog of the San Fernando Valley. Gazing out at the cantilevered homes that covered the valley wall, Mark suddenly felt homesick. Seeing those unfamiliar structures, supported by stilts, he missed the old-world beauty of England.

In the cavernous silence of the car the gentle beep of the phone sounded unusually shrill. Giles flinched but his expression never changed. Steven grabbed the phone before it could ring again. With an exasperated sigh, he handed the receiver to Mark.

"Kimbrough here," Mark said, checking his watch and confirming it was early evening in London. They were working late again. More trouble? Just what he didn't need with all this delay on the film. His assistant, Ed Jenkins, explained another suspicious fire had halted construction on one of Mark's projects. As he listened, barely hearing the details, the nettlesome thought that had accompanied him for the past few months returned: His luck had run out. After years of working himself up from nothing and overcoming personal tragedy, his hand had gone cold. They were little things really, like this fire. None of them alone would have been cause for alarm, but a series of unexplained problems seemed to be dogging him, threatening to bring down his empire. He dismissed the thought as uncharacteristically negative. These events were coincidences. Anyway, it would take a catastrophe to ruin him. He'd reached the pinnacle of financial success, not by taking outrageous chances, but by assuming well-calculated risks. His financial base was secure; he had nothing to worry about.

Mark hung up the phone and directed his comments to Giles. "Just my London office. It's cold and windy." Mark had hoped to engage Giles in some light conversation, but Giles merely nodded and turned to look out the window again.

"Making another big deal?" Steven inquired.

"No, just working on a few details." Mark kept his answer noncommittal, trying to end the conversation there. He would never discuss his problems with Steven. Mark knew Steven was jealous of his success. They were the same age, thirty-eight, yet Mark, who had started with nothing, had made a fortune. Steven had gone into his father's film business. Obviously, hanging on his father's star and having done nothing in his own right bothered Steven.

Their limousine drove into the Burbank studio leased by Hunter Films just as Nigel Hunter's Corniche glided up. Nigel stepped from his car; Mark was surprised at how agilely he moved. Nigel's body was an accordion of fat around a very stout frame. His thin white hair had been artfully arranged in a futile attempt to conceal his shiny bald crown. His face looked like the face of a former prizefighter, gnarled and scarred. When he spoke, Nigel's voice still had remnants of his Midlands roots.

"Father," Steven said, using the precise diction of the British aristocracy, acquired, Mark knew, through years of public schooling. "We arrived so late last night that I didn't call you."

"Humph." Nigel led the way into the studio's side door.

Why hadn't Steven spent the night at the home in the Hollywood Hills where Nigel was staying? It hadn't been that late when they'd arrived. Last night Mark assumed Steven had stayed with them in the bungalows at the Beverly Hills Hotel so he could hustle in the Polo Lounge. Now Mark wasn't so sure. Looking at the two of them, Mark was again aware of an obvious lack of warmth. While Steven pathetically tried to please his father, Nigel seemed indifferent toward his only child.

"We have a major problem down there," Steven said, looking to Mark for help.

Mark let him hang there. He wanted to see how Steven would handle this.

"We've brought some new footage of that seduction scene." This time Steven looked to Giles for assistance.

They came to an office at the end of a long corridor. Without warning Nigel halted, then swung around. "I thought I sent you down there to handle it."

Steven's face reddened. "I did, but Mark thought you should see this film."

Mark cringed at Steven's spinelessness. He had known all along he'd have to explain the proposed change to Nigel. He was neither afraid nor in awe of Nigel Hunter. Mark knew Nigel's abrasive manner was just a device for bullying those, like his son, who let themselves be pushed around. Beneath it all, Mark suspected, Nigel Hunter was a very compassionate man. He had solid business sense; Mark admired that. When Nigel needed to raise money for this film, Mark did not hesitate to invest. Mark knew he had Nigel's respect, not just because he was self-made like Nigel, but because Mark refused to let Nigel intimidate him. Mark stepped forward and opened the office door. "Let's go inside and discuss this."

They seated themselves around the oversized desk in Nigel's office. Mark came directly to the point. "When we arrived in Mexico, we found a woman who performs this part

much better than Melanie Tarenholt." He looked to Giles for
an affirmation. Mark was not in the habit of asking others for
support, but he had never participated in a film project before.
He wouldn't pretend he was an expert.

"No one could be better," Giles contributed. "She's absolutely top drawer." He paused and added, "Melanie simply
cannot act. I refuse to use her. Alexa's perfect."

"Alexa?" Nigel's voice rose incredulously. "Not Alexa Mac-
Kenzie, the author?"

"Yes," Mark responded, surprised at Nigel's obvious displeasure.

Nigel snorted loudly. "That broad's a pain in the ass! First
she refused to sell me the rights to her novel—she didn't want
her book ruined." He rose from his chair and lumbered over to
the small window overlooking the studio lot. "When I
brought her the perfect package, she insisted on script approval. Then after the deal was signed, she decided she
wanted to come along as script consultant. I agreed. But I'll be
damned if she's telling me how—"

"It didn't happen that way," Mark interrupted the tirade.
"She doesn't know we're suggesting she do the part. We had
her try to show Melanie what Giles wanted. When we saw
how good she was, Giles ran the camera."

"She's perfect," Giles repeated with quiet assurance.

Nigel's rheumy blue eyes were plainly hostile. "That's what
I heard about Melanie." He shot a lethal look at Steven, who
did not meet his father's eyes.

"I don't know about Melanie's contract," Steven mumbled.
"I'm not sure we can break it. Too expensive. We have plenty
of footage we can use."

The phone buzzed. Giles's frown deepened and the anxiety
in his eyes intensified when Nigel picked up the receiver.
They hadn't warned him about the trouble in Mexico yet.
Nigel would go off like a Roman candle if the Mexicans shut
down production. Undoubtedly Lloyd's would cancel their insurance too. Mark was concerned; they should have heard
something by now. He liked Giles and hoped Renata wasn't
going to cause him any more heartache.

Nigel tersely answered a few questions and it became clear
the call wasn't from Mexico. He hung up the phone and

smiled broadly, revealing a set of crooked teeth. Apparently it was good news from another front.

"Let's go see what you have in the can," Nigel said, pointing to the reel of film Giles held. "Have you had the sound put on it?"

"Yes," Giles responded. "We used an all-night lab."

On the way to the screening room Steven rattled on about Melanie's talents, box office following from her television show, and her contract. Mark sent Giles a look that said: Let me handle this. Mark glanced at Nigel and decided not to say anything. Nigel wasn't listening.

After they entered the small screening room Nigel wedged his bulk into a deep leather theater-style seat in the center of the front row. Mark and Giles took the seats on either side of him while Steven took the film to the projection room.

As they waited for the film to be loaded Mark decided to give Nigel some background. "When we shot this, Alexa had just come from the beach. We didn't use any makeup on her because we weren't expecting to film this. That's why you'll see sand clinging to her body, and she's wearing a bikini. You'll notice her hair looks as if she styled it with an eggbeater."

After a fractional pause Mark's attempt at levity paid off. Nigel threw back his head and roared. The overhead lights went off and the silver screen lit up.

Larger than life, Alexa's celluloid image filled the darkness and she began to speak. Her unbelievable presence, coming from an innate sense of timing and a reservoir of emotion, stunned Mark. His reaction was immediate and startling in its intensity. A throbbing tightness pulsed in his groin. He shifted uncomfortably in his seat. He had to admit he found Alexa incredibly sexy.

The camera dollied in for a close-up, magnifying each of Alexa's facial features on the large screen, but it was her matchless green eyes that reflected her anguish. "Please," Alexa whispered, "don't throw away the love we have."

Enhanced by Technicolor, her eyes became an ethereal green as tears sparkled on her lashes, seeped slowly from the corners of her eyes, and trickled down her cheeks. It was as if she was speaking directly to him. It seemed so real that he drew in his breath in astonishment. He longed to reach out to her, hold her, comfort her.

The scene ended and the lights came up slowly. Mark closed his eyes for an instant, replaying the dream he'd had last night. He saw himself on a deserted beach with Alexa. At the thought of her full breasts and her shapely tanned body, his pulse accelerated and his body tightened with anticipation. He blinked hard several times to banish the image.

Mark turned to Nigel. With his fingers interlaced across his massive stomach, Nigel stared at the now-dark screen. He twirled his thumbs around each other in a rapid circular motion. Finally Nigel turned to Mark.

"So? What's to discuss?"

# Chapter 4

Alexa raced through the hotel lobby. "Where can they be?" she asked Colin. "I prayed all night they hadn't been arrested."

"Don't worry. Let's check your room. Perhaps that's where they are." Colin sounded anxious despite his calming words.

As they hurried to her room, Alexa saw the storm's damage everywhere. Maids swept up broken glass and palm fronds, and from the walkway Alexa noticed a sizable chunk of the beach had been eaten away by the storm's angry surf.

"*Chubasco*," Colin said sardonically, "almost but not quite a hurricane. This isn't even the season for these storms."

Alexa frowned, thinking that compared with what might have happened to Linda and Renata, the terror of last night's storm seemed negligible. Had they been arrested?

Alexa inserted the key into the lock and leaned hard against the stubborn door. Aghast, she peered inside. The *chubasco* had centered its fury on her room. It looked as if there had been an explosion in a jigsaw puzzle factory: drawers were emptied and upended, clothes were thrown from the closet and ripped apart, the mattress was sliced open and shreds of ticking tossed about, furniture was upside down, and Alexa's precious papers were scattered like the remnants of a ticker-tape parade.

"They're in jail." Alexa sank down onto an upended chair. "It's my fault. I should have stayed and tried to explain. I should never have let you convince me to leave."

"Here, here, keep a stiff upper lip. Let's make a few inquiries before we assume anything."

Alexa and Colin were checking the pool area when Linda hailed them from the adjacent bar. Alexa bolted across the wide veranda cantilevered out over the Pacific Ocean. She stopped in front of the cushy lounge chairs where Linda and Renata were sitting. Sipping margaritas, they were casually watching the waves crash onto the beach below.

"I've been so worried about you," Alexa exclaimed. "What happened?"

"Is everything all right?" Colin asked.

"Yes." Linda directed her answer to Colin. "Thank you for coming to the rescue." She turned to Alexa. "The police didn't find anything. We convinced them it was a mistake."

"Thank God," Alexa whispered.

"*Señor* Avery," a waiter addressed Colin. "Please telephone London. Your wife is worried about you."

"She'll be up in arms when she finds out I spent the night with a beautiful blonde. I won't mention that it was in the city hall along with dozens of other tourists stranded by the *chubasco.*" Colin laughed. "I'll want to hear all about this later."

"What happened?" Alexa asked.

Abruptly Linda stood up. "Let's talk about this down on the beach."

Renata and Alexa followed Linda down the stone steps that were carved into the side of the cliff supporting the hotel. When they reached the sand, Linda sat down on the bottom step and motioned for them to sit beside her.

"Why all the secrecy?" Alexa asked impatiently.

"I don't want anyone to hear us," Linda said.

Renata leaned forward and picked up a handful of sand. "The police were tipped to search one specific room." She let the glistening sand filter through her be-ringed fingers onto the ground.

Alexa inhaled sharply, wondering how could she have been so insensitive. Drugs—Renata, of course. The police had been seeking Renata. That explained everything. A dismal feeling trickled through her. Renata didn't need any more trouble now when she'd resumed her career. Renata was well. Wasn't she?

Alexa gazed into Renata's sky-blue eyes fringed with spiky amber lashes and said, "They came to my room by mistake. They wanted you."

Renata brushed her russet bangs off her forehead, sending sparks of light off her rings. "No, Alexa, they were told to search your room."

"What?" Alexa said as Renata looked earnestly at her. She didn't smoke, only drank socially, and had never been involved with drugs. There had to have been some mix-up. "Are you positive?"

"Definitely," Linda responded. "John Dunfirth, the stunt man, speaks fluent Spanish. He overheard the police talking and he came to get us. We sent him for Colin."

Alexa's uneasiness increased; this was serious. All last night she'd told herself that there had been a mistake, that there was some logical explanation. The silence lengthened, interrupted only by the sound of the heavy surf breaking on the beach a few yards away. "You know I don't—"

"Of course." Renata placed her hand on Alexa's shoulder. "That's why we came to help you."

"What made you search my room then?"

A light puff of wind lifted Linda's silky brown hair. She brushed it back and shrugged her shoulders, wondering how she could explain this. "The second John came to us I knew you were in trouble. I had this feeling . . ."

"A hunch?"

Linda nodded, unwilling to put her thoughts into words. She had a well-honed sixth sense that often warned her. Past experience had taught her to listen to these feelings—or suffer the consequences. Since she'd spent the better part of the last decade paying for ignoring just such a feeling, Linda had let her intuition guide her on the raid. She'd been correct; someone had tried to frame Alexa.

"What did you do with my bag?" Alexa asked, not really believing in hunches, but reluctant to challenge Linda when she'd helped her. "Did you give it to the police? Do they want to talk to me?"

"No," Renata said, "we took care of everything."

"Renata did it."

"Did what?"

Renata giggled mischievously. "I couldn't flush the stuff down the toilet because they would have heard it. I pretended to be taking a shower while I poured it down the drain."

"Didn't the police ask why you were in my room?"

"Yes," Linda said. "I stayed very calm and said we were in your room because our showers don't work very well—which happens to be the truth."

"I saw you come out of the shower. I tried to come back but Colin pulled me outside and Linda slammed the door. What happened?"

Linda laughed. "They just gaped at Renata until one of them recovered himself enough to hand her a towel. While she dried off, they tore your room apart searching for the drugs."

"What happened to the bag?"

"I had it rolled up in the palm of my hand as I pulled back the shower curtain. But they weren't looking at my hand." Renata rolled her blue eyes and smirked. "After I dried off, I stuffed it into the wet towel. They never bothered with the towel because they handed it to me themselves."

"This sounds funny now, looking back, but it wasn't then," Linda said, her face solemn once more. "It was really serious; we were terrified."

"I know. It was horrible. Thank you . . . both of you and Colin. A simple thanks doesn't begin to cover what you did. I don't know what else to say. Who would have put that bag in my room? Why? If you'd been caught, you both would have been arrested because of me."

Alexa rose to her knees, leaned forward, and hugged first Linda and then Renata. She settled down on the sand again, shaking her head in disbelief. "I can't imagine who would want me in jail."

"Melanie," Linda answered with conviction, and Renata nodded.

"No." Alexa was shocked at the suggestion. "We just saw her in front of the hotel. She couldn't have been sweeter to me. She's leaving to do a television special in London."

"Leaving?" Linda's eyebrows shot up. "Her contract hasn't expired. What if she's needed here to film?"

"I guess she must have spoken to someone this morning when the phone lines were repaired. She seemed delighted. She said she was 'dying, simply dying,' to get out of this heat and return to London. I assume they're flying in another actress to do her part."

Linda remained unconvinced. "I'll bet someone told her yesterday they were going to cut her and she held you responsible."

"How could that be?" Alexa asked. "We don't know what they've decided. How could she?"

"Giles didn't call me last night," Renata said. "Evidently he couldn't get through. I have no idea what the decision was. But I agree with Linda. Melanie has a reputation for vindictiveness."

It was hard to believe Melanie would do this. Paul's face flashed before Alexa. The divorce still caused a raw ache each time she thought about it. He'd taken what he wanted from her already and wouldn't have had any reason to want her in jail. She couldn't imagine anyone who would.

"We can't prove anything, but in the future stay away from Melanie Tarenholt," Linda said.

Alexa followed them up the stairs to the lobby level. Tears filled her eyes when the full impact of what had happened hit her. She knew that plenty of cocaine came from Mexico. The Mexicans didn't mind making money off the illegal drug traffic, but if they caught you with it they could be merciless. Cold fear rushed over her as she envisioned months in a dreary Mexican jail, awaiting due process under a questionable judicial system. Alexa inserted herself between her friends and put an arm around each one's waist. "Thanks again. I'll never forget this."

Renata hugged Alexa. "I know what it's like to be in a pickle and have someone help you."

"You mean Giles?" Alexa asked. Linda had told Alexa how Renata's battle with drugs had ruined her stage career, but Alexa had never asked her about it. She was aware the British preferred not to become too personal until they really knew someone.

"Yes, I was a mess. I'd lost everything, including my career, but I was too far gone to care. That's what happens. You only care about your next high." Tears bordered Renata's blue eyes. "If it weren't for Giles I don't know what would have become of me. I had no money left, couldn't hold down any job, let alone work in the theater. He found me and paid for my treatment in a rehabilitation center. When I was well again, we were married."

Alexa couldn't suppress a stab of envy. Giles had enough love and faith in Renata to stand by her through the worst crisis imaginable. Paul's love had been fleeting, without commitment. "Why did you help me? It would have killed Giles if you'd been arrested. With your history, they would never have believed you."

"I couldn't have stood it, knowing you were in jail for something you didn't do."

"Now I'm going to help you," Alexa said. "When this picture wraps, I'm going to London with my play. You'll star in it."

"I'll design the costumes," Linda added.

"Do you really mean it?" Renata's voice was raspy, barely above a whisper. "I know we've been discussing it, but I haven't dared hope—"

"Of course I mean it. I wrote the play with you in mind. I'm planning on producing it myself." They came to a halt in front of her room; Alexa searched through her purse for the key and inserted it in the lock. "Linda, aren't you going to be working on another film?"

"No, this is my last. I've saved enough money to open a boutique featuring my own designs. And I'm going to persuade my old boyfriend to take me back."

"Really?" Linda had told Alexa about her divorce but she'd never mentioned a previous love. Using all her weight, Alexa shoved at the door and it squeaked open. The sight of her room siphoned Linda's comment from Alexa's mind.

"My papers," moaned Alexa. "All my research notes and story outlines were here. How'll I ever put them back in order?" She slammed her fist into the once-comfortable mattress, now reduced to a pile of ticking. "Linda, thank goodness you had my tote bag with the play in it."

"Tell us what to do," Linda offered.

"Gather up the papers and then we can sort them." Alexa shook her head, knowing this would take hours.

They collected her papers from the trash heap that had once been her well-ordered room. A loud double knock on the door alarmed Alexa. The police? Would they arrest her? A louder, more insistent knock followed. Alexa nervously brushed the ticking off her dress and walked to the door.

Linda expelled her breath in a relieved sigh when she saw it was Mark Kimbrough. He looked at her but gave no sign he recognized her before addressing Alexa.

"I want you upstairs for a meeting—now."

"I was just . . ." Alexa sputtered as she watched him survey the mess.

"Leave it," he said in a tone that permitted no discussion. "We're meeting in Giles's suite."

Neither of them spoke as they climbed the three flights of stone stairs to Giles's rooms. Alexa looked down, concentrating on each step.

Without knocking Mark opened the door to the suite and stepped aside for her to enter. Giles and Steven were seated in two oversized wicker chairs lined with plump blue cushions. Opposite them was a glass coffee table with several scripts and call sheets on it. On the other side of the table was a two-person wicker sofa that matched the chairs.

"Come, sit down," Giles gestured toward the sofa. "We heard there was a bit of trouble down here. Tell us about it."

Something in Giles's amber eyes instantly alerted Alexa. Was this what Mark was so hostile about? It was apparent that, without even asking her, they had convicted her.

"Tell us what happened." Steven's voice was soft and reassuring. At least he hadn't prejudged her.

"I don't know." How could she explain what she didn't understand? "For some reason—I don't know why—the police were told I had drugs in my room."

Mark sat down beside Alexa. "How long have you had this problem?" A cruel note underscored his words.

Alexa spun around to face him. "I don't have a drug problem." She snapped her mouth shut, shocked at her own vehemence. Mark, totally unaffected by her rancor, continued to stare at her.

"I've been all through this with Renata, and I know how

hard it is to admit you need help," Giles said. "You're just too talented to throw it all away."

Alexa jackknifed to her feet, hands on her hips. "I've never once—ever—taken anything."

Alexa crossed the room to the long expanse of glass overlooking the ocean. In the unpleasant silence that followed, Alexa stood shaking with fury at their injustice. What could she say? There had been a bag of coke in her room, and she was at a loss as to how to explain its being there. Through the glass she heard the waves breaking on the beach below. The sun hovered on the horizon and would be gone in another few minutes. How suddenly things change. When they had left for Los Angeles, she had been helping them solve the problem. Now she was the problem.

"The police found nothing?" Mark asked. "If they had found anything, they could have shut production down for days, weeks, or even longer. Lloyd's would cancel our insurance."

"Renata and Linda got rid of it." She looked directly into Mark's eyes, knowing how this would sound to him. His gray eyes narrowed; creases formed between his brows. She decided not to mention Colin's involvement.

"My God!" Giles put his hand to his forehead. "Not Renata. Where is she?"

"Nothing happened to her. Don't worry. She's with Linda in my room straightening out the mess the police left after they searched it."

"Why did your friends have to help you at all?" Mark came at her again. His eyes never left her face. He was carefully weighing her responses and judging her truthfulness.

"Someone wanted to have me arrested." Alexa offered the only explanation she had. Hearing her own voice, she knew she sounded unusually hesitant.

"Who? Why?" Steven asked, rising from his chair and crossing over to the bar. He fixed himself a drink. "That doesn't make any sense."

"How would your friends know to get rid of the drugs if you've never taken any?" Mark saw the obvious flaw.

"Linda had a feeling." Alexa had tossed logic aside and immediately regretted it. She should have thought longer before answering, put it another way.

"Not Linda Carlisle?" Mark asked, his tone even more derisive than before.

"This isn't getting us anywhere," Giles interrupted. "We can't have production shut down even for a day. You have to watch yourself, Alexa. Leave Renata out of your troubles. She simply must concentrate on her career." He seemed about to add something more but stopped. "Now, let's talk about that seduction scene."

Seething inside, Alexa nodded. They had found her guilty without knowing anything except that she had been accused. Now what did they want?

"We've decided Melanie isn't going to play that role," Giles continued. "We're going to release her tonight."

"That won't be necessary," Alexa said, still barely able to control her indignation. "She's left for London."

"Impossible," Mark stated flatly. "We haven't spoken with her yet."

"Colin and I saw her leave. She told us she was doing a special in London for Thames Television."

"It doesn't matter." Giles paused. "We want you to play the part. Nigel saw the footage of you and he agreed."

Alexa gasped. "You can't be serious. I'm not an actress."

"Luv," Steven assured her, "you will be when this film comes out. You'll get lots of parts. You'll be a star and Hunter Films will have discovered you."

"No" Alexa balked, terrified at the thought. "I can't. I refuse."

"Trust me, luv," Steven said soothingly. "We can turn this into a career."

"I have a career," Alexa countered in growing alarm, realizing they were serious. "You can omit the scene or use the footage of Melanie. I'm not doing it." She jumped to her feet.

"Wait, Alexa," Giles said. "Sit down. I realize you're a writer. No one knows this story, feels this story, the way you do. Will it be the same story without this scene?"

"No," Alexa admitted.

"Was Melanie playing it the way you wrote it?"

"No," she answered, again trapped by the truth.

"This is an opportunity, luv," Steven interjected.

Alexa glared at him.

"Alexa," Giles said softly, "I can direct you. You do have the talent. I'm completely certain of it."

Alexa shook her head, tossing her hair defiantly.

While Giles continued reassuring her of her talent, Alexa stopped listening. Things were happening too fast; she'd lost control. Her whole life had become a roller coaster ride—up and down. She was never in charge. Paul's treachery, the divorce, the drug raid, and now this. She had to stop it here.

Mark lightly touched Alexa's arm. She regarded him warily, brushing back wisps of hair that had fallen across her face.

"Are you concerned about taking your clothes off for this scene?" Mark's voice was unexpectedly soft.

Alexa hadn't thought he could be that sensitive. She looked down, concentrating on the tile floor. "Yes." She could barely hear her own voice. "Among other things."

"There's nothing pornographic or even the least bit tasteless about this film, you know," he added in a lower, more personal tone.

"I know. I wrote it." In her book it had only seemed natural to have the characters remove their clothes. But when Alexa had written this part, she had never imagined she'd be the one to perform it in front of a camera.

"We'll close the set," Mark assured her. "Only the essential personnel will be allowed. Will that help?"

Alexa shook her head and twisted a long strand of hair around her finger.

"Then *you* have to make the choice," Mark concluded with deliberate emphasis on the word you. "Either you do the scene or we leave it out entirely."

Alexa did not respond at once. Her thoughts circled and came around to the same point over and over. Without this scene her story's impact would be lost. Her choice was really no choice at all.

"All right . . . I'll do it—if you close the set."

"Of course," Giles assured her. He explained she would have two days to memorize the script and take preliminary tests for makeup and hairstyles. As he covered a variety of other details, a fresh wave of apprehension assailed her. She could memorize the part in no time, but could she do it? When the time came, could she take off her clothes?

Giles handed her a script. "Get some sleep, and don't worry."

Alexa slowly walked to the door, clutching the script. She turned and asked Giles, "Who would be included in essential personnel?"

"Alexa, please stop worrying."

Alexa rolled the script into a tight cylinder and moved into the hall. Turning, she was surprised to find Mark beside her.

"I'm not among those considered essential."

# Chapter 5

That was exactly what Alexa wanted to know. She refused to take her clothes off with Mark Kimbrough standing there glaring at her. She started down the stairs and realized he was beside her.

"Let's see about getting you another room. The hotel is full, but since Melanie has left, you should be able to have her room."

Without responding, Alexa continued down the stairs. Mark Kimbrough was an arrogant jerk accustomed to telling others what to do. She should check on Renata and Linda. *Speak up; tell him you're going to your room.* They reached the bottom of the stairs and turned toward the lobby. Reluctantly she admitted Mark was right. Getting another room was imperative. She couldn't possibly use the bed in her room tonight.

At the front desk Mark asked to see the manager while Alexa waited at his side. Smiling and waving, Linda came across the lobby toward Alexa, but when Linda saw Mark her smile faded and she turned away. Mark looked up and frowned at Linda's retreating figure.

The manager arrived and, with quietly restrained authority, Mark insisted her things be moved to the room Melanie had vacated. He collected all the keys to the new room and asked who would have pass keys. After making numerous inquiries about the hotel's security, Mark thanked the manager and walked away with Alexa.

"I think I've made my point. We know the manager and the head of housekeeping have pass keys. I doubt if you'll be bothered again."

Mark's hand was on Alexa's bare arm as he guided her across the lobby into the dining room. There was something about the casualness of his gesture she didn't like. That he could be so abrupt one moment and so personal the next confused her. She eased her arm from his grip. "When are you leaving?"

"I'm staying," Mark said as they followed the waiter out onto the restaurant's terrace. "I must be certain everything is in order before I leave."

Alexa looked around the dining room for a table they could join. There wasn't anyone to rescue her. Where had Linda gone? She would have to get through dinner with this man alone.

They were seated at a table on the terrace's edge. The sun had set over the Pacific, but enough light seeped up over the horizon to give the sky a coral glow under the encroaching canopy of night. The rustling of the breeze in the palm trees was overshadowed by the splashing of the waves on the beach below.

"See something out there?"

"No." Alexa met his fixed gaze with a cool glance. "Thanks for getting my room changed . . ." She paused for the right words, but none came. ". . . and taking care of everything."

Mark merely nodded.

"Why would anyone want to frame me?" she asked after they'd ordered drinks.

Mark shrugged, lifting his eyebrows slightly. Alexa was suddenly aware that, in his own way, Mark was handsome. The hazy lamplight on the balcony gilded his black hair and softened the expression in his intense gray eyes.

"I don't know. You tell me." Mark leaned back in his chair and studied her thoughtfully.

"I just told you," Alexa snapped, "I don't know."

He leaned forward and rested his elbows on the table.

"Alexa, we don't know each other at all. It's only natural for me to have assumed the worst."

"Why?" A fresh flare of hostility ignited deep within her.

"Are you aware that Mexico still uses the old Napoleonic Code?"

"You're guilty until you can prove your innocence?" she asked.

His gray eyes studied her intently. "They keep you in jail until trial—whenever that might be."

"You made your point. If they'd arrested me, I could have been detained indefinitely."

"What's across the Sea of Cortéz just east of here?"

"Mazatlan?"

"Sinaloa Province," he answered, his condescending tone sparking her anger once more. "It's where most of the drugs from Mexico originate. The bulk of it travels through Baja to California. The United States has put so much pressure on Mexico recently that the local authorities are anxious to show them they're cooperating. Nothing could please them more than to embarrass Washington by arresting Americans for drug trafficking. Didn't Giles warn the entire cast and crew the night you arrived to be careful?"

"Yes, but I doubt that it stopped anyone. All you have to do is walk behind the trailers and sniff the acrid air and note the technicians inhaling right down to their knees. That's the part of the problem you can smell. I wouldn't want to speculate about what goes on behind closed doors."

"I agree but it's you I'm concerned about."

"Why? Do you automatically assume all Californians have drug problems?"

"That's not fair and you know it. The U.K. has its share. Renata's an excellent example."

"She's over it and I've never even . . . You really don't care do you? Just don't let it interfere with production. Right?"

"We have millions of pounds and numerous careers riding on this film. We have to be careful. The Mexican authorities have already held up production once on a meaningless technicality that was undoubtedly an excuse to extort more money from us."

Rebuffed, Alexa mutely nodded. He was right, of course.

This was a business, and like any other business it deserved a professional attitude on the part of everyone involved. Taking this personally was terribly immature. She thought back to the hostile way she'd reacted to Giles's questions. Why was she so defensive? The answer came in one word: Paul. Over the years she'd allowed him to constantly put her on the defensive.

Mark reached across the table and cupped her chin in his hand, so she had to look directly into his eyes. She pulled away, her cheeks coloring at the intimacy of his gesture.

"Alexa, I believe you." His steady gray eyes never left hers. "I'm concerned because you are the most visible American on the set. If someone has set you up, that is probably the reason."

"I never thought of that. . . . Thank you," Alexa whispered. A jumble of confused thoughts and feelings rushed through her. Perhaps she'd been mistaken about this man. She should try to see his side of this. Undoubtedly he was saddled with the increasing debt caused by the various cost overruns and the pressure of keeping so many people on location. Who knew what other problems he had? Ashamed of herself for overreacting, she didn't know what to say. Miraculously the waiter arrived with the menus.

She retreated behind her menu and kept staring at it although she had already come to a decision. As usual the waiters operated on Mexican Standard Time—slow, very slow—so she had an opportunity to collect her thoughts. She didn't know what to make of Mark. He was abrupt and arrogant yet surprisingly sensitive. Somehow she sensed a darker side to him, a sharp undercurrent in his personality that warned her to beware. Not since Paul had anyone captured her interest, although several men had tried. The thought of Paul brought a familiar dull, aching pain, warning her to be suspicious of all men.

After they had ordered, Alexa stared out over the balcony, but the light had vanished and it was too dark to see much. She twisted a strand of hair around her finger. She liked to talk to people with backgrounds different from hers, but she had no idea what to say to Mark.

"Did you know the Baja peninsula was for a short time part of the United States?" Alexa knew this was pretty obscure, but perhaps Mark was interested in history. Doing research for her book had given her a depth of knowledge about the area.

Mark leaned back, adjusting his chair so that he could stretch his long legs. "Claimed is a better word. During the Mexican War several of your generals claimed this peninsula. About the same time your General Fremont grabbed California from Mexico."

Grabbed? Mark made the acquisition of California sound like a monumental land grab. She looked at him and realized he was teasing her. Was she ever going to adjust to the subtleties of British humor? Was she ever going to stop feeling defensive? His eyes swept over her and a grin tugged at the corners of his mouth. He wasn't just teasing her—he was baiting her.

Alexa couldn't help smiling at him, thinking he really had extraordinary eyes. They were dress-gray when he wanted to conceal his emotions, but now they were the soft, hazy gray of early dawn. For a moment it occurred to her he might be trying to seduce her. He was strange; she couldn't tell what he wanted. A distant bell told her to keep him at arm's length or she'd regret it.

"Actually, I found your book extraordinarily accurate."

"You did?" Alexa was unsure if he was complimenting her or teasing again.

"Lord Thomas Cochrane." Mark smiled. "Always admired his initiative. An impoverished nobleman with few prospects, he set out to make his fortune as a pirate."

"Eighteen twenty-two." Alexa laughed, feeling relaxed because they were discussing something she knew. "He was more than one hundred years too late. All the great names and fortunes had already been made."

"Can you imagine what Baja looked like when Cochrane sacked the peninsula looking for booty?" Mark shook his head and gave a rich, full laugh.

"Would we want to?" Alexa laughed along with him. How wonderful it felt to have him laughing with her, not firing hostile questions at her.

By the time they were served Alexa had explained how she had turned the Mexican episode of Cochrane's life into a best-selling novel. And as she listened to Mark, their conversation no longer forced, she discovered he was even more of a history buff than she. While they waited for the check Alexa slumped in her chair. Despite her best efforts her eyes kept closing.

"Knackered?"

"Totally. Colin and I had to spend the night on the floor of the town hall during the *chubasco.*" She pulled at the thin gauze dress she was wearing. "Luckily I changed into this before the police came, or I'd still be wearing that bikini I was in when I met you. Remember?"

Mark nodded very slowly. "I caught a bit of a glance of it." The word " 'glahance" was followed by an arresting smile with a decidedly seductive quality to it.

With a start Alexa realized she'd been correct—he was coming on to her. Mark continued to gaze at her, not even attempting to conceal his interest. She closed her eyes, pretending to have missed the implication in his words.

After they left the restaurant, Mark walked her up to her new room. Alexa turned to say good-night, but Mark stepped into the room and flicked on the lights.

This room was twice as large as her previous one and had a balcony overlooking the Pacific. Her things had been moved in and her papers placed in neat stacks on the dresser. Silently she blessed Linda and Renata for their efforts. On the nightstand was a huge vase of baby-pink rosebuds, evidently a legacy of the previous occupant.

Alexa turned to say good-night to Mark and saw him staring at the roses with a strange expression in his eyes. The happy look she'd seen during dinner had vanished, replaced by a startlingly bitter intensity.

"Melanie's," Alexa felt compelled to explain. "Someone sends them each week from London, I think." She held the door open, so he'd take the hint and leave.

Abruptly Mark turned to face her. "I'll help you with that script tomorrow."

Tomorrow? Mark planned on being with her tomorrow. The dinner had turned out better than she'd expected, but she had no intention of encouraging this man. Keep him at arm's length or even farther.

"Where will you be?"

"On the beach." Alexa sidestepped the question.

Mark stopped on the threshold and waited while Alexa
studied the Mexican tiles on the floor beneath her feet. With
his finger under her chin, Mark lifted her face up and lightly
kissed her. She backed away but he pulled her against him,
kissing her more deeply this time. An ache, intense and weak-
ening, filled her and she clung to him. She could feel the heat
of his firm body along the entire length of hers. The warmth
of her own body increased, and she recognized the spark of
sexual desire that hadn't been there for months. Somewhere
inside her head a warning signal flashed. She pulled back inside her room.

"Good-night," she whispered, pushing the door shut.

"Good-night, Alexa," she heard him say from the other side
of the door.

Alexa leaned against the closed door. Arm's length definitely wasn't going to be far enough. Thank goodness she'd
been deliberately evasive—there were so many beaches.

Mark adjusted his chair, stretching his legs out under the
table. The bright light of the midmorning sun transformed the
terrace of the Hotel Finisterra's restaurant from a romantic
café to a bustling coffee shop. While he waited for his order to
be taken, he stared across the table at the empty chair where
Alexa had been sitting last night. Seeing her the way she
looked then, caramel-blond hair deliberately clipped into a
stylish look of tousled disarray, wide green eyes, chin up and
cocked to one side in a defensive pose, Mark smiled.

*"Señor?"* the waiter inquired.

Mark wasn't hungry, but out of habit he ordered a large
breakfast. Waiting for his order, Mark gazed out at the Pacific.
He hadn't expected Alexa to respond to him so readily, to kiss
him with such passion. But the biggest surprise had been the
way he'd reacted to her. When he'd first seen Alexa, and later
during the film clip, he'd felt an undeniable sexual attraction
to her. Pure lust, he'd decided. But when they were alone and
talking, his attitude changed. With familiarity he usually became disillusioned by those women who from afar attracted
him. Their faces, their bodies, were frequently their only attri-
butes. Not Alexa.

*"Huevos rancheros,"* the waiter announced, waving a plate full
of questionable-looking eggs in front of him.

Mark took a forkful of the congealed mess and pushed the plate away, letting his thoughts return to Alexa. She was attracted to him, whether or not she cared to admit it. Her kiss had dispelled any doubts, just as her abrupt retreat signaled her insecurity. She'd been hurt, and badly. She was the kind of woman who would be cautious about an affair. Alexa wouldn't risk becoming involved with someone unless she was certain of him. Knowing this made him feel very protective of her. He'd been miserable when Caroline left him, so he could well imagine how Alexa felt.

"Hello," Steven said. Not bothering to wait to be invited, he sat down across from Mark.

"Hello," Mark replied in a toneless voice. He didn't like Steven any better now than when he'd met him at school years ago.

"How did you do last night?" A slight sneer marred Steven's fine features. His blue eyes, below his flawlessly combed blond hair, were alive with curiosity.

"Last night?" Mark asked evenly, not liking the direction the conversation was taking.

"With MacKenzie. Some piece, huh? Quite a body."

"She's a nice lady." Mark purposely emphasized the word "lady." He knew Steven had a reputation for being the biggest ass-man in the West End. His tastes ran, not to ladies, but to ambitious starlets hoping for career advancement.

"Right." There was a full-fledged sneer on Steven's face now. Impatiently he motioned for the waiter to bring a menu.

"Steven, why did you discharge Melanie over the telephone from Los Angeles rather than down here as we agreed?"

"I didn't." The too-quick reply and the way Steven averted his eyes assured Mark that this was exactly what had happened. "I don't have the foggiest idea how she got wind of it."

Why would Steven lie? It didn't matter that Melanie had been terminated over the telephone except that he concealed the fact. Why? Mark watched Steven feigning interest in the waves crashing on the beach. Some things never change. Steven was as deceptive now as he had been during their school days.

Breaking the unpleasant silence, Steven asked, "How's Warren these days?"

"Fine. I haven't seen much of him. I've been out of the

country most of the year." Mark was surprised Steven asked. He got along with Mark's best friend, Warren Rutherford-Jaymes, about as well as Steven did with Mark.

Mark couldn't resist countering, "And Jason?" Mark disliked Steven's close friend, Jason Talbott, even more than Mark disliked Steven. In fact, Mark hated Jason Talbott. Mark wasn't one for revenge, but in Talbott's case he planned to make an exception. It didn't matter that he'd already waited twelve years for the chance to avenge himself. He was a patient man. He'd wait forever if necessary.

"Oh, fine. You know, mountain climbing in the Himalayas, safaris in Africa, big game hunting—the usual," Steven replied in a transparently offhand manner. "What are you doing today?"

"Waiting to place a call to London," Mark answered, telling half the truth. The call last night after he'd left Alexa alerted him to still another problem.

"I thought I'd help Alexa." Steven grinned wolfishly and suggestively arched one eyebrow.

The waiter arrived with Mark's check and Steven's menu. "I doubt if she needs your help." Mark signed the check and said good-bye to Steven, confident that he wouldn't be able to find Alexa's beach.

Walking to his room, Mark focused on the problem. Windsor Airlines wouldn't survive the year unless the ticket fraud could be stopped. If the airline collapsed, thousands of Britons would lose their jobs. As he reviewed his months of work as a representative of the Commonwealth Trade Alliance, Mark knew all his progress to date would be forgotten if he couldn't prevent the airline's collapse.

"London please," Mark asked the operator once he'd returned to his room. He flopped onto the bed, waiting for the call to be put through. What had his assistant been able to find out? Had they been able to trace the laundered tickets back through the chain of travel agents?

"Hello, Ed?" Mark shook the receiver in a futile attempt to clear the static on the line. "Speak louder. This connection's bloody awful." Mark shook his head as he listened. "That's a bunch of crap. How can a travel agency buy a block of tickets and not know where they came from?" He stood up and unbuckled his pants. "Keep checking. They're fucking around with us. They know where those tickets came from." He stepped out of his pants and neatly draped them across the foot of the bed. "Keep on it. I'll be home in two days."

Frustrated, Mark slammed the receiver down. He turned to the dresser and sorted through his clothes until he found his swimming trunks. Once he had them on he stood in front of the mirror and assured himself the tan he'd acquired in California looked good. He went out the door and promised himself that in the future he'd work a bit less and holiday in the sun a lot more. He slung his towel over his shoulder and chuckled. Alexa would certainly be surprised to see him.

# Chapter 6

There she was. Alone. Stretched out, face down with her bikini top undone, Alexa lay on an enormous, multicolored beach towel. Her derriere, covered by a swatch of red fabric, was firmly rounded and sexy as hell. The sight of her sun-bronzed body made Mark's heart beat more rapidly than the strenuous climb up the hill had.

He stood on top of the steep ridge, riddled with cactus and boulders, that sliced the Banderas Bay into two unequal parts. On one side was a wide expanse of sand covered with sun-bathers from the movie set constructed on the slight rise just behind the beach. On the far side of the ridge, where Alexa was sunning herself, lay a secluded beach. A small ellipse of powdered-sugar sand wrapped itself around a tranquil cove of cobalt-blue water.

Mark paused a moment to catch his breath and then picked his way around the large boulders. Avoiding prickly cactus, he worked his way along the makeshift trail that twisted down the steep incline to the beach below. "How in bloody hell did she ever find this path?" Mark asked a thorny lizard lazily sunbathing on a rock.

He finally reached the beach and pulled off his shoes. The hot sand oozed up between his toes as he walked toward

Alexa. Against her back, the untied strap of her red bikini flapped in the fickle breeze. Mark stood beside her, casting a large, dark shadow across her golden body. A light film of suntan lotion made her skin glisten and smell faintly of coconut. He had an almost irresistible urge to lift the ruff of tawny hair, highlighted by pale gold streaks, from the top of her shoulders and kiss the back of her neck.

A cat's paw of wind off the bay floated over her, cooling her momentarily and lifting her long hair. Half asleep, Alexa slowly moved. She realized what had interrupted her nap—the sun had disappeared. It couldn't be rain because it rarely rained here, except for the *chubasco*. The memory of that terrifying storm snapped Alexa back to full consciousness, and she looked skyward for a do-it-yourself weather forecast.

"Mark!" Struggling to right herself, Alexa felt his bare foot pressing down between her shoulder blades.

"I wouldn't make any hasty moves if I were you." He laughed as he ran his big toe down her spine. "Unless, of course, you think this is the French Riviera."

Alexa felt her face go brick red as she remembered she'd undone her bikini top while trying to even out her tan. She reached back searching for the tiny hook.

"Need any help?" A shadow of amusement colored his voice.

"No." Rehooking her suit, Alexa righted herself and turned to face him. How had he found her beach?

"Thought you might like some lunch." Mark spread his towel out next to hers and placed the paper sack he was carrying between them.

Alexa hastily put on her sunglasses. From behind dark lenses she watched Mark sort out the mini-picnic. There wasn't a spare inch of flesh on his long-limbed, athletic frame. His broad shoulders were well muscled and lightly tanned. Dense, crinkly, black hair covered his chest and trailed down under the waistband of his bathing suit. She remembered the way she'd kissed him last night and her cheeks began to burn again.

"Here." With an encouraging smile Mark handed her a sandwich. She was obviously more surprised to see him than he'd anticipated. "And the all-American beverage available in every country on this planet." He gave her an ice-cold can of Coca-Cola.

"Thanks, I'm starving, but I'm too lazy to hike over that hill just for food." She popped the tab on the Coke and a cool spray misted her leg. "Hey, next time don't shake it," she teased, reaching for a napkin to wipe off her knee. She felt more relaxed now after the tension of the first few minutes.

"Yes, Your Highness." Mark made a mock bow from his crossed-legged sitting position. From behind his gold-rimmed Cartier sunglasses, Mark's eyes casually wandered over the full curves of her breasts threatening to spill out of her bikini top. Her taut nipples were clearly outlined through the thin fabric. He reluctantly took his eyes from the softly swelling arches of her chest and turned to look at the ridge. "How'd you ever find the path down here?"

When Alexa explained she borrowed a shovel from the properties department and used leverage to pry out the various rocks until she made the trail, Mark was incredulous. "You're not joking. Are you?"

"Nope," Alexa said firmly between bites of her sandwich. "That's how I did it. Some rocks were too big for me to move, so I made the trail go around them." She picked up the small bag of potato chips and placed the corner between her teeth and ripped it open. "Want some?"

"No." Mark finished his sandwich and stretched out full-length on his towel. Casually he rolled onto his side and propped himself up on his elbow so he could pick at the grapes while he watched her.

Alexa stared out at the waves gently lapping on the shore a few yards in front of her. She couldn't see Mark's eyes, which were concealed by his dark glasses, but she could feel them inspecting her. She found his nearness, his seeking her out on this lonely beach, both disturbing and exciting. She was determined not to encourage him. The way she'd responded to his kiss probably branded her as an easy mark. Why had she kissed him with such passion? It had been well over a year since she'd been with a man. Naturally, that explained her reaction to Mark.

"Let me hear you say your lines. Come on. Give it a go."

Alexa reluctantly retrieved the script from her sand-covered

Vuitton and handed it to him. "Start at the top of the page with the paperclip."

Mark gazed at Alexa's profile as she again turned to stare out at the cove. He wondered if she knew how adorable she looked with her cute little turned-up nose resolutely pointing dead ahead while she concentrated. Once again he was tempted, very tempted, to kiss her, but he didn't. He couldn't rush her or he wouldn't get anywhere with her at all.

"Excellent," Mark said after Alexa delivered her last line. She turned to face him and he slowly pulled her sunglasses from her face. He tipped down his Cartiers, peering at her over the top of the sunglasses. "Now try it with some feeling."

"I'll try," Alexa whispered. Saying anything to Mark as intimate as the lines in this scene would prove difficult. But it was probably a good test for the ordeal to come in front of the camera.

Once Alexa began reciting her lines and trying for the emotion that accompanied them, she forgot Mark. Once more the pain she'd experienced with Paul helped her pretend to be the character. She prayed she could use this technique when she actually had to perform the scene.

"Smashing," Mark said when she finished. He saw the tears in her eyes and reached over and ran his finger up the curve of her cheek. "Save it for the camera." He hoped his lighthearted remark would make her less self-conscious.

With the back of her hand Alexa wiped the tears away. Mark's masculinity and his ever-present sense of purpose had a magnetic pull on her. She blinked back an errant tear and saw a face from the past—Paul's. Once again she felt the tug of war between the past and the present. As usual the past won. Don't be taken in again, she reminded herself.

"Let's swim." She vaulted to her feet and sprinted to the water's edge without waiting for a reply.

When Alexa broke the spell and dashed to the surf, Mark followed. The sparkling sapphire waves tumbled gently onto the white sand. "Is it cold?" He saw goosebumps had prickled across her golden skin.

"Not really."

"Liar," he laughed after he stepped into the foamy surf. "It's March. The air's hot, but the water's still cool."

With a sidelong glance Mark watched Alexa. She stood there, hands on her hips, bringing her breasts into full prominence. A gentle breeze tossed her hair, sweeping it away from her face in sunstruck waves of gold.

"Race you to the rock," Alexa challenged, pointing to a large boulder in the center of the jumble of rocks protecting the cove. Without waiting for his reply, she dove into the chilly water.

The shock of the cold water momentarily took her breath away. She faltered for a few seconds before she found her rhythm. Kicking rapidly to warm herself, she swam toward the rock. She had no idea what she'd do or say to him once they reached the rock. The best plan would have been to return to the set, but it was too late for that now. Her hand touched the rock and she surfaced, sputtering for breath and tossing her hair back from her face.

"Where've you been?" Mark asked, his voice easy, masculine, deep.

Alexa looked up through the haze of salty water dripping into her eyes. She shook her head in disbelief as he helped her up onto the narrow shelf worn into the rock by the sea. "You're fast," she grudgingly admitted.

Mark settled back against the warm rock, letting its radiant heat warm his body. High above he saw the pristine blue sky that domed overhead and met the deeper blue of the Sea of Cortés. He closed his eyes and smiled to himself. Alexa had looked so chagrined to see him there first. She was more competitive than he'd realized. He liked that in women; it made them more interesting.

Conscious of how disheveled she must look, Alexa finger-combed her hair. Through her wet lashes she watched Mark drying in the sun. The water only enhanced his looks. His wavy black hair glistened in the sunshine while her hair was a tangled mess. His eyes were closed and pinpoints of water studded his lashes as they lay against his cheek. Droplets of water sparkled across the dense hair on his chest.

"See anything you like?" Mark's eyes flew open and he caught her looking at him. He grinned mischievously.

"I . . . I just wondered where an Englishman gets a tan like yours in March."

"Around the pool at the Beverly Hills Hotel. I sat there for days reading reports and waiting for the daily rushes from down here. I wanted to find out why this movie was so far behind schedule."

"Oh." Alexa settled herself against the rock and closed her eyes. She felt the familiar shadow block out the sun and sensed Mark was leaning toward her just short of touching. When his lips brushed hers, she froze, hands at her sides clutching the rock. She refused to return his kiss and he withdrew. Alexa opened her eyes and found him inches from her face. He caressed her, running his fingers along her cheek and down her neck.

"Alexa," Mark breathed into her lips as he kissed her again. This time Alexa parted her lips and slid her tongue forward to meet his.

Mark kissed her slowly and lingeringly, giving her time to respond. He hadn't intended to kiss her, knowing she was still wary of him, but he couldn't resist. She looked so damned cute, so sensuous in that red bikini with her erect nipples straining against the clinging fabric. Her wet hair, molded to her head, emphasized her luminous green eyes. He curved his hand around the back of her neck and stroked the soft skin behind her ear with his thumb. He drew her closer, reveling in the sensation of her soft, almost bare breasts against his chest.

The warmth rapidly building in Alexa surpassed the heat of the rock. Suddenly she didn't want to recall all the reasons she shouldn't be doing this. She snapped the door shut on her memories and gave in to the temptation she'd been resisting. Alexa murmured a small sigh of pleasure as the achingly pleasant sensation of being in Mark's arms took hold. Clinging to him, she sensuously slid her fingers through his thick, wet hair. The kiss, a deep, probing, magical kiss, lengthened as his tongue languidly worked its way across her teeth and then tangled with her tongue. She twisted in his arms so that she could feel the rough texture of his skin against her throbbing breasts. Her stomach fell in a pleasure-filled free fall. She wanted him, oh, how, she wanted him.

As he kissed her Mark felt Alexa's slow release, as if her defenses had collapsed and she had given herself up to the inevitable. Her fingers plowed furrows in his damp hair, sending waves of response through his body, hardening him. When Alexa arched against him and moved her breasts in a slow circle against his chest, his nerves went haywire. The gnawing ache in his groin increased.

Suddenly her palms were on his shoulders, pushing him away. Mark stopped kissing her but held her close. *What the hell happened?* He took a minute to let his breathing approach normal. "Alexa?" Her head rested against his shoulder; her eyes were squeezed shut. He gently leaned her against the rock and released her.

Alexa felt the welcoming warmth of the rock as Mark freed her. He'd be angry, and she didn't blame him. He'd think she was a tease. Alexa opened her eyes and found he hadn't moved. He sat there, still just inches from her, his gray eyes staring at her. His hair was mussed, and a wavy black curl had fallen onto his forehead. She could feel the heat of his body across the small space separating them.

"I just can't," Alexa tried to explain.

"I know. It's all right," was his unanticipated reply. He leaned toward her, visibly restraining himself from touching her.

"My husband . . . we were just divorced."

"It's been about a year, hasn't it?"

Alexa nodded. Where'd he get his information?

"It takes a long time. It took me three years." It was a long moment before his words seemed to reach her. Alexa's vivid green eyes widened and she looked confused. "In some ways I've never grown accustomed to Caroline's leaving me."

Alexa shifted uncomfortably. "Three years?"

Mark nodded his affirmation. His steady gray eyes never left hers.

Alexa was dumbfounded. The men she knew, with their masculine pride, would never admit their wives left them, or that recovery had taken so long. She hadn't anticipated his candor—it stopped her cold.

Mark waited, letting the impact of his words take effect. For a moment he thought Alexa might cry. It amazed him how the simple truth disarmed people in a way that no elaborate lie ever could. He'd dropped all pretense with her, revealing more about himself than he intended.

"You've been divorced three years," Alexa gulped, "and you're just now getting over it?"

Mark hesitated. He looked beyond Alexa at the surging sea.

He liked to maintain a certain level of evasiveness with people, holding himself back, avoiding real intimacy. "No, it's been twelve years." His own voice sounded strangely flat. "It took about three years before I adjusted to what had happened."

"Twelve years?" Alexa was too stunned to reason. "I . . . I hope it doesn't take me that long."

"It won't unless you let it."

"Meaning?"

"Don't be afraid to try again." A minute passed, rife with unspoken questions, while Mark waited for a response. When none came, he bent forward and kissed her lightly on the nose. "Don't be afraid of me"

"I'm not." Alexa's too-quick reply assured him that this was the case. "Are you recommending casual sex as some sort of home remedy?"

"Definitely not. I'm not trying to seduce you. I'm just getting a head start."

"On what?" Alexa asked, ignoring his disarming grin.

"On you. When you come to London with your play, I want you to know me, be comfortable with me. Then we'll see what happens."

Alexa had a sudden, primitive urge to run for cover. "Race you back!"

She refused to risk another glance at him and dove into the water, swimming as fast as she could. When the water became too shallow to swim she stumbled to her feet. Mark stood in the frothy surf, his hand extended.

"I give up." Alexa managed to laugh through the mat of tangled hair, covering her face.

Alexa and Mark were boarding the Volkswagen van, used as a shuttle between the hotel and the movie location, when a jet streaked noisily overhead. It tipped its wings in a wide arc over the Sea of Cortéz and turned north. Alexa watched Mark's eyes follow the plane, his smile turning to a frown as his brows drew together.

"The five-thirty flight to L.A." Alexa tossed her bag into the back seat of the van. Mark nodded absentmindedly and helped her inside.

On the drive along the dirt road back into the village, Alexa and Mark were the only passengers. The driver listened to the Mexican radio station broadcasting from the only other city of any size on the Baja peninsula, La Paz. Alexa looked back over her shoulder at the Sea of Cortéz, sparkling azure-bright in the late afternoon sun, until rooster tails of dust streamed out from beneath the tires, obliterating her view. Gazing forward again, Alexa peeked at Mark. He was still frowning thoughtfully and looking out the window. When the van careened around a curve where a small cluster of homes stood, it scattered a group of children playing in the dusty road and threw Alexa against Mark. Shaking her head in dismay at the Mexicans who loved to drive so fast, she clutched Mark's arm.

"Is something wrong?" she asked. Why had he suddenly become so quiet?

Mark saw the concern in Alexa's deep green eyes; he was unexpectedly touched. On the beach he'd thought he had broken through her emotional barrier, but she'd suddenly retreated. One step forward and two back described Alexa. He put his arm across the back of the seat and let his hand rest idly on her shoulder. There would be nothing wrong in telling her about the trouble at Windsor Airlines. It would probably be a good idea to share something that wasn't personal, to discuss something that wouldn't threaten her.

"I was thinking about the problem at Windsor Airlines."

Alexa waited. Perhaps he wouldn't want to talk about his business problems with her—Paul never had. When it was too late, Alexa's attorney had explained them to her.

"They'll be bankrupt within the year unless the ticket-laundering scheme that's plaguing them is stopped." Mark shifted slightly in his seat so he could face Alexa squarely. "Large blocks of tickets are purchased in Third World countries and redeemed in England. Airline tickets are good from country to country and can be exchanged for cash."

"How does that hurt Windsor Air?"

"Suppose you go with pounds to . . . say . . . Nigeria. There you exchange your pounds for the local currency. But instead of converting at one of the official money exchanges, you go to a black-market dealer. He'll give you double or triple the official rate to get hard currency—pounds, deutsche marks, or dollars. Now you have substantially more of the local currency than you could have obtained legally. Next you buy a block of airline tickets from a Nigerian travel agent. Since you have more local currency than the pounds you began with, you can buy many more tickets."

"I would then return to England and redeem the tickets for cash."

"Exactly. The airline is out the money and it will fly with empty seats. It's pure chaos. It's been a big problem for the United States as well."

The van fishtailed around a bend, forcing Alexa up against Mark. She'd been uncomfortably aware of his fingers lightly stroking her shoulder. It was a relaxed, seemingly unconscious gesture, but she felt it everywhere. When she tried to move, his arm tightened around her. She gave up and snuggled into the warm curve of his body.

As they drove along San Lucas Bay, Alexa watched the fishing boats, down from Los Angeles for the season, bob up and down. A spark ignited in the back of her mind.

"Wait a minute! Why doesn't Windsor Air take the tickets back to Nigeria, redeem them there, reconvert on the black market, and return home?" Even as she spoke, Alexa felt her confidence evaporating. This was too simple, too obvious.

"In the first place, black-market exchanges are illegal. In the second, removing large amounts of currency from these countries is prohibited. The airline would lose its operating permit." Mark squeezed Alexa and kissed the top of her still-damp head.

"I guess they use these countries because they need our money."

"Absolutely. They use poor countries with thriving black markets. In America, England, and other economically stable nations there isn't a black market because there isn't a need. These rings of criminals have hit most of the major airlines in all the industrialized nations. Before Interpol can catch up with them, they move to another country."

As Alexa thought about the problem, the van began the struggle up the long, perpendicular driveway to the Finisterra Hotel with its spectacular vista. Situated atop the high, narrow peninsula that was all that remained of the mountains that formed the spine of Baja before gradually tapering off for another quarter of a mile and collapsing into the ocean, the hotel commanded the best view in Cabo San Lucas. The awesome power of the Pacific pounded on the western side of the resort while to the east lay the picturesque serenity of the San Lucas Bay and the tiny village lining its shore.

The vehicle reached the summit and rolled to a stop in front of the open-air lobby. Mark helped Alexa from the van. Blowing through the lobby from the Pacific, a cool breeze lifted Alexa's hair. Mark guided her across the reception area to the bar.

"Do you have any idea who's behind this?" Alexa asked as Mark pulled out a chair for her at one of the tables facing the water.

Mark moved his chair closer to hers before sitting down. "We have some reason to think they're British." He didn't want to elaborate.

"Well, then it's simple. Put all the names of anyone British traveling to these countries in a computer and figure it out that way."

Mark's laughter was deep and richly masculine. Alexa felt herself flush. That was a silly idea—too simple.

Mark reached out and rumpled her already tousled golden hair. She was cute when she blushed that way. "You've been watching the telly too much. The criminals may never appear on a computer analysis. They may be using multiple passports or multiple entry points. It's even possible that they could be using military or diplomatic passports. In Third World nations, where security is often sloppy, those people are often just waved through passport checkpoints."

"But you believe it's more than one person."

Mark signaled for the waiter. "It has to be. Someone knows the market and at least one other person shuffles the tickets through a number of travel agents."

"A number?"

Mark waited for Alexa to order before he ordered and answered her. "Part of the problem is once the tickets are brought out of the Third World country they are then sold and resold—very quickly—through a network of shady travel agents. When they're redeemed, it's not by the person purchasing them."

"Oh, that does make it difficult." Alexa looked out at the horizon, where the sun was descending behind a bank of flossy white clouds. Iridescent shafts of light penetrated the spaces between the closely packed clouds. Something else occurred to her, but she hesitated before asking, "Do your investors stand to lose a lot of money if this can't be stopped?" Surely he'd suffer financially as well.

"No, Windsor Airlines is privately owned." After the waiter arrived with their margaritas, Mark continued, "I won't lose any money personally."

Then why did he care so much? Alexa took a small sip of the potent drink and stared at the sun as it dipped even lower into the sea, glossing the deep blue water with a coral sheen.

"I work most of the year with the Commonwealth Trade Alliance. My investment company is run from my London office by my employees. I'm not usually involved in its day-to-day operations anymore unless, like this project, something is amiss."

"I didn't realize you worked for the government."

"I don't. The Alliance is a private trade organization. I represent the Commonwealth Trade Alliance at meetings in various nations. We're trying to reverse the tide of cheap imports that have cost so many jobs in England. That's why I insisted the cast and crew of this film be British, and why we'll return to England to edit."

"I see." But Alexa didn't understand at all. What she'd learned about Mark today, personally and professionally, didn't match her first impression of him. He had a power and a depth that fascinated her.

The clouds had scattered, leaving a few fleecy puffs behind to catch the last light of day. The sun set in an awesome burst of color as Mark looked out across the water. What could be better, he thought, than watching the sunset with Alexa? Several other things he'd rather do with her occurred to him, but for now he had to be content to settle for the sunset.

Alexa touched his arm and cast him a radiant glance from beneath heavy lashes. She looked as if she sparkled from the inside out. "Look at that sunset. It's too beautiful to be described in words."

Mark merely nodded. How was it Alexa could make him ache with longing just by touching him? She had a natural, unaffected sensuality about her that he found extremely provocative. She sat there oblivious to the way she looked with her bronzed skin gilded a rosy coral by the setting sun. Her

hair itself was a shimmering sunset of tawny gold flashed
with pale blond streaks. She smiled again. A totally relaxed,
genuine smile—just for him. He put down his margarita and
reached for her.

# Chapter 7

Her white halter-top sundress swishing as she walked, Alexa hurried through the lobby oblivious to the admiring glances cast in her direction. Where was Mark? She checked the restaurant and found he was already seated at a table with Colin and Renata opposite him and Linda beside him The only available chair was at the far end of the table opposite Steven Hunter. Alexa hesitated This wasn't what she had expected when Mark asked her to join him for dinner. She'd hoped for something a good deal more romantic, like last night's dinner on the terrace.

Mark still hadn't looked up when Steven came jauntily walking over to her openly admiring what he saw. "I've saved a spot for you, luv."

Steven pulled out a chair for her as the group turned to greet her. Mark quickly glanced at her and beamed his approval. Alexa's spirits soared but did an instant nosedive when he returned his attention to Linda. Where had Alexa gotten the impression Mark and Linda didn't care for each other? They certainly looked chummy.

"All set for tomorrow?" Renata asked.

Tomorrow? She'd forgotten all about tomorrow. How could

she have? ". . . Yes." Tomorrow she would have to take off her clothes and film the scene.

"I'm not going to spend a lot of time rehearsing," Giles said. "I want you as natural and spontaneous as you were the other day with Colin. After you're made up and dressed, Linda will go over your marks with you. Then we'll shoot."

"Don't worry, luv," Steven said, his voice silky smooth, "you'll be so good they'll be howling for you to do more movies."

"I'm not an actress," Alexa hissed. Steven looked so taken aback that she was immediately sorry she'd overreacted. "I'm sorry. I become so nervous every time I think about filming that scene."

Steven smiled compassionately, reassuring Alexa. While he told her about Hunter Films' successes, she considered how very handsome he was. Unlike Mark, Steven wasn't overtly masculine. But with his fair hair and wide blue eyes, Steven looked as if he'd just stepped off the pages of *Gentlemen's Quarterly*. His Italian designer clothing echoed the perfection of his handsome face—stylish and expensive with just the right touch of casualness. He was too perfect, too polished, too processed, too . . . Hollywood. He was like so many show-biz types she'd come to know since writing her book. Their relentless, albeit synthetic, smiles were but a thin veneer, disguising their ruthless ambition.

"Alexa, do you have any projects you're working on that I might be interested in?" Steven asked, his smile appearing almost genuine; but when she told him about the play she could see he wasn't interested. "I've started my own production company and I'm looking for another action-adventure to film. I've got everything lined up to begin after this film wraps. But I'm not satisfied with the script that I have. Thought you might have something I could use."

"Aren't you going to be working with your father?" Alexa politely asked as she peeked at Mark. His eyes met hers and he winked. Alexa cursed the mariachi band for playing so loudly that it was impossible to hear any conversation from Mark's end of the table.

"No, luv," Steven answered, a strange expression marring his handsome face. "I want to get out on my own. My first project will be a low-budget film, but I'm confident of an enormous return. I could use you"—he reached out and squeezed her hand as she toyed with her fork— "if not as an actress then as a writer."

Alexa thought about the several story outlines she had. They were just rough ideas at this point, but perhaps one could be developed into a screenplay rather than a novel as she'd intended. There was no doubt about it—she needed money. After what Paul had done, she couldn't live on her existing funds for the several years it might take to write a first-rate novel like *The Last Chance.* "I have several outlines. They could be developed into novels or films. They're just ideas at this stage."

"Could I see them?" Let your agent know first, of course."

"I don't have one right now." She didn't add that her agent had known about Paul all along but failed to tell her. "The play has to be my first priority—"

Amused laughter from Giles cut into the conversation. "My brother—the shoe magnate."

"Really?" Alexa asked, anxious to be included in Mark's conversation. "Your brother owns a shoe company?"

"No, Alexa," Renata answered, "his brother supervises a shoe factory."

Mark caught Alexa's eye and smiled with that same virile appeal that had thrilled and frightened her all afternoon. With difficulty she concentrated on the conversation.

"He was out of work for over two years and was positively twitchy," Giles explained, "until Mark brought a new factory to the area."

"I didn't do it personally, of course. It was part of a Trade Alliance project to provide jobs for displaced workers in the area." Mark addressed the group, but his eyes never left Alexa's.

Alexa lowered her lashes and smiled at Mark. She wished there was some polite way of getting someone to change seats with her, but there wasn't. The waiter arrived and began taking orders at Mark's end of the table. Alexa noticed Steven's brows were knit together.

"Don't let him fool you." Steven lowered his voice and leaned toward Alexa. "Kimbrough's all do-gooder bullshit. He doesn't receive a salary, but don't think he doesn't make a

bloody fortune from all his whirling around the globe with
the Trade Alliance."

"How?" Alexa found it difficult to believe a man would
spend so much time doing something when he wasn't paid
even a token salary. Paul certainly never would have considered it.

Steven peered toward the other end of the table before answering in a still lower voice. "How do you think? Under the
table. He gets a cut from every deal he puts together." Steven
laughed cynically. "Of course no one's to know. Wouldn't be
ethical, but he doesn't fool me. I've known him for years."

Would Mark do something like that?

"Now, about your outlines." Steven's smile had returned.
"If I decide to use one, would you have time to work on it
while we're still in Mexico? I need it as soon as possible. I
want to begin preproduction work as soon as we wrap here."

"Yes, the play is finished." Alexa considered the situation
for a moment. "I've written plays. I worked with a theater
group, you know. I wrote my own plays, but I've only recently studied screenwriting, observing how they adapted my
novel. I'm not sure—"

"Do the best you can, luv. I need a great idea. I can always
rewrite where necessary."

All through dinner Steven talked nonstop about his plans
for his production company, but Alexa barely listened. She
kept casting sidelong glances at Mark. She didn't want to believe anything Steven had told her, but her common sense
insisted it was quite possibly true. Her ebullient spirits sank,
and the emptiness that had been her constant companion
since Paul left returned. Despite his pretensions, Mark was as
opportunistic and conniving as Paul had been.

"Alexa," Giles said after they'd finished eating, "you have
an early call tomorrow. Did you know?"

Alexa nodded; she'd been trying to forget. How was she
going to face tomorrow?

"Tomorrow night let's all celebrate," announced Steven.
"After Alexa finishes, you'll all be my guests at that little spot
down on the beach, Daiquiri Dick's."

"Good idea," Renata said. The gold light from the Mexican
lanterns made her hair look more ginger than red. Her deep
blue eyes twinkled as she looked at Giles.

"I guess I'd better go to bed," Alexa said, twisting a stray ringlet around her little finger.

When she stood up to leave, Mark caught her eye. "You'll be fine, Alexa."

"I'm coming with you." Linda rose and followed Alexa. "I'm really knackered."

On the way upstairs Alexa couldn't keep from asking, "Linda, for some reason I had the impression you and Mark didn't care for each other."

Linda hesitated, wondering if she wanted to reveal anything this personal. Although she liked Alexa and understood how upset the divorce had left her because she'd been through a similar situation, Linda had never discussed her problems with anyone. "Mark has every reason to dislike me." Linda realized there comes a time in every friendship when you have to take that extra step toward intimacy or forever remain superficial friends. "I told you about my divorce but not the whole story."

Alexa recalled Linda had told her she'd been divorced for two years and had a young daughter in London. Apparently there was more than what she'd discussed previously, but then Alexa hadn't been completely candid about her divorce either.

They arrived at Alexa's door. "Come in for a while." Cautiously Alexa opened the door and peeked in. Was she ever going to stop anticipating that the police would be waiting for her?

"Let's sit out here," Alexa said after they were in her room and she'd opened the balcony door. She gestured to the two wicker chairs.

Linda slid into a chair and gazed out at the Pacific. The full moon shot ribbons of wavering light across the rippled water, reminding her of the night she'd met Ian. The water on the Thames had sparkled under a hunter's moon, putting stars in her eyes so she didn't see what a phony Ian Carlisle was. "As I told you, I married Ian after knowing him for less than a month. When I immediately became pregnant, I was determined to make my marriage work."

"You mentioned he was unfaithful." Like Paul. A surge of compassion for Linda and a fresh wave of sadness at what Paul had done came over Alexa.

"Yes, Ian began almost the minute we were married. Everyone knew but me." Linda's terse laugh was filled with bitterness. "It amazes me how everyone can hardly wait to tell you they knew all along—after you find out."

"I know what you mean," Alexa said, swinging her feet up onto the balcony's rail. "Everyone was so informative after I discovered Paul had someone else."

"Ian never loved me," Linda said, her voice cracking with emotion.

"Linda, I'm certain he did. You're so beautiful, so talented." Alexa stopped, not knowing what else to say. It was impossible to believe Ian could not have loved Linda with her willowy figure, complexion like fresh cream, and wide violet-blue eyes set off by chestnut-brown hair.

"Ian married me for my family's connections. You see, Alexa, even today in England background is everything. I had entrée to all the proper people. Ian had an investment company, and after our marriage he found many clients in my family's circle of friends." Linda paused, despising herself for what she'd done, and hating confessing it to a friend whose opinion she valued. "There's something I must do when I return to London, and that's why I need Mark. By the way, I insisted on sitting beside him at dinner although I knew he was saving the seat for you."

"Really?" Alexa said casually, but Linda could hear the smile in her voice. Good, she thought, there wasn't anything better for a broken heart than a new love—or an old love rediscovered.

"I've known Mark for years," Linda continued. "His best friend, Warren Rutherford-Jaymes, is the man I've always loved. The problem was I met Warren when I was too young —just eighteen. We dated for the next two years while I attended St. Martin's School of Art. Then we were informally engaged for the next two years. Warren didn't want to rush me. He was six years older and felt I needed to start my career as a designer before we married. I met Ian when Warren was out of the country on a business trip. Ian was so exciting! He constantly told me he loved me and sent me gifts and flowers. Warren had been warm and comfortable, not exciting. Then Ian pressed me to marry him. Instead of waiting to see if our relationship would last, I eloped."

This didn't sound like the practical, rational person Alexa knew, but women in love did strange things. "Didn't you explain to Warren how you felt?"

"No, we were married before he returned. I didn't even ring him up; I left him a note."

"A note?" Alexa jerked her feet down from the rail. "A note —after four years?"

"Yes, it was the most cowardly thing I've ever done." The light from the room behind them illuminated the tears in Linda's eyes. She fumbled in her purse and managed to find a tissue, thinking she should be past crying over this. "I can't believe I behaved so badly to someone who loved me and had been so kind."

"Did you ever talk to Warren?" Alexa recalled how she'd waited for some sort of explanation from Paul, but none ever came. She couldn't believe Linda had been this callous.

"No, I should have. It wouldn't have made it right, but it would have been the proper thing to do. Warren must have been deeply hurt and humiliated. All of our friends travel in the same circles. Everyone knew I jilted him, just as later they all knew Ian cheated on me."

"What does Mark have to do with all this?"

"I forced myself on him tonight because he's been ignoring me for years now. I wanted to talk to him, to let him know I've changed. Warren and Mark are like brothers. I want to soften Mark up a bit before I go to Warren. As soon as I return to London I plan on asking him to give me another chance."

In the silence that followed Alexa listened to the breaking of the waves on the beach below and the sharp cawing of a seagull strutting along the rail of an adjacent balcony. Another chance? Alexa knew she'd never give Paul another chance. It was over; he was remarried. "Why didn't you go to him right after you left Ian?"

"I was upset and humiliated at what Ian had done. I just wanted to hide, so I took the job with Hunter Films. I've lived out of England for the last two years while I waited for my life to come around." Linda kept her tone matter-of-fact. It wouldn't do any good telling Alexa how difficult it had been leaving her young daughter in England during this time, but it wouldn't have been good for Holly to be shuttled about while Linda traipsed around the world with Hunter Films. Now, no matter what happened with Warren, she would be with Holly once more. Now Linda had the funds to open her own boutique, and her life would be back on track where it had been before Ian detoured her.

"I know just how you felt. I insisted on being a consultant on this movie just so I could get away from my problems. I said I wanted to learn about screenwriting, but I wanted to hide."

"Alexa, it was worse with Paul than you've told me, wasn't it?"

Bone-tired, Alexa had to face an ordeal tomorrow. How much did she want to upset herself by discussing Paul tonight? But she went ahead, telling Linda everything, including the fact Paul had concealed his long-term affair with the woman he married two days after their divorce became final.

"I'm sorry, Alexa, it was really cheeky of me to put all my problems on you after what you've been through. I never would have had I known." Linda sensed Alexa was avoiding the core of the betrayal. "There's more, isn't there?"

Alexa blinked hard, refusing to let tears come. "Yes, I found out Paul stayed with me until he was certain I signed the movie contract. You see, California's a community property state. Paul waited to divorce me until 'my little project' as he called it, was sold to a publisher. He waited until my agent negotiated the movie rights and I signed the contract. Then he left. I hadn't wanted to make my book into a movie. I was afraid it would be ruined, but Paul insisted. When we divorced, he received half the money and I got half of his debts. I didn't know how great his—or I should say 'our'—losses in the market had been until my attorney told me. Now I have very little money."

"That's not what hurts, is it?"

"No, if he'd loved me as much as I loved him, we could have solved our financial problems. I didn't care about the money except now I have to be practical. Writing for a living is a hit-and-miss proposition. I'll have to make the money I do have last, so I won't have to take another job to support my writing."

"Come to England. We'll help each other." Linda looked at her watch, thinking how furious Giles would be if he knew she'd kept Alexa up this long. "It's monstrously late and you have an early call. I'm leaving straight away."

Alexa followed her to the door. "I dreaded talking about this, but now that I have I feel better."

"Holding it inside only prolongs the hurt." Linda hugged Alexa, squeezing her tightly. "Get some sleep. I'll see you in the morning."

After she said good-night to Linda, Alexa walked over to the vase of pink roses. Absentmindedly she plucked the wilted flowers and tossed them into the wastepaper basket. Who had tried to have her arrested? Why? Tomorrow was just hours away. How was she going to do that scene?

She pulled one of the still-fresh roses from the arrangement, removing one petal at a time. Deep within her something clicked, like a revolver being cocked, sending through her a mysterious yet unmistakable warning . . . tomorrow.

# Chapter 8

Mark checked his watch for the third time in the last fifteen minutes—almost noon. They should be filming Alexa's scene by now. How long would it take? Hours probably. Everything about making a movie took longer than expected. He returned his attention to the stack of papers before him. The daily camera and production reports were still a mystery to him, but he had begun to understand the average daily footage sheets and the count of script pages filmed per day. The cash flow charts needed no explanation: the bottom line. Every business had one, and it gave Mark immense satisfaction to finally understand some phase of film making. Dammit, he cursed under his breath, seeing the trail of red ink all too clearly. Hearing a noise, he turned and saw Linda Carlisle at the trailer door. "Are they shooting yet?"

"Yes, but they aren't ready for Alexa. Making a movie is a dicey business requiring a good deal of patience. It'll be another two hours before they need her."

Mark couldn't see Alexa, with all her restless energy, waiting patiently. "Should we keep her company?"

"You may if you like. Come on."

Mark pushed the sheets aside and followed Linda out the door. They fell in step together, heading toward the trailers.

"I'm busy being a go-fer, meaning I go for things. I'm but one of several assistants to the director, which means I get all sorts of odd jobs. Hence my title," she bowed, "go-fer."

Mark laughed and studied Linda closely. Still beautiful, she seemed much more mature than the girl Warren had been in love with years ago. But then again, he'd been very different himself back then. Time does that for you, he decided, time and experience.

"Mark, how well do you know Alexa?"

Mark gauged his response carefully. "I've seen a bit of her since I've been down here. She's extremely talented."

"Absolutely," Linda answered, "but I'm not sure she's aware of it. She's frightfully insecure and defensive at times."

"Yes, her divorce is undoubtedly the root of the problem."

Linda halted and looked up at Mark curiously. "Alexa told you about Paul?"

"Yes." *But not all that she could have,* he added silently.

"She made a serious mistake and she knows it." Linda dug her foot into the sand. "We all make those mistakes, you know."

For a moment Mark thought Linda was referring to his divorce from Caroline. The mournful look in her eyes changed his mind, and he touched her shoulder lightly. "I know what you're trying to tell me," he said gently, "what you wanted me to know last night."

"I've made a terrible mistake." Linda stared down at her feet. Mark, does Warren ever mention me?"

"No." Mark was certain Warren still cared for Linda. He hadn't been able to commit himself to a woman since she'd left him. But Mark refused to interfere in his friend's business.

"I didn't really think so." Linda stopped and nodded toward the hut housing the numerous portable generators necessary to run the power-hungry equipment used in filming. "I've to check on something. Maybe you can help me by explaining to Alexa what's going to happen when we start shooting."

"You'd better fill me in because I haven't the foggiest."

After Linda gave him a quick rundown, Mark walked toward a long, narrow trailer divided into several side-by-side compartments. The honey wagon, with its cramped stalls, served as a holding area for bit actors whose status on the set didn't merit them a trailer of their own. The intense light of the midday sun reflected off the trailer as Mark rapped on the third door.

"Who is it?"

"Mark. Are you dressed? May I come in? Linda sent me over to explain a few details to you."

"Oh, aah . . . sure. Come in."

Mark stepped into the tiny cubicle, bracing himself as the cool air from the air-conditioner engulfed him, causing the thin film of perspiration on his skin to chill. Alexa lay on a narrow daybed. Her leonine hair had been coiffed into a prim mass of curls popular in the early eighteen hundreds. She wore a thin wrap robe that clung suggestively to her soft curves, making it obvious she had nothing on beneath it. He smiled to himself; no wonder she hesitated.

Mark reached for the only chair in the cramped room, swung it around backward and sat down straddling it, facing a sepia-tone poster of Judy Garland someone had taped to the formica wall. Placing his arms casually across the chair's back, he asked, "How're you doing?"

"Fine, I guess." Her eyes refused to meet his. Her tone was polite and nothing more. "Are they ready for me yet?"

The coolness of her voice surprised Mark. Was she uncomfortable because she had so little on, or had she regressed again? A bit of both, no doubt.

"No. It'll be about two hours more."

"Grrrreat," Alexa moaned.

There was a loud knock on the door and from the other side came, "Don't touch her. I don't have time to redo any of her makeup."

"Don't worry, Carl," Alexa said, raising her voice and propping herself up on one elbow. "That's the head makeup artist. They've spent hours making up every inch of my body. In the nineteenth century women didn't sport bikini lines."

With difficulty Mark suppressed a grin. The thought of Alexa's body with nothing on it but bikini lines was very appealing. "They erased the lines? How?" Keeping her talking was the only way he knew to overcome her insecurity. She obviously wasn't thrilled to have him here. "Are you going to let me in on it or is it a trade secret?"

"I'm not sure what they used, but it took hours. They stood

me up like a scarecrow and painted me all over with a muddy mixture of clay and iodine and who knows?" She shrugged. "They waited for it to dry—which took forever—then washed it off."

"How could you come out all one color if you were already darker in some spots?"

"They used various shades of the same glop."

"Aaah." Mark liked the idea of Alexa being lighter in some places than in others. "You look a little too red. Are you supposed to?" He sensed that degree by degree she was relaxing.

"So they tell me." Alexa shook her head. "Apparently the cameras have filters or something. It'll look perfectly natural on film. Next they washed and styled my hair and applied twenty-five pounds of makeup to my face."

"I noticed. You don't usually wear any." Except for last night, he added to himself. She'd made a special effort to look good for him, and he'd been trapped at the other end of the table. The thought of food reminded him it was lunchtime. "Have you eaten?"

"No, I'm too nervous to be hungry, but I'd love a Coke."

"I'll get you one straight away," Mark said, sliding off the chair backward and coming to his feet.

Alexa breathed a sigh of relief watching Mark leave. She wasn't comfortable sitting here with nothing on but the cotton robe. He wasn't supposed to be on the set when they filmed the scene. He'd told her that himself. Why was he here now?

Linda let herself in. "Where's Mark?" She turned the chair around and sat down. She'd already decided they would be a perfect couple. Despite his reputation as a confirmed bachelor, Linda sensed Mark still suffered from the fiasco with Caroline Hampton. He probably needed a good woman, just as Alexa needed a good man.

"He's getting me a Coke. Is it going to be much longer?" Alexa wound a lock of hair around her finger.

Linda reached over and took Alexa's hand away. "Mustn't muss. There's been another delay. It'll be two hours at least. Mark will keep you company. I've boodles to do."

Linda hoped Alexa wouldn't be too upset to perform. After all, she wasn't a professional. It was obvious all this waiting was making her nervous. It was making Linda edgy too. She supposed that was because talking with Mark made her miss Warren all the more. She wanted to wrap this picture as quickly as possible and return to London.

Alexa nodded unenthusiastically. Last evening she'd have given just about anything to be near Mark, but today she wasn't so sure. He was probably just like Paul—ruthless and ambitious. She wasn't certain she wanted to know him any better.

"Linda, do you think Mark makes money under the table from his activities with the Trade Commission?"

"Of course not! What would make you even think such a thing? Look, I know what you're going through—I've been there. But every man isn't like Paul or Ian. Don't blame Mark for what Paul did or expect him to behave as Paul would. Being a trade adviser is like being on a Presidential commission in your country. He'd never embarrass himself by exploiting his position."

Linda shook her head with complete conviction. "Why would he? He's already made a fortune. I imagine he does it to help his family."

"What family?"

"Mark's parents are dead, but he has oodles of relatives in the distressed area outside Manchester where he grew up. He spends lots of time trying to redevelop the region. Remember last night when we discussed Giles's brother and the shoe factory? That was one of Mark's redevelopment projects." Linda paused, realizing Alexa was behaving normally considering her traumatic divorce. She'd met an attractive man, and now she was throwing up roadblocks because she was afraid. "You're interested in Mark, aren't you?"

"No!" Alexa denied emphatically and then hesitated. "Well . . . maybe a little."

Linda laughed again, tossing her dark brown hair from side to side. "It's all right. Just take your time. Who knows, maybe when we're in London . . ."

Alexa recognized the wistful note in her friend's voice. Didn't she owe Linda the truth? This affair with Warren had taken place years ago. It was totally unrealistic to expect him still to be in love with her.

"I think . . ." Alexa began cautiously, "you must talk to Warren to clear your conscience. But I'm not too certain he'll give you another chance. Do you have any reason to believe he still cares for you?"

"None at all. But sometimes, when our eyes have met across the room at a party, I've had a feeling . . ."

"Then talk to him and see—"

The trailer door swung open, letting in a blast of white-hot heat. "Sorry it took so long. I stopped to say hello to Renata." Mark started to hand Alexa the Coke.

"Hold it," Linda said. "We're moving Alexa to the wardrobe trailer where they'll dress her for the scene. It'll be a bit longer before they call for her, but the air conditioning is working better in there."

"Don't they usually dress first and then go to makeup?" Mark asked.

"Usually," Linda answered, "but Alexa had body work. It won't matter; her gown buttons down the front." She turned to Alexa. "Ready?"

Alexa carefully swung her legs down to the floor, clutching at the top of the wraparound gown. As she struggled to pull on her sandals with one hand, Mark's arm circled her waist, supporting her. The warmth of his hand penetrated the sheer fabric.

"All set?" Mark asked when the second shoe was on.

Alexa swallowed hard and nodded, turning slightly in his arm to face him. "Thanks." She caught a whiff of his woodsy aftershave lotion. In his slate-gray eyes there were tiny pinpricks of silver she'd not noticed before. His arm tightened around her waist and the bittersweet thrill of desire radiated through her. There was no denying it; she was attracted to this man.

Outside, Linda pointed to a trailer standing off to one side near the light trucks. "Over there Mark. I'll be back for you, Alexa, about a half hour before we need you. Mark will explain everything."

There was no one in the wardrobe trailer when they walked in. Dressforms stood watch over racks of clothing that filled the deserted room.

"They're probably at lunch. Let's wait over there." Mark indicated two chairs facing each other with a small, low table in between. He pulled out one chair for Alexa and seated himself opposite her in the other. With his foot he scooted the table aside and leisurely stretched out his legs. He gave her a devastating smile as he popped the Coke open and handed it to her.

"What are you supposed to tell me?" Sipping the drink, she met his fixed grin with what she hoped was a composed look.

"Tell you?" Mark scooted his chair forward so that he was beside her but still facing in the opposite direction. "Mmmm . . . oh, yes—what to expect." There were many things he'd like to tell Alexa, but Linda wanted him to remind Alexa of a few details. His job was to relax her so she'd give a first-rate performance. He could see the longer she waited, the more anxious she was becoming.

"You've probably heard it all before." Mark reached for her hand and gently placed her fingers in his palm. "Does this body makeup come off?" He inspected his thumb.

"The stain doesn't come off except with soap and water." Alexa inched her fingers forward until her entire hand was in his. "They said it'll take a week or so. I think Carl was worried about the makeup on my face." Alexa felt a sudden rush of color to her cheeks.

"I see."

The heat of his hand sent a delightful sensation of awareness through Alexa. She had the urge to lean sideways, kiss him, and worry about Carl later. Instead she whispered, "What are you supposed to tell me?"

"Don't be surprised if this short scene takes longer than you expect. It may require several takes before Giles is satisfied." Mark carefully placed a finger under her chin, lifting her head so he could look directly into her green eyes. "It won't mean that there's anything wrong with your performance, so don't let it upset you."

"All right." Alexa had heard all of this before, but something about the way Mark expressed himself reassured her.

"The other thing to remember is that most of the film that is shot is never used. They'll edit out what they don't need, and it will be left on the cutting room floor." A disturbing thought hit him, causing a familiar knot of heat to form in his stomach. He jerked his hand from beneath her chin.

"What's wrong?"

*Steven,* Mark thought, *son of a bitch.* He tried to cover his concern by raising her hand to his lips and slowly kissing her fingertips. He would have to make certain that Steven didn't keep the "outs," the unused footage, of Alexa's scene. Mark had heard about Steven's ribald parties where he showed "screen tests" of starlets. The thought of Steven or even worse, Jason Talbott, watching Alexa perform in the nude infuriated him.

*There's something he isn't telling me.* She took a long drink of cola while she formed the question. "Mark . . . if they asked someone special to you . . . like your girl friend to do this scene, would you let her?"

Mark saw the confusion in Alexa's eyes. *You are special to me; you just don't know it yet.*

Alexa waited, hating herself for asking. She could imagine what Mark's girl friend would be like. He had one, of course, or several. None of them would be doing this scene.

"Alexa, you're not having second thoughts, are you?"

"Please answer my question." Alexa jerked her hand from his.

Mark could see he didn't have a diplomatic way out. He reached for her hand again, ignoring the hostile look in her eyes. "I would have told you not to do it." Alexa started to speak but he raised his hand to silence her. "Not because there is anything wrong with the scene, but I'm a trifle too Victorian. Look," he said gently, "you felt the scene was important enough to this story to fight to keep it in the movie. Do you still believe that?"

Alexa nodded slowly.

"So do I. So do Giles, Nigel Hunter, Renata, Linda—everyone. But more than that we believe in you, in your ability to make this scene work. Don't let my old-fashioned ideas upset you."

He was straightforward and honest; she had known he'd tell her the truth. "It's just my middle-class morality working overtime. I made this commitment; now I'm going to do the best I can."

"It'll be all right, I promise." Mark spoke the words into her hand, but his eyes were on hers. His gray eyes were as soft and reassuring as his words had been.

Alexa shifted in her chair to be nearer Mark. She brushed back a stray lock of his thick black hair. With deliberate slowness she skimmed through his wavy hair, letting the curls slip sensuously through her fingers. The woodsy scent she'd smelled earlier wafted up at her. "Mark," she whispered.

Alexa spoke his name so softly he almost thought he'd imagined it. As her fingers laced through his hair, a shudder of passion coursed through his body. Just one kiss, one long, long kiss. Damn all that makeup!

Mark reached over and slid the gown from Alexa's shoulder. Her skin was peach colored in the dim light of the trailer. "I wouldn't want to upset Carl," he whispered, slowly kissing the base of her neck.

Alexa drew in her breath and held it as Mark's lips kept moving lower. His hand slipped under her breast, the warmth of his palm flowing through the filmy fabric. She released her breath in a long sigh.

Mark lifted her breast slightly, caressing it slowly. Beneath the fabric he felt the nipple harden. He slipped his hand into the deep vee of her gown and under her bare breast. Her fingers tightened around a handful of his hair.

Alexa's heart clamored crazily at the initial shock of his lips on her breast. An even more intense message of desire swept over her, and she moaned softly. Releasing his hair, she stroked his head gently. Her breast surging at the intimacy of his kiss, Alexa felt the rush of heat between her thighs.

Suddenly there were loud voices outside the door.

"Carl," Mark said as he raised his head and deftly closed her gown. "He has X-ray vision. He's coming for me." Amusement flickered in his eyes while he smoothed his hair into place.

The door popped open, letting in a rush of hot desert air and intense sunlight.

Straightening her gown, Alexa tried to hide the flood of color she felt staining her cheeks.

"We were looking for you in the honey wagon. I'm Helga," said the stout woman. "This is my assistant, Teddy."

Helga gave skinny Teddy a thump on the back, which brought him forward onto the balls of his feet. When he regained his balance, Teddy nodded. Helga turned to Mark. "And you are?"

Mark extended his hand. "Mark Kimbrough."

Helga's eyes roved over Mark in a brief but obviously approving appraisal as she pumped his hand. She crossed the room and grabbed a lacy white gown from a rack. "This is Alexa's costume," Helga proudly announced to Mark, totally ignoring Alexa. "A replica of a nineteenth-century nightgown."

Mark looked at the frothy lace creation, trying to imagine Alexa in it. He saw her in lace, all right, but something black and slinky, something that showed off her soft curves instead of hiding them beneath yards of confectionlike lace and ribbons. "Nightgowns certainly have improved since then. Nowadays someone would get married in this."

Alexa stifled a giggle when she saw how horrified Helga looked. "But, Mark, this is supposed to be the nineteenth century."

Mark responded with a devilish grin and a dismissive shrug of the shoulders.

"Here are the rest," Helga jerked her arm toward another rack.

"The rest?" Alexa jumped to her feet. The scene called for a nightgown that she would immediately take off.

"Certainly. For retakes. In that scene you practically tear your gown off to get at him, ducky. What if you ruin it on the first take? Wrinkle it? Get makeup on it? We'll be ready with another." Helga's firm voice left no room for argument.

She plunked the gown she'd shown Mark onto the rack. "Come, Teddy me boy, we've work to do." With Teddy literally in tow, she disappeared behind a rack of clothing.

Alexa stood mesmerized by the array of white gowns and the scene they represented. Without turning she felt Mark move up behind her, stopping inches from touching her.

"Remember what I said?" His low, steady voice reassured her. "There's certain to be more than one take. You must expect it, anticipate it. You'll be fine."

Slowly Alexa nodded. His confidence was contagious. It was something Paul had never given her because he didn't have it himself. That was why he'd never encouraged her and why he always chipped away at her self-esteem.

"We might as well sit. Tell me about your family," Alexa said, knowing if she dwelled on the scene she'd become even more anxious.

"There's really nothing to tell," Mark answered as they sat down again. "I'm an only child. My parents passed on years ago, but I have several aunts and uncles and passels of cousins. How about you?"

Alexa realized Mark had turned the conversation to her life once more. She'd noticed how effectively he'd done that before when he didn't wish to answer.

"I'm an only child as well. My mother died two years ago just before I finished the book." A too-familiar pang of loneliness overcame her. She paused a moment for the ache to pass. "I never see my father. They were divorced when I was four."

"You miss her terribly, don't you?"

"Yes, she was my best friend."

*And your husband wasn't,* Mark wanted to add.

The trailer door flew open and Linda sailed in on a gust of warm air. "You're up as soon as we get you dressed and"—she paused to inspect Alexa's makeup—"you've been careful. No redo necessary, just a touch-up. Not bad for all these hours."

"Have they closed the set?" Mark asked.

"What are you?" Linda joked. "Her personal manager?"

"Something like that." Mark knew how much more secure Alexa would feel knowing the set was closed.

"They're taking care of it right now. You and Steven are excluded."

"Right. I'd just make her nervous."

"Keep an eye on Steven then. He seems to think his presence is necessary."

"I will." Mark seethed at the mention of Steven. The outtakes. Perhaps a better strategy than mentioning them to Steven would be to contact Nigel Hunter directly. As executive producer, Nigel would team up with Giles to supervise the final cut. Mark would remind them to dispose of the outs. That way he wouldn't give Steven any ideas he didn't already have.

"Run along now. I need to work with Alexa," said Linda.

Time had run out, Alexa realized. Was she ready to face the camera?

"Helga," Linda called, disappearing behind the racks of clothes, "I need you."

"Alexa," Mark said, "chin up. You'll be fine. I'll be waiting for you. Tonight I'm going to make sure I'm with you at dinner."

"Don't forget." Alexa wanted to ask him to stay, to be there if she needed him. But he'd make her nervous when she had to undress.

# Chapter 9

Alexa shifted slightly in his embrace, conscious of the coarse fabric of his fully clothed body against her naked one. Except for their labored breathing, no sound disturbed the uncommon stillness. She rapidly unbuttoned his shirt, crushing the crispness of it beneath her fingers. While he slid it off, Alexa undid his belt and then unhooked his trousers. The buckle clanked as his pants dropped to the floor and he stepped out of them. Wantonly Alexa wriggled against his torso, her nipples hardening as they brushed against the rough hair on his chest.

"Tell me you love me," Alexa whispered. Her fingers wound through his hair, her body arching seductively against his.

His only reply was a punishing kiss; his hands clasped her bare buttocks, his nails digging into her soft skin.

"Please say it," she pleaded, "just once."

He shoved her onto the bed and climbed on top of her, brutally thrusting at her. Alexa tasted the salty tang of his skin as she bit into his shoulder to stifle a scream. Scalding tears streamed from her eyes. Finally he collapsed on top of her.

"Cut!" Someone in the background yelled.

"Kill the baby," someone else screamed, and the overhead lights went out.

Colin rolled off Alexa. "Are you all right?"

Nodding, Alexa pulled the sheet over her nude body.

Colin nonchalantly turned on his side and braced his jaw against his palm.

"Do you think we're finished?" Alexa asked, keeping her eyes on his face. "This is the seventh take. Do you always do this many?"

"Frequently we do." Colin ran his finger down her bare arm. "They'll let us know. Pretending something as intimate as this is difficult. You're tops. You should consider an acting career."

"After what happened on the first take?" Alexa felt her cheeks grow warm at the memory. She'd been fine—until she had to remove the nightgown. Then she'd stood there stark naked for a full minute until she heard herself mumble something about not being an actress. Mercifully someone had yelled, "Cut," and Linda dashed up with a robe. "I panicked."

"Nonsense. Stage fright. I have it still. You were fine on the next take."

Alexa noticed Colin tactfully didn't mention it had taken the better part of an hour to calm her down. After filming resumed Colin had made no mention of her breakdown. He treated her with all the respect due a professional actress. Colin Avery had proven not to be an ego-driven superstar, but a genuinely nice man. That he'd taken such a risk by helping her evade the police still surprised her.

"I don't know how to thank you for what you did the other night," she said, thanking him for the dozenth time. "I'd be in jail now if you—"

"Forget it! I wouldn't let that bitch Melanie get you arrested."

"Thank you. I don't think Melanie did it. Why would—"

"Blast!" Colin groaned at the approaching makeup unit. "Another take."

Wearily Alexa allowed them to dress her in a loose wrapper and lead her off to the portable makeup station to have her hair and makeup repaired. Dammit, how could she do the scene again? They fussed over her with a Turkish towel, drying the fine film of perspiration caused by the sweltering heat of the bright lights. Another of Helga's creations appeared, and Alexa was ready again.

"Standing by in one minute," someone shouted. "Everyone out!"

A blur of jeans-clad technicians checked camera angles and then rechecked them. Lights were double-checked, and camera monitors were cross-checked while Alexa waited.

"Clear the set . . . please!"

"Open your mouth," an assistant commanded and Alexa's jaw obediently dropped to receive the spray of mouthwash. "There, you're ready to kiss him again."

"Places. . . . Quiet!"

Alexa stiffened. Once more with feeling, she thought, concentrating on the past. On Paul.

"Everyone quiet. . . . Light it up. . . . Cameras rolling. . . . Action!"

The clapperboard snapped shut, the assistant called off the scene and take number, and Alexa stepped in front of the camera again. A chill of apprehension, an inexplicable foreboding tiptoed down her spine. A single thought niggled at the back of her mind—she shouldn't be doing this.

The van slammed to a stop in front of Daiquiri Dick's and Colin slid the door open for Linda and Alexa. Bouncing out, she felt ridiculously happy—it was finally over. She could hardly wait to see Mark.

"They've been down here for hours. They're probably all snockered by now." Colin laughed, ushering them up to the entrance.

Just a few yards from the high tide line, the restaurant was no more than an open-air grass hut. Alexa forgave Dick for the mediocre food because he made the best margaritas in Cabo, and his restaurant had a terrific view of San Lucas Bay.

Inside, the darkness forced them to pause for a moment to get their bearings. Mexican lanterns hung aloft gave the dried palm fronds forming the ceiling an amber glow. On the tables candles planted in empty, long-necked bottles of Corona beer provided hazy light. The band loudly played an off-key rendition of "I'm So Excited."

"Over here," waved Steven.

But Alexa's eyes were on Mark. Weaving around tables, he

quickly crossed the room. His navy Polo shirt hugged his wide shoulders, and crisp white trousers outlined his thighs and emphasized his long legs. Alexa threw her arms around him, welcoming the feel of his strong frame as she hugged him. Mark squeezed back, surprised at Alexa's obvious display of emotion. The shooting had taken so long he had no idea what state she'd be in when she finished. If he didn't have to leave tomorrow, he would have insisted on postponing this little celebration.

"It's over," Alexa said with obvious relief as he guided her to the table. "Thank you," she told the group. "I'm sorry I was a crybaby about such a small part, but it was really difficult for me."

Mark could detect the choked tone in her voice and knew it had been very trying for her. He had known it would be. Alexa wasn't the type to do something like this casually.

"Would you like a margarita?" Mark asked.

"Make it a double," she answered. While Mark ordered her drink, she glanced around the table. At the opposite end sat Steven, scowling. She blew him a kiss and he responded with a weak smile. Across from Steven, Linda sat chatting with Giles and Renata while Colin wearily slumped in the chair beside Alexa. Good friends—all of them. A warm feeling of camaraderie filled Alexa. She realized what she'd been missing for years: real friends, and a sense of truly belonging.

The waiter arrived with the margaritas. Alexa ran her tongue along the rim of the glass, savoring the salt before she took a sip. Slowly she sipped and leaned back, conscious of Mark's arm casually draped across the back of her chair. "I'm going to miss everyone when this is over."

"Does that go for me?" Mark moved closer, looking into her bright green eyes.

"Does what go for you?" Alexa said, coyly lowering her lashes while she took another sip.

Amused, Mark grinned. *She's so damned sexy.* That she could flirt with him at all was progress. "Are you going to miss me?"

"Sure," Alexa replied, deliberately being flip. She reached up and brushed back the wisp of hair that had fallen across Mark's forehead. "When are you going?"

"Tomorrow at nine."

"No! Why?" He'd caught her off-guard. She knew he would have to go. But why did he have to leave so soon?

"I have to be in Brussels in two days for a Trade Alliance meeting." Mark kept his tone light. She didn't need to know how very much he'd rather stay here with her.

"Can't someone else attend the meeting?"

"Afraid not." Mark stopped. Shafts of gold from the candles sparked Alexa's green eyes; her unhappiness at his words was apparent. He hadn't expected her to show this much emotion, but it was what he needed to know. She was the first woman he'd been truly interested in for years, and he wanted to know how she felt about him.

"We could be here through April or mid-May. Do you think you'll get back?"

"Out of the question. My schedule has been set for over a year." Mark did not add that he planned to free himself from as much travel as possible, so that he'd not have to leave England as often once Alexa arrived. Anyway, at the rate his business problems were compounding, they demanded he remain home. "Our timing should be perfect. I'm going to be in London in mid-May. I won't be leaving the country much after that." Mark smiled. "Let's make the most of tonight."

Alexa concentrated on rubbing the remaining salt from the rim of her glass with her finger. She gingerly licked the crystals from her fingertip before taking another sip. There was a gentle hum deep in her head. The tequila had taken effect, causing her thoughts to jumble disjointedly, but the implication in Mark's words had been all too clear. What should she say? This was just too fast. She couldn't decide what to do, nor could she dispel the delicious sense of anticipation she felt at the thought of Mark making love to her.

Alexa's nervousness made it obvious to Mark she'd not tried to heal the scars from her divorce by jumping into bed with men. It occurred to him there might not have been anyone at all.

"Are you hungry?" he asked.

"Famished," Alexa admitted, relieved to change the subject.

Giles heard her. "They've closed the kitchen, but we've arranged for a family-style service. We'll all share."

"Great." Alexa laughed self-consciously. She felt Mark's eyes on her, studying her in an unsettling way.

Alexa tipped her head back, swirling her tawny gold hair across her shoulders as she laughed. Casually Mark moved his hand from the back of her chair to her shoulder, where her hair danced softly when she moved her head. The pale green dress she wore was a backless affair clearly disclosing she wasn't wearing a bra and emphasizing the fullness of her breasts. Without moving his hand, Mark slowly rotated his thumb against her soft skin.

Alexa felt the goosebumps spring up across her back and tried to ignore Mark's hand. Not daring to look at him, she glanced down the table and saw Steven. He had been watching her with a sullen expression on his face. She smiled and he responded with a faint nod. He's angry, Alexa realized, asking herself why. This dinner, she remembered—he'd planned it for her, and she'd blithely flown into Mark's arms. She'd make it up to Steven later, but not tonight, not with Mark leaving tomorrow.

The waiter arrived with huge, steaming platters of food. Reluctantly Mark eased his hand off Alexa's shoulder.

No longer hungry, Alexa pushed the food around on her plate, thinking. She wouldn't sleep with him just because he was leaving tomorrow. If anything happened between them, it would have to be in London.

"Let's dance," he said, taking her hand.

When they reached the tiny dance floor, the band was playing a waltz and it was all but impossible to move, the area was so tightly packed. Deftly, Mark drew Alexa to him and spun her into the center of the crowd. Alexa kept herself rigid in his arms. She felt Mark's leg flex slightly between hers as they moved to the beat. He placed her hand on the solid wall of his chest. His hand now free, he lightly fluffed her hair aside and touched the back of her neck. His thumb slowly rubbed across her bare skin, forcing her to relax and sending prickles of awareness racing down her spine. Alexa put her head against his shoulder, inhaling his warm, woodsy scent.

Mark drew Alexa closer. The supple softness of her body molded against his sent a jolt of desire mingled with an aching tenderness through him. There was no doubt about it, he decided, he communicated better with Alexa physically than verbally. In the future he'd have to remember that.

Alexa felt Mark's heart thumping against her breast. Tentatively she slipped her arm around his waist. His hand left her neck and slowly trailed down her bare back, sending shivers of anticipation through the pit of her stomach. For once she was thankful for not being taller. She didn't have to look him in the eye and have him see how very attractive she found him. How much she wanted him.

The band finished the song, and the throng around them clapped, but Mark and Alexa didn't move. When the strains of another waltz floated over the crowd, Alexa and Mark swayed with the music. Another couple bumped into them, forcing Alexa to look up and see Mark tenderly gazing down at her.

Mark watched Alexa's lashes, a golden fringe against her emerald eyes, flutter as she smiled at him. Heedless of the crowd around them, Mark lowered his lips to meet her soft, warm ones. His hand clutched a fistful of golden curls at the nape of her neck, holding her still as his tongue parted her lips.

That wasn't just a kiss, Alexa realized when he pulled away. It was a promise of things to come. She shakily put her head on his shoulder, knowing her resolve to resist him had been destroyed. Mark leisurely moved one hand up and down her back, lightly stroking her bare skin with his fingertips, leaving her breathless. They were barely moving now, only pretending to dance. His large hand caressed the small of her back. Roaming lower, he fondled the soft curves of her bottom. Slowly and deliberately he pressed her against him, his arousal evident. Mindless of her actions, Alexa rose on her tiptoes and brushed her yearning body against his bulge.

"Don't you think it's time we went back to the hotel?"

Alexa stood in front of Daiquiri Dick's with Mark, waiting for one of the two cabs still operating after midnight to come by. The lights of the Finisterra Hotel winked seductively in the distance. She snuggled against Mark's body and pointed to the stone arch known as Land's End that marked the tip of the Baja peninsula. "Isn't it beautiful? Finisterra means land's end."

The full moon proudly rode the rocky crest above the arch, spilling shimmering light onto the water below. The silvery rays accentuated the ragged peaks of the timeworn coastline, while moonlit shadows deepened the irregular crevices the wind and the water had eroded in the sides of the ridge. The sky above was miles of black silk with stars flickering like courting fireflies.

Alexa tipped her head and sent a cascade of golden curls across Mark's shoulder. He kissed the top of her head and squeezed her gently. Alexa was attractive, not glamorous with that hard edge of chic many women coveted, but beautiful in her own way. She'd removed the heavy makeup she'd worn for the movie, leaving her face the way he liked it best—natural.

Alexa looked up at him and saw a silvery sheen brightening his eyes. She lowered her gaze to the firm outline of his mouth, so inviting, so close. She parted her lips and leaned forward slightly, silently asking to be kissed.

Mark's strong fingers closed across the back of her neck as his lips came down on hers. There was no fierceness to his kiss, only a gentle, seeking sweetness that left Alexa straining toward him begging for more. With a sigh of surrender, she curled her arms around his neck, running her fingers through his jet-black hair. She slid her hand under his collar, savoring the warmth of his flesh against her fingertips. With tantalizing slowness, Mark moved his hand from under the weight of her hair to her jawline. Lightly, he traced the outline of her cheek with his thumb while he deepened the kiss.

Just then a car full of locals screeched into the parking lot. Silently Alexa and Mark pulled apart and looked down the stretch of golden sand known as Medano Beach while the noisy group went inside.

"I . . . I wish you didn't have to go," Alexa whispered, the words catching in her throat, her body aching for the return of his touch.

Mark drew her to him, his arms tightly encircling her. "I know," he replied, his warm breath ruffling her hair. "I wouldn't leave unless it was absolutely imperative I be in Brussels."

Mark pulled away from Alexa and reached into his back pocket. "This is my business card. On the back I've written my private number at home. You'll be able to reach me there late at night. When you arrive in London, ring me immediately." Mark opened her Vuitton tote, inserted the card into the inside pocket, and zipped it shut. "Will it be safe in there?"

"Yes, that's a good place for it. Everything that's valuable to me is inside my bag. All my notes, story outlines, and travel documents are there. I'm not taking any chances by leaving them in my room."

"That's why it's so bloody heavy." Mark grinned and slung it over his shoulder as the taxi pulled up.

Alexa slid into the far corner of the back seat. Mark climbed in and extended his long arm, pulling her to him across the worn leather seat.

"What you need is a good night's sleep," he whispered as she rested her head on his shoulder.

*Wrong,* Alexa thought, cuddling up against him. *That's not what I need right now.* I can sleep tomorrow. She reached up, traveling the blunt edge of his jaw with her fingertip, and kissed him. His hand rested lightly on her knee as his tongue explored the smooth interior of her mouth. Moving his hand across her thigh to the rounded fullness of her hip, he gently squeezed her firm flesh.

Vaguely, Alexa was aware of the old Chevy sputtering and coughing while it wound its way up the steep grade to the Finisterra Hotel. As she acknowledged the desperate ache in her chest and the warm fullness between her thighs, she admitted she wanted Mark tonight, not two months from now. Boldly, she inched her hand across his upper thigh.

Without warning the taxi lurched to a halt in front of the hotel's entrance. Mark paid the driver and then helped Alexa from the car. Neither of them said anything on the way up to her room. Mark inserted the key into the lock and opened Alexa's door a finger's width.

She realized it was very late. Only the sound of the waves tumbling on the beach below broke the deathly quiet. And the incessant pounding of her heart. Why didn't he ask to come in or something? But still Mark didn't move or say anything.

"There's a fabulous view from my balcony . . . would you like to see it?"

Mark expelled his breath in a silent whistle. For a minute there he thought she wasn't going to invite him in. Tomorrow he wanted her to remember this had been her idea. He sensed her insecurity and knew she wasn't ready for this. She might resent him later. He wished he could be here to reassure her, but he couldn't. To hell with tomorrow; it would have to take care of itself.

Alexa hurried into her room and hastily slid open the balcony door. "L-look," she stammered, gesturing to the beach below and beyond it the Pacific. "There's a full moon."

Pretending interest in the view gave Alexa something to do during those first few unnerving moments. The ocean dancing in moonstruck waves stretched endlessly before them. The silence between them, punctuated only by the lulling, rhythmic splash of the surf breaking on the shore below, seemed endless as well. She could feel Mark's warm body next to hers, but she lacked the courage to look at him. A panicky feeling filled her lungs and breathing became more difficult. She'd invited him in, but he'd have to do something now. Since her divorce Alexa hadn't slept with another man. She wasn't ready for this. Her body, so eager earlier, turned to lead. Inviting him in had been a mistake. Why couldn't she have seen it? How could she gracefully get rid of him now?

Mark watched Alexa's hands tightly clasp the railing. She didn't deceive him by feigning interest in the view. She'd asked him in and now she was terrified. It was exactly what he'd expected. He had finally begun to understand her. This was why he hadn't wanted to make their first night together his last night in Mexico. What Alexa MacKenzie did not need was for a man to make love to her and then disappear. Yet, how could he leave now without her feeling he'd rejected her?

Mark moved behind Alexa, putting his arms on either side of hers and covering her hands with his own as she clung to the rail. He bent down, kissing her softly on the cheek. With a brush of his nose, he pushed back the champagne-colored mass of hair and kissed the warm skin behind her ear.

"Just think . . . China's right out there," Alexa mumbled. She tried to remain coherent as Mark's lips parted and he flicked his tongue along her ear. "If we could swim that far."

"The Philippines."

"What?" Alexa whispered, although she no longer had the least bit of interest in swimming to China. Even the pounding of the surf had taken on a faraway, muffled sound. He pressed moist kisses along her neck. He breathed his response into her ear. "Swim. You'll come to the Philippines, not China, if you maintain a straight course."

Alexa's throat constricted. Let someone else swim. "Are you always this precise?"

"Yes." Mark pried Alexa's hands from the rail and turned her to face him. "Please don't be afraid of me."

Alexa looked up at him. The light of the moon etched the hard planes of his face, making him appear even more masculine, more virile. "I haven't made love to anyone since my divorce," she whispered.

He saw her eyes were misted with so much hurt, so much pain. "I know. It'll be all right."

He kissed her slowly and thoughtfully. Just as he'd suspected, there hadn't been anyone since her husband. She hadn't used sex as a panacea for a broken heart. While that knowledge elated him, it made him uneasy. This had to be good for her. He didn't want her to regret that he was the one.

"It's been months for me," Mark said. And it wasn't any good then, he realized. Casual sex usually wasn't. Threading his fingers through her tawny gold hair, he whispered, "I've been waiting for you."

# Chapter 10

"Alexa . . . Alexa," Mark whispered. He took her face in both his hands and tipped it back, gazing down into the green-gold of her eyes. The gleaming moonlight wove silver threads through the honey-colored strands of hair framing her face. Her uncertainty triggered some primitive urge in him to protect her and possess her all at the same time.

Mark's voice had a gentle, persuasive quality to it. He was reassuringly open and sincere. She hadn't missed being with a man until she met him. "Mark—I," Alexa said, twisting her face away from his lips. There were a thousand reasons why she should ask him to leave.

"It'll be all right. I promise."

Before she could respond, Mark's lips were on hers, gently kissing her. He wound his fingers through her hair and braced the back of her head, holding her lips to his. The unhurried kiss was intended as an enticement, an invitation. He slipped his warm palm down her back, gently pressing her against his solid frame. She drew in her breath when his tongue parted her lips and languidly brushed against her tongue.

Alexa's thoughts were a jumble of incoherent images and a face from the past—Paul's. A multitude of emotions that had been threatening to surface each time she had performed the scene overwhelmed her. She tried to move away, to pull herself from Mark's grip, but he refused to release her,. His wide hand splayed across her back, Mark whispered a dozen reassurances. No longer supporting herself, Alexa leaned against his sturdy frame. The seconds passed and a warm glow ignited within her. Like the wave of a magician's wand, his lips banished her lingering doubts.

Mark felt Alexa's resistance ebb away as she clung to him, pulling him closer. He held himself back, allowing Alexa to become accustomed to him. A sweet, fragrant smell driven by the heat of her body rose from her skin as her fingers kneaded the muscles at the base of his neck and inched up through his hair. Mark squeezed his eyes shut, savoring the sudden rush of pleasure her touch sent through his body.

A shiver of pure delight raced through Alexa. She felt alive, utterly female, for the first time in more than a year. She'd be able to handle this just as long as she didn't fall in love with him. She was an intelligent, independent woman; surely she was capable of controlling herself. All she had to do was to remember not to expect anything to come of this.

"I'm sorry I have to leave," Mark whispered. "Don't forget you have my number in your bag."

"I won't."

Alexa's tongue darted back and forth between his parted lips. Seductively she brushed her hips against his. Mark couldn't stop the low moan building in his throat. Alexa had his number, all right.

"How do you get this off?" she muttered, toying with the tail of his Polo shirt.

Mark released Alexa and with one continuous motion pulled the shirt over his head and tossed it backwards into the room.

"Ummmm." In the moonlight Alexa studied his tapered chest and massive shoulders. The crinkly black hair that fanned out across his chest glinted in the uncertain light of the moon. She reached out to feel the rough texture, weaving her fingers through the curly hair and caressing the firm muscles that lay below the surface. The thump of his heart and the aroma of his skin aroused her as much as his kisses had. Gently she kissed his chest, trailing her kisses slowly down to his nipple. Her tongue slid out from between her moist lips and moved in slow circles, raising his nipple through the whorl of crisp hair. His breathing became uneven and an almost imperceptible shudder rippled through him.

"How I've wanted you," Mark whispered, drawing Alexa up to kiss his lips once more. Tonight Alexa was his because she wanted to be, not because he'd forced her. He would take her completely, erase her doubts, while satisfying some deep inner longing within himself.

Mark pressed Alexa against the balcony rail, forcing her into the heat and growing firmness of his lower body. His rigid arousal pushed against her. As she dug her fingers into the firm flesh of his back, he felt the trail of tiny, half-moon imprints her nails carved into his skin. An almost savage intensity replaced his earlier restraint. She inhaled sharply as his hand plunged down her back and skimmed along the base of her spine.

When Mark raised his head and backed away as if he were trying to retain some measure of self-control, Alexa boldly reached up and ran her fingers through his rich black hair. Without a word, Mark lifted Alexa off her feet and carried her into the room, stopping beside the bed.

Pools of blurred moonlight splashed across the unlit room, highlighting the darkness of his hair and the metallic silver of his eyes. Vaguely she was aware of the freshly made bed, of the faint scent of roses, and of the slight breeze billowing the drapes; but her attention was focused on Mark. He tugged impatiently at the top of her dress, forcing it down from her shoulders into a bunch at her waist. As the fabric passed over them, her breasts sprang free. Mark froze.

"Oh, yes."

Cupping her breasts, he gently kissed each one, sending ripples of pleasure down to her toes and back again. Her hands slipped into his thatch of thick hair as he folded her into his arms. The roughness of his chest against her aroused nipples brought a wanton sigh to her throat. Deliberately she teased him, thrilled with her newfound feminine power, gliding up and down against the raspy grain of his chest. Her moan of pleasure echoed his. Alexa flexed and twisted erotically against Mark as she shed her dress. After it dropped in a crumpled heap on the floor, she sidestepped the garment and kicked off her sandals.

Alexa swayed against Mark, kissing him fervently as his hands came down her naked back to the silky bikini she was still wearing. Cupping her buttocks, he brought her up onto her toes and held her firmly against his arousal. She pressed against him, straining to feel him through his trousers.

His hands moved inside her panties and slowly caressed her bare bottom. Her breath came in such uneven, staccato bursts that kissing him was no longer possible. She buried her face in the hollow of his neck while he spent agonizingly long minutes tracing the rounded curves of her buttocks. Only when Alexa sighed and twisted impatiently did Mark inch his hand lower. With a light touch, which was maddeningly arousing, he teased the delicate swell of her upper thigh, gliding his fingertips across the smooth skin but refusing to touch her where she needed it most. He fluttered his fingers along the cleft of her derriere, coming closer and closer until, at last, he touched her downy hair. Running his hand under her bottom, he intimately stroked the tender flesh between her thighs. Hot waves of desire spiraled through her. Stretching up on tiptoe, she made herself stand still, allowing him to feel her. With every touch of his fingertips, Mark moved his hand higher, expertly probing the tender flesh. The slip-sliding movement of his fingers took her breath away.

"Oh, Alexa." Feeling her respond like this, whispering his name and clinging to him, stunned him. The more her passion heightened, the more aroused he became. He held her firmly against him and slowly inserted his finger into the satin heat of her body. Moist and hot, the soft core of her body yielded to his touch. After giving a startled gasp, she stood perfectly still, permitting him to caress her.

His unexpectedly gentle touch unfurled a sweet burst of sensation deep within her. She held her breath and clung to him, allowing him to languidly stroke her. Gently his hand moved back and forth. Each motion brought an unanticipated rush of delight. Shivering with pleasure, Alexa ground against his rigid shaft. A tremor was building deep inside her, and she had no other thought now except surrendering completely to him.

"Don't," she groaned plaintively when he withdrew.

With a snap and a zip, Mark released his trousers. A muffled sound followed as he shed his clothing and it fell to the floor. The shadowy light of the moon revealed the surging fullness of his arousal. A thrill of anticipation accompanied by a prickle of apprehension jolted Alexa when she saw he was even larger than she'd expected.

Mark yanked the bedspread off and hastily turned back the sheet. Gently he lowered Alexa onto the crisp white linen. Stretching out beside her, Mark propped himself up on one elbow and stared down at Alexa. He reached over and spread her golden hair across the pillow. The moonlight from the open balcony door bathed the bed with a soft glow and cast an opalescent sheen over Alexa's honey-gold hair. Her eyes, usually dominated by emerald irises, were dilated with arousal, making them black encircled by a luminous aura of green. She wanted him, of that Mark had no doubt. But he didn't want her simply ready for him; he wanted her desperate to have him. He needed to make certain that when he left tomorrow she wouldn't forget him.

His tongue searching, he kissed her for the longest time before slipping his hand down to find her breast. Heat coursed through Alexa and her heart hammered incessantly in her ears as he explored the fullness of her breast and circled the nipple with his thumb. Her body, quivering now, arched against him. Mark slowly outlined the taut curve of her stomach with his fingertips. Reaching the elastic edge of her panties, he paused, waiting a long moment while Alexa held her breath before he slid his hand over the top of the silky fabric to cover the moist mound between her thighs. Alexa exhaled sharply. The heat from his hand instantly penetrated the fabric as his fingers lightly skimmed across the satiny panties. Alexa clasped his head to her breast and mindlessly entangled her fingers in his tousled hair. Aching with need, she wondered what was taking Mark so long.

"Now, Mark, now."

"Not yet, angel, we have all night." *Take it easy,* he thought, *not too fast . . . make this last.* His warm fingers slipped into her panties and across the mound of flattened hair between her thighs.

He bent down to her breast and drew the crested nipple into his mouth while he used his hand to gently explore the warm, wet recesses between her thighs. With calculated leisure he fondled her, bringing her almost, but not quite, to

where he wanted her. Alexa's hips churned; her passion made
him painfully aware of how hard and achingly hot he was.

Alexa reached for him, running her fingers through the dark
cloud of hair on his chest and slowly following its path across
the hard, flat planes of his stomach to the turgid thrust below.
Groaning, he froze.

"Don't stop," she pleaded, moving against him, encouraging him.

"Touch me, Alexa . . . touch me." His own voice sounded
faraway. All he could hear was the rapid pounding of his
heart and his own labored breathing. Holding back was becoming painful now.

As she closed her hand around him, he responded to her
command with warm, agile fingers that trailed an erotic path
between her thighs. Exalted at his male strength, she gauged
his size with awe. He pushed himself into her hand, silently
urging her to tighten her grip. When she did, the thrill of his
heightened arousal made her bolder. Was there anything else
on earth that was as hard as steel yet silky smooth? she wondered.

"Harder, angel, you won't hurt me."

Alexa squeezed, moving her hand rapidly back and forth
while she matched the rhythm with her body. "Mark," she
heard herself breathlessly repeating his name.

Impatiently Mark slipped her silky bikini down over her
hips, and Alexa fluttered her legs to get rid of them. He moved
over her, parting her thighs. She was driving him crazy. If he
waited much longer, there wouldn't be anything left to wait
for. He surged forward, encasing himself in her. He felt her
body stiffen and she gasped. Knowing he'd used more force
than he intended, he stopped. "Are you all right?"

"Don't stop!" Alexa panted. *Was she all right? Never better—just
don't stop.* She churned in that instinctive, primitive cadence
beneath his steady thrusting. She gave a satisfied moan and
smiled to herself. No, he wasn't too big for her after all. He
was just right. Everything about him was just right. His smile
. . . his kiss . . . his no-nonsense approach to life. Just right.

Mark thrust urgently and deeply, and Alexa lifted her hips
to meet him. *Hang on.* Mark bit an imaginary bullet. *Make this
good for her.* Sensing she was about to climax, he moved his
head aside to let a shaft of moonlight illuminate her face.

More important than his own satisfaction was hers. Watching her carefully in this totally unguarded moment, tiny sparks of light came from her half-closed eyes. The cascade of rumpled gold hair glistened in the moonlight as a look of delight flashed across her face.

"Mark," she sighed, undulating uncontrollably beneath him, clutching a fistful of his hair.

Mark quickened his pace, concentrating on himself now, contracting his body again and again and again. The blood pounded in his brain and coursed white-hot through his veins as he drove himself back and forth with a passionate fury he never knew he possessed until his body exploded with indescribable pleasure. Gasping for breath, he rolled over onto the pillow beside her.

Alexa reached over and brushed her hand through his hair. Her touch was almost unbearable in its tenderness. She was the affectionate, sensual woman he'd known was hidden behind the hurt and insecurity. Had he ever felt quite like this? For years now he thought he'd been making love, but he'd merely been going through the motions, seeking physical gratification.

Utterly dazed, her entire body flooded with pleasure, Alexa snuggled against Mark. She liked the way she fit into the curve of his body— as if she belonged there. Why did Mark have to leave? She turned her head to face him. The opal moon cast milky light across his handsome face. His velvet-gray eyes were gentle, full of warmth, understanding . . . and perhaps something even deeper.

Mark studied Alexa carefully. He could sense how much she needed to be held and reassured. His gut twisted painfully —if only he didn't have to leave so soon. With her eyes closed and a floss of honey-blond hair strewn carelessly across his arm, she looked childlike, angelic. The sight of her touched him more sweetly, more profoundly than any of their lovemaking. With one finger he traced the delicate curve of her cheek up to her hairline. He selected one lock of hair and wound it around his finger the way he'd seen her do so many times. Silently she burrowed against him, hugging him. He released the curl, spreading it out across the pillow. *You have absolutely no idea what you do to me.* An aching pang of tenderness crept through him. After making love he seldom did much talking, but tonight there were so many things he needed to say.

"Alexa," he whispered softly as he kissed her turned-up nose, "Alexa?"

Carefully he drew the tangled sheet over her and tightened his arm protectively around her. Poor kid, it had been such a long, grueling day. She'd fallen asleep even before her pulse returned to normal.

# CLOSE-UP:
## *London's West End*

# Chapter 11

Alexa peered through the airplane's Plexiglas window, straining to see what was below. Water. They were still somewhere over the English Channel.

"See land yet, luv?" Steven asked, taking another drink of vodka before turning a page of the London *Times.*

"No."

Alexa continued to gaze out the window. Lush green, gently undulating land hung with a heavy mist finally came into view. Below, the bosky countryside gave way to a wide meadow carpeted with yellow wild flowers. Alexa's spirits lifted—London couldn't be far now. Allowing Steven Hunter to convince her to spend a few days, which turned out to be ten, in Marbella had been a mistake. She should have loved the Spanish Costa del Sol with its whitewashed villas filled with the young Turks of Europe's jet set and the late nights spent dancing at Regine's. But Marbella, the upstart rival of Cannes and Monte Carlo, seemed just like another watering hole for the *sans souci* set to Alexa, who preferred the laid-back atmosphere of Cabo San Lucas. She regretted losing valuable time in planning the play. And she hadn't been able to see Mark.

"Well," Steven snorted, "I'm not surprised."

"About what?" Alexa kept staring out the window. The mist had thickened, obscuring her view, but every few seconds patches of English countryside came into view through the gaps in the fog.

"Kimbrough owns half of Windsor Air."

Alexa spun around. Mark had said he didn't own any part of the airline. But that had been two months ago; perhaps something had happened since then. "Are you positive?"

"The *Times* is never wrong." He handed her the financial section.

Alexa read the article carefully and saw Triad Investments owned half of Windsor Airlines. There could be no mistake; the *Times* was the most respected newspaper in Europe. "I guess he just bought it," Alexa mumbled.

"No, luv," Steven corrected. "These things take months and months of negotiations. A year even. I overheard him on the car phone when we were in Los Angeles. He owned it then. I know what he's up to. Triad will suck the life out of an ailing company and then sell its assets. That's how Kimbrough made his money."

"Fasten your seat belts, please," came the voice over the intercom.

Alexa stared out at the bank of billowy white clouds they were now descending through. Why hadn't she heard from Mark? In the two months since she'd slept with him, he hadn't called or written. Nothing. She had his number in her bag. She planned to call him as soon as she arrived at Steven's town house. Surely he had an explanation for this.

"Luv, aren't you excited about our film?" Steven asked as they left the plane and headed toward the Customs area.

"When I sold you the screenplay, it became your property, *your* film." She purposely emphasized the word "your." "I haven't changed my mind. I'm here to produce the play for Renata."

"All right, luv." Steven turned toward the queue of British subjects waiting to clear Customs. "Let me know if you change your mind."

Alexa stood in the line marked "Non-Commonwealth Passports." Waiting her turn, her thoughts returned to Mark. Why couldn't he have found the time to call? Was she just a one-

night stand? She wondered if she should call him. What if he
didn't want to see her?

When Steven opened the door to his Waverton Street town
house, they heard the telephone ringing. The chauffeur who'd
met them with the Hunter Films black Bentley limo brought
their bags inside while Steven ran to answer it. Alexa glanced
around at the high-ceilinged foyer painted stark white except
for the black-and-white marble floor set in a checkerboard
pattern. A white marble staircase with a gleaming chrome rail
rose abruptly to the next floor.

Strolling into the living room, she studied the area in disbelief. Could this be a Mayfair town house? For over two hundred years Mayfair had been the most prestigious neighborhood in London. Built as town homes for the nobility, houses
were narrow three-story affairs complete with staff quarters
and mews areas behind, which had housed the carriages and
horses. The original residents had also owned vast estates
with acres of green space, so few Mayfair residences had gardens of their own. Standing beside each other like a platoon of
soldiers, the town houses had common walls and were set
within a few feet of the street.

In present-day London, real estate had become so expensive
that the mews had been split off and refurbished as sophisticated flats. The old town houses had been restored and sold
for millions of dollars, placing the Mayfair district beyond the
reach of most Britons. Consequently, the area now boasted
numerous embassies, including the American embassy, famous hotels, and five-star restaurants. Today's Mayfair residents were more likely to be oil-rich Arabs, who'd become so
much a part of London in recent years, or wealthy British
entrepreneurs, than to be the descendants of the titled elite
responsible for establishing the area generations ago.

Even knowing all this, Alexa had been fooled by the exterior—red brick with Georgian motifs—which looked very inviting, very British. But where were the cozy fireplace, the
warm wood paneling, the yards and yards of chintz, and the
clusters of faded family photographs in antique silver frames?
Not here. Apparently the interior had been completely torn
out and redecorated in what Alexa supposed would be called
Italian modern. Pure white prevailed as the dominant color,

with hidden light from the ceiling illuminating black lacquer accent pieces.

Alexa checked herself for any visible dirt before collapsing onto the white silk sofa. It was a low-slung piece with oversized pillows that left almost no room to sit. She stared over the black lacquer coffee table decorated with a lone Oriental silk flower arrangement at the enormous black-and-white abstract covering one wall. Unable to decide what it was supposed to be, Alexa turned her attention to the black marble fireplace with the self-lighting gas log.

Steven walked in. "Would you like a drink?" He opened a black lacquer cabinet that concealed the bar and splashed Absolut vodka into a tall tumbler.

"I never drink before five," Alexa responded, unable to disguise the reproach in her voice. How many vodkas had Steven consumed since they left Marbella? "Which way to my room?"

"You may have the entire second floor." Steven flashed his little boy smile. "Sorry, but it hasn't been redecorated yet."

Fabulous, Alexa thought, I love it already. Would there be a telephone up there?

"Unless," Steven continued, "you'd be more comfortable with me on the first floor. I have a custom-made bed by Spurlucci."

"Thanks, but I'll be fine." She rose to leave.

Steven's blue eyes clouded. "Suit yourself, luv." His tone implied that it was her loss. "That was Audrey Throckmorton on the phone just now. Be ready at six-thirty. She's giving a bash tonight for her husband, Sir Alec."

"Go without me. I don't mind." Alexa tried to ease out of the invitation without offending Steven. "I'm too tired to socialize." What she really wanted to do was scream that she was sick of his friends. After ten days of nonstop partying at Jason Talbott's villa in Marbella, another party was the last thing she had in mind.

"I'm afraid I must insist you come, luv." Steven's smile, radiating sincerity and charm, would have won him a role as a born-again preacher in any movie. "I told Audrey you were my houseguest and I'd be with you. She'll set a place for you." He turned to refill his glass. "Besides it'll be a chance to introduce you to some financial people. Run along, luv. Have a bath and a nap."

Alexa tramped out of the room. Returning to the entry, she threw a tote over each shoulder and tugged her heavy suitcase up the stairs, wondering why Steven didn't have live-in staff. Struggling with her bags, she realized Steven had cleverly twisted her around his little finger—again. She resented it. It would be rude to refuse his request to attend the party. She supposed she should be grateful he'd helped her solve her financial dilemma by purchasing her screenplay. Instead of paying her cash, he'd agreed to let her use his town house rent free while he was away filming, and he'd given her half a point of the net on his movie. Steven had also promised to arrange for her to meet some British theatrical backers, so she could obtain financing.

As much as she appreciated everything he'd done for her, Alexa wasn't comfortable with him. An inveterate socializer, he never missed a party. But when he arrived, he never stood still. Afraid he might miss something, he constantly prowled, meeting and greeting. He never allowed himself to sit down and enjoy anyone he'd met. Alexa preferred small groups where she could get to know people.

She reached the landing and set her luggage down. Her bags were too heavy to lug any farther until she knew where to put them. She flicked on the light in the first room she came to and her jaw dropped in amazement at the Italian-modern bordello with mirrors covering the walls and ceiling. On a raised dais proudly stood a round bed covered in white raw silk with a sculpted black lacquer headboard depicting an egret in flight. Shafts of light shot down onto the bed from a concealed source in the ceiling while an enormous white moiré chaise posed in front of another black marble fireplace that had never known the presence of a genuine wood log. On the hearth was a white arctic fox rug. Alexa's heart wrenched for the animal who had been so needlessly slaughtered.

"Change your mind, luv?" Steven's voice came from behind her.

"No. I thought you said the second floor."

"I did, luv." His voice sounded slightly slurred. "In England we number the first floor above ground as one, not two."

"I'd forgotten." Alexa stepped into the hall.

She wearily pulled her suitcase up the stairs. She and Steven had been at odds since they'd left Mexico. There he'd readily accepted the fact that she was committed to the play until he'd bought her script. Then he persistently tried to change her mind, encouraging her to assist him in filming his movie.

"It's dinner jackets tonight," Steven called up to her. "I'll wake you at five. Will that be enough time to dress?"

"Fine," Alexa responded as lightly as she could. "Is there a telephone upstairs?"

"No, luv. There's one in the library and one in here."

Alexa beamed when she reached the second floor and saw her room. The dark suite with high ceilings and Victorian molding definitely had not been redecorated. In the corner a fireplace with a delicately carved mantel held a collection of crystal candlesticks and a Herend figurine. Above the mantel, a gilt-framed mirror graced the chimneypiece, and on the hearth a brass scuttle held several oak logs.

An eighteenth-century four-poster bed covered in a faded rose-print chintz dominated the room. Its canopy was the same material lined in a muted shade of pink, while off to one side a worn wing-back chair stood beside a small, round table draped in the same faded fabric.

A quick glance around the room confirmed there was no closet. The tall, burled walnut armoire flanked by a series of botanical prints would have to hold her clothes. Now this is England, she thought, flopping onto the bed and closing her eyes.

When Steven had said he'd be wearing a dinner jacket, Alexa hadn't given it much thought. As soon as they arrived at the party, she recognized her mistake. She knew dinner jackets were called tuxedoes at home, but she hadn't realized how formally the British dressed. In Los Angeles women frequently wore short cocktail dresses when men wore tuxedoes. In England the women adhered to the rules and wore long gowns. Alexa immediately saw she was the only one in a short dress.

There was nothing she could do about it now, she decided. She didn't even have a long dress with her. Sipping her champagne, she tried to hide her embarrassment by admiring the ballroom. High above her head a coffered ceiling of dark walnut mellowed into a rich, creamy paneling that covered the walls. Forming one wall, tall leaded-glass windows overlooked the terrace. Deep-blue velvet drapes lined with a watered blue silk were tied back with thick gold cords. Soft, hazy light sparkled from three imposing old Waterford chandeliers. The dance floor, a herringbone parquet of rosewood polished to a satiny sheen, reflected the chandeliers. Delicate gilt chairs lined the dance floor where the guests were now gathered for cocktails.

Steven guided Alexa through the groups of guests, introducing her, as he had in Marbella, as an American actress. She seethed, interrupting him frequently to add that she was a writer. Alexa was immensely pleased when several guests recognized her name and told her they'd read her book.

Standing with Steven in a small group, Alexa listened to him explain his new film company. In the distance she heard an achingly familiar voice. Her entire body stiffened. She tuned out the conversation around her and stared down at the steady stream of bubbles erupting in her champagne glass. It couldn't be! Yet it was the same rich baritone she'd heard a thousand times in her dreams.

Mark's resonant voice came from a small cluster of guests a few yards away. Alexa moved closer to the tall but very portly man to her right. Peeking around his bulky frame, Alexa saw Mark. His broad shoulders looked spectacular in his black silk dinner jacket. A perfectly knotted formal bow tie topped a dazzlingly white dress shirt with rows of neat little tucks down the front that gave him an air of elegance and sophistication she hadn't noticed in Mexico. Looking relaxed and happy, his gray eyes were warm and he was animatedly talking with someone Alexa couldn't see.

Why hadn't she taken the time to go downstairs and phone him this afternoon? Now he'd see her with Steven and have the wrong impression about why she was staying with him. There was nothing she could do now except go over and say hello and wait for an opportunity to explain the situation to him privately. As Alexa moved, a passing guest brushed her arm, splashing her champagne over her hand. Hastily she pulled back her dress before the liquid could spot it.

"My dear, I'm ever so sorry. Terribly clumsy of me," said a

tall, loose-limbed man with thinning copper-colored hair and quick, intelligent hazel eyes. He whisked out his handkerchief and patted her hand dry.

"I'm Chauncey Beddington. I don't believe I've had the honor."

"I'm Alexa MacKenzie."

"You don't say? *The* Alexa MacKenzie?"

She noticed the vague look of boredom etching his patrician features had vanished. She nodded as Chauncey continued to dab solicitously at her hand and block her view of Mark. The worst possible news came from Chauncey's lips next. He'd read her book three times and loved it. It appeared he'd be content to spend the night discussing it with her. She knew of no polite way to escape a man who'd given twenty-three hardback copies of her book to his friends. Pretending to listen attentively, Alexa shifted her stance so she could catch a glimpse of Mark.

He moved out of the group, sending her stomach into one long free fall. On Mark's arm was the most stunning woman Alexa had ever seen. She had the very tall, lithe, almost boyish figure of a high-fashion model. Her midnight-black hair was pulled back into the type of sleek chignon popular with Parisian models. A considerable amount of artfully applied makeup enhanced her vivid blue eyes and high cheekbones. Her flawless white skin, obviously a stranger to the sun, perfectly offset a black satin gown that fit across one shoulder while leaving the other completely bare and then tightly clung to her long-limbed figure as it fell to the floor. The dress was most certainly an exorbitantly expensive designer original. Everything about the woman screamed glamour, sophistication, and haute couture.

She ducked in front of the lanky Chauncey so Mark wouldn't see her. She reached for a strand of hair and twisted it around her finger.

"Alexa, there you are. And Your Grace," Steven said. "I see you've met Alexa."

Totally numb, she stood there as Steven threaded his arm through hers, amiably discussing mutual acquaintances with Chauncey Beddington. No wonder Mark hadn't called. Why would he when he had someone like that? Alexa felt a hot flush flare up under her deep tan when she recalled the way she'd behaved with Mark. She'd spent the last two months building that night into something it wasn't.

"How'd you manage that, luv?" Steven asked as Chauncey strode off across the room.

"Wh-what?" Alexa stammered, releasing the lock of hair.

"What's the matter with you? Didn't you hear what His Grace said?"

"N-no," Alexa confessed. She hadn't been listening to him. His Grace? Chauncey must be a duke.

"He's gone to find Audrey. He wants to be your dinner partner. Don't you know what an honor it is for the Duke of Reston to request that you be his dinner partner?" Wordlessly, she shook her head and tried to ignore the empty ache in the pit of her stomach. "It'll make you someone of significance. By the time the dancing starts, everyone will know you. Get hold of yourself. This is going to be your big night."

Thankfully, Steven moved to the opposite end of the room, away from Mark. Although there were about one hundred guests, she realized she couldn't possibly avoid Mark all evening. Steven continued introducing her to various people, and Alexa forced a smile in response to their endless banalities. They were talking with a cluster of guests when she saw Mark approaching. She inched behind Steven, certain that Mark had not yet seen her, determined to postpone the inevitable for as long as possible. As she watched Mark with Miss Haute Couture, a tight knot of jealousy formed in her chest. Mark and the glamorous creature were obviously well acquainted. The way his arm circled her waist and drew her to him as he escorted her through the crowd suggested a certain intimacy that made Alexa's spine prickle. The woman stopped as if to finish a private conversation before joining their group. Her red lips whispered seductively into his ear while she brushed back an errant lock of his hair from his forehead with her long, frosty-white nails. When she finished, Mark laughed, his light metallic eyes twinkling brightly, and he pulled her even closer.

The group stepped aside, making room for them. There was a strange, hollow feeling to Alexa's body now, but pride guided her, ordering her to retain her composure and smile.

"Mark, great to see you," Steven greeted them with a wide smile, "and Charmaine. Lovely as always." Steven slid his arm

possessively around Alexa's waist. "Mark, you remember
Alexa."

"Yes . . . of course." Mark's gray eyes were cool, and he
looked blankly at her as if he were trying to recall just where
they'd met.

Alexa nodded, her smile on hold.

"Charmaine, this is my newest star, Alexa MacKenzie.
Alexa, this is Charmaine Crowne."

"Hello," Charmaine responded smoothly with that clear,
precise diction and cadence Alexa had come to associate with
the British upper classes. Charmaine's silvery voice and the
aura of poise and immutable self-confidence she exuded in
every graceful line of her body told Alexa her instincts had
been correct. Everything about Charmaine indicated impeccable lineage and a privileged heritage. Undoubtedly she could
trace her ancestors back to the Magna Charta.

With one flutter of her long, wispy lashes, Charmaine's
gaze swept over Alexa's face, found nothing of interest, and
fell to her gown. Alexa knew the sheer, Grecian-style white
silk dress shot with minute gold threads was inappropriate
attire. It hung in graceful folds across the bodice, snugly
wrapped her waist, and skimmed across her hips; but it was
too short. It was evident to Alexa the hours she'd spent in one
of Marbella's numerous chic boutiques agonizing over such an
extravagant purchase had, in Charmaine's estimation, been
wasted.

Unwilling to trust herself to speak, Alexa nudged her flag-
ging smile back onto her lips. Someone asked her a question,
but the blood was pounding so loudly in her ears she couldn't
concentrate. There was a fractional pause and before Alexa
could say anything, Steven answered for her.

"Alexa's living with me. She's a fabulous actress, you
know. She had a small part in my last film."

Silenced by surprise and embarrassment, Alexa stared into
her champagne glass.

"Excuse us," Mark said, hailing a passing acquaintance.

"I need another drink," Steven said. He spun Alexa around
and guided her in the direction of the bar.

Mortified, Alexa still couldn't speak. What had Mark
thought? Apparently he didn't care. Nothing about that night
in Mexico had been special to him.

"Isn't she a heart-stopper?" Steven said, handing his glass across the bar for a refill.

Her self-control returned and with it her anger. "Dammit, Steven, why did you say I was living with you?"

Ignoring her question, Steven continued, "Charmaine Crowne. The soon-to-be Charmaine Kimbrough."

They were engaged? Alexa forgot how angry she was with Steven as the full impact of this statement hit her. Weakly she reached out for the fresh glass of champagne the bartender proffered.

"Jason says they'll announce any day now. It's about time. They've been together for two years."

Two years? What a fool I am, Alexa thought, a dull ache filling her heart. She saw the look of triumph in Steven's eyes. Did he know about that night? He probably did. Movie companies had their own set of jungle drums. Word traveled swiftly and there were no secrets. People seemed to know things even before they happened.

"I don't know how Mark gets those women to marry him. Like Caroline Hampton. He convinced her to marry him and used her fortune to start his business. When it became a success, he divorced her." Steven shook his head in disgust. "It isn't Charmaine's money he's after, although she has an enormous trust fund. It's her father's connections. Kimbrough's grooming himself for a political career."

Alexa stared down into her glass. The light refracted off the bubbles as they burst to the surface, all her illusions about Mark Kimbrough exploding with them.

"We all tried to warn Caroline, but she wouldn't listen," Steven continued. "She was in love with him. Even her father, who was bitterly opposed to her marrying beneath her, couldn't stop her. In the end she still loved him. Cried all over town that he'd filed for divorce and wouldn't take her calls. Then she began to drink heavily."

Alexa took a big gulp of champagne that almost refused to go down. Shattering her hopes into a thousand pieces, the agonizing reality hit her. Mark was just like Paul. Why hadn't she been able to see through him? What did psychiatrists say? Women usually choose the same type of man over and over again. She despised herself for her weakness. To make the same mistake twice was totally unforgivable.

"What happened to Caroline?"
"She was killed."

Across the room Linda spotted Alexa standing at the bar
talking with Steven Hunter. She hesitated a moment; she disliked Steven. For the past weeks she'd watched Steven manip-
ulate Alexa. Linda had tried to warn her that Steven was using
her, but Alexa was too sweet to see it. The man delighted in
dangling beautiful starlets under his friends' noses. With
Alexa he'd outdone himself. Not only was she a big name, but
she could stop a man's heart across the room, particularly in
that dress.

Scanning the area, Linda took in the eclectic mix of party
guests: titled names, young moguls like Mark Kimbrough,
politicians, and a dash of arty types. She knew exactly why
she'd been invited. Her family's title had been severely impoverished for decades until the fact her brother was a bar-
onet no longer mattered. He worked as a solicitor, a damn
good one. Her family's title aside, Linda realized she'd been
invited because everyone was curious about where she'd been
for the last two years. *Let them wonder.* Linda crossed the room,
oblivious to the admiring glances she received in her strapless,
shimmering rose-colored gown.

Someone tapped Alexa on the shoulder. She spun around to
find Linda Carlisle smiling at her.

"Alexa, where have you been? When did you get in?"

"This afternoon, and am I glad to see you." Alexa threw her
arms around her friend, hugging her tightly. She wanted to
find out what had happened to Caroline, but now wasn't the
time, she thought, leaving Steven at the bar and following
Linda. "What's up?" Inside, Alexa was a knot of nerves, but
she felt immensely relieved just to be near Linda.

"Warren's here. I want you to meet him." Linda had been
back for two weeks, but he'd been out of town until tonight.
She'd surprised him earlier by greeting him as he walked in.
He'd obviously not expected to see her, for he muttered a cool
hello before pointedly turning away. She wasn't giving up
that easily.

"There he is," Linda whispered. "Over there with the short
blonde in the red dress."

"You mean the little cherub who appears to be permanently attached to his arm?"

Linda giggled, but Alexa's laugh caught in her throat when Mark and Charmaine joined Warren. Mentally she gave herself a hard shake, recalling Mark's lie about Windsor Air and his shabby treatment of his wife.

"Warren, I'd like you to meet a friend of mine," Linda said when they joined the group. "This is Alexa MacKenzie."

Alexa tossed her head, sending her hair fluttering across her shoulders. From somewhere she found a social voice and a social smile she'd been unaware she possessed. "Hello," she said, extending her hand to a short, rather stocky man with rusty-blond hair and a face lightly dappled with freckles. Warren had an irrepressible grin and a glint of teasing laughter in his brown eyes, suggesting a man of warmth and charm. He wasn't as attractive as Alexa had expected, but she instantly liked him.

"Julia Hartley," Warren responded in cultivated, upper-crust English, indicating the pink-cheeked blonde clinging possessively to his arm.

"Happy to meet you," Alexa answered. She noticed Julia wasn't looking at her. Instead, she stared with politely disguised hostility at Linda.

"I understand you're a writer." Warren addressed Alexa, but his eyes were on Linda.

"Yes," Alexa answered. She let her gaze casually drift over the group. She met Mark's eyes and saw, although his face was a composed mask of English civility, his eyes were chips of gray ice. "I'm here producing a play for—"

"Alexa, daaaarling," twittered a high-pitched female voice. "There you are!"

Alexa turned and found herself being effusively hugged by Melanie Tarenholt, who immediately launched into mindless prattle about how she'd missed Alexa. Melanie wore a poison-green lamé dress with a neckline that really did give new meaning to the word plunging. A white boa, like a feathery garland, draped her shoulders. Every time she gestured with it, the boa emitted a burst of sweet perfume.

"You've all met my friend Alexa?" Melanie fluttered a set of false eyelashes. "We just made a picture together. Alexa does this naughty nude scene." She flittered the boa under War-

ren's nose and giggled, indicating the word "naughty" did not
cover the scene.

Alexa choked, groping for words. Her friend? Naughty
nude scene? Alexa felt shame rising in a hot wave to her
cheeks. "It wasn't—"

"I'd love to see it." Warren smiled mischievously.

Charmaine arched one delicate eyebrow, letting Alexa
know quite definitely that any nude scene was vulgar. Mark
stood there, his smoky gray eyes gazing at her impassively.

"It's done in extremely good taste," Linda interjected.
"Wasn't it Mark?"

Mark's eyes coldly assessed Alexa. "I wouldn't know. I
haven't seen the footage."

He spoke the words quietly in a deceptively casual tone, yet
each word stung her. How could he? A fast-rising anger
singed through Alexa.

"My agent simply wouldn't allow me to take off my clothes
like that," Melanie bubbled, waving her boa for emphasis.
"Alexa has so many talents. She's doing another movie with
Steven Hunter."

"I'm doing a pla—" Alexa started to protest.

"No wonder you needed a holiday. You've been so busy."
Melanie gushed on, refusing to let Alexa have a word. "Didn't
you simply adore Jason Talbott's villa in Marbella? Isn't Jason
simply the most fascinating man?" A look of smug satisfaction lurked behind Melanie's overbright eyes.

"I-I hardly know him," Alexa stammered. It was true. In
Marbella, Jason had made a half-hearted attempt to seduce
her before moving on to easier game. Alexa felt her composure slipping. Everything Melanie said had an element of
truth to it. A detailed explanation, if she could manage to get
one in, would make Alexa look ridiculous. She was on the
verge of saying something terribly crude just to shut Melanie's mouth.

"Noooow, don't be modest. Jason told me what a sensation
you were. He invited you for a few days and you stayed ten.
It isn't just any woman who can interest a man like Jason
Talbott."

There was a subtle light in Warren's eyes as he cast a glance
at Mark. Their expressions were polite but withdrawn.

"He didn't. . . . I'm not—" Alexa began anxiously, when

Melanie again cut her off. Melanie giddily chatted on about how wonderful Jason was. Alexa stood there in witless confusion. Melanie refused to give her a polite way of denying these insinuations. Fury and humiliation were overwhelming her when Chauncey Beddington appeared.

"My dear," he said, extending his arm, "Audrey is seating everyone."

When they found their places, they were joined by several other couples at a table for twelve. The last couple to arrive was Mark Kimbrough and his dinner partner, the dowager Duchess of Dunfey. Their seats were directly opposite Alexa. Miraculously, a huge formal arrangement of red roses and tall candelabra made a clear view of Mark difficult, and conversation across the wide table was impossible.

Alexa tried to concentrate on the attentive Chauncey, but too often she found herself listening for the sound of Mark's voice, for some morsel of his conversation. She'd convinced herself that Mark was different, and now she was shocked to feel how miserable the truth made her. All through dinner the constant pull of his presence kept her laughing nervously, but pride prevented her from looking at him.

Linda kept her eye on the adjacent table, where Warren had been seated, waiting to make her move. After the cold terrine of grouse liver and truffles in a green peppercorn sauce had been consumed, the waiters scurried about clearing the tables and removing the wineglasses for the next course. In the flurry Linda left her table and walked up to Warren.

"May I speak with you privately?" she asked, making certain she spoke loudly enough for his dinner companion to hear. "It won't take a moment. You'll be back in time for the next course."

Her heart pounding lawlessly, Linda watched as Warren Charles Geoffrey Rutherford-Jaymes, the future Viscount of Attenborough, stood. She'd known he wouldn't refuse her request. They'd both been raised with the same upper-class breeding that demanded politeness and civility, particularly in front of others.

"What is it?" Warren asked as she took his arm and led him outside the dining hall into the portrait gallery.

"Let's sit," she said, wanting to get him into a position where he couldn't easily walk away.

Warren reluctantly sat at one of the tête-à-tête tables. His steady brown eyes never left her face, but his usual smile was absent.

For a speech rehearsed so many times, over so many years, the words still caught in her throat. "Warren, I'd like you to know how terribly sorry I am for what I did."

Silence.

"You were wonderful to me. I didn't realize what I had until I'd lost it."

Warren looked at her blankly as if he had no idea what she was talking about.

"I loved you . . . love you very much, you know. I don't know what came over me with Ian."

"Thank you for telling me," he said in a neutral tone that chilled her more than the angry words she'd expected.

"I behaved so badly," she said, ignoring the persistent quiver in her voice. "I'd like you to give me another chance."

"That was then and this is now," Warren said, coming to his feet in an easy, casual movement. He moved around behind his chair and placed both hands on the chair's back. "It's over. We can't re-create the past . . . even if we wanted to. Take care of yourself," he said as he walked away.

After dinner was finished, Chauncey escorted Alexa into the ballroom, where a band was playing. She glided around the room in Chauncey's arms, asking herself how she ever could have believed Mark, a disreputable liar with a thirst for money and power, was special. Any woman who did not realize Mark Kimbrough was six feet three inches of heartbreak lying in wait would get what she deserved. Fate had been kind to her, Alexa decided. She'd been shown the truth while there was still time to get away. She willed herself to have a good time and forget Mark.

A succession of dance partners, whose names and faces Alexa knew she'd never remember, twirled her around the dance floor. Fueled by the champagne, she laughed and talked nonstop. She repeatedly told herself not to look at Mark, but she couldn't help noticing he danced continuously with Charmaine. She could see they were perfect together—tall and dark like a matched pair of sleek thoroughbreds. They were carelessly at ease in their elegant evening attire, wearing it with the assurance of those completely accustomed to formal affairs—and to each other.

Dancing each dance with a different partner, Linda patiently explained again and again where she'd been and that she was home to stay. Laughing female voices combined with the men's deeper tones as snatches of conversation filtered through the dance music. The entire time Julia remained with Warren. Linda realized if she was going to find another chance to speak with Warren, she'd have to make it happen herself. Just then Mark whirled by with the regal Charmaine in his arms. Earlier Linda had wondered what had happened between Mark and Alexa, but she hadn't had the chance to ask. Mark caught Linda's eye and smiled. She quickly shifted her glance to the sidelines where Warren stood sipping an after-dinner drink with Julia. When the next number began, Linda noticed Mark was leading Julia onto the dance floor. Linda didn't hesitate.

Just after midnight Alexa was once more dancing with Chauncey. He was the type of man any woman would want, Alexa thought. He had wealth and charm and even a title. Why then wasn't she attracted to him? Dancing nearby were Mark and Charmaine. He held her very close and she was laughing her soft, husky laugh and gazing up at him. As they waltzed by Alexa, she saw Charmaine's fingernails gleaming through the thick hair at the nape of Mark's neck. He was slowly sliding his hand up and down her back along the edge of her gown, his thumb skimming along just under the rim. A backwash of bittersweet memories swept over Alexa. She giggled at something Chauncey said, her smile paralyzed in place.

# Chapter 12

Alexa turned off Shaftesbury Avenue and hurried down Earlham Street past the rows of vendors' stands and turned onto the short side street marked Tower. Sprinkling lightly now, rain gilded the cobblestones, making them slippery. The wind rose, blowing through her sweater; the heaviness in the air signaled an approaching storm, not just a brief shower. What had happened? When she had arranged to meet Linda and Renata to decide which theater to lease for the play, the sun had been shining.

The rain-bloated clouds now darkened the sky and the old buildings created deep shadows, making it difficult to read the address Alexa had scribbled on a scrap of paper. Could this be it? She eyed the Cheong-Len Chinese Market suspiciously, then looked across the narrow street. The old brick building with the Georgian facade and side yard enclosed by a wrought-iron fence appeared to be her destination. Over carved double doors, which obviously had not been opened in years, ornate Gothic letters announced: Regency Theatre.

Alexa tugged on the door; Renata and Linda had said to meet them inside. With a groan the stiff door opened, and she stepped into the foyer. A wave of chill, damp air and the scent of mildew hit her. From a frayed cord a single light bulb, long since deserted by the protective fixture, swung back and forth, alternately illuminating and darkening the small area.

"Hello?" Alexa called, her voice reverberating thunderously in the emptiness. "Hello?" She brushed through a set of mildewed drapes dividing the lobby from the theater. In the distance she detected light seeping out from under the drawn curtain enclosing the stage. She waited a few seconds until her eyes adjusted to the dim light. "Linda? Renata?"

No answer. Walking down the aisle toward the light, Alexa surveyed the theater. With cobwebs draped like sheeting across the armrests, tattered seats of what she supposed once had been red cut velvet formed lopsided rows. A faded floral carpet worn thin in numerous places and filled with the dust of countless soles ran down the aisle.

"Alexa, we're up here," Renata called, peering out from behind the sagging stage curtain.

"What do you think?" Linda asked, her blue eyes widening expectantly as Alexa joined them.

"I . . . I . . . well," Alexa stammered. They both looked so pleased, so optimistic.

"Not what you were expecting, is it?" Renata waved a ring-crowned hand at the footlights.

"No," Alexa confessed. "When was this place last used?"

"About ten years ago," Linda answered. "It's not easy to find an available theater in the West End. Most are booked years in advance."

"You've had an agent looking?" Alexa asked, winding a strand of hair around her finger. "This is the best we can do?"

"Yes," Renata assured her as she turned to go backstage. "We'll show you two others nearby, but this is the best."

In shock Alexa followed them into a warren of minuscule rooms, a thespian's junkyard, filled with discarded props and broken-down sets where rat droppings, like confetti, covered everything. She couldn't imagine her play opening here. "Are there any plans to renovate this place?"

"The agent says the owner will give us a generous improvement allowance if we agree to a two-year lease," Linda responded.

How generous was he prepared to be? Alexa wondered. Could they simply napalm it and start over?

"Let's walk over to the other two theaters," Renata suggested when they again reached the mildewed lobby.

"Aren't we near the Ambassador Theatre?" Alexa asked as she stepped onto the sidewalk and ducked under Linda's umbrella.

"It's around the corner."

That reassured Alexa. *The Mousetrap,* London's longest-running play, had been there for nearly four decades. At least they were in the right neighborhood. The breeze subsided momentarily, but the rain continued to come down. Alexa cursed. Why hadn't she bought a raincoat in Spain instead of that useless cocktail dress she'd worn to the party? The memory of the party brought Mark's image to her—again. Despite the shock of all that had happened, tears refused to come to ease the ache in her heart. She was still stunned to have learned Mark had used his wife for her money in much the same way Paul had used her. In Mexico he'd seemed so sincere, so honest. But he'd never called her. Why should he? Miss Haute Couture obviously kept him busy. The fact was Alexa had been a one-night stand—nothing more.

"Where is Steven?" Renata called out over the hiss of the rain. "I thought he was coming with you."

"He's gone to the country for a few days," Alexa replied as evenly as she could. She didn't add he hadn't mentioned his trip. This morning after Linda had called, she'd found his note.

The next two theaters were smaller and more like old-time music halls. No wonder the agent had given them the keys; no self-respecting thief would bother with these dives. Compared to them, the Regency Theatre was positively pristine.

"The Regency isn't what I had in mind," Alexa said as they stood outside the last theater waiting for a taxi to happen by or for the downpour to stop.

"This isn't the States," Renata explained. "Our theaters are very old. The theater is in every Englishman's blood. We'll go anywhere to see a good play—music halls, taverns, church basements, village greens—anywhere. We don't have to be in a glitzy American-style theater. It's the play that counts."

Reluctantly, Alexa nodded her agreement. She reminded herself the English were the most avid theatergoers in the world, seeing on average three times as many plays in a year as an American saw in a lifetime. "You're right. That's why I want to produce this play myself. At home I could never expect to produce a play. Women aren't given the chance."

"You'll be fine," Renata said. "People won't judge you because you're female. If you produce a good play, that's what will count. But you have to decide if we want to open in the West End, or should we look farther out?"

"The West End," Alexa answered emphatically, knowing it was the same as opening on Broadway. "You belong here, not in some neighborhood theater."

"Then we'll have to make do with the Regency."

"Let's dash around the corner to the Bombay Café and talk about it," Linda suggested. "We can wait out the shower there."

The "dash" around the corner proved to be more than three blocks, and by the time they arrived Alexa was shivering uncontrollably. Shower, she thought. In L.A., where it seldom rained, this would call for Noah's Ark.

"After lunch we're taking you shopping," Linda said, looking down at Alexa's ruined leather pumps, "for a proper brollie, a Burberry raincoat, and a pair of Wellies."

Sipping hot tea and waiting for their order, a flush of warmth spread through Alexa, and with it the desire to forget who she was and even where she was. The weather mirrored her mood—dismal. Everything had veered disastrously from the course she'd envisioned. How could she help Renata if she had to produce a play in that ramshackle theater? Even more important, when was Steven going to help her get financing? Nothing in her life mattered now except her friends and her career. She needed to concentrate on making this play a success. Then, when the movie was released, she'd have three hits to her credit—a book, a movie, and a play. Her career would be firmly established. She would earn enough money to take off for a few years and write another long novel.

"Did you see what happened Saturday night?" Linda asked, sensing Alexa's thoughts were far away.

"When? I guess I had more champagne than I should have."

"You were fine." Linda smiled, thinking again how insecure Alexa was. "I spoke with Warren."

"And?" Renata asked, leaning toward Linda.

Linda briefly recounted what she'd said to him on the dance

floor. "I told Warren that I understood how he felt but I wasn't giving up. And that every time he sees me to remember I love him. When you love someone, you shouldn't give up easily—particularly when you've caused that person great pain. You can't expect one 'I'm sorry' to cover it. I intend to prove I mean it."

"Good," Renata said, tossing her red hair emphatically and pointing a ringed index finger at herself. "Giles never gave up on me. He said he'd do anything for me . . . except support my coke habit." The quartet of rings flashed as she dabbed at her nose with a handkerchief. "By the time I came to him I was almost dead. But I knew he loved me and I wanted to start over." Renata paused for a deep breath. "Do you know what he told me? He said he loved me and had been waiting in hell for me. I had to be hospitalized. It was dicey for a while, but I knew I could never let him down. Go ahead, Linda, prove to Warren you love him. Maybe he's been waiting in hell and is afraid to take another chance on you."

Alexa blinked back an unexpected tear. "I guess . . . it can't hurt to try."

The waiter arrived with a tureen of curry and plates of rice. The pungent odor from the hot curry filled Alexa's nostrils. Suddenly she was very hungry. When the waiter returned with an enormous pitcher of water, Alexa asked, "What's that for?"

Renata laughed. "This is three-alarm curry. You may need water to put out the fire."

Gingerly Alexa ladled a spoonful of curry onto her rice and tasted it. "Wow!" She grabbed her glass of water and took a gulp. "This is hotter than Texas chili."

"You'll get used to it," Linda said. "It's the British answer to Mexican food."

While they ate, Alexa gained the courage to ask the question that had been bothering her. "Do either of you know how Mark's wife died?"

Renata shook her head, but Linda answered, "In a motorcar accident."

"Anything mysterious about it?"

"No, her Rolls hit a patch of ice on the road near her father's estate. It skidded over the embankment and down into a ravine, killing her straightaway."

"Had she been drinking?" A vision of Steven lurching toward the car as they left the party came to Alexa.

"It's possible." Linda's sky-blue eyes narrowed. "She drank heavily after the divorce."

"Do you know what caused the divorce?" Alexa asked.

"I have no idea," Linda said. "I doubt that they had much in common; they were so different. But Mark's too much of a gentleman to discuss it. Why?"

"Well . . . I . . . just wondered," Alexa said. Obviously her friends were deceived by Mark's charm. They didn't see that Caroline's broken heart had driven her to drink.

"Mark has done a smashing job with this Windsor Airlines thing, don't you think?" Renata asked.

"Absolutely," Linda agreed. "England needs more men like him. Without his money Windsor Air would have collapsed, or we'd have another government-owned airline. Apparently he's put an end to that ticket fraud scheme as well."

Alexa bit back a scathing retort, wondering why Mark hadn't told her he owned Windsor Air. She recalled Paul and all the things he'd so cleverly concealed; Mark was just like her former husband. "Let's discuss the play."

"Giles can't help us," Linda said. "He's involved in post production work on the movie. The first cut deadline is in mid-July. He'll advise us, but he's frightfully busy."

"If you approve, he's arranged for you to interview one of his protégés, Archibald Twicksby," Renata said. "He's a young but talented director."

"I appreciate the recommendation. I'll check him out." Now if only Steven could find the time to introduce her to potential backers. "Money's the main problem."

"It always is with a play," Renata said. "It works itself out. You make adjustments, reorder priorities, whatever."

Alexa frowned. Everything she'd done so far had been first rate. Putting on her play in that broken-down theater wouldn't do—not at all. "Let's go talk to the agent. We need to find out how much the owner is willing to give us to improve Mildew Theater."

Just as Alexa had feared, the owner offered an improvement allowance too small to be significant. To make matters more complicated, they would have to supervise the renovations.

"Are you positive we can do this?" Alexa said as they rode

in a taxi toward Harrods to purchase rain gear. "The allowance isn't nearly enough, and we don't know anything about construction."

"We'll make do," Renata said firmly. "It's not as bad as you think. A thorough cleaning and a bit of paint will serve as a magic wand. I've been on the stage for twenty years. I have all sorts of connections. We'll use them."

Magic wand? That's exactly what it would take to transform that toady old theater into anything resembling what Alexa had in mind. "What about the broken seats? The upholstery? The lights?"

The taxi pulled up in front of Harrods. "Don't worry," Linda assured her. "We'll go black."

"Black?" Alexa slid out of the taxi, thankful it had stopped raining.

"The workers are on the dole," Renata explained. "The government pays them because they're unemployed. We'll have to pay them in cash. It's how most work is done here these days. They make more collecting from the government than they can from a regular job. We can cut costs that way. Everyone does it."

"There's nothing more I can do, luv." Steven leaned toward Alexa and ran his finger up the rise of her cheek. "No one is willing to risk money backing a play with Renata as the star."

"Maybe if I'd gone with you . . ." Alexa's voice trailed off.

"Steven's done his best. I've even asked a few people I know," Jason added. There seemed to be a certain telepathy between them. Almost before one spoke the other picked up his thoughts.

Alexa eyed Jason suspiciously. Straight from central casting, Jason Talbott was every inch the handsome but haughty aristocrat. Beneath his sleek auburn hair, his dark brown, almost black, eyes reflected his indifference. Unless he'd yawned he couldn't have looked more bored.

"Look, I didn't promise you I could raise the money," Steven continued, signaling the waitress for another drink. "I said I would try. Our deal was the exchange of your script for my town house, not for me to find your financing as well."

"I know," Alexa snapped and immediately regretted it. In the week since he'd come back from the country, Steven had tried to raise the funds necessary to produce the play. It really wasn't his fault no one wanted to take a chance on Renata. "I'm going to get the money somehow. Renata's counting on me."

"Why Renata Tremaine?" Jason asked, his contempt obvious.

"She's a friend, a good one." Alexa decided not to mention the incident with the Mexican police. Although she could not immediately say why, Alexa felt the less Jason knew about her, the better. "I wrote the play specifically for her."

Jason shrugged dismissively, his auburn hair catching the light and reflecting its gold tones. "I have all my capital tied up in more lucrative ventures."

Alexa found Jason's condescending attitude irritating. The simultaneous demise of Renata's career and her own play was a frightening prospect becoming more real each day.

"Why don't you come with me while I make my movie?" Steven asked.

"I can't do that. I'll find a way to finance my play."

"Suit yourself, luv."

Steven was really two people; one she liked very much and one she somehow mistrusted. But he'd done what he'd promised by trying to help her. It was really up to her to find the financing. This was her problem, not Steven's.

"She should have been here by now," Jason said, his eyes focused beyond them, circling the room with obvious irritation. He left the table and walked toward the entrance.

"His wife?" Alexa asked.

"Lord, no!" Steven shook his head. "They have an understanding. He goes his way; she goes hers."

"Oh." Dismayed, Alexa peered around Legend's bar. The nightclub famous as the gathering place for the money men of show business in Britain had a nose-in-the-air ambience. Alexa never felt comfortable in places like this where everyone was intent on seeing and being seen. Steven had insisted she accompany him. No one, he'd told her, knew who she was, and no one was likely to find out if she spent all of her time working on her play. Here I am, Alexa thought, take a good look, because I'm not coming back.

Alexa blinked twice, disbelieving what she saw. Coming

toward them, Jason's arm encircling her waist, sashayed Melanie Tarenholt.

"What's she doing here?"

"Relax, luv. She and Jason have been an item on and off for years."

"Really?" Alexa was amazed. An out-and-out womanizer, Jason idly collected beautiful women. And as she had noticed in Marbella, women adored him. Enthralled, they listened to every word he uttered, laughing more than necessary and giving him more attention than he returned. Melanie, Alexa observed, was an exception. Jason gazed down at her with nothing less than a rapturous smile.

"Alexa." Melanie blew her a kiss as she slid into the booth and a wave of cheap perfume invaded the small space.

Alexa stared at Melanie. Beneath those platinum tresses a coiled viper waited to strike. There'd be no point in confronting her about the insinuations she had made at the party. What could Alexa say? You exaggerated? You implied that Jason and I . . . Then it hit Alexa. How could she have been so stupid? Perhaps Melanie actually believed Alexa had something going with Jason and she'd become jealous. That would certainly account for Melanie's behavior. The jealous, possessive feeling Alexa had felt when seeing Mark with Charmaine came hurtling back to her. Alexa gave Melanie a tight half-smile. She had Alexa's sympathy, but not her trust. Undoubtedly Melanie was guilty of nothing more than bad taste in lovers. Alexa understood that perfectly. She'd made the same error—twice.

"All right, hold it. Smile." A flash of blinding light and a loud pop sounded as the photographer caught the four of them point-blank.

"Why did he—" Alexa blinked away the white-hot circle of light.

"Melanie," Steven answered. "She's big news in the tabloids."

Still seeing a bright starburst, a feeling of uneasiness came over Alexa. She didn't want her picture in one of those papers. In the short time since she'd come to London, she'd become acquainted with their virulent brand of yellow journalism. The antithesis of the London *Times,* these papers were obsessed with escapades, real or imagined, of royalty and stars.

As the prime-time queen of a British soap opera, Melanie was front-page material.

"How was Italy?" Melanie asked when the photographer moved away.

Steven straightened in his seat. "Fine. Just sorting out some of the usual preproduction problems."

"Aren't you filming in the Sudan?" Alexa asked, stunned.

"Location work's in Sudan, luv." Steven shifted uncomfortably, his blue eyes avoiding hers. "Studio work will be done in Rome. It's cheaper than London."

Why did Steven say he was in the country, implying the English countryside, if he went to Italy? Alexa wondered. He was mercurial. One day he was charm itself, with a beguiling smile he could summon at a moment's notice. He'd spend hours confiding in her about his plans for the future and then become cold and secretive.

"Have you seen much of Mark Kimbrough?" Melanie asked.

"Only briefly that night at the party when I saw you."

"Really?" Melanie smiled as if someone had presented her with the crown jewels. "I thought—" she paused dramatically and snuggled up against Jason. "Well, in Mexico you two seemed . . . cozy. But you know how Mark is."

*I do now,* Alexa thought.

"Mark has tied up a lot of his capital in Windsor Airlines." Jason's handsome features registered his contempt. "That could be a big mistake."

"He's taken on more than he can handle this time," Steven added with a smile.

With a quicksilver change of expression directed at Steven, Jason continued, "Mark Kimbrough may just find his little empire in Carney Street."

"Where's—" Alexa started to ask.

"Bankruptcy, luv." Steven downed the rest of his drink.

# Chapter 13

Because the sky was a cloudless blue and the sun brilliant, the day seemed to have more promise for Alexa than the previous two rainy days had. During that time she had asked everyone she knew for the funds for her play. She'd contacted most of the cast and crew of *The Last Chance* to obtain their ideas. She'd received many suggestions, only to have those people politely refuse her request. Take heart, she told herself, while she walked to her first appointment of the new day. She had faith in her play. As her best work to date, it suited Renata perfectly.

Hours and several uncomfortable conversations and polite rejections later, Alexa slowed her pace as she shuffled along the narrow street, her shoulders slumped. It's supposed to be easier than this, she told herself. The British had hundreds of plays going all the time. As conservative as they might be in many things, they'd generated most of the innovative theater productions in the last twenty years. She had counted on this artistic entrepreneurialism. At home she'd never be given a chance to produce her play. Here unknowns and women were accorded the respect Broadway reserved for proven winners.

It was more than just Renata's reputation causing the problem. The financial people didn't know Alexa and were unwilling to trust her. An American novelist who'd never written a play before and a proven drug addict were viewed as a deadly combination. She couldn't really blame anyone. She realized no one would give them the money except as a personal favor. As it had so many times since she'd come to London, Mark Kimbrough's name came to mind. He knew Renata and liked her. He also knew Alexa and must at least respect her professionally even if he had rejected her on a personal level. But she refused to let that bastard make another nickel off her. It was bad enough her movie, when it was completed, would add to his impressive net worth. She didn't want him to make any money from her play. There had to be another way.

The sky was aswirl with thickening gray clouds and in the distance she could hear muted thunder, softly ominous. Standing on Wardour Street in front of the office buildings housing the giants of the British film industry, Alexa fought her fatigue, her frustration, her despair. She mustered her courage for one last attempt to obtain the financing. Her mouth was dry with apprehension as she entered the building. What would she do if Nigel Hunter turned her down?

After waiting an hour because she had no appointment, a secretary admitted Alexa to the chrome-and-glass office suite. Her footsteps were silenced by the dense white carpet as she crossed the room and nervously extended her hand. "Thank you for seeing me." Staring directly into Nigel's rheumy blue eyes, she said, "I'm trying to raise money for my play. It—"

"With Renata Tremaine?" Nigel cut her explanation short, curtailing her carefully marshaled arguments.

"Yes, she's perfect for my play." Alexa could sense she wasn't doing well at all. Nigel seemed disinterested, barely polite. She reached for a lock of hair and wound it around her finger.

Nigel lumbered over to the floor-to-ceiling expanse of glass that formed one wall of his office. Alexa could see his profile as he stared out at the surge of lightning tracing its blue web across the sky.

Mentally, Alexa crossed her fingers. She had to admit Nigel's gruff, abrasive manner unnerved her. She would never have had the courage to come to him now except Steven had told her how impressed his father had been with her acting. Apparently Nigel had overridden Mark's decision to use Melanie and had agreed with Steven that Alexa could better perform the part.

"All right," he said softly. Nigel turned to her, "I'll give you some money on one condition."

Alexa stepped from the taxi in front of the large Georgian house. Formally clipped greenery traced a foot-high wrought-iron fence, and clusters of impatiens lined the walk, spilling their tendrils of color onto the gray stones. As she clanged the brass knocker, it began to rain again, a mossy scent filling the air. Typical May weather in England, Alexa decided, showers followed by sunshine and then more showers. She wondered where she'd left her umbrella this time.

"Hello, Malcolm. Linda's expecting me," Alexa said when the houseboy admitted her.

"Alexa, come in here," Linda poked her head out of the library door. "It's a bit chilly. I thought a fire would be rather nice, even though it's summer. Is something the matter? You look upset."

"I wanted to talk to you alone before Giles and Renata get here." Alexa sank into a soft leather sofa, twisting a lock of hair around one finger. "Steven couldn't find anyone to invest in my play. He's tried, but no one's willing to take a chance on Renata. I've been trying myself for the past three days. I know how much Renata's depending on this. I'm putting all my own money into my play."

"Can you afford to do that?"

"Not really, but I'm willing to take a chance on what I believe in, and I believe in my script and in Renata. Please don't mention to her what a risk this will be for me. I'm certain she thinks I have plenty of money. She needs to concentrate on her career, not to worry about my finances." She unwound the hair, then rewound it tighter this time. "I don't have all the money. I've got about half."

"I wish I could help," Linda said. "All my money is tied up in the shop. We're staying here with my brother until my boutique makes money."

Linda was interrupted by Malcolm announcing Renata and Giles had arrived.

"Hello," Alexa said, hugging Renata and smiling at Giles. This was the first time she'd seen him since she'd come to

London. Alexa knew he'd been extremely busy with the post-production work on *The Last Chance.* "How's the editing going?"

"Fine," Giles said. "I may need you one morning for a bit of voice work. I'm not certain yet."

"Let me know." Alexa paused. "Have you seen any of the footage of me?"

"Just the rushes. In the next few weeks when we edit the first cut, I'll have another look. Don't worry, I'll see you're not overexposed," he said, rumpling her hair. "I have the final cut."

Alexa nodded. She knew he had insisted upon the right to the last cut of the film before it was printed. Otherwise producers, known for their commercial rather than artistic tastes, usually had the last cut. Somehow she wasn't reassured, but she put her uneasiness aside. She had enough to worry about. However the scene turned out, she'd have to live with it.

"Let's have tea in the conservatory," Linda said, leading them down the hall and into a large room dominated by floor-to-ceiling windows overlooking a small garden filled with foxglove and a trellis laden with pink roses. Unlike the well-worn library with its masculine smells of leather and tobacco, this room was an utterly feminine area decorated in confectionlike prints of lavender and pinks.

"Alexa's raised half the money for the play," Linda announced with a proud smile.

"Fabulous!" Renata's smile sparkled as brightly as her rings, generating a fresh surge of enthusiasm in Alexa. Friends were worth the risk.

"Who's the angel?" Giles asked from his place next to Renata on the overstuffed pink sofa, using the industry term for investor.

Alexa hesitated. She hated deceiving her friends, but Nigel had been quite specific. There would be no mention of his investment.

"I put up one fourth and Steven put up another quarter." Alexa flicked a wave of hair through her fingers. This was close to the truth. She had put up a fourth, and Steven would receive credit for Nigel's investment.

"Steven?" Renata's face registered surprise. "I thought he was putting everything into his new production company."

"Why would he invest in a play?" Giles asked. "His movie is so low budget that he's filming in Africa with some unknown Italian director."

"He believes in Renata," Alexa compounded the first lie with another, "and he wants to be successful independently of his father." This wasn't exactly a lie, Alexa assured herself. She'd promised Nigel not to say he was the one with faith in Renata. Apparently he had confidence in Alexa's ability as well. He'd encouraged her to come to him with any future film projects.

"What I need to do now is raise the other half of the money." Alexa noted a shadow of alarm had replaced Renata's happy smile.

"I wish we could help," Renata said in a choked voice, her tear-brightened eyes widening. "We haven't much money. I haven't worked, except for that small bit in the film, in three years. All the money Giles has earned has been used to pay off my debts. We won't receive any more money until *The Last Chance* shows a profit."

Giles reached across the sofa and drew Renata to him in a gesture of such tenderness that Alexa had to look away. "Don't worry, we'll get the rest of the money somewhere."

"Surely we can find someone willing to back a play starring Renata," Linda said as she passed the tea cakes around.

"Let's go over who you've seen," Giles suggested. "Perhaps you've overlooked someone."

Alexa ran through the potential investors she'd personally visited, including Chauncey Beddington. "He'd be happy to invest but he can't until after the first of the year. Something about his trust has a limit on the capital he is permitted to withdraw in a year. He's at the max for this year."

"I see." Giles nodded thoughtfully and took a bite of a sandwich. "I believe we've overlooked Mark Kimbrough. He's quite fond of Renata, and he knows I'll take a personal interest in helping make this play a success."

"I don't want to ask him." Alexa had known that sooner or later Mark's name would come up. "I don't think he has the money," she hedged, using the bankruptcy comment Steven had made as her escape hatch. "This Windsor Air thing may ruin his business."

"Not bloody likely," Giles said. "The *Times* says the trouble is over and they're making money again. Mark's brought them through the crisis."

Alexa rose and walked over to the window. The rain fell steadily and in the fading light the pink roses seemed unusually bright. How could she let pride stand in her way? If there was any chance Mark would lend them the money, she should take it.

"I'll ask him."

# Chapter 14

Alexa sat on the edge of the chair, her spine stiffly erect, and handed the proposal across the desk to Mark Kimbrough. "I'm looking for investors for my play."

Mark accepted the document while Alexa adjusted her suit jacket, smoothing out nonexistent wrinkles.

"With Renata Tremaine?"

"Yes, I may have mentioned it to you in Mexico."

"I remember." Mark scanned the pages, stopping now and again to read a section more closely.

Did he remember anything else? Alexa wondered. At the sight of him, in his Gieves and Hawkes suit, looking like an advertisement for his Savile Row tailor, the knot of apprehension in her chest tightened.

"I've never financed a play," he said, his voice cold. "Real estate. That's my field."

"We . . . I thought perhaps . . ."

"How many investors have turned you down?"

"They're reluctant to invest." She deliberately evaded his question. "Because they don't believe Renata is well. She is and this play will put her on top again."

"Who is this . . ." Mark flipped the pages of the proposal. "Archibald Twicksby?"

"The director—"

"I can see that. Where did he come from? Does he have experience in the theater?"

"Yes, he trained with the Royal Academy of Dramatic Arts. He's a protégé of Giles Acton."

"Then his experience is mainly with films, not theater."

"Yes, but his early training was in the theater."

"I understand." Mark's mouth tightened. "Unlike American actors, most Britons train on stage first, but that doesn't mean they're fully qualified for that field. If Twicksby has worked with Giles, films are his forte."

"Renata and Giles seem to think he's the best available director for my play." Alexa could feel the heat prickling up her neck. "I've interviewed him and I'm satisfied that we'll work well together."

"I see." His voice clearly indicated his doubts. "Has he ever directed a play before?"

"No."

Mark again directed his attention to the proposal. With one hand he rapidly flipped his Mont Blanc pen over and over. Each time it hit the heavy oak desk it made a dull thud.

"And you?" he asked.

There was a catch in her throat, a moment of uncertainty before she realized he wanted to know about her experience in the theater. "I've written and produced five plays."

"Really? Where?"

"West Coast . . . California." Alexa knew being deliberately evasive would work against her. "At a small neighborhood theater."

"Amateurs?" Mark stood up, his tall frame backlit by the leaded-glass window behind him.

"We were very professional," Alexa continued, although Mark had turned to look out the window. "With Hollywood so close we had to be."

"Really?" he said without turning.

"Yes, I shouldn't have any trouble with Renata, Giles, and Archibald to help—"

"Why is Steven Hunter listed as coproducer?" Mark turned to face her. "I thought he was leaving to make a movie. I didn't realize Steven had any experience with stage productions."

"Aaah . . . he." Alexa hesitated. Nigel couldn't object to her using his name in a low-key way. "Steven says I'm to go to Nigel anytime." She prayed Nigel's name would act as some sort of talisman.

Mark slowly slid into his brown leather chair as he regarded her pessimistically. She shifted in her seat. The mammoth desk wasn't wide enough to protect her from his penetrating gaze. A buzz sounded from the monitor on Mark's desk, and he frowned as he switched it on.

"You have a call on line two."

"Take a message. I said not to interrupt me."

"It's Barnaby Apsford at Windsor Airlines."

"Excuse me," he said to her as he picked up the telephone. She witnessed a momentary crack in his aloof composure. "Barnaby," Mark said. His voice had a deep, troubled timbre to it.

Alexa sat watching him while he listened intently. Although she despised herself for noticing, he never looked better. She forced herself to concentrate on those words, "Windsor Airlines." The agony of Mark's duplicity knifed through her again. Why couldn't he have simply told her he owned part of the airline? What difference would it have made? As he had countless times before, Paul's smiling face as he told her another lie came to mind. He's just like Paul, she thought, wondering how many lies Mark had told his wife before he discarded her.

"Do you have any idea where they were purchased?" He bent his head to one side to keep the phone braced against his shoulder while he rapidly made notes. "Really? . . . They've moved then. . . . That's such a small country. Start contacting travel agents there. Let's stop this before it gets any worse. . . . Check with Interpol." Mark returned the receiver to the cradle. "Just a minute," he said to Alexa and left the room.

When she'd entered his office, she'd been too nervous to notice her surroundings. Now she looked around curiously. Unlike so many of the offices she'd visited lately, with their glitzy modern interiors of chrome and glass, Mark's office had retained the historic charm of the building. A Heriz rug in muted tones of rust and blue partially covered the oak plank floor. Volumes of leather books, many appearing to be quite old, sat on library shelves along with dozens of art objects he had obviously collected during his travels. On the far side of the room, before a small fireplace, was a sitting area with two wing-back chairs upholstered in a blue and rust plaid. Between the chairs a low table held a cut crystal decanter of brandy and several glasses. The only concessions to modern convenience were the telephone and a small computer terminal. The office had such a masculine, personal touch that she suspected no decorator could have designed a space so well suited to the man.

"You were saying?" Mark seated himself again.

"Th-that Nigel will help if I need him."

"And you?" he asked, flipping the pen over and over.

"Me?" His unwavering stare unnerved her. "I-I'm investing as much as I can afford."

He continued regarding her solemnly and playing with the pen. The thought that he would help had been a false hope, she realized.

"The Regency Theatre, I don't believe I know it."

Alexa felt a flood of color rush to her cheeks. "Probably not. It hasn't been used in several years."

"How many?"

She paused before saying, "Ten."

"Why not?"

"There's been some . . . aaah . . . deferred maintenance."

"It's a shambles."

"The owner will give us an allowance for improvements."

Mark checked his watch. "Let's call the agent and get the key."

"Why?" Shock had almost prevented her from speaking.

"I want to see it."

"The Regency?" He wanted to see it. Imaginary cameras rolled and she saw his beautiful leather shoes scrunching rat droppings. "I gave the key to Renata. She's over there rehearsing."

"Are you positive you need to see it?" Alexa asked Mark as they walked up to his maroon Jaguar sports coupe.

"Definitely," he answered, holding the door open for her.

Alexa settled into the beautiful leather seat and ran her hand across the burled walnut paneling on the dashboard. It was old, a classic, but expertly maintained, evidently a treasured possession. When he turned on the ignition, the powerful engine purred to life and Mark deftly moved the vehicle into the late afternoon traffic.

"The investors will have to sublet the theater should the play close."

"Of course." She hadn't thought of that because she had never considered the possibility her play might fail. Her nerves tightened another notch. He would see the condition of Mildew Theater and never invest a tuppence. It would require fancy mental gymnastics to conceive of a successful play in that theater.

The traffic along Shaftesbury was at a standstill. The sports car, designed to zip along at thousands of RPMs, rolled forward and stopped, rolled forward and stopped.

"Did you get to Morocco while you were in Spain?" Mark broke the uncomfortable silence.

"Yes," Alexa answered. Where had that question come from?

Shifting again, Mark eyed her suspiciously. "Did you enjoy it?"

"No . . . yes . . . Well—"

"Which?"

"I was frightened."

"Why? Steven would have protected you." A distinct note of sarcasm colored his voice.

"I was alone. Our tour had to have armed guards. It was so dangerous they made us leave our passports on the ferry so they wouldn't be stolen."

"You were by yourself? You had no business being there alone."

"Nothing happened. I was silly to be afraid. On the way back I went to see the Rock of Gibraltar. I never knew all that stuff was in there." She rambled on aimlessly about the contents of the rock even though she could see he wasn't listening.

As Mark pulled into a parking space near the Regency, a fresh pang of anxiety assailed her. Bringing him here was an idea conceived in pure desperation.

The instant Mark pulled the door to the theater open for her, Alexa could smell the mildew. What was the point of even going in? But she couldn't turn back. Mark's hand held her arm, guiding her into the lobby.

"Roof leaks," he observed tonelessly.

In complete shock Alexa stood rooted to the spot.

"Old buildings," Mark went on, oblivious to her, "you have to expect that."

He gripped her elbow firmly, drawing her into the theater before she could comment on the lobby. As they walked down the aisle toward the stage, Alexa inspected the area in disbelief. Whoever had cleaned the lobby had waved the same magic dustpan over the theater. Gone were the cobwebs and pounds of dust, leaving the place looking like an impoverished dowager instead of the down-and-out bag lady Alexa had expected.

"Hello, Mark, Alexa," Renata waved to them from the stage, where someone had replaced the broken footlights and repaired the sagging curtain.

"Renata," Mark responded, beaming at the redhead.

"You're just in time." Warren popped up from a seat in the front row. With Linda at his side, he grinned broadly at them, his gold-flecked eyes bright. Warren continued his easy bantering with Mark about the productions at the Regency he remembered from his youth. Warren's unaffected charm and his easiness with Mark were apparent. Linda, too, spoke to Mark with the unawed familiarity of a close friend. Alexa hardly knew how to speak to him except defensively.

Alexa found her way onto the stage. The myriad of props still cluttered the area, but someone had swept away the rat droppings. "Who cleaned this place?" Alexa whispered.

"I did," Renata grinned. "Better?"

"I'll say."

While the group chatted, Alexa watched silently. So Warren had come by to see Linda. Maybe he was still interested, she thought, deciding it was too bad he didn't have any money to invest. It seemed that Warren's funds, like Chauncey Beddington's, were tied up in some sort of trust. Perhaps though, Warren could persuade Mark.

"Alexa, let's look at the office." Mark's voice interrupted her thoughts. "Since your proposal didn't include an expenditure for office space, I assume you'll use the manager's office."

Alexa nodded and led him up the back stairs. Festooned

with cobwebs, a single lamp lit the small office, illuminating a
tiny desk still laden with papers, a rusty file cabinet, and a
sagging sofa. Several ancient play posters were haphazardly
nailed to the walls. The room had a dusty, stuffy smell to it
that made Alexa want to hold her breath. A scuttling sound
came from near her feet as a mouse skittered across the floor
and slid under the sofa.

"It's not going to work. I've participated in numerous real
estate projects. What the owner's offering isn't enough. The
roof leaks. The lobby's the most noticeable, but it leaks everywhere. New carpets, upholstery . . ." He shook his head, his
eyes a metallic silver in the dim light. "The wiring undoubtedly isn't to standard."

"Don't worry about what the owner's offering. We can
make it. We're going black—" she stopped midsentence, noticing the sudden change in his expression.

"No, you're not!"

Why was he so upset? With a blunt swipe, common sense
returned. Mark, she remembered, with his political ambitions
and visible public profile on the Trade Alliance, could never
condone anything illegal. Everything he did would have to be
above reproach. She should have known this. "Everyone does
it," she whispered.

"I'd never put my money into a venture unless it was totally legal." In two strides he covered the length of the office,
turned, and paced back again.

"What are you two doing in there?" Renata's voice came
through the closed door.

"I'll have to think about your play," he said, leaving the
office. His voice underscored the word "your," implying it
would never be his play.

Tight-lipped with anger at her own blunder, Alexa followed him. Her insides were a house of cards that had tumbled into a heap in the pit of her stomach. She'd lost any
chance she had to convince him to help her.

"We're going to Morton's for a drink," Warren informed
them when they joined the others in the lobby. "Come with
us."

"All right," Mark agreed, his tone emotionless.

"I have an appointment," Alexa excused herself with a lie.

How could she face her friends when she'd just bungled everything?

Alexa made herself speak to Mark. "Thank you for seeing me. I appreciate your considering my play." When he responded with a curt nod, she turned to the others and said good-bye.

She stepped out of the theater into a light drizzle. Dusk had fallen, deepened by the shadows of the buildings along the narrow street. She hadn't realized how late it had become.

"Need a ride?" Mark asked from behind her.

"No," Alexa replied, startled. She'd assumed he'd stayed behind with the others while Renata locked up. "I'm grateful you took the time to come here."

She pivoted and walked away. She'd gone a block and a half before she realized she didn't have her umbrella and she was going in the direction opposite the Underground station.

# Chapter 15

Three o'clock, three o'clock, three o'clock. Each step she took hammered out the time as she walked to Mark's office. At three o'clock she would know if he was going to give her the money. Alexa took a deep breath to still the butterflies fluttering through her stomach as she made her way around the construction barricade blocking the sidewalk. Acres of scaffolds accompanied by tall cranes covered the financial district, turning the already-narrow streets into frustrating roadblocks. Alexa disliked the cubistic high-rises all this construction represented. Too much of the picturesque London with its ghosts of the past had given way to a modern, linear skyline. She wondered if any of the chrome-and-glass edifices that had altered the city were the result of Mark Kimbrough's real estate ventures.

The square-mile financial district had once been the heart of the city, and so Londoners affectionately referred to it as "the City." It still had its own Lord Mayor and Council operating independently of the rest of London. Even the Queen had to obtain permission to enter. Once the City had been a fort, before the Romans expanded it and built a wall around it. Later a maze of narrow streets developed, radiating out from the wharves on the Thames. Now the area was packed with various financial institutions, reflecting the newly burgeoning British economy. Not only were they acquiring American companies, in effect buying back the colonies they'd lost, but the British were giving their country renewed financial vigor.

Near St. Paul's, Alexa entered Mark's offices in a quaint old building. A discreet brass plaque above the old-fashioned frosted glass doors read: Triad Investments. Judging from the offices listed on the directory, Mark was involved in many diverse projects, including real estate, international investment, property management, and something called multinational acquisitions. The scope of his holdings was far greater than she'd anticipated. Surely he could afford to back her play.

She crossed the small lobby, noting that the dentil molding with its finely carved design added an elegant touch to what at first appeared to be a rather modest reception area. A single oil painting by Hogarth graced the paneled walls.

When she stepped up and pressed the button, the brass, birdcage-style elevator immediately and soundlessly appeared. Unlike most of the old lifts Alexa had ridden since coming to England, this one had none of the frightening jerky movements. She assumed it had been refitted with a more modern hydraulic system. Through swirls of brass curlicues, Alexa watched the walls of the elevator shaft pass by. The knot in her stomach tightened when she pulled back the door and stepped into the hall in front of Mark's office. *Accept whatever he has to say,* she reminded herself. *Don't be upset when he says no.*

"Alexa MacKenzie," she said, presenting herself to Mark's secretary. "I have a three o'clock appointment."

"Mr. Kimbrough has been unavoidably detained," responded sandy-haired, freckled Mr. Coombs from behind his horn-rimmed glasses.

Her courage ebbing away, Alexa found a chair in the empty waiting room. Why wait? she asked herself. It had been over a week since she'd seen Mark. If he'd been going to lend her the money, he certainly would have contacted her before now. Undoubtedly he was just being polite by asking her to come to his office. If there was one thing she'd learned since coming to England, it was that the British were unfailingly polite, even when they said no.

Alexa straightened her suit jacket and examined the waiting room. It had the same old-world atmosphere Mark's private office had. The fine English antiques and the beautiful Aubusson rug covering the oak plank floors gave the small room an aura of the past. Prismatic light came through the leaded-glass panes of the mullioned windows, splashing a soft rainbow of color across the room.

Time elapsed. . . . Where was he? Alexa stared distractedly at the hunt scenes lining the paneled walls. She'd leafed through numerous issues of *Acquisitions Monthly* and *Financial Times* left about the waiting area.

"Will it be much longer?" Alexa inquired of Mr. Coombs after two hours had passed.

"I really couldn't say."

Frustrated, Alexa sat down again. She had to see Mark. If there was any chance he'd help, she had to know. Could he be deliberately making her wait like this? Was he hoping she'd become discouraged and leave? Just the thought of having to postpone producing the play and the heartache it would bring Renata left a sick feeling in the pit of her stomach.

Finally, in a whirlwind of activity, Mark came through the door, nodding curtly to Mr. Coombs and going into his office without looking in her direction. Immediately Mr. Coombs, pad and pen in hand, responded to some imperceptible command and followed Mark into the office. It wouldn't be long now, she told herself.

In the twenty minutes that followed she checked her watch twenty-five times. She decided that he'd forgotten her. The rosy haze of light faded as the sun dropped lower in the sky, robbing the windows of their sparkling light.

"Miss MacKenzie," Mr. Coombs said, emerging from Mark's office and holding the door open for her to enter.

Alexa vaulted to her feet. *Wait . . . get hold of yourself.* She paused to smooth the wrinkles from her suit and to affix her most confident smile before entering.

"I apologize for keeping you waiting. I had an emergency meeting." Mark's words were conciliatory, but his tone was positively forbidding. "Sit down."

Alexa sank into the chair opposite his desk. Mark appeared distracted as he rifled through a stack of papers. A muscle in his cheek tightened, hardening the outline of his jaw. Apparently she couldn't have come at a worse time. She tightened her grip on the arms of the chair, forcing her voice to remain casual. "Should I come back? Would tomorrow be a better day?"

"That won't be necessary." He continued searching through the pile of papers.

*Dammit,* Alexa thought, *get on with it. Just say no and let me leave.* He handed a sheaf of papers to her. She met his gaze, her heart pounding in her chest. At first she'd assumed he was returning her proposal, but this document had to be at least twenty-five pages long.

"You're going to invest in my play," she whispered.

"If you accept my terms."

What terms? Amazed at the incredible legalese, Alexa slowly turned the pages. The text was riddled with the word "whereas" and phrases like "parties of the first part," "pertaining to," and "accepts liability for."

"You've retained the services of a solicitor, I assume?" His unenthusiastic tone chilled her.

She nodded, blessing Linda's brother for volunteering to help. He'd die when he saw this document, but she'd definitely need him to decipher all this legal mumbo jumbo.

"I'll review the most important points with you now. That way we'll know if we're in agreement before you ask your solicitor to ratify this."

Again Alexa nodded, forcing herself to smile. No one else would lend her the money—she needed Mark. He could dictate any terms he wished.

"First, there will be no work done on this play at any time that is not strictly legal. All government policies and union rules will be strictly adhered to." He leaned back in his chair, sizing her up. "Do you know how to fill out the cards?"

"Cards?"

"I rather thought not." His lips curved into a thin smile and a spark of mockery lit his slate-gray eyes. "National Insurance cards for every employee. They'll have to be filled out each week and stamped."

"I can learn—"

"No one works without a card. No going black."

"Of course, I—"

"I'm on page seven—the budget. Each category—salaries,

publicity, costumes—will have strict financial guidelines. You're to remain within these boundaries. If you're going over budget, I want to know before it happens. Understand?"

"Yes," she maintained levelly. She struggled to retain that euphoric feeling she'd had moments ago when she'd realized he would invest in her play. At this point he couldn't still be considered an angel. Investors were never allowed to take charge like this. He'd cleverly elevated himself from investor to coproducer. And he had hemmed her in financially by reducing her already sparse budget. If she wasn't extremely frugal, she'd have to come to him for money again and again.

"The next section, page fifteen, deals with your contract."

"M-my contract?" Alexa stammered, caught off-guard.

"Certainly. Everyone will operate under a contract. I can't risk money to have people leave this production if something better comes along. Two years. You'll remain with the play for two years—the length of the lease on the Regency. By that time the play should be well enough established not to require your services."

"Two years?" she responded, dismayed at the distressing quiver in her voice. She'd counted on staying with the play until it opened and perhaps for a few months after. A year at most. But two years? That was a long time, and she wouldn't be able to go on to any other project. She'd have to remain in London.

"Agreed?" There was an ironlike grimness to the set of his jaw as he stared at her for the longest moment.

She smiled straight into his eyes, challenging him. "Yes."

Alexa realized what he intended to do. He wanted to offer her the money, so everyone would regard him as a hero. But he'd intentionally made the terms objectionable, trying to force her to refuse his offer. If she accepted, she could hardly be called a producer. A manager working for Mark Kimbrough would be more like it, but she didn't have any choice.

With an angry gesture he flipped the pages. "I'm on page twenty now."

Alexa quickly read the page. The lease and the improvements were to be overseen by Triad. "Why?"

"If this production fails, I want to be able to sublet the building. You have no experience in building renovation. It's foolish for you even to try when I do it all the time."

"I see." Alexa stifled the urge to issue a cutting remark. She was absolutely certain now that he was determined to make her reject his offer. She wanted to supervise the improvements. There would be adjustments to lighting and sound he wouldn't know about or understand. And as bad as it was, she didn't want the Regency ruined. London's gracious old buildings, as Alexa had previously observed, had surrendered to a surge of commercial greed. She was determined not to let that happen to the Regency.

He quickly read a memo, wadded it up, and tossed it in the direction of the wastepaper basket. "Turn to the last page. Read this part carefully. Be certain you understand it."

Alexa quickly read the page and then slowly reread it, trying to make certain she hadn't misunderstood it. This was impossible! She and Renata would be required to submit to weekly drug tests. In Mexico Mark had said he believed her, but apparently he hadn't. Why else would he humiliate her like this? Unless this was a last-ditch effort to make her reject his offer.

"If at any time either of you tests positive, we close the production. No second chances." His voice had a fine edge of hostility to it now. Above glacial gray eyes his brows drew together in a frown.

"I see." She tried to control her anger, but she could hear its undertone in her voice in spite of her effort.

Alexa kept her eyes on the page. How could he do this? Weekly tests? It wasn't necessary for either of them; he knew that. How could she agree to this contract? She'd be committed to two years, and she'd have to keep a constant vigil so she wouldn't go over budget and have to ask him for more money. She felt her anger rise like a red-hot wave, washing her cheeks with color. She reached for a lock of hair and twisted it around her finger.

She reminded herself that losing her temper would only put her at a disadvantage. "Is there anything else?"

"You understand then why these tests are necessary?" His voice was unexpectedly soft, and yet his words were sharper than a slap.

She knew all right. This was his final attempt to make her refuse his terms. He had her backed into a corner and he knew it.

"I understand," she responded with scathing disgust. She had the unexpected pleasure of seeing his face stiffen in annoyance. She wasn't giving in so easily.

"Then you consent?" he asked, his words coming out from between clenched teeth.

She realized he was taking perverse pleasure in shaking her. She didn't want to disappoint Renata, but was she being fair to herself? Would it be worth it to put herself through all this just to have a successful play to her credit? Would it be worth it to save a friend's career?

Unexpectedly her mind replayed that last night she'd spent with Mark in Mexico. That memory, painful and belittling, made her nerves tighten another notch. Why hadn't she realized what type of man he was? Her previous sense of disillusionment had been replaced by anger now that she realized how ruthless Mark Kimbrough was.

This was it. She had to give him an answer. She was upset and no longer thinking clearly. All at once she had the urge to scream, or cry, or even throw something at him. She had never disliked anyone more in her entire life. She glared at Mark but saw instead Renata stepping out of the shower and facing the Mexican police.

"I accept your terms."

# Chapter 16

Alexa rose from her chair and briskly walked to the door.

Shocked, Mark could only stare as she whirled out of his office defiantly tossing her tawny gold hair and slamming the door. Her abrupt departure caught him completely off-guard. Goddammit! Why couldn't she ever talk things through? What was the matter with her? During the entire meeting her thinly disguised hostility had angered him. Didn't she realize he was trying to help her? Evidently not. Why did he even get involved? Now of all times, when his business was in serious jeopardy, he'd just sent his personal life careening out of control by lending her the money. But he hadn't been able to refuse her.

Mark went to the leaded-glass window and gazed out through the twisted diamonds at the dome above St. Paul's. Like the distorted glass, his life was totally out of focus. He was making a fool out of himself over a woman who obviously preferred the company of another man. Mark had known something was wrong when she hadn't returned any of his calls to Mexico. He'd assumed she hadn't received the messages or that his busy schedule caused him to miss her return calls. He'd rerun the memory of that night in Mexico countless times, and with each replay a deep ache he couldn't control accompanied his thoughts. What the hell had gone wrong? The time he'd spent with her had been a trap sprung with such suddenness he hadn't realized he'd been caught until it was too late to get away.

Avoiding her after she'd appeared at the party and he'd found out she was living with Steven had been a wise decision. Cut your losses. It was a sound business principle that had taken on new meaning when Alexa had moved in with Steven Hunter. Now what had he gotten himself into? Certainly more than he'd bargained for, he decided, as he mentally reviewed his diminishing bank account.

A knock on the door was followed by Warren's voice. "Tom said you were alone. Are you ready?"

"Ready?" Mark asked, sinking into his chair.

"The opening. Remember? Linda's boutique." Humor lurked in Warren's brown eyes and, as always, he was wearing a happy expression.

"Tonight?" Mark was exhausted. The troubled meeting at Windsor Airlines and the scene with Alexa had drained him. "I think I'll pass. I don't expect to be buying women's clothes anyway."

"You look whacked. Trouble?" Warren asked, seating himself in the chair Alexa had vacated.

Mark nodded. "This Windsor Airlines thing. They're at it again."

"More bogus tickets? Are you in trouble? Financially?"

"I will be soon if I can't stop them. I haven't an endless supply of cash to pour into that airline."

"Don't worry," Warren said, thinking his friend looked more pressured than he'd ever seen him. "You'll get to the bottom of this. You almost caught them last time." He checked his watch. "Speaking of endless supplies of cash, I just ran into Alexa getting off the lift. How'd the meeting go? She seemed upset."

"About as well as the Windsor Airlines meeting this morning—a disaster. I can't seem to say anything right to her. Whenever we talk, she becomes hostile, defensive. Undoubtedly Steven's convinced her that I'm some sort of monster."

"Did she understand why you wrote the contract that way?"

"She said she did." Mark ran his fingers through his hair. "With her it's hard to tell sometimes."

"Then maybe it's the way you're talking to her. You can be pretty cold sometimes. You're not, but you seem that way."

"I've never had your ability to talk to women."

Warren laughed, his eyes reflecting his innate good humor. "You always got the girl; I always got to talk to her."

Mark chuckled; Warren never failed to amuse him. His only really close friend, Warren always seemed to know just what Mark's mood was without asking.

"I'm serious. I know you. You're hard-lining it with her because of Steven. It may work in business, but not with Alexa. She's too sensitive."

"I suppose you learned all this in the two times you've met her?"

"Yes, and from talking to Linda."

Mark walked over to the sitting area and poured them both a brandy. Warren was right, Mark decided; he was trying to hurt Alexa. He knew how sensitive she was—Mexico had taught him that. It was childish to want to hurt her. Yet the thought of her spending every night in Steven's bed enraged him. She never would have contacted him had she been able to raise the money elsewhere. Her ambition was a chip he intended to play.

"You're right." Mark handed Warren a snifter of brandy. "I thought Alexa would have more sense than to take up with Steven. I was wrong again. As the past has proven to both of us, women are a good deal more skilled at deception than men."

"I doubt she tried to deceive you. I don't think she cares a fig for Steven."

"No? She insists he be listed as coproducer even though he won't be around to help her. She'll do all the work while he takes all the credit. Sounds as if he's got her right where he wants her."

"Give her a chance. She'll be onto Steven in no time. You hoped he was behind that flurry of black-market tickets from Morocco, didn't you?"

"I thought it was a possibility. Talbott's villa's not far away. It would have been easy for Steven or Jason to get to Tangiers and back without being missed. But if they were behind that ticket swindle, one of them would have taken Alexa there when she wanted to go. It would have been the perfect excuse."

"Have your agents been able to develop any leads?"

"They're still investigating, but every day the trail gets colder. Right now we've got our hands full with a raft of black-market tickets from Pakistan."

Warren wanted Mark to accompany him to the opening. It would be much easier to keep this visit impersonal if the two of them were together. "I think you need to get your mind off the whole bloody mess. Alexa will be modeling some of Linda's new designs at the opening tonight. Come with me. Try a little brotherly love on the lady."

The evening traffic was slow and go as Warren maneuvered his green Aston-Martin through the crowded streets. Mark watched Warren, his wrist casually draped over the steering wheel, looking ahead into the knot of vehicles. He appeared to be relaxed and happy, but Mark knew better. Warren was nervous about seeing Linda.

"Are you two going to be an item again?" Mark kept his voice casual.

"I don't know." Warren stared at the cluster of taillights ahead of them. Piccadilly's perpetual traffic jam at Green Park brought them to a complete halt.

"I spoke with Linda in Mexico. She wants another chance. I really think she's changed." When Warren didn't immediately answer, Mark was silent. In a way he was jealous of his friend. Linda would chase Warren until he let her catch him. Meanwhile Mark couldn't get anywhere with Alexa even by lending her money when no one else would. Hadn't Caroline taught him you couldn't buy love?

Warren stared ahead into the sea of taillights as the sports car inched along. He hadn't realized how much he missed Linda until she'd told him she loved him. Then he began seeing her with too much frequency to be just coincidence. Each time, she'd smile that slow, seductive smile he'd never been quite able to forget.

Last week he'd run into her coming out of the Corsair Club. She'd been with her brother, who was also a member, but he'd quickly—too quickly—excused himself. Before Warren knew it he'd asked her to tea and they'd ended up at the

Regency. He'd been amazed at how much Linda had changed. Her youthful innocence had disappeared, leaving a more mature, and far more interesting, woman.

But could he forgive her? He doubted it. Even now he remembered the gut-wrenching feeling of betrayal he'd experienced when reading her note. That she'd fallen for another man had surprised him. Her dismissing their relationship with a terse note had devastated him. A woman capable of such actions could never be trusted.

Warren hadn't seen her since that day at the theater. He was going to this opening, he told himself, not because she'd asked him to come, but to see if she'd fulfilled her potential. Years ago Warren had agreed to open a boutique for her as soon as she finished school. She'd thrown her career—and his love—to the four winds when she eloped with the Australian four-flusher, Ian Carlisle.

"Did you tell Alexa you bought the Regency Theatre?" Warren asked, needing to change the subject. He'd been dwelling on Linda too much lately.

"No," Mark answered, "I don't want anyone to know."

"It might help if she knew how much work you went to putting this deal together. You didn't have to buy the theater because the owner refused to bring it up to standard. You could have found another one."

"There wasn't any other one. I checked."

They were silent as the car crawled along Brompton Road past Harrods and turned up Beauchamp Place. Warren considered this elegant little street, with its Regency shops and iron balconies, the perfect antidote to the overpowering Harrods. Linda had shown good judgment in locating here along with the other glitzy boutiques of London's top designers like Bruce Oldfield and the Emanuelles. Princess Diana and the legions of upscale shoppers, known as the Sloan Rangers for their preference for shops within striking distance of Sloan Square, all shopped on Beauchamp Place. When they weren't picking up holiday togs at Monsoon, they were buying pricy lingerie from Janet Reger.

Warren slipped his sports car into a parking space Mark would have sworn was nonexistent. "You should tell her. She doesn't have a crystal ball, you know," Warren said. "She has quite a bit invested in this too."

"One quarter of the play. I have half," Mark said as they got out of the car.

"Alexa put up every cent she has."

Mark stopped short. Ahead the lights of the boutique glittered, and he could see it was packed with people. "Impossible! She had an international best seller and sold the movie rights. She has to have more than that."

Weaving their way through the crush at the door, Warren said over his shoulder, "Linda was quite certain."

"There's she is." Mark nudged Warren. "Let's go say hello to Linda."

As they twisted their way across the crowded room, Mark kept looking around for Alexa, realizing the delay in their meeting must have made her late for the opening. He heard her low, throaty laugh and stopped in midstride, turning to see her modeling a frothy white gown.

A portly man whose protruding stomach made him look more pregnant than fat and his moonfaced friend were frankly admiring Alexa's low-cut neckline. She brushed back a wayward wisp of golden hair and laughed again, the light catching her cat-green eyes. The silk gauze dress fluttered, revealing a handkerchief hemline, and an image of her at Audrey's party in that shimmery white gown came back to him. She'd looked so incredibly sexy in that Grecian number that clung suggestively to her figure. He'd never wanted anyone more than he had wanted her that night. He'd made a complete ass of himself by playing up to Charmaine in a futile attempt to make Alexa jealous.

A playful elbow in the ribs brought Mark's attention back to Warren. "I said we're impressed with your boutique, Linda. Aren't we Mark?"

Mark nodded. He was impressed all right.

"Don't mind him," Warren continued with laugh, "he's just admiring your designs."

"Did you see Renata's gown?" Linda asked them both, but Mark noticed her eyes never left Warren's.

Mark felt a stab of envy. No woman had ever looked at him with such undisguised love. Casually he let his gaze wander over the crowd to Alexa. She stood talking to a cluster of middle-aged ladies who had no business even considering buying the dress she was showing them. When Alexa moved on, she looked up and Mark caught her eye. He pinned a warm smile on his face. Her gaze wavered; he kept smiling until she responded with a brief half-smile.

"Giles has asked us all to dinner," Linda said. "I guess we have some celebrating to do. Renata's so excited you're financing the play that we could hardly get her dressed."

"Sounds like fun. Doesn't it, Warren?" Mark answered, realizing his friend hadn't quite come to terms with the new Linda. Unless he went with him, Warren wouldn't go.

"I think we have plenty to celebrate—the play, your boutique." Warren stopped a passing waiter and took two glasses of champagne. He handed one to Linda, letting Mark take his own. His eyes met her violet-blue ones as she took the glass. He had to force himself to look away. Why did she have to wear that halter-top creation? The plum-colored chiffon deepened the color of her eyes and floated sensuously down her willowy frame.

"Isn't that Charmaine?" Linda asked Mark, her eyes still on Warren.

Christ! Mark thought. He should have known she'd be here. A living clotheshorse, Charmaine knew every trendy boutique and elegant salon in London, Paris, and Milan.

She glided up, holding her champagne glass like a scepter. "Mark, how are you?"

Mark dutifully bent to kiss her proffered cheek. "Fine."

"Linda, this a delightful little shop. I know the neighborhood well. I purchase most of my gowns just up the street at Bruce's."

"Bruce?" Mark had no idea who she meant, but he knew a double-edged compliment when he heard one.

"Bruce Oldfield," Charmaine laughed. "He's the top designer in London." She directed her next remark to Linda. "Of course, some of your designs are interesting. I prefer to wear black"—Charmaine paused and cast a glance in Alexa's direction—"sometimes white—if it's not too casual."

"I designed that gown specifically for Alexa," Linda answered. "In fact, every gown she and Renata will model tonight I created specifically for them. Any woman purchasing one of my dresses will know it was designed just for her."

Warren silently applauded Linda. Once she'd have withered if the premier fashion maven had slighted her designs. The years had given Linda a sense of purpose and a determination that had been missing before.

"Look, there's Chauncey," Charmaine said. "Let's go say hello." She tugged on Mark's arm.

"You go. I'll be along." Mark watched Charmaine move through the crowd to join Chauncey Beddington.

"Don't let Charmaine bother you," Warren told Linda. "You've got a smash here." He meant it. Anyone could see Linda had more than just a flair for design. She had a unique talent.

There was a loud commotion at the door followed by bright slashes of light from exploding flashbulbs. A throng of paparazzi hovered at the entrance as a low, expectant murmur filled the room.

"Expecting any celebrities, royalty?" Warren joked. "Princess Diana perhaps?"

"Not really," Linda answered. "Just the usual assortment of titled elite, but no one meriting this."

Inwardly Mark groaned. Being taller than either of them, he saw her first.

Linda gasped. "I never invited Melanie Tarenholt!"

# Chapter 17

Mark quickly checked the crowded boutique for Alexa, but she was nowhere in sight. Apparently she'd gone into the dressing room to change into another gown. After Melanie's outrageous behavior at the party, he hoped Alexa would stay out of sight until she left.

"How could she come without an invitation?" Linda fumed.

"Relax," Warren said. "It's free publicity. Tomorrow it'll be all over London that Melanie attended the opening of Changes."

"I don't want anyone to think I designed anything she wears!"

"Don't worry," Mark backed up Warren, "few people actually notice how she's dressed, but it will give you a lot of exposure."

"Well, I'm not sure . . ." Linda hesitated.

Mark sympathized with Linda. Melanie Tarenholt had absolutely no taste at all. Everything she wore was two sizes too tight and had a neckline that stopped just shy of her navel. On the other hand, Charmaine always dressed tastefully, but her clothes were too dramatic. She usually wore something black and shriekingly chic, the type of clothing that turned heads when she entered a room. He disliked it when women

dressed in outrageously fashionable attire. He always had the
feeling they were wearing clothing that would show other
women how fashionable they were. Mark doubted if
Charmaine cared whether or not her clothing pleased him as
long as her name appeared on the best-dressed lists.

Mark again checked the crowd for Alexa, but she hadn't
reappeared. Her style, he decided, was no style at all. She had
a casualness about the way she wore her clothes, as if she'd
just reached into the closet and donned the first thing she'd
found. Her tousled mane of sun-streaked hair and her lack of
makeup added to her natural, outdoor appeal. Women were
supposed to look like that, not like mannequins or harlots.

Melanie's too-loud laugh drew near. Mark turned to see her
twitching through the crowd, her hips swaying like a fan-
dango dancer's. She stopped frequently to say hello to the
important people while a bevy of photographers and reporters
recorded everything. Before he could slip away, Melanie spotted Mark.

"Mark, darling," Melanie beelined up to him and threw her
arms around him, kissing him on the cheek. She obligingly
remained in his arms wagging the longest false eyelashes this
side of the Thames while the cameras flashed.

"Hello, Melanie." He extricated himself from her arms and
took two discreet steps backward. Where on earth did she get
that God-awful perfume?

"Linda, I absolutely, positively adore your enchanting boutique," gushed Melanie.

"Thank you." Linda's voice was cool.

"Warren, darling," Melanie flung herself at Warren. He
managed to escape with a quick hug.

"Have you seen Chauncey Beddington yet?" Warren gestured to the corner where Charmaine and Chauncey were engaged in conversation. "He's over there." Mark noticed the
mischievous twinkle in Warren's eyes.

"Boys," Melanie addressed the paparazzi clustered around
her, "the Duke of Reston is one of my oldest, dearest friends."

"Chauncey, darling," Melanie twittered, elbowing her way
toward the corner.

Just then Mark caught sight of Alexa. She was coming
down the temporary runway that had been installed for the
opening. Her tawny hair, flashing with platinum lights,

swished across her shoulders. She wore a diaphanous evening gown of clinging silk that emphatically outlined her luscious curves. Mark didn't know what to call that particular shade of green. It was somewhere between sea-green and emerald—the exact color of Alexa's eyes. A closer inspection revealed the dress wasn't actually transparent. The high neckline, a spider's web of emerald silk, laced into a bodice that clearly revealed the shadowy cleft between her breasts and emphasized their upward tilt.

For a moment the steady buzz of conversation in the room died down as Alexa pranced to the end of the runway. She did a slow pirouette and it became obvious she was unaccustomed to professional modeling. Despite this, she moved with an untutored grace that one is either born with or never will possess. The rear view of the dress disclosed it was totally backless. She faced forward again, smiling and oblivious to the sensation she was creating.

"What do you wear under that?" Warren asked Linda.

"Whatever God gave you," Linda whispered and winked.

Without revealing anything, the dress actually concealed nothing about Alexa's figure. Mark grabbed another glass of champagne from a passing waiter. Alexa stepped off the runway and moved into the crowd. The talking resumed, but Mark noted too many men stopped in midsentence as she passed by. He swirled his champagne until it eddied into a miniature whirlpool and then he downed it in one gulp.

"I'll take it," he said.

"I don't think you have the figure for it," Warren laughed.

"I'm serious," Mark told Linda.

"Mark, that's the most expensive piece in my entire collection. I really—"

"Send me the bill. Give it to Alexa." he paused and looked into Linda's blue eyes. "Just don't tell her it's from me. You couldn't sell that dress to anyone else. No one else will look that good in it."

"Linda, darling," Melanie whirled up to them, "I simply must have that dress."

"With her bovine figure?" Warren whispered to Mark.

Mark stifled a laugh. How did Melanie think she could support her tits in that creation? There was no possible way to wear a bra in that number. The dress totally depended on the wearer's figure for its effect.

"I'm sorry, it's sold," Linda said.

"Sold? How can it be sold?" Melanie huffed. "She just came out in it. Did someone buy it right off the hanger?"

"Yes," Warren said, "some people know just what they want."

"Well . . . I never," Melanie moved away.

"I wonder," Mark heard Charmaine at his elbow, "if you could make that gown for me in black?"

"I'm sorry, I only do one of each gown. That way every woman knows she has an original."

"I see." Charmaine arched one fine eyebrow. "Mark, will you walk me to my automobile. I have another engagement."

Mark couldn't refuse her although he knew her father's chauffeured Rolls would be in the usual spot, double-parked in front of whatever building Charmaine had entered. She possessively threaded her arm through his. When they reached the door, Mark glanced back over his shoulder. Alexa stood amid a throng of admiring men. Approaching her, Melanie brought the coterie of photographers. Startled, Mark noticed Alexa's welcoming smile directed at Melanie. The two stood, chatting like old friends, while the ever-present cameras recorded their reunion.

Alexa slipped into her own cotton dress. With a sigh she ran her fingers over the cool green silk of the dress she'd just hung up. She'd never been in a dress quite like that one. Provocative without being too sexy, too risqué, it fit her as if it had been sewn onto her. She never believed haute couture could be worth it, but now she was convinced.

"Alexa, are you in there?" Renata's voice came from the other side of the dressing room door.

"Yes, I'm dressed. Come in."

"Let's hurry." Renata's red head poked around the door. "Giles is at Reflections saving us a table. You go get Linda while I hail a taxi."

How could she tell Renata about the drug tests? The delayed meeting with Mark had made Alexa late for the opening. She'd sailed in with just enough time to tell Renata and Linda that they had the financing. Renata had been ecstatic, and as the night progressed, she'd become happier with each clothing change. Now she was positively glowing. Alexa would have to explain it to her over dinner. She made up her mind to soft-pedal it, pretend it was no big deal. Since she'd agreed in principle to the terms, there was no reason to upset Renata.

"Linda, where are you?" Alexa called into the dimly lit stockroom.

"I'm here checking inventory," Linda said, her mind still on the unbelievable success of the opening and the fact that Warren had been at her side most of the evening. "Do you know I sold almost everything I showed tonight? Now what am I to do? I'll have nothing to sell when the shop opens to the public."

"That's fantastic!" Alexa hugged her. "You'll design more—sell more. Are you ready to join Giles?"

"Yes, of course." Linda clicked off the light. She wouldn't miss it. Warren would be there. "Alexa, the green dress—"

"I'll get it," Alexa said, turning toward the dressing rooms.

"No, leave it . . . I—" Linda faltered, hating not being able to tell her the truth. "I want you to have it."

"You have no idea how much I love that dress. I've never been in anything quite like it. I wish I had the money, but I don't. Sell it to someone else. You can't imagine how many people asked me about it."

"I know." Linda's voice sounded unsteady. "I must have sold another dozen dresses and taken orders for another score just because you looked so good in that dress. I'm giving it to you."

"You can't be serious. It's too expensive. I just can't let you do that." Alexa felt the tears coming. The fact that Linda even wanted to give her the dress was unbelievably touching.

"I insist. You've done wonders for my boutique by modeling for me tonight. I designed the dress just for you. It's yours —I won't take no for an answer. I think you're a very special person. You've put your whole career on the line for Renata. I want you to have the dress."

"You can't imagine how much this means to me." Alexa choked back the tears. "I really love it. I've never been in a dress that made me feel so . . . so beautiful."

"Just promise me you'll save it for someone special . . . really special."

Bubbling with laughter, Alexa followed Linda and Renata through the bar. Reflections was one of the many new bistros that had sprung up in London over the last five years. A duplicate of dozens of new-wave restaurants that mimicked their American counterparts while leaving Alexa more nostalgic than ever for "old" London, Reflections had a bar area twice the size of the dining room. Fighting their way through the jungle of ferns, almost too green and too large to be real, and past scantily clad waitresses, they came to the dining room. Emitting a warm glow, shell-shaped sconces illuminated the apricot-colored walls. Banquettes of a deeper peach print and chairs upholstered in matching fabric stretched out across the crowded room. Enormous potted palms were strategically spaced to give the illusion of privacy between the tables.

When they found their group, Alexa hesitated, torn by conflicting emotions. Why in hell was Mark here? She'd seen him leave with Charmaine. After Renata sat down beside Giles, Alexa moved aside, letting Linda take the empty seat next to Warren while she had no choice but to sit next to Mark.

He looked at her speculatively, easing into a smile. Without looking Mark in the eye, Alexa nodded a brief hello and turned her attention to Giles. "Well? What do you think? Isn't Changes a smash?"

"Yes," Giles agreed, "I can see where a good deal of our money will be spent."

"It was quite a bash," Warren said, pretending not to have noticed Linda had maneuvered herself into the seat beside him.

"Melanie Tarenholt is really cheeky to show up without an invitation," Linda said, trying to draw Warren into a discussion.

"Linda, I'm sorry," Alexa said. "I invited her. I spoke with her a few days ago and told her to come. She thought her invitation had been lost." Alexa felt everyone's eyes on her. "I didn't think it would be a problem. The press follows her everywhere. I thought it would give Changes some free advertising."

"Just what I told her," Warren said. "It's publicity money can't buy."

"I suppose Warren is right," Linda answered.

"I didn't realize you two were friendly," Renata added, using her ring-laden fingers to hook her red hair behind one ear.

"We have a lot in common," Alexa answered, feeling the sudden necessity to defend someone she really did not like.

"Like what?" Mark asked. He said it in a playful tone, but Alexa could tell he was serious.

"Like Jason Talbott," Alexa answered, seething with anger that he dared question her choice of friends.

Everyone stopped talking and an uncomfortable silence, magnified by the noise around them, filled the small space. She glanced at Mark. His gray eyes had darkened, but his face remained impassive. She hesitated a moment, baffled. What the hell was wrong? "It's simple," she continued. "Melanie loves her career and Jason."

"In that order?" Warren's voice was uncharacteristically sarcastic.

"Look, Melanie loves someone who's a louse. She knows it, but she still can't help herself. I know how she feels—I've been there. I feel sorry for her. She's not so bad if you give her a chance."

It seemed as if everyone breathed a sigh of relief at once. Alexa didn't look at Mark, but she could feel his eyes on her.

"Don't waste time feeling sorry for Melanie." Renata's voice was unexpectedly cold. "Alexa, you're too soft a touch."

Mark remained silent, but Giles's forehead, beneath his woolly gray hair, creased into a brief, censorious frown. "Stay away from her. She's trouble."

"We'd better order. It's getting late." Warren signaled for the waiter.

Alexa slowly twisted a quarter-turn in her chair away from Mark and let her hair swing forward to veil her face, avoiding all eye contact with him. Everyone else seemed to be in the best of spirits, but then they were unaware of the stiff terms Mark had imposed on the play.

Linda edged her chair closer to Warren's and kept her voice low. "Thank you for coming to the opening. It meant a lot to me."

"I always believed in your talent." Warren looked into her

violet-blue eyes and struggled to keep his tone casual. "You should have done it years ago."

Linda placed her hand on his arm, gazing into his serious face. "I've spent the last seven years paying for my mistake. There wasn't a day that went by that I didn't tell myself what a fool I'd been."

"Why did you stay with him then?"

"Because of Holly. She's the only good thing in my life since I left you."

"But you left her for almost two years." Warren had no idea how a mother could leave a preschooler, seeing her only on brief holidays. He supposed it indicated some inner flaw he'd failed to see, just as he'd never expected her to cast him aside with a note. He'd been too mesmerized by Linda's beauty and the soft, silky feeling of her when they made love, as well as the fun they had together, to see her faults. He saw them all clearly now.

"I left Holly," Linda's voice faltered, "for her own good. When Ian and I divorced, I had no money, no way to earn a living. Nigel Hunter gave me a chance. Nothing I could have done would have paid as well as working for him. I'd always be scraping by, asking my family for money for Holly's schooling. I knew that if I took the job, I'd have the capital to start the boutique within a few years. It might have taken me ten if I'd stayed here. But I had to be working on productions in various countries. Holly was better off living with my brother and attending nursery school here where she had, not only her cousins, but my parents to love her." Linda paused a moment, glancing up at the waiter standing at her elbow. She ordered the first thing that came to her mind and waited until Warren ordered before continuing, "I'm finished regretting the past. When I came home, I started over. I have the career I always wanted and Holly. If you give me another chance, you won't regret it."

Warren didn't respond. Linda's sincerity was unmistakable. And her explanation of why she'd left her daughter made sense. He had to admit some part of him wanted to forgive her while another part reminded him of her past behavior.

Across the table Mark asked, "More wine?" forcing Alexa to look at him.

"No . . . thank you." She squeezed out a smile in response

to his friendly grin. He didn't deceive her for an instant. He could discuss the play with Giles and Renata all he wanted, but Alexa knew he'd done his best to sabotage it.

As they finished their after-dinner drinks and coffee, Alexa knew she couldn't postpone telling Renata about the drug tests. If she objected, Alexa had to know it before she wasted the solicitor's time going over the contract. "Renata, about the play. There's a very unfavorable clause in the contract. If you disapprove, I won't go ahead with the deal."

For the second time that night a moment of suspended animation settled over the group, while everyone stared wide-eyed at her as if she'd struck an exposed nerve.

"What clause?" Renata asked. Uneasiness clouded her blue eyes.

"You . . . and I will have to take weekly drug tests." Alexa couldn't keep the bitterness from her voice.

Renata's mouth curved into an eager, delighted smile. "Oh, Alexa, from the way you sounded I thought something was wrong."

"You don't care that each week we'll be humiliated by having to submit to a drug test?"

"It was my idea."

"Your idea?" Alexa felt the blood leave her face for a moment and then rush back to fill it.

"Yes, athletes do it in America. Why not here? After two years of passing the tests, no one will be able to say either of us has a problem." Renata reached across the table for Alexa's hand, but her eyes were on Mark. "Didn't you explain the situation to her?"

"What situation?" Alexa couldn't keep the hostility from her voice. How had Mark managed to convince Renata this was her idea? She glared at him without even bothering to conceal her contempt.

"It seems that you were unable to obtain financing because the word is out that you have a drug problem," Mark answered.

"The word came through the entertainment circles," Giles said, his amber eyes dead serious. "Even before we returned to London everyone here knew about the raid. Lloyd's had blacklisted both of you even before we finished shooting."

"Blacklisted," Alexa whispered, barely able to hear her own voice, "what does that mean?"

"They refuse to insure anything either of you two appear in because of the drug risk," Mark answered.

"Then how is the play being insured?"

"We're self-insured," Mark answered in a quiet voice. "We pay for any problems we have."

Alexa sat there unable to finish her coffee. Blacklisted? Another thought occurred to her. Why hadn't Steven told her? He had to have known she had been blacklisted.

While Giles settled the bill, Warren watched Alexa and Mark. He'd been warm and friendly to Alexa all evening, but she'd remained aloof, barely civil. Evidently she had more problems than Linda indicated. Now he wondered if he should have encouraged Mark. Warren noted both Alexa and Mark were silent as the group moved outside. The attendant brought up Warren's Aston-Martin first, and he and Mark turned to say their good-nights. Warren deliberately spoke to the group, making no move to single Linda out. He slid behind the wheel as the attendant closed the door, waiting for Mark to come around and get in. Hearing a tap on the window, Warren turned and saw Linda. He rolled the window down.

She put her head through the opening. "Remember what I told you: I love you."

She leaned forward and kissed him. It was a light butterfly of a kiss, nothing more, but it sent Warren's heart spinning. She lingered, just inches from his lips, a low smoldering light firing her deep blue eyes. Then she was gone.

Barely conscious that Mark was in the car, Warren zipped out into the traffic. He adjusted the rearview mirror; Linda was still standing on the curb, staring after him.

# Chapter 18

Her head bent as if she were studying the computer screen before her in the Regency's office, Alexa watched the cat rub his burnt-orange fur on Mark's navy blue suit. He raised one elbow to fend off the persistent animal but otherwise kept concentrating on the reams of paper before him. Minutes passed and the cat gave up trying to get Mark to pet him. The cat sat down on one of the stacks of papers on the desk before Mark and began picking his teeth with his hind paw. He could really be a disgusting animal sometimes, Alexa thought. Twice the size of the average tom, he had a coat that was a patchwork of scars. One ear was bent in half and had a chunk missing, obviously proclaiming there had been at least one fight when he had not been the victor. He was so bedraggled and mean looking Alexa had been unable to resist bringing him to the Regency as the resident mouser. But she had to admit if he hadn't been a cat he'd have looked like something the cat dragged in.

"Does this animal have a name?" Mark asked.

Alexa's head snapped up to meet his slate-gray eyes. "T.S.," she answered, lowering her gaze to the blank computer screen.

"For T. S. Eliot?" Mark's voice was glacial.

"No, for tomato soup." Alexa knew that would end the

conversation and it did. She needed to say something else to him but she didn't know how. In the weeks since he'd funded the play, Mark had relentlessly organized the internal operations of the production, becoming in essence her coproducer. He never interfered with her creative directives, but he insisted she use his accounting systems and computer programs.

What she needed to tell Mark now was that she was sorry. She wanted to apologize for the outrageous way she'd behaved at the restaurant. If the emotion she'd felt that night had been simple anger, she'd be able to apologize now. But it wasn't. She had to admit it went much deeper than that. Much. Through all the past weeks when they'd been setting up the books, beginning renovations on the Regency, and working together with tight-lipped efficiency, Alexa had been unable to make herself say those three little words. Words that would have cleared the air, words that would have shown she wasn't as immature as she seemed, and words he deserved to hear. Words her pride refused to let her say.

She flicked off the computer and rose from her seat. "I'm going out to check on rehearsals."

Alexa took the North London line to the edge of the city where their temporary rehearsal hall was located. A daily trip was probably unnecessary at this point. The director had things well in hand, but somehow she couldn't help herself. She needed to talk with them. Since Steven had left weeks ago, she seldom saw anyone outside of the theater. The boutique kept Linda busy, and when she wasn't working, she was with her daughter. Renata rehearsed and went home to Giles. Alexa worked on the play and then returned to Steven's town house and continued working. Face it, she told herself, you're lonely.

She stepped from the train, the July sun warming her and bringing out that inevitable optimism summer always brought out in her. She walked to the rehearsal hall thankful she and Twick and Renata worked so well together. Threesomes were notoriously difficult, but in this case that did not apply.

"Hi," she whispered, collapsing into a chair beside Twick as he sat watching a group of actors rehearsing a scene.

Archibald Twicksby, Twick to his friends, grinned at her. Short, wiry, with nut-brown hair cropped close along the sides and combed heavenward, Twick looked as if he'd re-

ceived a mild electric shock. A fourteen-karat gold safety pin
pierced his right ear and dangled below the lobe. Initially his
punk appearance had concerned Alexa, but from their first
conversation she knew she could work with him. He immediately grasped her concept of the play, and in the weeks that
followed he'd proven to her that Giles was right about
Twick's directing abilities. One day, Alexa was certain, his
name would be synonymous with superb directing.

Not for the first time Alexa was thankful Mark had never
shown any inclination to visit rehearsals. As domineering as
he was concerning the finances, he never once strayed into the
creative domain. Alexa glanced around the room at the assembled cast and crew. She could imagine what Mark would
think when he met Twick and the rest of the group. They
were an odd assortment of people ranging from young kids
with the London-street-scene look Twick embodied to older
semiretired crew members Renata had recruited. All of them
were professionals and Alexa doubted she'd have found a better group if she'd had the pick of everyone available. She did
have to admit, however, they looked like a British version of
Coxie's army. As worried as Mark was about his investment
now, he'd be terrified when the renovations on the Regency
were completed and the cast moved into the theater to re-
hearse and he saw this group.

"Take ten," Twick yelled when the scene was over. He
turned to Alexa. "Well, are we stuck with the Tannoy?"

Alexa stared at the sweater in her lap. "I'm working on it.
Don't worry, we're not going to use that old sound system. I'll
take care of it."

"I was over there yesterday," Twick persisted. "The super-
visor tells me the specs don't call for replacement of the Tannoy."

"I'll take care of it."

"Alexa!" Renata came bouncing over. "What do you think?
Isn't Twick doing a super job?"

"We were discussing the sound system," Twick said.

"What did Mark say?" Renata asked.

"I haven't had a chance to speak with him." Alexa was
ashamed of her outright lie.

"Are you free this evening?" Twick asked. "I want you to
hear something."

"Yes," Alexa reluctantly agreed, knowing Twick would spend the time badgering her about replacing the Tannoy.

"I'm on next," Renata said. "I'll see you later."

Alexa's mind drifted to the Tannoy problem while she watched Renata and Twick going over the scene. When she'd prepared the original budget, she'd not included any allocation for improvement of the sound system. It was adequate for carrying the spoken word throughout the theater, but when music was played on the Tannoy the technological leaps made over the last forty years were painfully obvious.

Locked into a budget that earmarked funds item by item, Alexa had nowhere to turn. There simply was no room in the budget for improving the sound system, and she refused to ask Mark for another pence. It would only emphasize her tactical error in not anticipating the problem, and it would give him the opportunity to refuse her. She was stalling now, hoping somehow another budgeted item would come in enough under allotted cost to allow her to upgrade the sound system.

After the rehearsals were over, Twick drove Alexa back into Soho in his antique Morris Minor. They parked and walked several blocks to Le Pussy Cat Sex Shoppe. Taking the back stairs, they came to Quinton Malmsby's loft.

"Okay, Quint," Twick said after introductions were over, "let's hear what you have."

Alexa collapsed beside Twick, flopping onto a Futon that obviously served as a bed. She tried not to stare at the young man with the neon orange hair and thick black brows sitting before an enormous keyboard. Unlike any machine she'd ever seen before, this keyboard had numerous lights, levers, and buttons. It looked like a Martian's idea of a piano.

"First," he said, his voice surprisingly soft despite his discordant appearance, "Renata's theme. Then you'll hear the villain's introduction, a variety of tunes for scene changes, the quarrel, and the love scene."

Inwardly Alexa groaned. How could she tell them, when they'd obviously gone to so much work, she couldn't afford music and certainly not an original score.

Quint took a moment to flip a few switches and make some adjustments. Loud music suggesting bumps and grinds filtered up from the bar below, filling the tiny loft and vibrating through the Futon. She shook her head at Twick, knowing this score was another of his highly creative ideas. He had more original thoughts on lighting, staging, and sets than she had ever imagined possible. It was hard to keep up with his continual flow of creativity.

Quint hit the first note and Alexa jumped as the room filled with what seemed to be a full orchestra. Note after note lilted across the loft, blocking out the noise from below. Mesmerized, Alexa listened to tune after tune. By the time Quint played the love song, her eyes were brimming with tears. She jumped up and bounded over to him.

"I've never heard anything like it. It's beautiful." Alexa sat down beside him and gave him a quick hug.

"It's the synthesizer," Quint explained. "It simulates with absolute perfection all the instruments known to man. The beauty of it is that it takes but one person to play it."

"Show me how it works," Alexa demanded. "Play Renata's theme again."

Effortlessly Quinton played Renata's theme, and when that was finished Alexa wanted to hear the love song again. Another hour went by as she carefully listened to the entire score once more.

"It'll never work on a Tannoy?" she asked Twick.

"Never."

"We've got to have it." She stopped; she couldn't lead them on. She couldn't afford it. "I-I mean it's wonderful, some of the best music I've heard ever . . . really. I just don't have the money."

"I'm willing to give you the music for full credit and a percentage of the record and tape sales after the play opens." Quinton's anxious look made him appear far younger than his midtwenties.

"I know someone in Germany who's developed a sound system and a series of remote speakers," Twick said. "They haven't been marketed yet, so I'm quite certain he'd let us test them. All we'd have to do is buy the master unit and install the speakers. It would take some special wiring, but that's about it." Twick gave her a wide that-solves-your-problem grin.

"Just a minute," Alexa said, "let me think." She'd never wanted anything before as much as she wanted to add this musical score to her play. Suddenly she had an idea how she could raise the money. "Do either of you know a studio that could produce tapes and records at a low cost, and I mean *low."*

"Nonesuch Studios in Liverpool. Why?" Twick's brown eyes narrowed inquisitively.

"I'm thinking of *Evita* and *Cats* when they came to Los Angeles," Alexa said slowly. She was almost afraid to tell Twick what she was thinking. It might be too off-the-wall even for him. "They were London productions, of course, and L.A. waited months for them to come, but the music always preceded the production. We all knew the tunes even before we saw the play. Do you follow me?"

Twick's jaw hung slack for a moment. "You mean record and release a soundtrack before the play opens?"

"Why not? Won't all London await Renata's play? We'd get plenty of publicity and income from the music."

"Why not? Why the hell not?" Twick rubbed the gold safety pin dangling from his ear. "But aren't you skipping over the main problem, the Tannoy?"

"Not at all," Alexa assured him, "not at all."

The next day, Sunday, Alexa went to the Regency to take a closer look at the Tannoy. To her surprise Mark was there going over the weekly reports. He looked more relaxed, more casual in an open-neck sports shirt and slacks than at any time she'd seen him since Mexico.

"Any problem?" Alexa asked.

Mark looked up and shook his head. T.S. was perched on the small desk Mark used when he came to the office. Purring raucously, the cat was giving himself a bath. Walking over to her computer terminal, Alexa stifled a grin. The cat evidently adored Mark, taking all his efforts at ridding himself of T.S. as playful gestures. The animal had yet to bag his first mouse, but as Alexa watched him roll onto his side and clean his hindquarters, she appreciated his comic relief. Mark jerked a pile of computer sheets from beneath T.S., who took no notice of the disturbance.

Alexa booted up and waited for the upcoming week's payroll to come up on the screen. She stared at the green screen, not seeing the rows of names and numbers. Quietly she rose and walked to his desk.

"Yes?" Mark looked up.

Alexa sat in the chair beside the desk so she could be at eye level with him. Not for the first time she noted the weary lines at the corners of his silver-gray eyes. She wondered if he'd been able to solve his problems at Windsor Air. Last week he'd bought out the principals and now owned the airline outright.

"Mark, I can't tell you how sorry I am for the way I behaved that night at Reflections. I don't know why I acted that way. . . . I guess I was still upset about the raid in Mexico. I thought you hadn't believed me. I had no idea I'd been blacklisted. I'm sorry. I really appreciate what you're doing for Renata by lending us the money. I apologize for being so immature."

Mark waited. He seemed to expect her to say something else, but she was at a loss for any other words. "I'm sorry," she whispered, "terribly sorry."

# Chapter 19

During the following week Alexa never saw Mark. He came late at night to check the construction work and to leave her brief notes about the production. She needed to find out when he would be out of town for three or four days. She knew he traveled frequently on business, but she wanted to know if he'd be gone over a weekend when the construction crew would be absent from the theater as well. Obtaining this information would prove difficult, considering Mark never told her any of his plans.

From the office's single window the midday sun scattered its golden light across her desk as Alexa packed her red tote for her trip to the rehearsal hall. Just then the door swung open and Mark entered, as usual without knocking.

"Would you be interested in helping select the fabric for the reupholstering?" he asked, whisking the snoozing T.S. from his chair and dropping his attaché onto the desk.

"I'd love to." She smiled brightly at him. If she was ever going to learn anything about his schedule, they'd have to be on speaking terms.

"Let's go," he said without returning her smile.

Alexa had assumed Mark would take her to one of London's design studios, but when he entered a mirrored-glass high-rise in the City and pressed the button on the lift marked penthouse, she asked, "Where are we going?"

"Manchester." Mark's terse reply cut off any further discussion just as his monosyllabic answers during the drive over had stifled conversation.

They reached the top floor and Mark guided Alexa through an unmarked side door onto the roof, where a black helicopter, resembling a futuristic bumblebee, sat poised atop an orange target painted on the roof. All black glass except for polished chrome runners and blades, the helicopter had the Triad logo, a stylized T with a silver lightning bolt through it, on its side.

Mark helped her into the back seat, which was surprisingly large considering the machine's streamlined appearance, and gave the pilot instructions to take off. With a muffled whir the copter shot straight up before rocketing forward. London's skyline, ancient spires crosshatched by reconstructive scaffolds and multistoried modern edifices, whizzed by as she stared out awestruck through the tinted glass. Mark pulled out a laptop computer from his attaché and began pressing numbers.

In minutes they'd left the city and were out over the verdant countryside. They rocketed over the beflowered meadows and bowers of wild flowers and quaint villages in full summer glory.

Alexa leaned forward and asked the pilot, "How fast are we going?"

"Just over two hundred and fifty miles an hour." The pilot caressed a multitude of winking lights that covered the instrument panel. "She's a jet chopper. We'll be there in half an hour."

"Oh," Alexa said, recalling having been told helicopters were used in Great Britain in much the same way private jets were used in the U.S. With shorter distances to cover, helicopters were more suited to the terrain.

They touched down on a green field beside a series of brick buildings etched with soot. The still-spinning blades created a cyclone, whipping Alexa's hair into her eyes as she stepped from the helicopter and followed Mark to the vintage Bentley waiting on the adjacent lane.

"This is a Trade Alliance redevelopment project," Mark explained, indicating the timeworn buildings the Bentley passed.

Inside a building on the perimeter of the complex, they were taken to a design room where two runs of fabric were stretched across a thick oak table that had been gouged and scarred by tailors for more than a century.

Mark fingered a heavy damask with an ivory background and a golden swan surrounded by clusters of mossy green laurel leaves. "This is a reproduction of the fabric used when the Regency opened in eighteen ninety-three." He turned to the other sample. "And this is a duplicate of the material used to reupholster the theater in the nineteen thirties."

Alexa recognized the embossed scarlet fabric that had covered the seats in the theater when she'd first seen it. It was pretty—the traditional red that had been used in theaters for most of the century—but the ivory, with its delicate design, was incomparable.

"Which do you prefer?" Mark's crisp, businesslike tone had softened considerably.

"Well," Alexa hedged, "is there a price difference between the two?"

"The cost of refurbishing will be paid by Triad." His tone had once again taken on an icy edge. "Which do you think would be best?"

"The swan. There won't be a theater as beautiful in all London." Alexa could imagine the soft ivory fabric highlighted by the gold leafing in the theater. Nothing in London could possibly compare. "But will it be ready in time?"

"This will be a special order," Mark answered, leading her from the room up a flight of stairs into the manager's office.

"I'm so sorry, Mr. Kimbrough," the manager said. "Had I known you were coming—"

"It's all right. This is Alexa MacKenzie. She'll be working with me. We've decided on the swan design. We'll need it in a month."

Alexa thought she saw the man gulp, but he responded, "Of course."

The manager's deferential treatment of Mark assured Alexa that Mark had been the power behind this project just as he had been behind the shoe factory where Giles's brother was employed.

"You'll have the order ready by the end of the month?" Mark asked and the manager nodded. "I'll be out of the country the last week, but Alexa will supervise the installation."

Alexa froze. Of all the good luck! Mark would be out of town for an entire week. She'd found out when he'd be gone without asking any suspicious questions. Now all she'd have to do would be to juggle the computer records so he wouldn't realize she'd spent the costume money on the sound system.

On the flight home Mark relaxed and told her what he planned for the Regency. Restorations of old buildings, it seemed, were his hobby, and he planned to restore the Regency to its previous grandeur.

Under the encroaching canopy of dusk, they touched down on the iridescent orange helipad. Mark clutched her arm while the still-moving rotors whished the air around them and they dashed for the building's entrance. His black hair had been tossed in a thousand different directions, giving him a more youthful appearance. His hand was still on her arm and he was walking closer than necessary as they came up to the lift. He reminded her to select an agency to do the advertising campaign.

"I'll be by Wednesday afternoon to look at what you have, if you're available."

He turned to face her and she felt that quiver of anticipation she'd been unable to dispel despite all she'd learned about him. "I'll be there," she said.

By five o'clock Wednesday, Mark had still not arrived and Alexa had completed the day's work and part of the next day's as well. She scooped a tin of Whiskas cat food into T.S.'s bowl and left it outside the office door. The cat, who ignored his job description as resident rodent hunter, showing no enthusiasm for the rat population, materialized out of nowhere and planted his face in his bowl. The only two things the cat cared about were food and Mark Kimbrough. Alexa switched off the lights and inserted her key into the stage door's lock.

"Am I too late?" Mark's unexpected voice from behind made her jump.

"N-no." She swung around. Mark leaned against the side of the building, his shoulders slumped, his tie loosened, and the top button of his shirt undone. His face had a pinched, drawn look to it, and in the shadows he looked years older.

"Have you eaten? The Ivy Grill is just around the corner," she said, thinking he certainly didn't look as if he was in the mood to review the ad proposals.

"Good idea." They headed toward the café. "I'm sorry I'm late. I was in a meeting all day and forgot I'd promised to come by."

"No problem," she assured him and then chatted on about the play until they reached the restaurant. Alexa continued to carry the conversation while they ate. Mark seemed preoccupied, barely listening to her. "I'm really excited about the ad proposals we have, but let's do it another day."

He straightened in his chair and managed a half-smile. "That bad?"

"What?"

"Do I look that bad?" he asked, wearily.

*No, that good. Too good.* "You look tired—knackered, right?"

"I was up most of last night."

"Then you need your rest tonight. We'll do it another time."

Mark nodded and Alexa kept up the cheery one-way conversation until they arrived back at the Regency.

"I'm getting a second wind. Let's see what you have."

Alexa hesitated, fumbling with the key. Advertising represented one of the play's largest budgetary allocations. Mark would scrutinize it even more closely than he had less expensive items. She wanted him fresh and well rested before he saw what she had in mind. "You're sure? I'm here every day."

He took the key from her and unlocked the door. "I'm positive."

Reclining beside his empty bowl and giving himself his umpteenth bath of the day, T.S. leaped to his feet when he saw Mark. With long, loving swipes he rubbed his orange fur onto Mark's trousers. Alexa swallowed a smile as Mark sidestepped the purring feline and walked into the office.

"I had each agency do a poster design as well as a proposal. The poster will be used for the ads and playbills as well," Alexa said, handing him a packet from one of the agencies he'd suggested. Alexa fiddled with some papers while Mark spread the proposal across his desk.

"Uh-huh," he said, after reading the material and examining the mock-up poster.

Alexa handed him the second proposal. He glanced at the poster and then to her. "Better, don't you think?"

"Yes." She scooted the purring T.S. from the chair beside his desk and sat down.

When she handed him the third poster, his eyes sparked. "Outstanding," he said, smiling at her. "This is it! If their proposal's in line, let's use them. Is it?"

Nodding her head, she tried to hide her excitement.

"What agency is this?" Frowning, he checked the letterhead. "Wilkens and Wilkens? I don't recognize the name."

Alexa drew in her breath, "They're young—just out of school. They've a loft in Soho. You can see they're talented."

"Phenomenally, but can they produce everything we need?" Mark picked up the poster, which was deep green except for a silver razor's edge outlining the svelte figure of a woman in a long, clinging gown. Her head was a wild flurry of saffron-colored curls. With his finger, he traced the single strand of hair that flowed off to one side and formed the word RENATA. Below her name smaller silver letters announced the play's title: *No Chance.*

"I'm certain they can do it. They're new in the business"— she heard the breathless rush of excitement in her voice and took a breath— "but talented. They immediately understood the image I described to them when neither of the other two agencies gave me what I wanted."

"This"—Mark waved the poster in front of her—"was your idea?"

"What could be better than the red hair and the single word "Renata"? The whole campaign will center on Renata and her return. The play will be secondary. Well? What do you think?"

"Think? What do I think?" He brushed his fingers through his hair. "I think you're incredibly talented, *but*"—he paused to emphasize the word "but"—"I think we need to talk this over."

She felt a rush of heat to her cheeks at the unexpected compliment. Perhaps they could work together in spite of everything.

"First, let's talk about the agency. No one is more in favor of giving young Britons a start than I, but there are some business concerns we need to address before we award them a contract. Often fledgling businesses fail to deliver product, not out of any intent to defraud, but out of poor business practices. They may not have adequate cash flow to cover expenses. They might take our money and spend it to pay for a previous project's debt and when it comes time to, say, run our posters, they'd be out of funds. We'd have to come up with more money. And that I would not allow."

"But they've—"

"Hear me out, Alexa. I didn't say we wouldn't work with them, but if we do it will be up to you to closely supervise their account. I have a tremendous number of problems to deal with right now."

She wanted to ask him about his problems but didn't want to press their newfound relationship. "I'll be very careful with the Wilkenses," she said.

"Fine. Now about Renata. By basing your entire ad campaign on her, you've subjugated the play to her. If *anything* happened to her, it would ruin any chance the play has of being a success."

"She *is* the play," Alexa insisted. "I wrote it for her. She isn't doing drugs any longer; I'm not worried about that."

"What if she's run over by a car or breaks a leg?" he asked.

"It isn't fair to you, is it?" Alexa asked. "You'd lose your investment if anything happened to her."

"I'm willing to go along with it," he said, "as long as you are. It's a brilliant campaign. Just so you realize what you're risking."

"Since we're talking about risk taking, I have another idea." Alexa watched him draw in a deep breath.

When she explained her plan for selling tickets earlier than usual through their own box office at a discounted price, he was skeptical.

"I want everyone primed for Renata's return," Alexa said. "If they buy a ticket early, they'll be eager for it to open. We can take the money and have you invest it. That way we could be making money even before we open."

"The ticket brokers won't like it. There won't be anything they can do about it unless the play's not quite a hit but isn't bad enough to close either. Then they could steer business away."

"It'll be a hit. Come to a rehearsal. You'll see."

It took a little convincing, but he finally agreed to try her ticket idea.

That Saturday evening she prepared to go out with Chauncey Beddington. Hidebound by three hundred years of titled wealth and tradition, he had an overbred gentlemanliness about him that she found difficult to relate to. No excuses, she told herself as she dressed, the man's a bore, but you're lonely. As usual, Chauncey was punctual and they arrived at the exclusive private club, the White Elephant, before their table was ready. They were seated in the cocktail lounge having a drink, when Alexa heard a cultivated woman's voice behind her.

"Chauncey, how wonderful to see you."

Alexa turned to find Charmaine Crowne walking up to their table. Beside her, nodding a cool hello, was Mark Kimbrough.

"And . . . aaah . . ." Charmaine turned to Mark for help.

"Alexa MacKenzie," Mark said.

"Yes, of course. How are you?" Charmaine asked, beaming all the while at Chauncey.

"Fine," Alexa replied, gazing down at her white gown. Jeez, of all the luck. Why had she chosen to wear the same dress she'd worn to Audrey's party?

Before Alexa could reply, Chauncey insisted they join them for a drink. Clad in a short black dress shot with silver metallic ribbons that wound around her and came to an enormous cluster of bows at the top of her derriere, Charmaine held center stage. An oversized silver bow perched on her chignon had a veil that spider-webbed across her head and face, giving her a nineteen-thirties look.

"I hear the play's going awfully well," Charmaine said. "You must be terribly grateful to Mark."

"Alexa has had all the creative ideas," Mark said, smiling at Alexa.

Charmaine surveyed them over the rim of her wine goblet. She's jealous, Alexa realized with a start. Despite her money and her beauty Charmaine wasn't entirely certain of Mark.

"Look, there's father," Charmaine said, indicating a silver-haired, distinguished-looking man with the same ice-blue eyes she had.

"Father," Charmaine said after the men had exchanged greetings, "you remember Alexa. At Audrey's party we all admired her dress."

Thurston Crowne nodded politely, but Alexa doubted he'd even noticed her at the party.

"You certainly are getting a lot of wear out of your dress," Charmaine added, her eyes on Mark, then on Chauncey.

Heat prickled across Alexa's cheeks, but before she was forced to respond, the waiter came to take them to their table. As they walked away, Mark caught Alexa's eye and gave her an unexpectedly warm smile.

In the dining room Mark's party was seated near their table. Several older men had joined the Crownes' group.

"I say," Chauncey commented, "perhaps the rumors are true."

"Rumors?" A sinking feeling coursed through her.

"It looks to me as if those gentlemen are trying to persuade Mark to seek a seat in Parliament."

"Really?" The heaviness in her chest lightened.

"You're looking at all the really politically influential men in England," Chauncey assured her.

But Alexa wasn't looking at those men at all. While she listened to Chauncey drone on about the possibility of another cold winter, Alexa stole glances at Mark. Every so often he'd look their way and she'd grin at him, knowing that beneath the black veil, arctic-blue eyes caught every smile.

While Chauncey ordered after-dinner drinks, Alexa excused herself and found the ladies' room. When she came down the hall past the telephones on her way back to the table, she saw Mark.

"Alexa," he said, stepping directly in front of her, "what are you doing tomorrow?"

# Chapter 20

Alexa gazed out the Jaguar's window as it sped through the countryside. When he'd asked her what she was doing Sunday and she'd replied she had no plans, she'd thought Mark wanted to work on the production. He'd surprised her by arriving at her door expecting her to go for a picnic.

"Where are we heading?" She turned to him, noting the relaxed way he leaned against his door with his elbow resting on the lowered window. Dressed in perfectly creased white linen slacks and a short-sleeved navy sport shirt, he looked far more casual than she felt in her coral halter-top sundress.

"Just beyond Pildowne Crossing. Ever been there?" He turned toward her and gave her a slow, easy smile she hadn't seen since Mexico.

She shook her head. A date. This was actually a date, and she hadn't even realized it until now. Why? He was practically engaged to Charmaine. What was he up to? She couldn't afford to alienate him, but she had no intention of letting their relationship become anything more than business.

"You'll like it. Kent is the garden of England."

So far she had to agree. Lacy, opalescent clouds drifted across the brilliant sky while gently undulating meadows splashed with yellow and gold wild flowers welcomed the

August sunshine. They turned off the highway onto a two-
lane road flanked by ferns so tall they towered above the Jaguar. Mark never slowed down as he took the irregular curves
with practiced ease until they pulled into a cluster of homes
and a few stores surrounded by three-hundred-year-old oaks.

"Pildowne Crossing," Mark announced as he turned the
Jaguar off the main thoroughfare onto a one-lane unpaved
road that was still deeply rutted from the spring rains. With
tall oaks forming a cathedrallike ceiling above them, they'd
gone several miles down the lane before Mark turned onto an
even narrower dirt road with a simple sign that read: Wyndham Hill.

"What do you think?" he asked, pulling to a stop in front of
a stone manor house that had to be hundreds of years old.

Right out of a travel brochure, Alexa thought as she looked
at the rambling structure. Thick ivy twined its way up the
weather-beaten stones and garlanded the stately chimneys.
Leaded-glass windows winked, reflecting golden sunbeams
across a small courtyard. Clusters of wild flowers, tended by
Mother Nature, sprang from the unmowed lawn.

"I love it!" Alexa answered, surveying the overgrown rose
garden. Courting blue jays flashed through the tall oaks flanking the drive, and in the distance, a mourning dove cooed to
its mate. "Who owns this?"

"The bank," he said, stopping the car. "Hold on," he called
as she stepped from the car.

"Hurry up!"

He caught up with her and they walked together along the
cobblestone path toward the front door. The greenery tracing
the courtyard fence had spilled over the walkway and had
encroached upon the mossy stones.

"The electricity has been shut off," Mark said as they entered.

Inside the vaulted entry hall, a sweeping spiral staircase invited an image of a fairy-tale princess floating down the steps
in her ball gown. Shafts of wavering light caught dust motes
as they danced on the breeze drifting in from the open door.
The air had a heavy, stale smell to it as if this was the first
time in months the empty house had been opened.

"This way." Mark put his hand on her shoulder and guided
her into a huge hall. "The great hall," he said, indicating the

wide room with heavy exposed beams crosshatching the cathedral ceiling. Three brass chandeliers, designed to hold candles, not electric lights, hung from the wide central beam.

"Look at that fireplace," Alexa said. She walked up to the stone hearth and stood before the opening. "I could fit in here," she said, stooping over and wriggling into the opening.

Mark reached for her hand and pulled her out. "What do you think?" he asked without releasing her hand.

"I love it. I just wish we had lights. We could see better." She brushed a smudge of soot off her bare shoulder.

When they came to the library, Alexa had to suppress a fierce stab of envy. Floor-to-ceiling oak shelves held hundreds of leather-bound books. A tall ladder on a rolling stand allowed access to the top shelves. Against one wall an exquisitely carved fireplace boasted an exceptionally wide mantelpiece that held several hand-tooled and gold-leafed books.

"They left their books but took the furniture?"

"Undoubtedly they sold the furniture piece by piece. I doubt if any of the books on these shelves are particularly valuable," he said, taking her out of the library and down the hall. They paused on the threshold of the dining room, which was floored in a herringbone pattern of chestnut and walnut.

"I'm considering buying this place. I need a weekend retreat within commuting distance of London. What do you think?"

He gazed down at her with earnest gray eyes. What did she think? She was positively green with envy. As soon as she got her hands on some money she planned to buy a cottage in the country. "I like it. I really like it. It'll take lots of work. Let's see the rest."

"I'm going to do some research into the architectural history of Wyndham Hill. The owner, an elderly lady who's retired to Portugal, didn't seem to know much. She thinks the staircase was carved by Grinling Gibbons, but she's not certain."

"Let me help." The words slipped out of Alexa's mouth before she realized what she'd said. "I'm good at research."

"Great, I'm really tied up these days. Just find out who and when and then let's decide upon the best way to duplicate the fabrics and furniture of the period."

Mutely, Alexa nodded. Had he meant to say that? "Let's decide." Did he really plan on having her help? What about good old Charmaine? Maybe they weren't a sure thing after all. She felt a warm glow flow through her. *"Let's decide."* Stop it, *Alexa! Lead with your head, not your heart.* She reminded herself that this was the man who had never bothered to call her after that night in Mexico. *Be smarter this time. Don't let yourself be taken in again.*

After inspecting the upstairs living quarters, which were badly in need of refurbishing, they returned to the car for the picnic hamper and blanket.

"This way." Mark guided her around toward the rear of the house.

"It's so quiet," Alexa whispered. Only the golden-toned warbling of a meadowlark lilted across the bosky stillness.

"The nearest neighbors are in Pildowne Crossing. That's three miles away. I see too many people in the city. I need to get away."

A brook, banked by clumps of periwinkle-blue wild flowers, meandered through the tall grass and disappeared into the forest. The scent of wild honeysuckle laced the air while squadrons of unseen birds harmonized in the trees and flitted through the dense underbrush rimming the field. They stopped at the tall elm that stood on the brook's edge and Mark lowered the basket to the grass. "Looks like a good spot for a picnic. What do you think?"

"Perfect."

He spread the blanket on the grass and then patted it, indicating she should sit. Alexa lowered herself to the plaid blanket. The smell of damp grass and moist earth combined with that of the honeysuckle. It really was perfect. Mark smiled at her while he spread an unbelievable number of packages from the basket.

"Fortnum and Mason's?" she asked, inspecting the cold poached salmon, game pie, and assorted cold meats and cheeses.

"Cumberbatch's" Mark answered, pulling a bottle of wine from the hamper.

"Cumber—"

"My housekeeper, Mrs. Cumberbatch. She made everything. Mrs. C's getting a little too old for this." Mark opened another container, revealing cold breast of capon and a side dish of some sauce Alexa couldn't immediately name. "She doesn't like me waking her after midnight and demanding a picnic be ready first thing in the morning. After sixty they get a little cranky."

Sixty? Cranky? A grandmother took care of Mark? She smiled in spite of herself. He hadn't planned this picnic. Last night . . . why he must have thought . . . Well, she *had* tried to make Charmaine jealous by flirting with him. An image of that first picnic in Mexico came back to her. Despite her reservations about Mark; that same uneasy yet exciting feeling crept through her.

"Wine?" he asked, extending a glass of Chardonnay, which she accepted.

For the next two hours they chatted companionably about renovating Wyndham Hill while they feasted upon Mrs. Cumberbatch's goodies. Alexa tried to keep a psychological distance from him, but too often she found herself wishing she didn't know so many distasteful things about him and that this was the beginning of their relationship.

Mark stowed the empty containers in the hamper and placed a basket of strawberries alongside a container of Rodda's Cornish Clotted Cream. When she reached for the strawberries, Mark handed her a slice of cake.

"Mrs. C's rum cake. Perfect with strawberries and clotted cream." He winked at her and gave her an eager smile.

When they'd finally finished everything and repacked the hamper, Mark lay back looking up at the midafternoon sun as it splintered light through the elm's dense foliage onto their blanket. Alexa turned her head away, willing herself not to notice how attractive she found him in spite of everything. She forced herself to concentrate on the murmur of the breeze through the treetops and the soft hiss of the brook.

"Alexa." Mark rolled onto his side and propped himself up on his elbow. "I'd like to explain something to you."

Something in his tone forewarned her and Alexa straightened, sitting upright, waiting.

"About Windsor Airlines."

She struggled not to look shocked, but judging from the change in his expression, she hadn't succeeded.

"When we were in Mexico, I wasn't completely honest with you. I knew Windsor was in trouble, and I knew I'd lend them money to refinance if they were unable to solve their problems. I should have said this to you instead of going on and on about the Trade Alliance. I am active with the Trade Alliance, but I risked my own capital to help Windsor Air."

"How long had you been working on the refinancing?"

"We were just in the talking stage when I mentioned it to you. I should have told you the precise truth."

Alexa noted the weary lines, which had been absent all day, clustering around Mark's eyes. She stretched herself out opposite him and braced her head against her cocked arm. "It's all right."

"No, it's not. Absolute honesty is the best avenue. I should have told you I anticipated lending them money if they were unable to evade the black marketeers."

She hesitated, wondering if Steven had misunderstood the car phone conversation he said he'd overheard. Given the animosity between Mark and Steven, it was even possible he'd deliberately tried to make Mark look bad. It didn't matter, she decided, as the memory of that night in Cabo returned, bringing with it the belittling image of Mark and Charmaine. No wonder he'd never called. Now he had that same "trust me" look she'd fallen for in Mexico. What did he want this time? She considered the situation for a few seconds and decided to turn the tables. She wanted the new stereo system to be installed before he realized what had happened.

"Mark." She cast him her most bewitching smile. "I'm the one who has something to be sorry for . . . the drug testing. It was all a horrible misunderstanding. My fault really—"

Before she could finish Mark reached for her, pulling her into his arms. Warm and firm, his lips met hers, demanding she part her lips. When she did, his tongue swept her mouth. In a series of darting little forays, he discovered her tongue and caressed it tenderly, lingering over it and circling, circling.

She relaxed, letting him kiss her while she tried to concentrate on how she'd dupe him. With a groan Mark moved over her, pressing her into the soft earth beneath the blanket. He drew back; his smoky gray eyes were heavy-lidded with passion. Selecting a lock of her hair, he caressed it gently before he kissed her again. Stroking his tongue in and out between her soft, parted lips, he kissed her until she barely heard the burble of the nearby brook or the birds chirping in the trees above them. It wasn't until he slid his warm hand over the tops of her alert nipples that she became aware of the moist, hot heat building between her thighs. He wasn't doing this to her—not again. She wedged her hand between his chest and hers and pushed.

Shit! Mark rolled onto his back and stared at the canopy of trees. He hated himself for wanting her, but undeniably he did. Wavering patches of sunlight and shadow flickered through the trees leaving alternate splashes of dark and light. Just like Alexa, he thought, light and dark, on and off, back and forth. "Alexa, what the hell do you want?"

"Mark . . . I . . . we can't."

He sat up and looked down at her. "Why in hell not?"

She rose to a sitting position, curled her bare feet under her, and peered up at him with a hesitant smile. "We're in business together. It isn't a good idea to—"

"And Mexico never happened?" He tried to keep the sarcasm from his voice but the look on her face told him he'd hit the mark.

"It shouldn't have. I needed—"

"To get laid?" he asked, watching her nod self-consciously as her cheeks turned pink. "No, you needed more than that—you still do. Does Steven give you what you need?"

She shook her head, sending waves of honey-gold hair fluttering across her bare shoulders. *Let me give it to you.* She turned and stared off at the copse of birch trees across the meadow. He reached up and cupped her chin in his hand, forcing her to face him. "What do you need from me?"

She turned her head downward and placed a soft kiss in the center of his palm before she gazed up at him again.

"I want us to be friends. Start there and see what happens. I'm lonely and confused and under pressure with this play. I lied about just needing to get laid. I said that because it was easier than admitting I'm afraid. Let's take this slowly and see."

"All right, let's take this a day at a time, but don't ever lie to yourself. Don't tell yourself that there's nothing between us." He slid his arm around her bare shoulders.

Alexa snuggled against him, tucking her head into the curve of his neck. Did she have any idea what she did to him? he wondered. She could be immature and insulting and still get him to forgive her. He'd brought her to Wyndham Hill today to see her reaction. He wanted a place where they could be alone. Her unabashed delight with Wyndham Hill mirrored his own. There was no question in his mind that she felt something for him. But what was holding her back? Steven? Her ex-husband? Chauncey?

They sat for the longest time, silently watching the glowing crimson sun slip behind the trees, lengthening their shadows and claiming the meadow and the wild flowers. One by one the birds abandoned their tunes and returned to their nests until only the bittersweet refrain of the meadowlark could be heard.

"We'd better go," he said, reluctantly releasing her.

When they reached the car they stood hand in hand and looked back at the house. The sky, deepening to a plum twilight, cast soft purple-gray shadows across the ivy-clad walls.

"It's sad to leave it," Alexa said, moving closer to him.

"We'll—" he stopped himself from saying "be back." "Start researching. I'm leaving town first thing in the morning, remember?"

She smiled up at him with an eager, delighted look in her clear green eyes. "I remember."

On the drive back into London Mark kept the conversation upbeat and impersonal. She still needed time, but he couldn't help feeling that today he'd made more headway with her than he had in the last three months. When he dropped her off, he walked her to the door, reminding her to watch the budget. "Stay on top of that ad campaign and personally oversee the installation of the seats."

"Yes, sir!" She gave him a mock salute and gazed up at him through those incredible lashes. "Anything else, *sir?*"

"Call my secretary if you have any problems. They'll send someone over or get in touch with me—whatever it takes."

"Mark." She moved close to him, her erect nipples brushing the thin cotton shirt he was wearing. "I had a wonderful time today. That house is fabulous."

On her tiptoes, Alexa looped one arm around his neck and kissed him on the cheek. Hell! He wasn't letting her get away with that. He pulled her to him, kissing her and devouring the softness of her lips insistently until she swayed against him. Inhaling the sweet, flowery traces of perfume lingering on her skin, Mark ran his hand along her bare back until he felt the gooseflesh rise beneath his fingers.

He wanted to hear her say his name in that soft, seductive voice again and again, but he pulled away. "You're right," he said with a grin. "There's nothing between us."

# Chapter 21

"Mr. Kimbrough's asking for you," the stage manager called to Alexa.

She checked her hair in the dressing-room mirror and gave it a quick run-through with the brush before reaching for one of the lipsticks on the carousel. Don't give him any reason to be suspicious, she reminded herself.

She came through the wings and down the stairs into the theater. In the dim light she could make out the image of a tall man seated in the back row, listening to the rehearsal. At the sight of him, the knot of apprehension in her chest coiled tighter and tighter. Since the Wolfschmidt sound system wasn't being used, he couldn't have guessed what she'd done. But when the lights were on and he began inspecting the newly installed upholstery, that would be the real test. Would he notice the much larger Tannoys had been replaced by smaller speakers?

"Welcome back," she whispered, sliding into the seat next to Mark.

"Hello," he said with a warm smile, but immediately returned his attention to the scene being rehearsed.

Out of the corner of her eye, Alexa noted he looked tired and that he needed a haircut. He couldn't have been back in town long—a day or two at most. For the last three days she'd been uneasily anticipating his return. When she diverted the money from the wardrobe account to cover the sound system installation, had she done anything that would alert him? If he found out she'd used those funds and had gone "black" to pay for the system's installation, there'd be no telling how he'd react. He'd made it absolutely clear that no one was to be paid under the table, and she'd defied him by doing just that.

Alexa turned and gave Mark her most enchanting smile. "Well?" She inclined her head toward the stage.

"I'm impressed. The place looks terrific. The fabric is just right—much better than the red. Everything was completed without a hitch?"

"No problems. We're finished now." She raised her eyes to his and found him watching her with more than just casual interest. She wiped her damp palms on her jeans.

"I'll want to take a closer look later," he whispered, returning his attention to the stage.

Alexa swallowed a laugh. Mark had read the script, but he'd never seen a rehearsal because they'd been unable to use the theater until recently. This was the first time he'd seen the kids in the street scene. Their attire defied description: Leather and chains seemed *de rigueur*, as did the chalky white makeup and black lipstick and eye shadow. But if he had any negative thoughts, he kept them to himself.

"Does this look *anything* like the mildewed cavern I brought you to?" Alexa asked after the rehearsal finished and she took Mark into the lobby.

He shook his head, but his eyes never left hers. A dizzying jolt of excitement thrilled her. He wasn't even bothering to look around. She walked into the office, explaining in rapid-fire succession what she'd done since he'd left.

Mark paused to swoop T.S. from his chair. "No problems on the ad campaign?" he asked, sitting down.

Alexa showed him the artwork the Wilkenses had done. Through all her explanations Mark kept nodding and watching her intently. A sudden weightlessness, a curious expectancy thrust up against the underside of her heart. The invisible web of attraction she'd always felt for Mark surfaced once more while she tried to remember all her reasons for distrusting him. She had to fight the overwhelming urge to confess everything to him and beg him not to be angry. His steady gaze flustered her and she stammered nonsensically when she handed him the computer printouts covering the last two weeks.

"I'll read them later," Mark said, stuffing them into a briefcase already so full he had to force the top down to latch it.

Alexa said a silent prayer that he wouldn't have time to read the reports too closely. Surely he had more pressing business. With luck she would be able to replace the funds before he discovered what she'd done.

Mark set the briefcase aside and waited for Alexa to say something. All morning she'd seemed nervous, excited. Had she spent as much time thinking about him as he had her? He'd hardly been able to wait to see her. If it hadn't been so late last night when he arrived home, he'd have called her. The week he'd been gone had been so long and empty that it frightened him. He'd even found it difficult to concentrate on the Trade Alliance meetings and the persistent problems at Windsor Air. After seeing her, would he be able to give his undivided attention to the myriad of business problems he knew were piled up on his desk?

"That's it," she said.

She couldn't know his heartbeat had accelerated. Even her most casual movement reminded him of her sexual attractiveness. Did she have any idea how sexy she looked in those jeans? Beneath her heavy sweater the free bob of her breasts indicated she wasn't wearing a bra. Now that he thought about it, he'd never seen her in one.

"I have to get over to Triad. I came in last night. This was my first stop."

"Of course," she answered, walking over and opening the door for him before he could finish.

"What's the rush?" he chuckled, inclining his head to the chair beside his desk. "I want to talk with you."

Slowly Alexa crossed the room. "Yes?" Her voice seemed unusually hesitant.

"About Wyndham Hill. Did Mr. Coombs call you?" When she nodded, he continued, "Then you know I own it."

Alexa jumped up and hurried over to her desk. She bent over, giving him another provocative view of her rear, and pulled a maroon notebook from the bottom drawer of her desk. With an expectant, eager-to-please expression, she handed it to him. "My research on Wyndham Hill. I completed it last night."

Astonished, Mark leafed through the pages. Here was more work than he'd expected to have in six months. Genealogies, garden plans, furniture inventories, and clippings of newspaper accounts of past events at Wyndham Hill filled the binder.

"When did you find the time?"

She shrugged, a faint blush highlighting her cheeks. "I'm a professional researcher really. That's how I did the book on Cochrane. I knew where to go. I've even located some of the original furniture. There's a list at the back of the notebook."

He cleared his throat, pretending not to be affected by her obvious enthusiasm for the project. She couldn't know how much she meant to him. He'd taken great pains to hide his feelings from her and now wasn't the time—not yet.

She stood before him with her hands shoved into her hip pockets, her firm breasts jutting out. Tugging on her lower lip with her teeth, she looked acutely uncomfortable. The animated sparkle had died from her eyes, and her face had turned a vivid scarlet. *How was it he could never think of the right thing to say?*

"Alexa, thank you."

"Then you like it?"

He stood up and gripped her upper arms with both his hands, forcing her hands up out of her back pockets. "Of course, I like it. It's wonderful. I just never expected—"

"You said you wanted me to help," she mumbled, her nervousness painfully apparent.

"Yes, I'm very pleased." He drew her into his arms, looking into her vivid green eyes. "I'm not much good with words." He paused for a deep breath. "I'm touched that you went to so much trouble. Nothing could make me happier. This is just the first step. I want you to help me restore Wyndham Hill."

A delighted grin replaced her frown and she smiled. For a heartbeat the office became so still that he could hear T.S. purring. Slowly Alexa rose on tiptoes and parted her lips to receive his kiss. With a soft, seeking kiss, he told her what he'd been unable to say. Months of desire and anger and frustration flowed between them. Her soft breasts molding against the contours of his chest, she wound her arms inside his jacket and around his back. He ran his hand across her cute bottom and up under the sweater. Hot and hard, he felt his prick rising, obliterating his other thoughts. He physically needed to make love to her, but he realized this wasn't merely a sexual urge. It was a desperate desire to possess her, as if the physical act would somehow bind her to him. Stroking her back languidly, he said, "You know what I'd really like? To spend an evening going over your notebook at this intimate little restaurant I've found. How about tonight? Say eight o'clock?"

"Tonight?" Alexa jerked out of his arms, a peculiar, concerned expression in her green eyes.

"You have plans?" he asked, willing her to volunteer to break her date.

"No . . . but"

"Cumberbatch's Trattoria. The best food in London. Seven?"

Pensively Alexa stared down at the tops of her well-worn Reeboks. "Don't you have plans?"

"Yes, but as soon as I get to the office I intend to cancel them. It's a big party. They won't miss me."

His explanation left her looking even more perplexed. "We could do it another night . . . sometime next week," she muttered, her eyes flittering from side to side, as if seeking some way of escape.

"Alexa, I thought we were going to be honest with each other. What's the matter?"

"Your birthday."

Christ! He'd forgotten it. How the hell did she know? He watched as she spun around and went back to her desk. From a drawer she slowly drew out a package wrapped in brown paper.

"I didn't have time to wrap it."

He took the heavy object from her. Her winsome, little-girl smile tugged at his heart as he pulled the thick paper off a set of brass bookends. The pair of lions, one male with his paw on a round ball representing the world and the female with a cub at her feet, were brilliantly polished. He examined them closely and immediately determined they were at least two hundred years old. "Where did you find these?"

She gave him an impish smile. "They'd been on the library

mantel in Wyndham Hill for over two hundred years. I found
them covered with dust in an antique shop."

"You shouldn't have."

"I wanted to."

He didn't know what to say. She couldn't possibly afford
something like this. "Then we must go to dinner."

"No." Alexa shook her head, tossing clusters of honey-gold
curls across her shoulders. "The party. It's for you. Everyone
will be there. You can't—Charmaine's gone to a good deal of
trouble."

"Dammit! I hate surprise parties."

Just the phrase "surprise party" brought back the memory
of that night, years ago, when Caroline had thrown him a
surprise party. Everything about it had been a surprise, all
right. He'd been surprised to learn all their friends knew his
wife was having an affair. He'd been even more surprised
when he'd learned who her lover was.

"Mark," Alexa gazed innocently at him. "Don't you think
you could go along with it? Pretend. Half of London will be
there."


For the third time Mark tried to make the bow tie necessary
to top off his dinner jacket. In disgust he stared at the flawlessly cut dinner jacket and starched white pleated shirt with
its stiff collar. Somehow this getup reminded him of his days
at Bilbrough Hall with the regimented formal attire. He saw
himself as he'd been upon entering the school: a lonely,
skinny kid committing innumerable social blunders.

He slung the wrinkled tie aside and took another from the
box marked Westscott's. The Jermyn Street men's accessory
shop knew enough to sell the ties by the dozen. Once wrinkled, they weren't worth a damn. This time he concentrated
on the length of black silk, tying the formal knot more easily
and thinking things had definitely changed since those days at
school when Warren had befriended him. Now he had major
problems, not just adolescent insecurities. Someone was deliberately and systematically trying to destroy him. At first he'd
merely thought he'd developed a case of paranoia, but now he
was positive. He'd assumed Windsor Air was experiencing the
same black-market ticket problems confronting other airlines,
but when the problems increased dramatically after he'd

bought it, he became suspicious. And now, rafts of counterfeit tickets were afloat as well as the black-market tickets.

Had it just been Windsor Air he might have dismissed his concerns, but his other projects were suffering as well. Unexplained fires . . . labor disputes . . . banking hassles. Someone had even given his expensive computer system a virus that jumbled all the information, rendering it inoperable. Triad Investments, a name once synonymous with well-run projects, was quickly becoming a jinx. All he needed now would be to have trouble with the play. Not that there was that much money involved. There wasn't, but he couldn't face Alexa if something happened.

On the ride to the Crownes' Lowndes Place mansion in elegant Belgravia, Mark continued considering his difficulties. If he was right, something would happen to the play, and most likely it would involve Renata. Once again Alexa's image came unbidden to him. No one knew how he felt about her except Warren. It suddenly occurred to him if anyone knew just how much he cared, she would be vulnerable. It might be best to keep their relationship quiet. Wyndham Hill. There they could be alone. In time he'd get to the bottom of this sabotage. Until then he'd better pretend there was nothing but a business relationship between them.

He drove up to the Regency-style villa, admiring the numerous trees and gardens in the area. In some ways Belgravia, with its verdant squares and tree-lined streets, was more beautiful than Mayfair, where he lived. The attendant took his car, adding it to the collection of Rollses, Bentleys, Aston-Martins, Jaguars, Mercedeses and chauffeured limos lining one of the most prestigious streets in London. He'd purposely been late to give everyone time to assemble before he came. He wondered if Alexa had arrived yet. He intended to ask her to go to Wyndham Hill with him the next day. Earlier he'd tried to catch her at the theater, but she'd left. Tonight he needed to settle things with Charmaine. He'd already explained to her that he didn't want to commit himself and that he had no intention of remarrying. What he'd really meant, what he suspected most men meant when they said this, was he didn't wish to commit himself to her. She'd said she understood, but when he'd returned from Mexico and stopped sleeping with her, Charmaine had shown him a side of her that he never knew existed. In her well-bred, understated way, she'd become aggressive. She constantly called him, inviting him to a number of affairs he cared nothing about. Unfortunately, he'd let her convince him to escort her to the Throckmortons' party. That night he'd given Charmaine every reason to believe he did care, and not even his apology the night of the boutique opening had dissuaded the woman. When her father, Thurston Crowne, had asked him to dinner to discuss a business venture, Charmaine had invited herself along.

Mark ambled up the tiers of stone steps, pausing to greet Oliver, the doorman. When he started to open the carved double doors for him, Mark shook his head. He took a deep breath and stared at the mansion, lit up like a castle in a fairy tale. Bracing himself and summoning a half-smile, he nodded to Oliver and the door swung open.

"Surprise!!" chorused a throng of people, some of whom Mark had trouble remembering.

He let his jaw drop in mock surprise and saw Charmaine gliding up to him.

"Happy birthday, darling," she murmured, handing him a Hennessy and soda.

"Charmaine, you shouldn't have." He dredged up a smile. "What am I going to do with you?"

She winked suggestively and gave him a seductive smile that made him wish he'd kept his damn mouth shut.

"Let me take you around," she said, looping her arm possessively through his.

Mark checked the clusters of guests for a honey-blond head. She wasn't here yet. He tried to concentrate on Charmaine as she gestured to the circle of people looking expectantly at him. He could have sworn he'd never met one of them. He was right. Charmaine proceeded to introduce him to the group. He nodded politely, never really hearing a single name. He completely tuned out when the group began discussing politics with an intensity that wasn't diminished in the least by the fact they were all in complete agreement.

Out of the corner of his eye he looked at Charmaine. As usual she was garbed in outrageous designer plumage. Floor length and as tight as good taste would allow, the black gown clung to her thin frame. Down one side a trail of rhinestones traced a leaf pattern. Her hair, instead of being caught back in the familiar chignon, was piled atop her head into an elaborate cluster of curls through which a pair of black diamond-studded chopsticks protruded. He took a deep breath and subtly let his eyes skip over the crowd for Alexa.

He had finished his Hennessy and soda before he realized what was happening. Under the guise of a birthday party, this was the Crownes' way of parading him before Thurston Crowne's political cronies. Although all Mark's friends and acquaintances were there, politicians he'd never have numbered among his friends were out in force. Apparently that night at the White Elephant, the Crownes hadn't believed him when he'd told him he had no political ambitions.

"Happy birthday." Warren put his hand on Mark's shoulder.

Mark kept smiling and nodding to people as they squeezed their way through the crush of guests and found a quiet corner. "Where is Linda?" Mark asked, thinking Alexa could very possibly come with her.

"I don't know. I haven't seen her," Warren said, not adding the past weeks had been longer, more agonizing than he cared to admit, even to Mark. Knowing Linda was his—if he wanted her—was more difficult to bear than losing her to another man.

Mark frowned, thinking if there was one person in the world who deserved to be happy, it was Warren. In all these years he'd never gotten over Linda. Hell, maybe it would work this time.

"What about this?" Warren inclined his head toward the assembled crowd. "Do you have political aspirations you haven't told me about?"

"You know I don't."

"I guess the Crownes haven't gotten the message." Warren leaned toward Mark and lowered his voice. "Half this crowd looks as if they'd wandered in from the Carlton Club."

Mark laughed, agreeing that the conservative club was well represented here. "I'm not cut out for politics. I'm too outspoken. And I don't intend to find my private life smeared over the pages of the tabloids again. Once was enough."

"There's Linda. Excuse me." Warren moved toward the

foyer. "Let's have lunch or dinner next week," he threw over his shoulder.

Alexa wasn't with Linda. Mark checked his watch. Where the hell was she?

"Darling, I want you to meet Vernon Harrington." Charmaine appeared at his side with a tall, thin man with white, wavy hair.

Mark sipped his drink and listened to Harrington give an ill-informed analysis of Britain's trade problems. Nodding politely but never hearing a word, he kept his eye on the foyer for new arrivals. Chauncey Beddington walked in with a petite blonde at his side. The knot already burning in Mark's stomach turned white hot.

"There's Chauncey," Charmaine cooed, pulling Mark along with her.

As they came closer the blonde turned around and Mark let out an inaudible sigh. It wasn't Alexa. Mark waited until he could politely escape before going to find Linda. She'd know what was keeping Alexa. It took him a few minutes to locate Warren and Linda in the library. Sitting on the sofa, they were talking quietly with their heads together, looking very much in love.

"Excuse me, you two," Mark interrupted. "Linda, I'm wondering what's keeping Alexa."

Linda gave him a blank look and then her blue eyes widened. "She wasn't invited."

# Chapter 22

"He's serious about Alexa, isn't he?" Linda asked Warren as soon as Mark left.

"I hope not. I know she's your friend, but she's got a chip on her shoulder where Mark's concerned. He doesn't deserve that." Warren didn't add Mark had enough business problems for twenty men right now. He didn't need Alexa to give him any more trouble.

Linda hesitated, wondering how to answer. Warren had eagerly sought her out tonight after weeks of avoiding her. She didn't want to argue with him, but she had to be honest. "Alexa is the best friend anyone could ask for," Linda said, and then recounted all she'd done to help Renata. "Her problem stems from her divorce. Her husband hurt her badly. She doesn't trust men, not even one like Mark Kimbrough. I've tried to tell her that he's different, but she can't see it. It'll take time, that's all."

Warren was silent as he thought for the thousandth time he shouldn't take up with Linda again—she'd only hurt him. But still some inner voice reminded him how happy he'd once been. She'd apologized over and over. There was nothing to do now but make a choice—forgive her or walk away once and for all. The memory of the loneliness, the search for someone to take her place was still too acute. The time he'd spent with Linda, although years ago, was still the happiest time he could remember. The golden years. He'd always thought of them that way. She'd made a mistake, but did she —did he—have to pay for it forever?

"Let's talk about this at my place," Warren said.

A tight, hot knot of anticipation formed in Linda's chest as they made their excuses to the Crownes and left.

As soon as Linda entered Warren's Adam's Row town house, tears stung her eyes. The Mayfair residence had been in Warren's family for generations. His parents lived on their Derbyshire estate while Warren had lived in the town house since college. Like most English homes passed on from heir to heir, this house had changed little since the turn of the century. How often she'd dreamed she was here again! Nothing had changed—yet everything had changed.

"Oh, Warren . . ." She turned and found herself in his arms. *Don't cry now. Don't spoil it.*

Warren held her tight, breathing in her floral perfume and the smell of her freshly washed hair. He cleared his throat, not knowing what to say. Having her seemed right. So right. The moment she'd walked in, time rolled back. She seemed more like the old Linda—fresh and beautiful as an English rose. And innocent. Oh, so innocent.

"Darling," she whispered, her voice choked with tears. "Take me upstairs. Let me make love to you."

In the darkness Warren grinned. This was the new Linda, taking the initiative.

Upstairs, Linda continued to take charge, removing his clothing, kissing him, loving him, thrilling him beyond anything he'd experienced since she'd left. Everything about her lovemaking was achingly familiar yet completely new.

"I love you," she whispered when she'd undressed them both and they were on his bed.

Warren looked into her sky-blue eyes, speaking to him across the years, welcoming him home. And in the depths of her eyes he saw life as it always had been—happy and full of promise.

He sucked his breath in, realizing he'd become rock-hard in a matter of minutes. Linda moaned, whispering something into his parted lips as she slid her hand up to the juncture of his thighs. Hot and pulsating, his erection slid into her hand. His whole body throbbed for her, leaving him dismayed at the intensity of his need. Other women had come and gone, but there'd been only one woman who could make him feel like this.

She brought his erection up between her satin thighs into the moist, pulsing heat.

"Darling . . . darling," he moaned.

"I hope the advance ticket sales and the soundtrack pay off," Renata said as she sat in the recording studio in Liverpool with Giles and Alexa. "I think Mark could use some good news about now."

"Oh," Alexa asked, "why?" She was still so elated from hearing the demo tape of the soundtrack that her mind wasn't on Mark for the first time in days. She'd taken an advance from her publisher for her new book and had used it to finance the tape project. She'd put half of her share in the newly formed company in Mark's name.

"Haven't you been following the Windsor Air fiasco in the papers?"

Alexa shook her head. All of her time had been consumed by the play and the research on Wyndham Hill. She couldn't recall just when it was she'd last had the time to read the paper.

"According to the *Times,*" Giles said, "Windsor has been unable to solve that recurring black-market ticket scam, but now they've been hit with bogus tickets. Apparently some popular flights have been double and even triple booked. Irate passengers have been stranded or have had to take other airlines, and Windsor has had to refund their money."

"Can't that be sorted out with a computer?" Alexa asked. "In the U.S. travel agents and airline ticket counters check space, dates, and I don't know what on the computer. Couldn't the tickets somehow be checked?"

"I don't know that much about it," Giles answered, "but from what I gather, computers aren't used in many of the Third World nations Windsor services. Apparently the bogus tickets originated in those countries."

Alexa considered all of this carefully. No wonder Mark had looked so weary lately. Phantoms of conscience danced through her head, overridden by the thought that soon money would be rolling in and that would counteract her deception. It was a childish way of attempting to right a wrong, she knew, but it was all she could do. It wouldn't be a significant amount of money, considering the large-scale consumption of funds airlines took, but it might give him a psychological boost.

The next day they toured Liverpool's Brackton Theater. Although much smaller than the Regency, everyone agreed it was just right for the play's trial run.

"Renata is so good that I almost feel we're wasting money spending January playing in the provinces," Alexa said. "The expense of keeping the cast and crew here will be astronomical."

"You're wrong," Giles interrupted. "Every play needs fine tuning. We're all too close to it to see it. Little things make the difference between a successful production and a loser. Every London play has a trial run somewhere in the provinces. It gives the director"—he turned to Twick— "a chance to make adjustments before facing a more critical audience in London."

"Maybe we should investigate doing these drug tests in a lab closer to the theater," Alexa said when she and Renata came into the Regency after ten o'clock Monday morning. "It means Twick has to wait an hour before you arrive."

"Mr. Kimbrough's waiting for you," called one of the crew.

Alexa's spirits did a nosedive. Mark! What could he want? She adjusted the green tam on her head and took a deep breath before opening the office door.

"Hi," Mark said. His long legs stretched before him and crossed at the ankles, he sat idly petting T.S., who was perched on the desk purring. "Where've you been?"

"The lab," she answered, taking her coat off and then removing the tam. His ebullient spirits assured her he hadn't found out about the Wolfschmidt.

"I tried to get you this weekend."

"I went up to Liverpool to check out a theater to use in January," she answered, noticing he looked relieved. "How was the party?"

Encased in fine English tweed, his shoulders seemed broader

than usual as an appealing grin brightened his face. "I survived," he chuckled, then tipped his chair back and clasped his hands behind his head. "Barely. I didn't realize you weren't coming to the party."

"What brings you here this early?" Alexa asked, not commenting on being omitted from the guest list.

"I'm waiting for a delivery."

"Of what?"

"What would you say to a new sound system?"

A chill skidded through her body. She spun around and sifted through a stack of computer reports on her desk. "None was specified in the original construction plans." She tried to keep the quiver from her voice but clearly heard it anyway.

"Because I didn't know when they'd have a prototype ready for installation. There's this new British company with fabulous small speakers, but I wasn't sure when they'd be delivered. I didn't want to hold up the renovations."

Of all the luck. There'd be no way of keeping the truth from him now.

"Hey," Mark chuckled, "you don't want it. I'll send it back."

Alexa didn't know where she found the strength, but she forced herself to turn and face him. He looked so pleased with himself that her heart went out to him. "Maybe that would be best."

"What do you mean?" he asked quietly. Too quietly.

"We have a new system," she said, her voice trailing off as the numerous clever ways she'd conjured up to explain the situation to him eluded her.

"When? I didn't notice anything on the reports. How did you pay for it?" His voice, still perilously low, held an ominous note, like distant thunder.

"I used funds allocated for costumes. I have money coming in December. I'll put that into the account to cover the costume bill, which won't be in until January."

He vaulted to his feet. "I don't recall any installation bills on the computer reports."

Alexa swallowed hard before saying, "There weren't any."

"You went black after I *specifically* asked you not to?" His eyes narrowed and he stared at her for the longest moment. Finally, he asked, "Why? Why didn't you come to me?"

"Because I didn't want you to know."

The words detonated as soon as she uttered them, bringing the truth: She'd been deceiving him all along.

# Chapter 23

"I can't believe it," Renata said, waving her hands in the air and sending sparks of light from the rings on her fingers. "It's even better than I dared hope," Alexa admitted. "I give full credit to the Wilkenses' ad campaign." She nodded at the glossy green poster on the office wall. Highlighted by swirling, bright red hair forming the word Renata, the print dominated the tiny office.

"Quint came by this morning with the demo tape. Have you heard it on the Wolfschmidt yet?" When Alexa shook her head, Renata continued, "It's terrif, but it does mean adjusting our timing a bit to allow for the music. Twick's working with us on it."

"Good," Alexa muttered. Just the word Wolfschmidt gave her a hollow, aching feeling. "I did see Quint though. He tells me the studio already has a backlog of orders just from what little air time the soundtrack's had."

"The money's rolling in—just the way you predicted. Omigosh!" Renata said, checking her watch. "Seven o'clock. Got to run. I have to be at the BBC studios in Ealing at eight. I'm doing another interview."

"Good-night," Alexa called to her as Renata whirled out the office door.

Things couldn't be going better. Everyone thought Alexa had the Midas touch. The ad campaign had come in under budget, and the soundtrack's sales were already taking off. Advance ticket sales had put lines around the block from the first day. She should have been walking on the ceiling, and yet she was miserable.

She stared at Mark's chair, which the snoozing T.S. had had to himself for the last month. The moment she'd said she didn't want him to know, Mark had stalked out the door. She'd called his office, leaving numerous messages, but he'd never returned her calls. She thought about using the private number he'd written on his card but decided against it, sending him a letter instead. In it she'd explained her actions and told him she'd purchased an interest in the soundtrack in his name. She'd received a terse reply from the Triad solicitor stating any further attempts to involve Mr. Kimbrough in her "ventures" would result in legal action.

An hour later Alexa left the theater and went home. She stepped out from the Underground tunnel into a damp black night. How she dreaded the lonely nights. At the theater she tried to shut Mark out of her mind and concentrate on the play. Her invisible companion, he frequently intruded while she worked. What would he do here? What would he think about this? If she didn't drive herself, force herself to go non-stop, his memory threatened to overtake her days as it had the empty nights. Forced to admit she cared for him intensely despite what he'd done to his wife, Alexa faced the eradication of a lifetime's assumptions about love. Could she really have fallen for a fourteen-karat heel—again? The last time she hadn't known—this time she had no excuse.

She gathered her raincoat more closely about her as she hurried through Shepherd's Market. Closed for the evening except for the pubs and cafés, the market was an island of nineteenth-century England surrounded by sophisticated Mayfair with its swank Bond Street shops and enormous Oxford Street department stores. She often shopped here because she enjoyed the quaint shops and stone-paved streets that hadn't given way to twentieth-century modernization or allowed themselves to be cutesied up for tourists.

Although it was only early October, the bite of winter filled the air. By the time she reached the town house, she was thoroughly chilled and it was raining. She fumbled in her purse for the key. A misty halo encircled the moon, diffusing the light across the entrance and making it difficult to see anything. In the distance she could hear the telephone ringing. Her heart skipped several beats before she forced herself to be realistic. Mark wasn't going to call; let the damn thing ring.

Upstairs in her room, the slow, monotonous drip of rain from the eaves was accompanied by an eerie wind, shuddering and moaning its loneliness through the barren trees. She shivered, reluctant to remove her raincoat just yet. Before getting to work on her novel, she needed a hot bath to banish the chill. In the adjacent bathroom Alexa filled the tub and shook Gilbert and Soames bath salts into the hot water before climbing in and settling back. Heaven. Absolute heaven. Her thoughts were wandering over the work she'd already done on her manuscript and what she should do tonight when she heard the phone downstairs ringing.

She slid from the tub, grabbing her robe on the fly and bounding down the stairs. Slipping and almost falling on the polished marble, Alexa came to a breathless, dripping halt just as the phone gave another loud double ring.

"Hello."

"Alexa?" The male voice sounded familiar, but she couldn't quite place it.

"Yes?" she answered, trying to keep the disappointment from her voice.

"This is Warren."

Warren? She did a quick mental calendar check and decided Linda was still in Paris buying for the boutique. "How are you?"

"Great. I spoke with Linda this morning. She told me to make you stop working so hard and have dinner with me. Have you already eaten?"

"No."

"How about Le Caprice," Warren said, naming one of the poshest restaurants in London. "Should I pick you up in an hour?"

By the time they'd entered Le Caprice, the "in" spot for the affluent younger set in St. James's, Warren had Alexa smiling and laughing. His infectious humor and his open, engaging manner made Alexa aware of how incredibly lucky her friend was. The glow in his warm brown eyes as he said Linda's name told Alexa all she needed to know. No matter how vile her friend's past behavior, Warren had forgiven her.

"Alexa, I'm about to do something I've never done before, and that is stick my nose in Mark's business," Warren said, his buoyant personality suddenly grave. "No one knows I'm discussing this with you. I don't want anyone to find out, not even Linda. My regard for Mark's friendship is too great."

"All right. What's the problem?"

"I hoped you could tell me. I thought perhaps you two had something going, but Mark refuses to discuss you."

"He's never going to speak to me again," she said, her voice breaking, "ever."

"Do you want to talk about it?" Warren asked as the waiter came up with the menus.

Briefly and with harsh self-criticism, Alexa explained the situation with the soundtrack to him.

"Wait a minute. Back up. It started long before this, didn't it? When Mark came back from Mexico, he told me he'd met an interesting woman. It was the first time I'd heard him say that in years. Then you appeared at Audrey's party with Steven, and Mark was livid."

"He was?" she asked, feeling a tiny spurt of hope.

Warren smiled and nodded. Alexa was an unusual, complex woman. She'd walked in tonight unimpressed by being given the most important table in the house and had failed to notice when he'd ordered a vintage bottle of Chateau Margaux. She was equally unaware she'd captured the heart of one of Britain's wealthiest and most elusive bachelors.

"What did Mark say when I came with Steven?" Alexa prompted after they'd ordered.

"Nothing. But I know him well enough to tell a lot by looking—at both of you. He financed your play when no one else would, and yet, that night at the restaurant, you were inexcusably nasty. You both behave so volatilely with one another that it's apparent you each care very much for the other."

"I care, but Mark—"

"Go to him. Explain."

"I've called. I've written."

"Eat your dinner before it gets cold," Warren said as their

entrées arrived. He took his fork in his left hand and began eating his Dover sole. Pausing, he asked, "You call what you did trying? Linda cornered me every chance she got."

Alexa forced a bite of venison down. How could she tell Mark's best friend that it was more than just this standing between them? What he'd done to Caroline couldn't be easily explained.

"He may not forgive you immediately. Mark's unbelievably stubborn at times, but he cares. He'll come around. What you did wasn't as bad as marrying someone else and leaving your boyfriend a three-line note." Warren took another bite, chewing thoughtfully, deciding where to begin. "There are a few things you should know about Mark. We met years ago at Bilbrough Hall. Because his family was very poor, Mark was attending on a government scholarship. His father drove a lorry and his mother worked as a piano teacher. Like all prestigious schools here, Bilbrough Hall has a rigid dress code. Mark came in a jacket with pinstripe trousers several inches too short for him. You could have put three fingers between his shirt collar and his neck. The first night at dinner it was apparent he'd never seen more than one fork at a place setting. Snickers echoed up and down his table, and the boys moved away, leaving him. I'd been sitting at another table. I didn't realize what had happened until I looked over and saw this gangly kid staring at his plate and eating alone. You should have seen the look on his face when I came over and sat with him."

"I'll bet," Alexa said, her heart going out to the deserted boy and blessing Warren for his sensitivity.

"It proved to be the best move I've ever made." Warren took a sip of wine. "We became fast friends. He showed everyone. When it came to sports, Mark had no equal—especially soccer. He'd grown up in a tough neighborhood in Manchester while the rest of us had led pampered lives. If you can excel there, you can play anywhere."

"What about his studies?"

"Always at the top of his class."

"Then he made friends after the first weeks?"

"It may be hard for you to understand, being an American, but class distinctions have always been quite important in England. We don't talk about them much anymore, but they're there. Most of the boys accepted Mark—sports is a great equalizer—but a couple of them spent the next years reminding him of his roots. No matter how many awards he won, on the field and off, they managed to let him know they hadn't forgotten."

"Did it bother him?"

"He never let it show. At Parents Day he proudly introduced his father and mother to everyone. But whenever there was a party, Jason and Steven made certain all the girls knew how poor he was. At that age girls can be quite snobbish."

"Jason Talbott and Steven Hunter?" Alexa asked, incredulous.

"Didn't Mark tell you? The four of us have never gotten along. It's always been us against them. Of course, we're all too old for that now."

"You mean Jason and Steven actually did things like that?"

"Definitely, right up to graduation day. Mark and I went on to the London School of Economics, while they joined the *sans souci* set. We haven't seen much of them in years. So when you moved in with Steven, Mark was shocked."

Alexa sighed, "I didn't realize. I really liked Mark in Mexico, but when I came here he seemed so different. Cold, rude. I've never slept with Steven," Alexa felt compelled to explain. "I'm using his town house. Nothing more."

"Does Mark know that?"

"He never asked."

"Go to him. Explain all this. Put all your cards on the table and give him a chance."

"No. I care but maybe it's better this way," she said, trying to swallow the lump in her throat. "I'll get over it. If he feels anything at all, it'll pass. I'm not denying I've been in the wrong, but I don't think I could accept what he did to Caroline."

"What are you talking about?"

When Alexa said that Mark had used Caroline's money and left her, Warren slowly shook his head. "Alexa, what you've heard was the tabloid version of their divorce. That wasn't the way it happened at all. Mark met Caroline when she returned from some finishing school in Switzerland and was living with a group of girls in London. Blond, beautiful, blue-eyed, and blue-blooded pretty much described her. They began dating, but no one thought it would last. Caroline was a compulsive shopper and partygoer; she had no other interest in life. I thought Mark would be bored with her in two minutes. I was wrong. He looked into those baby blues and was smitten. Then I thought she'd tire of him; he didn't have enough money to run with her set. Again I was wrong. Apparently Mark has other qualities women appreciate."

Alexa felt her cheeks warm but kept her tone cool. "What did her parents think?"

"At first they thought it was a phase and she'd get over it. But when Caroline brought Mark home and had the audacity to introduce him at a family gathering, her father forbid her to see him." Warren slowly shook his head. "Frankly I think that cinched it. Nothing is more tantalizing than forbidden fruit. If her father had ignored the situation, I'm certain she'd have grown tired of Mark. He was far too intellectual for her and too poor."

"But surely he saw something in her . . . besides her obvious assets," Alexa said. "Hadn't he dated much before?"

"Quite a bit actually. Women have always found him attractive, even the snobs. Caroline hung on him, made him feel important. He once told me that she really needed him."

"They married without her parents' permission?"

"No, they gave it, reluctantly I assume. They threw an enormous bash of a wedding. I hoped for the best and prayed the marriage would work out. But Caroline soon tired of living on a tight budget in a flat that was one cut above a bedsitter. She spent money they didn't have and complained, but Mark put up with it. He thought Caroline needed those things because she'd always had them. He worked nonstop building a small inheritance from some distant relative into an empire. He never took a pound from the Hamptons, although they wanted to put him into business. And he refused to let Caroline use her sizable trust."

"He didn't marry her for her money?" Alexa whispered, numb despair coming over her at this updated version of reality.

"Absolutely not. And by the time they divorced, Mark had made a good deal of money. He settled a large sum on her to make certain she was comfortable."

"Why did they split? If he was making the money to support her lifestyle, she should have been happy."

"Understand one thing. Mark Kimbrough is an insular man; it's nearly impossible to get him to discuss sensitive matters. He never told me exactly what happened, but he caught Caroline cheating on him; and he left her."

"Oh, no," she muttered, realizing they had more in common than she'd ever suspected.

"At first he heard nothing from Caroline, but then things with her lover went awry. He never told me who it was, but I think he was a French count she'd met in Marbella earlier that summer. At any rate, she began calling his office and my town house, where he was living. She cried and pleaded with him to come home, but he never gave in."

"But if he loved her . . ." Alexa pushed her plate away a fraction of an inch and the waiter hovering at a discreet distance instantly removed it.

"He did mention that if he reconciled with Caroline, it would only happen again and again."

A melancholy silence followed as Alexa sat with a deep, aching sense of loss that went beyond words. She'd constantly misjudged Mark, blaming him for what he'd never done.

"About a year after the divorce Caroline was killed in a motorcar accident. Mark blamed himself because she began drinking heavily right after he left her. She was dead drunk that night when she got behind the wheel. Someone tipped the newspapers that Caroline Hampton had been tragically killed because she was unable to recover from Mark's leaving her. The tabloids speculated he'd made his fortune from her trust fund. Later Edward Hampton, her father, refuted this in several interviews, but no one seems to remember those things."

"Surely none of his friends believed it."

"Of course not. A great many people knew better, but it left him quite bitter about life—and women. Until you came along."

"And I blew it. I really blew it."

"Alexa." Warren took her hand, squeezing it gently. "Go to him."

# Chapter 24

"Hello, luv."

"When did you get back?" Alexa called to Steven as she came in the living room the following evening.

"I flew in from Rome this afternoon. I've a few days off before we go on location in Khartoum. Thought I'd check in with a few old friends. Do you mind?"

"N-no, of course not. This is your house. Anytime you want to come home—it's just that I hadn't heard from you."

Steven patted the pristine sofa. "Come here, luv. Tell me how things are going."

Alexa plopped down beside him. "Steven, did you know Lloyd's had blacklisted me?"

"I heard something about it, but I assumed it was just a rumor. I suppose I should have investigated, but I was terribly preoccupied with my film. In Rome I heard it was true. I'm sorry." His blue eyes were fixed on her; his sincerity was unmistakable. "It worked out though, didn't it? How's the play going?"

She admired him for telling her the truth. He was extremely self-centered at times, but he'd been immersed in the preproduction scramble on his film. She started to tell Steven he'd been wrong about Mark and Caroline but stopped, remembering Warren had told her how carefully Mark guarded his privacy. If he hadn't told Warren the details of his breakup with Caroline, Mark certainly wouldn't want Steven to know his wife had been cheating on him.

For the next hour Steven listened attentively to every detail about the play. Nodding now and again or laughing at the appropriate moment, he made it seem as if nothing in the world could be more important than what she was saying. When she finished telling him all about the play, he insisted on taking her to dinner. She hesitated; she'd planned on going to see Mark tonight. But what would one more day matter? Mark undoubtedly had a date tonight anyway.

Steven took her to Annabels, the exclusive membership club on Berkeley Square. No sign marked the entrance, only a discreet brass plaque with the number 44. Alexa noted Steven and the doorman were on a first-name basis as they side-stepped the group at the door and were immediately seated. Steven spent the first hour they were there hopping up and down greeting friends he hadn't seen in weeks. Alexa indulged him; Steven needed this. By the time their food arrived, Alexa was thoroughly enjoying herself. She'd been too long without someone to talk to, she told herself.

"How's your film going?" she asked, realizing he hadn't mentioned it.

"I'm running a bit short of money," he answered.

"Then why are we here?"

"This dinner wouldn't pay for a single costume. Besides, by the time the bill comes in, I'll have plenty of money. This is just a temporary shortfall. The studio work cost me a bit more than I anticipated. Then the Italians went on strike. Their labor disputes set us back several weeks."

"Oh, Steven, what a mess."

"I was hoping you could help me," he said, giving her a forlorn, little-boy-lost expression. "Could you lend me some money?"

Suddenly she knew why he'd been so nice and why he'd invited her to dinner. He wanted to borrow money. "I haven't a spare pound. I put all my money into the play, remember?"

"Of course." He gave her a stunning smile, assuring her he should have chosen a career in politics. "I have a very lucrative investment that will pay off shortly. You'd get your money back plus an enormous interest payment. Couldn't you lend me funds from the play's account? Kimbrough wouldn't have to know."

"No, I can't risk it. Renata's career is riding on this play. Movie financing is a monetary twilight zone. Anything could happen to your production and you might need all your investment to keep going, and I would have to shut down the play if you didn't repay me. Besides, it's dishonest. I won't do it."

The next day, Saturday, proved to be one of the longest days of her life. Knowing Steven was sulking around the house, she kept to her room until she could no longer stand it. She slipped out and walked up South Street to Park Lane, while the autumn sunshine and westerly breeze followed her into Hyde Park. Squads of late-fall chrysanthemums bordered the paths as the usual jog and pony show captivated her. After strolling for hours, Alexa consumed her umpteenth Cranks salad for dinner and took in a neighborhood play before returning to Steven's town house. He'd told her he had an eleven-o'clock flight to Rome. He should have left for Heathrow by now.

As soon as Alexa opened the door to her room, she knew something was wrong. She'd set up one corner of the room as an office, placing her portable typewriter on the chintz-covered table. Against the wall she'd piled the notes and books she was using to write the novel she'd promised to deliver. The overstuffed chair served as the receptacle for whatever she carried home from the theater. On Friday she'd tossed the play's ledger, her idea notebook, checkbook, and computer runs onto the chair. Someone had neatly, very neatly, stacked everything on the chair. Why? No one ever came into her room except the Pakistani daily, Mrs. Raj, but she'd not worked today. It could only have been Steven unless he'd had someone over while she'd been out. But what had he been looking for? She'd told him everything about the play.

She considered the possibilities for a moment and then yanked the checkbook from beneath the computer reports. She flipped through the pages until she found her last entry. The next check was in place, waiting for her to fill in the blanks. She tossed the checkbook down, deciding her imagination was running amok. Just because Steven had asked to borrow money didn't mean he'd take a check when she refused to help him. She stood there wondering why someone had touched her things. She seized the checkbook once more and methodically turned the pages, one by one. Two thirds of the way through, she discovered the missing sheet. Someone had removed an entire page of checks from the notebook-style checkbook.

Her stomach twisted when she remembered handing Steven a bank signature card. As coproducer he was authorized to sign checks. Of course that had been a formality. He wouldn't be around to do any of the accounting. But legally he could take the money and there wasn't a damn thing she could do about it.

She rummaged through her Vuitton and came up with Mark's business card. Clutching it, she raced down the stairs. Almost midnight. Would he be home? Would he have someone with him? More important, would he help her? She slid to a stop in front of the phone. As she dialed, she tried to think what would be the best way to approach him.

After the first ring he answered, "Kimbrough here."

Just the sound of his voice sent a sharp ache through her body.

"Kimbrough here," he repeated impatiently.

"M-Mark, it's Alexa. Please don't hang up. Something has happened. I need to see you right away. May I come over?"

Dead silence. Her stomach fluttered.

"It's the middle of the night. Can't this wait?"

"Tomorrow may be too late."

"All right," he said before the dull buzz on the line told her he'd hung up.

Running full speed up South Audley Street, Alexa was approaching the American embassy on Grosvenor Square when a crack of thunder and a jagged arc of lightning illuminated the enormous eagle perched on the embassy's roof. Where in hell had this storm come from? The harvest moon, which had earlier smiled on her from a star-spangled sky, had vanished, leaving a thick, angry mass of clouds. Instantly the rain fell in sheets with no visible room between the drops, making it all but impossible to see through the curtain of water. She raced up Lees Place past the wrought-iron gate marked Shepherd's Close and stopped in front of Number 8 Lees Place.

She stood under the small portico. A shaft of blue-white lightning flooded the entrance, revealing the graceful Georgian door flanked by narrow panels of leaded glass and the graceful fanlight above the door. She clanged the heavy brass knocker and waited, shivering. It took a few minutes before the door swung open.

Heart-stoppingly handsome, Mark stood there casually attired in navy corduroy slacks topped by a nubby blue sweater that added bulk to his frame. The startled expression on his face told her she looked like something T.S. had found in an alley.

"Come in."

Her Reeboks squishing noisily, she walked in and stood there dripping all over his polished parquet floor. "Mark, I need help."

He raised his hand to stop her. "Before you catch pneumonia run upstairs and get out of those clothes. Bathroom's second door on the left. Leave your things outside the door and I'll toss them in the dryer. You can wear the robe hanging on the back of the door."

Her squeaking shoes echoing across the stunning entry with its vaulted ceiling and multiprismed chandelier, Alexa climbed the walnut staircase to the next floor. Inside the bathroom decorated in masculine tones of chocolate and camel, she pulled off her clothes. Teeth chattering, she put them outside the door. She was toweling off when Mark knocked.

"Blow dryer's in the drawer," he said.

She put on the heavy navy terry-cloth robe and inhaled sharply as the woodsy aroma of his aftershave wafted up at her. No matter what he said about the checks, she wasn't leaving here until she'd apologized to him. Again.

She found the dryer, but when she picked it up, she discovered it was still warm. Turning, she looked at the shower door. Water droplets covered the beige tile. While she ran through the storm, he'd quickly showered. So he hadn't been out with anyone.

She walked into his study, the robe trailing below her knees and draping from her arms like a monk's habit.

"Well," Mark asked. "What's so important?"

"I'm about to lose all the play's money."

"I'm through helping you."

"Please," she said, "hear me out. I need your advice."

He gestured to the burgundy sofa in front of the fire, indicating she should sit. She eased into the butter-soft suede, curling her chilled feet under her. He sat in a chair next to the couch and eyed her balefully while she explained the situation to him.

"What do you want from me?"

"Do you know of any way I can stop Steven from cashing those checks?"

Silence. His eyes roamed the bookshelves lined with leather-bound volumes while she found a tangled curl and twined it around her finger.

"I can't help you. I'll get your clothes," he said. "They should be dry by now. Then I'll drive you home."

He returned with her things, handing them to her without a word.

"Mark, isn't there something I can do to protect the play? I'm not asking for myself, but dozens of people are relying on me to make this play a success. If you can think of anything, anything at all, tell me."

"Get dressed."

She hugged the bundle to her chest. His cold dismissal was unmistakable, but she refused to leave without telling him how she felt. "I'd like you to know I'm sorry for what I did. I should never have tried to deceive you. You were right that day on the beach in Mexico when you said it takes time to get over the hurt of a divorce. Things from my past and things I'd heard about you colored my judgment. I know I never should have diverted the funds, but I did it to help the production, not for personal gain." Through a shimmer of unfallen tears, she finished, "What else can I say except I was wrong and I'm sorry."

He shrugged and walked away.

She fled down the hall and into the bathroom, leaning against the closed door. She squeezed her eyes shut, but hot tears plummeted down her cheeks. She dashed to the basin and splashed cold water on her face until the tears stopped.

When she returned to the study, she found Mark sitting at his desk. His shoulders squared and his jaw set, he bent over a multipage document. "Come here."

Alexa went over to the desk and stood there. She waited,

staring down at the toes of her Reeboks, which had curled in the dryer.

"There might be a way out of this," he said, scribbling on a legal pad. "You'd have to agree to it."

"Anything," she whispered.

"There's a clause in your contract stating if there is a misappropriation of funds or a failure to operate within the legal guidelines, the agreement can be terminated. Technically this gives me the right to withdraw my funds, thus closing the play. What I could do is let you sign a document admitting your misappropriation. I could remove both you and Steven from the production. Another production company could be formed and the play would go on. What do you think?"

Like a pendulum gone wild, her thoughts swung from preserving her position as producer to saving the play.

"Let's do it," she said. She stood there, sick at heart. She'd get credit for her work as writer, but all her hours putting the production together would go unheralded.

"Is there any way Steven can withdraw the funds before you take care of this?" she asked.

"No, tomorrow's Sunday. He can't do anything until Monday. Before the bank opens I'll have my solicitor ready the necessary documents to close the account. You come by tomorrow afternoon to sign the legal papers confessing your misappropriation."

"All right. Thank you."

"Understand one thing," he said. "I'm doing this for Renata and Twick and the others who've operated professionally and don't deserve to have this play close. If it had been you alone, I'd have enacted this clause when I discovered the other sound system."

His vehemence startled her, leaving her momentarily speechless. Of course he was angry. He had every right to be.

His next words came out from between clenched teeth. "I don't want Steven Hunter to have anything more to do with this play. Am I understood?"

# Chapter 25

"A badge?" Alexa asked when the attendant in the Triad lobby told her she couldn't go upstairs without proper identification. She wondered if Mark was carrying this security thing too far. In the three weeks she'd been a Triad employee, the once-quaint lobby had been taken over by an attendant-guard who refused to permit anyone to enter without strictly checking their identification.

"Yes, miss," he replied and nodded to a man standing nearby. "Go with Mr. Sargent."

As she followed him, she noted the beautiful oil by Hogarth had been replaced by a botanical print. On the next floor the security offices had been shoehorned into a small room that had evidently been previously used to store supplies. In one corner a Polaroid camera had been mounted on a tripod and a laminating machine stood atop the small desk.

"Is all this necessary?" Alexa asked as the bright light clicked on and Mr. Sargent took several shots. "I just came by to get the payroll checks signed."

"Yes, with all the bombings and terrorist threats in London these days, one can't be too careful."

While they waited for the shots to develop, Mr. Sargent asked her a few questions "for his files." The basics had been covered in the personnel record that she'd filled out when Mark formed a new production company naming Alexa as producer and himself as coproducer, excluding Steven completely.

"Choose one," Mr. Sargent said, indicating the color snapshots.

Alexa grimaced and chose the one in which she looked the least wide eyed and startled. Watching him clip the photo to size and laminate it into a badge, Alexa thought about Nigel Hunter. He certainly hadn't seemed to care that the production company had been dissolved. She still regretted she'd been unable to explain the situation to him in person. She'd tried to reach him for days, but he was always "unavailable." When he finally returned her calls, he sounded indifferent, disinterested. She'd expected one of Nigel's usual blustery lectures, but it hadn't come. No, he hadn't known Steven's film was short of funds. No, he hadn't seen Steven when he had been in town. And no, he hadn't heard from Steven since he'd arrived in Khartoum.

The interoffice telephone buzzed and Mr. Sargent picked it up. "Security." He nodded his sandy head. "Yes, she is." His brown eyes widened for a moment and then narrowed as he focused on her as if noticing her for the first time. "I'll tell her." He replaced the receiver, saying, "Mr. Kimbrough wants to see you as soon as you're finished here. I'll escort you upstairs."

Alexa kept a composed look on her face but couldn't stop her pulse from accelerating. What did he want?

"You're to go right in," Mr. Coombs said after she'd been taken to the executive offices.

Alexa smoothed her tangled hair, which, as the photographs had clearly disclosed, had been less than artfully rearranged by the stiff November breeze, and walked through the door. Seated at his desk, Mark had the telephone braced between his head and his shoulder while he rapidly flipped through a document. He motioned for her to take the chair opposite his desk.

Under the warm coat she was still wearing, a tiny shiver gripped her as she sat down. Her instinctive response to him was unbelievably powerful. He was special. She'd been a fool not to recognize it from the very first.

"Alexa," he said as he replaced the receiver. "I had a call from Warren and Linda this morning. They're getting married."

"Wonderful!" she blurted out, but the unenthusiastic look on his face told her he had his doubts. "I knew it. They were meant for each other, even if it's taken all these years for them to get together. When?"

"This evening at seven," he said, his voice flat. "That's why I called you in. They'd like us to be there."

"Sure." Alexa went ahead and let her voice sparkle. Even if Mark disapproved, she refused to let him dampen her happiness for Linda. "Where? Just tell me and I'll be there."

"Torquay—a village down the coast. I'll drive us, but it'll take us a few hours to get there. We'll need to leave straight away if we're going to make it. Go home and pack what you need. We'll be staying the night at the Boughwood Inn. My helicopter will pick me up at dawn because I have to leave for Australia. I'll need you to return my car to Triad's garage."

Alexa splurged on a taxi to get home quickly and pack. When she called the Regency to tell them she wouldn't be back, Bob Wickson, the new assistant Triad insisted she employ, told her Jason Talbott was trying to reach her. She almost didn't take the time to call him, but decided he might have a message from Steven.

"Jason? Alexa MacKenzie returning your call."

"How are you?" Jason's voice was velvet.

"Fine. How can I help you?" Alexa asked as she mentally reviewed her wardrobe, trying to decide what to wear to the wedding.

"Why so businesslike? Haven't you time for an old friend?"

*Friend?* "Jason, have you heard from Steven? Is that why you called?" The checks had never been cashed, and a part of Alexa still wanted to believe Steven wasn't at fault.

"No, I called to tell you I'm picking you up for dinner at eight. It's about time we got to know each other better."

"I-I can't. I'm—" Her thoughts whirled, seeking a graceful way out without mentioning the wedding. She knew Warren and Linda wouldn't want Jason Talbott to know about the marriage even before they'd told their family and friends. "I'm going to the country. Thanks for asking."

"When will you be back?" he asked impatiently. "We'll go out then."

"I'm not certain. I'll call you," she said and hung up without waiting for him to reply. She tossed the paper with his number on it into the wastepaper basket before she bounded up the stairs to pack.

Alexa stood before the mirror holding the exquisite green dress Linda had given her against her oversized sweater. It really was too dressy and far too revealing for a seven-o'clock wedding, but she hadn't anything else to wear. After all, Linda had given it to her and said save it for something special. This was special. Maybe if she wore her black velvet jacket over it. That's it, she decided, slipping the jacket from the armoire. If she kept the jacket on the entire time, the dress would appear less formal and less revealing.

The Jaguar roared westward along the A30 as Alexa smoothed her damp palms on her wool slacks. So far Mark had failed to say anything more than was absolutely necessary. She realized this ride might be her only chance to talk to him, and yet she had no idea where to begin. He had his eyes fixed dead ahead although the afternoon traffic was light.

"Torky, you said?" Alexa asked nervously. "I've never even heard of it. What's it like?"

"T-o-r-q-u-a-y. We pronounce it so it rhymes with porky. It's one of the more popular holiday resorts on the Devon coast." He turned, giving her a flash of teeth that was supposed to pass for a smile. "You should be at home there. Palm trees and balmy breezes. Year round it has the mildest climate in England."

"Really? I've been meaning to get out this way but there hasn't been time."

"There's lots more to England than London," Mark said, returning his gaze to the road. "Most Americans never take the time to discover the best of the U.K."

Alexa knew his comment was directed at her, but she met his fire with patience, knowing she deserved it and much, much more. "I plan to—"

"Why don't you take the car and drive around Devon over the weekend? Just because I'm leaving doesn't mean you have to come back. Drive out on Dartmoor. It's one of our largest national parks. Just don't get lost."

For the next two hours Alexa kept the mostly one-sided conversation going. She purposely avoided any topic that would annoy Mark. Concentrating on questions about history and geographical features, Alexa forced him to talk to her. He answered her questions tersely and unenthusiastically.

Mark detoured from the main route to drive along the coast and show her the red sandstone cliffs, pebble beaches, and sandy coves that characterized the Devon shoreline. They drove into Torquay at almost five o'clock.

"Imagine the shocked citizenry when Sir Francis Drake sailed in here with the first ship he'd captured from the Spanish Armada," Mark said.

"Here?" Alexa asked.

"Not exactly," he said, pointing across the water. "Across Tor Bay at Brixham, but everyone in Torquay could see the ships."

"It looks more Mediterranean than British," commented Alexa as she peered out at the waterfront harbor with its sailboats and yachts. The palm-lined waterfront walk led to a park and pavilion built in the British Raj–style architecture of Queen Victoria's era.

"You're right, it is reminiscent of Cannes or St. Tropez. Its prevailing wind is from the southwest, which gives this part of the coast a milder climate than most of England enjoys," Mark said as he turned the Jaguar up the hillside road overlooking the harbor to a small, postcard-perfect fieldstone inn.

After they were shown their rooms, they found Linda and Warren in the tiny dining room of the Boughwood Inn having tea. They looked so much in love that Alexa couldn't resist peeking at Mark to judge his reaction. His open, relaxed smile contradicted his earlier skepticism.

"Congratulations," Mark said, kissing Linda on the cheek before turning to shake Warren's hand.

"Sit and have tea with us," Warren smiled, his warm brown eyes glowing. "How was the drive?"

"Super," Alexa answered. "I never knew how beautiful the Devon coast was."

"It's our favorite area. We've let a small cottage at

Brixham," Linda said. "We're staying there a week before returning to London."

"Then we're taking Holly with us to Hong Kong while I take care of some business," Warren told them as one of the staff placed a fresh pot of tea and two more cups on the table. "I guess I'm going to be an instant father."

"You'll be perfect," Linda assured him. "Warren and I feel the three of us need the time together to bond as a family. Since Ian and I were divorced, Holly's spent most of the time in my brother's house. I'm afraid it's quite confusing to a child to have a father who has returned to Australia, an uncle who's been like a father, and now, a new father. It'll take some time, but we're going to do things right this time." She didn't add Warren's acceptance of Holly had been the last hurdle concerning her. Would he be able to accept another man's child? He had. And the way Holly delighted in him removed all Linda's doubts.

"Sounds good," Mark said, stirring sugar into his tea and adding a generous splash of thick cream. "When will you return?"

"Not until the first of the year," Warren said. "After I've finished working in Hong Kong, I'm taking my girls to Chamonix. It's time Holly learned to ski."

Alexa stared into her teacup, wondering where she'd be at Christmas. With Renata and Giles in the United States for the multicity screenings of *The Last Chance,* qualifying it for Academy Award consideration, and Linda off with Warren, Alexa suddenly felt lonelier than ever. Once the theater troupe went on hiatus, she'd have time to concentrate on writing her book, but somehow that had no appeal for her.

"Alexa, let's go upstairs and get ready. We'll be down in an hour," Linda smiled over her shoulder at Warren as Alexa led her from the room.

While they climbed the narrow stairs to Linda's room, Alexa asked, "What's the plan? Mark said you'd be married at seven."

"Then we're going to celebrate by dining with our best friends before we drive on to Brixham."

"Tonight?" Alexa asked. "You're not staying here tonight?"

"No, is that a problem?"

"No-No, of course not. I just assumed . . ."

Linda knew exactly what Mark and Alexa had both thought. She and Warren deliberately planned on leaving them alone after the wedding.

"Alexa, do you think you could help me by moving some of the boxes I left at my brother's into Warren's town house? We'll be living there after the first of the year. I'd ask my brother, but he's done so much for me and my sister-in-law will be busy managing Changes."

"Sure, no problem. We go on hiatus the first week in December. Could I do it after that?"

"Anytime really. There's a key at my brother's. Why don't you stay at Warren's—I mean our—town house during December? If Steven comes back, you might not be comfortable where you are."

"Thanks, I may do that even though I doubt he'll come back. He doesn't wrap until just before Christmas. He mentioned something about holidaying in Marbella with Jason after that."

Linda opened the door to an antique-filled room overlooking the harbor. It was a smaller version of the charming room where Alexa had put her things. Across the bed lay an ivory raw silk suit with a slim skirt and a jacket with a saucy peplum flounce.

"How beautiful," Alexa exclaimed. "I'm not sure I've brought the appropriate dress. I'm wearing the green dress you gave me. I know it's too formal for this, so I'm wearing my black velvet jacket with the silk ruching. That should keep it from being too—" The shocked look on Linda's face stopped Alexa.

"Don't you dare!" Linda shook a beautifully manicured finger at her. "It's perfect for the wedding just the way it is. If you're going to be cold, wear the jacket over your shoulders when you're outside only. Otherwise carry it over your arm. You'll ruin the whole effect of that gown if you cover it up with a jacket. There isn't a man alive who can resist you in that dress. Speaking of resisting, how's it going with Mark?"

"It's not," Alexa sighed. "He's written me off. All the way down here I tried talking to him— believe me he's no longer interested. If he ever was."

"That's because you've lost your instruction manual," Linda said, drawing out a Janet Reger special, a wispy lace bra-and-panty set. Following it came a matching silk slip with transparent lace insets across the chest.

"Manual?" Alexa mumbled, staring at the black silk negligee Linda tossed on the bed. The openwork lace bodice was held together by three narrow satin bows. Alexa had visited Janet's shop, just down the street from Changes, and knew these creations were exorbitantly expensive. Linda wasn't usually this frivolous. But why not? This was her honeymoon —already postponed too many years.

"The instruction manual in womanly wiles, subtitled the art of seduction. Every woman is born with one and adds to it as she moves through life. You must have lost yours. You sat through tea turned away from Mark, not toward him. Never once did you smile at him or flirt." Linda pulled a half dozen more sexy nighties from her suitcase. "What did you tell me when I came home from France? You love him. Remember? Well, find that manual."

"I'll try," Alexa said, wondering if Linda knew just how stubborn Mark Kimbrough could be. "I'd better go get dressed." When she reached the door, Linda called to her and she turned in time to catch the black negligee. "What?"

"It'll be a little long for you, but I doubt he'll notice." She winked.

"But we're not—"

"Alexa, it's hard for a man to remain angry at you when he's making love to you. Believe me, I know."

Mark checked the nick on his chin. It had finally stopped bleeding. He stood back and inspected his image in the small mirror, checking his dark navy suit and burgundy tie. He carefully splayed a matching burgundy handkerchief and tucked it into his breast pocket. He withheld the impulse to ask himself what Alexa would think. If she'd wanted him, she'd have made a move before now to pursue him. Instead, she'd accepted his arrangement of keeping her at a distance without once even trying to see him. It was apparent she wasn't going to be like Linda, who'd chased Warren until he'd let her catch him. Mark thought he'd grown accustomed to the fact she didn't care—until today. The drive down had been longer than he'd anticipated. All she'd talked about was history and geography until he felt like a goddamned tourist manual.

Downstairs, he waited with Warren. Linda and Alexa were already ten minutes late.

"What time are you supposed to be——" Mark stopped in midsentence. Coming down the stairs, Alexa was wearing that green number he'd bought for her. Even sexier than he remembered, the gown clung provocatively to every curve. Christ! He quickly looked away, concentrating on the floral arrangement gracing the Pembroke table to his left.

"You look beautiful," Warren said, admiring the way the ivory suit followed the graceful curve of Linda's hips and emphasized her long legs. Not only was she a beautiful woman, but she was the only one for him. Time had proven that. In a way, the last years with all their heartaches, made him appreciate her all the more. She'd changed—for the better—in so many ways.

Alexa handed Mark her coat and he stood there a moment feeling foolish before he realized she wanted him to help her put it on. She let him slip it over her shoulders before looking up with a sultry promise in her eyes and murmuring a breathy thanks.

When they climbed into the back seat of Warren's Rolls for the short ride to the chapel, Alexa slipped across the leather seat and sat so close to Mark that their thighs touched. Not giving her any encouragement, Mark waited to see what she'd do next.

While Warren and Linda spoke privately with the parson, Alexa and Mark sat in the front pew.

"It's wonderful to see someone you care about happy, isn't it?" Alexa whispered, squeezing his arm and looking up at him with bewitching green eyes.

Mark refused to give her the satisfaction of agreeing with her or looking at her. He stared at his knees but instead caught sight of her shapely ankle and vampy shoe. Her legs were demurely crossed at the knee and she idly swung one foot back and forth. It was difficult to believe even a foot could be sexy, but hers was. Everything about her sent out an electrical pulse. Still, he felt like strangling her when he remembered how she'd tried to deceive him. Then the image of her standing there looking sexy as hell in his bathrobe while she apologized came back to him. He'd let her off the hook—again—by keeping her with the play. He simply didn't have the heart to take it away from her. After all, she was the creative genius behind it. Right now none of that mattered. He wanted her to come to him, to show him she cared. He wasn't making this easy on her—not this time.

"We're ready," Warren said as the parson took his place.

Mark moved up beside Warren while Alexa stood next to Linda. The service began and Linda listened carefully, looking directly into Warren's eyes, promising him a lifetime of love.

A hundred haunting shadows from the past swept over Mark, blocking out the minister's words until Warren nudged him and he remembered to produce the ring.

When the service was over, Warren took Linda in his arms and kissed her for a full minute. Christ! Mark thought, this marriage had better last. Alexa came up beside him. Tears sparkled on her long lashes, making her eyes the same luminous green he remembered from the film clip.

"Here," he said gruffly, handing her a handkerchief and wondering how he could be crazy about a woman who didn't have the sense to remember her umbrella or come to a wedding with a handkerchief.

"Mark." She touched his arm as he started to move away. "Wait for me." She tucked her hand through his arm and gave him a slow, suggestive smile that made his heart flip over.

On the ride to the Fox and Hounds Restaurant, she moved closer and slipped her hand into his. He kept talking but couldn't bank the surge of anticipation he felt. Unable to deny himself her touch, he let her hold his hand. Still, he kept himself in check, barely acknowledging her presence. When he did, he made certain she knew it was because he had no other alternative. Tonight her tight-lipped withdrawal had vanished. She seemed totally oblivious to his indifference because she kept looking at him and smiling entrancingly through lowered lashes.

She handed him her coat to check as soon as they entered the restaurant. He took it deliberately, not looking at the provocative gown, but as he followed her across the restaurant he admired the graceful curve of her bare back as it met the gentle rise of her bottom. He didn't need to see the front to know how seductively her breasts swayed as she walked. And he couldn't help noticing that the men at the tables they passed watched her go by. An unexpected surge of jealousy seized him, but he took care to hide it behind a mask of indifference.

"What should I have?" Alexa asked him after they'd been seated and handed menus. "This seems to be regional fare."

Mark bit back a smile as she used the question as an excuse to inch closer to him on the banquette. While she read the menu he studied her. She'd taken a good deal of care with herself tonight. Her hair had been brushed back over one ear and fastened there with a glitzy comb. She'd taken time to apply makeup, especially eye makeup.

"Devonshire is known for its cream and cheeses and generally hearty country fare. I'd suggest . . ." She looked up at him and he forgot for a moment what it was he'd planned to suggest. ". . . ordering a bottle of champagne for a toast. How about it Warren?"

"Definitely."

Warren was too busy gazing into Linda's blue eyes to handle ordering champagne, so Mark took over and ordered two bottles of the finest, Dom Perignon '53. Then he helped Alexa select a leek soup made fresh with Devon cream and chestnut-stuffed game hen. She again slid her hand through his. Every time he looked at her, his pulse thrummed and his willpower dissolved a little more. The way things were going, he'd be a fool not to let her seduce him tonight.

Linda had a difficult time concentrating on dinner. She was anxious to get to the cottage in Brixham. It wasn't as if they hadn't made love. They had—just this morning. But tonight would be special; they were married. Marriage meant a commitment. A commitment she'd waited years to make.

Across the table Linda saw Alexa had taken her advice. She was practically in Mark's lap, and any fool could see he was loving it despite his aloof attitude. *Keep it up, Alexa, he's worth it.*

After dinner they drove along the shore through a light rain back to the Boughwood Inn. The moon's silvery light kicked across the choppy bay and caught the raindrops as they hit the water.

"Stay here, Linda," Warren said when they pulled up in front of the inn. "I'll get our things. We'd better get to Brixham before the rain gets any worse."

As the men saw to the luggage, Linda squeezed Alexa's hand and winked, whispering, "Stay with it."

Mark helped Warren with the suitcases and returned to find Alexa waiting for him in the small lobby.

"I guess walking on the promenade is out of the question," she said, smiling coquettishly.

Mark shrugged. Walking was the last thing he had on his mind. He took a quick peek at the shadow between her breasts. All through dinner it had been almost impossible to keep up his unapproachable demeanor. Walk? Hell, he wanted to tear that shimmery green dress off her and kiss her until she was breathless. But he refused to make a move.

"Does your room have a fireplace?" she asked. When he nodded, she continued, "Why don't you run upstairs and light it? I'll go into the bar and see if I can get us some cognac."

Mark steeled himself not to look shocked. Christ! She'd just invited herself to his room. His stomach did a backflip. All night he'd been tiptoeing along the edge of a cliff, waiting for her to push him over. And now she had. He hadn't suspected she would have the nerve. "All right," he said when he'd played the moment as long as he could. Hoping his eyes didn't betray him, he turned and went up the stairs.

Mark tossed his jacket and tie onto a chair before he built the fire. As he watched the kindling catch, he couldn't stop the surge of anticipation that was already hardening him. At the thought of slipping that green gown from her luscious breasts and finding those pink nipples beckoning him, he could almost forgive her for anything—almost. He reminded himself not to make this easy for her. Play with her a bit.

Mark ignored the first soft tap on his door. He sat on the loveseat in front of the fire and waited for the second rap.

"Who is it?" he called as if he was expecting any one of a number of friends to drop by.

"Alexa . . . let me in," came the muffled answer.

He sauntered over to the door and opened it. Alexa stood there in a slinky black nightgown. Slit up one side to her thigh, it revealed a sizable portion of her leg. But that was nothing compared to the sheer lace bodice that barely covered her breasts and couldn't begin to conceal her alert nipples.

Three small black bows seemed to be all that was holding the damn thing together.

"Are you going to make me stand in the hall all night?" She smiled, handing him a bottle of cognac and two brandy snifters.

# Chapter 26

"No, come in."

Struggling to regain his composure, Mark took the bottle and glasses. For once the tight, hot knot in his stomach had nothing to do with his persistent business problems. He'd expected almost anything, he thought, as he watched her sashay across the room and make herself comfortable on the loveseat, but not this. She wanted him—no question about it. Now that he had her on the hook, he intended to enjoy her. Warren had been correct. Being pursued could be a thoroughly enjoyable experience—if the right woman was chasing you.

For a moment he stood there awkwardly. Then he remembered the bottle he was holding. Christ! *Le Paradis*. She'd even splurged on his favorite cognac. Mark poured two snifters of the amber liquid and handed her one. He eased himself into the loveseat, making certain to sit as far away from her as the small space allowed.

"Warm it in your hands," he said when he realized she was going to take a sip. He cradled the glass between his palms, showing her what he meant. It was apparent she didn't have much experience with fine cognacs.

"What did you want to talk about?" he said, being deliberately coy.

She shrugged, her green eyes dancing above a saucy smile until she lowered her lashes to study the glass in her hands. While she wasn't looking, Mark noted the sheer black lace couldn't hide the creamy lushness of her full breasts—or her erect nipples. All he'd have to do would be untie one tiny bow—

"Thanks for Bob Wickson." Alexa said, looking up unexpectedly and catching him. "He's making my job much easier. Now I don't have to take work home at night. I'm able to write in the evenings. I should have no trouble making my May deadline."

"I'm glad you weren't threatened by him." Mark pulled his gaze back to her eyes, velvet-soft in the firelight. "You know he's a distant cousin's kid, don't you?" Fixing wide green eyes on him, she nodded and he continued, "You'd be astonished at the long-lost relatives who'll find you once you become wealthy. But I really don't mind. Bob will be an excellent manager one day. I thought the play would be a good place for him to get experience."

"Has Steven tried to cash any of the checks?" When he shook his head, she added, "I'm hoping he won't. It'll restore my faith in people."

Mark refrained from commenting. Nothing Steven Hunter did could restore Mark's faith in him. "Do you expect him home for the screening of *The Last Chance?*"

Alexa shook her head, tossing a floss of golden hair across her lace-covered shoulders. "He'll be on location right up to Christmas."

"What about Nigel? Have you seen him?"

"N-no, I haven't seen him in months."

Mark took a sip of the cognac. Like warm silk it slid down his throat, leaving a golden afterglow. Where the hell was Nigel these days? No one seemed to have seen much of him since they'd returned from Mexico. Mark recalled their conversation about Alexa's outtakes. Nigel had assured him it had been handled. Catching Alexa's eye over the rim of his glass, Mark decided he'd give Nigel another call. Although the editing had long since been completed, the final cut signed off, and the private screening date set, it never hurt to double check.

"Are you nervous about the screening?"

"Yes," she said, "and no. Giles told me it's been expertly cut. My scene won't reveal any more of me than was absolutely necessary." She paused and took a sip of cognac. "I'm still concerned. Just the idea that I'll appear nude on film still upsets me."

"I'd never know it." Mark twisted the knife, knowing how vulnerable she was on the subject. "Judging from the dress you wore tonight and this getup."

"You didn't like the green dress?"

The hurt look in her eyes forced him to backtrack. "It was beautiful, but too revealing. It's nothing compared to what you have on now. Do you always come to a man's room dressed like a pro?"

"I've never come into a man's room dressed like this. I wore this just for you. . . . You must know you're special."

"If I'm so special," he said, unable to stop himself, "why didn't you return my calls to Mexico? Why didn't—"

She catapulted herself across the small space and came to rest across his lap, bumping his hand and spilling the cognac on his trousers.

"You called? You *really* called?" she said, throwing her arms around him and hugging him.

"Of course I called. A dozen times at least. Didn't you get my messages?"

"No." The shocked look of disbelief in her wide green eyes told him she was telling the truth. "The hotel must have . . . It doesn't matter. What counts is you did call." She leaned forward and softly kissed him.

"Alexa, why did you move in with Steven?"

Without hesitating she told him about her divorce and her financial predicament. She'd gone through much more than he'd ever realized. Her confession banished the doubts he'd harbored for months. While she talked, he couldn't resist stroking her rounded bottom. Sliding his hand over the filmy silk, he resisted the temptation to slip his hand into the slit that exposed her thigh. All day he'd wanted to take her into his arms and now here she was. Nothing could be sweeter than touching her while she talked. But it wasn't enough. Not nearly.

"There's never been anything physical between us," she finished. "It's always been business."

"And what is it between us?" he asked.

"Whatever you want it to be."

Those silken syllables, spoken with incredible softness, caused a thick, tight knot to lodge in his chest. Backlit by the fire, her hair formed a glowing nimbus around her face. He had to steel himself against her overwhelming power.

"It's up to you. Show me what you want," he said.

Staring with misty green eyes at him, she reached up and brushed his cheek with her fingertips. Her hand slid into his hair, winding the loose curls around her fingers. She drew his head closer, her flowery scent twining around him. Her touch had a delicacy he hadn't remembered. Without moving he let her kiss him. Her tongue traced his lower lip, caressing it and urging him to open his mouth. She fluttered her tongue, demanding he let her in. But he held his ground, making her work for it. She sat up in his lap, pressing herself against him with uninhibited eagerness. Through his shirt he could feel the full mounds of her breasts and the pulsing of her peaked nipples. Involuntarily he lowered his jaw and her tongue darted forward, searching for his.

For some minutes she seemed to be content to kiss him, long and lingeringly, but with undisguised passion. The longer she kissed him, her tongue tangling with his, the more he allowed his inhibitions to uncoil. Then she drew back, breathing heavily, and began unfastening the row of buttons on his shirt. All the while she kept her other hand twined through his hair, caressing the back of his neck. A warm ache built steadily in his groin, but he kept his arms loosely clasped around her, letting her take charge.

"Take it off," she commanded when she'd unfastened the last button.

He shrugged out of his shirt and tossed it aside. She made a throaty sound, almost like a purr, and reached forward to touch his chest. He'd never considered the abundance of hair on his chest to be particularly attractive. But she seemed fascinated by its denseness, because she kept running her fingers through it, bringing it upright. Her fingers worked like magic, fluffing the matted hair and stiffening his erection until he jabbed into the soft underside of her thigh as she lay across his lap.

While she worked on his chest, curling the hair through her

fingers with tantalizing slowness, he watched the rounded crests of her breasts beneath the black lace. They were so minimally covered he could see the dusky pink aureole around her burgeoning nipples. He longed to lower his head to her breasts but reminded himself this was her show.

He had no idea what she was going to do until she reached for the bows holding her gown together. With three quick snaps of her wrist, she released them. Her breasts sprang forward, lush and full with deliciously peaked nipples. She shifted on his lap, changing the angle of her body until she faced him. With heavy-lidded eyes, she inhaled sharply and moved forward, forcing her erect nipples through the nest of curls on his chest until they met his bare skin. Then she moved languidly up and down, back and forth, brushing the taut nubs through the tight curls. Spasms of heat shot from his groin, sending ribbons of desire through his entire body.

"You have a wonderful chest," she whispered as she moved to kiss him once more.

Mesmerized by her eyes, her mouth, her touch, and the thousands of feelings she aroused in him, he couldn't keep his hands off her. He ran one hand up her leg and under the silk negligee.

She pushed his hand away. "Mustn't touch. Let me show you—"

"How about showing me on the bed?" he managed to say.

She stood up and slowly shimmied until the whisper of black silk dropped to the floor. His heart skipped two beats and then began to trip erratically. From the golden tumble of her hair as it fell across her full breasts to the darker blond triangle of curls capping her thighs, she was everything he'd ever wanted in a woman. Inwardly he smiled. Last time he'd seen her she'd been all one color. Now faint traces of bikini lines left tantalizing white patches of skin. Extending her small hand for his larger one, she pulled him upright.

She led him to the canopied bed and he stood there while she fumbled with his belt. When she finally unhooked it, she ran her hand slowly downward, circling his shaft and squeezing it before she unzipped his trousers. It was impossible to count the beats of his heart as it quickened even more. He let his pants drop to the floor and stood there watching her tugging at his shorts. He chuckled at the startled look on her face when his prick sprang free. She recovered, returning his smile and giving him a little shove to indicate he should be on the bed. He flopped backward saying, "I hate making love with my shoes on."

She jerked his loafers from his feet and peeled his socks off before climbing onto the bed beside him. Her body pressed against his, a mass of golden curls fanning out across his chest. With aching slowness, she kissed his chest, nipping playfully as she moved downward. Changing positions, she inched lower, tracing lazy circles across his taut stomach with the liquid tip of her tongue. She slid lower and his breath caught and he automatically tightened his groin muscles. Bending forward she sent a fall of rumpled curls across his thighs as she stroked his turgid shaft with her fingertips. Her lips seared across his inner thigh. Hot and moist, her mouth closed around him. He threw his head back, expelling his breath in a long sigh. The sweet suction sent a scarlet rush of heat through his entire body.

He reached down and caressed her head, running his fingers through her hair. He'd been too long without her to take much of this. "Come here," he said, pulling her upright. The glow of the fire warmed her skin to a golden honey color as she gazed down at him. Undisguised love in her eyes, she moved over him, her satiny legs straddling his. His breath caught and held as he guided her down while he drove sharply upward, filling her.

Christ! She was tight. Ready for him, no doubt about it, but tight—even tighter than he'd remembered. She wriggled forward and dipped her head to kiss him. When she sat upright again, her bare breasts swaying from side to side, she rhythmically moved up and down. He placed his hands on her hips to show her what he needed as their heated breathing filled the still room.

"Wait," he cried, pulling her down to him again. He pushed on her thighs, indicating she should straighten her legs out over his. If he didn't slow down now, he wouldn't be any good for her.

Reclining lazily on him, she eased her hand upward to smooth the damp hair from his temples. "How I've missed you, needed you," she whispered, her body churning again, finding a new, more satisfying rhythm. "Don't let me go."

"Darling," he heard himself mutter as he clasped her face between his hands and pressed his mouth to hers, devouring its softness.

She arched her body and accelerated her pace. She whimpered and he realized that there wasn't any chance he'd climax before she did. She'd missed him every bit as much as he'd missed her. He ran loving hands over her curved buttocks, urging her on while he held himself back.

"Mark," she gasped, drawing his name out in a whispery moan as she buried her head in the sensitive curve of his neck. Quivering, she whispered, "Oh, yes . . . oh, yes."

Mark smiled into the darkness, inhaling the flowery traces of perfume clinging to her neck. He kissed her and kissed her, waiting for the spasms to lessen. Burning with a longing that was more than physical, he held her until her breathing became less frenzied. Never leaving her, he rolled her onto her back. Trembling, he drove into her; her body arched up to meet his. Her smooth legs wrapped around his hair-roughened ones, pulling him deeper and deeper. She dug her nails into his shoulders and then raked down his back. Heightened by the flicker of pain this caused, he thrust with increased force. He felt himself shuddering toward climax when he realized she was on the verge of coming again.

"Harder—harder," she begged.

With rapid jerking movements, he used more force than he'd ever used with a woman. Finally, a fierce heat coursed through his body, bringing with it sweet release.

Spent but reluctant to let her go, he rolled onto his side, his body still linked with hers, cradling her in his arms. He'd never thought anything could top that night in Mexico.

"Nobody does it better," she whispered, running her hand over the moist skin of his shoulder and down the slope of his waist to his hips, "nobody."

He wound his fingers through her hair, smoothing it against the pillow. "You're not going to fall asleep on me this time are you?"

"Not on your life!"

She hooked one silky leg over his, trying to keep him as close as possible. He kissed the top of her head. The contentment and happiness that had so long eluded him no longer concerned him. He had what really counted now. He'd been right to make her come to him. It was the only way he could be sure, really sure, she cared. It simply wasn't possible for a woman to surrender her body the way she had unless she'd already given her heart. He couldn't take any chances with their happiness even if it meant he'd have to keep their relationship private.

"Alexa," he said, "don't mention this to anyone, not even Renata or Linda. There are some things going on that I need to straighten out. Trust me."

"I do trust you. I won't tell anyone."

"I'm leaving for Australia first thing in the morning. I'll be back in two weeks. I should have things straightened out by then."

"Two weeks?" she moaned. "I don't know if I can wait that long. After tonight I may just . . ." She wound her arm around his neck and kissed him.

He detected a faint stirring in his groin. She was right. Two weeks was a helluva long time. "Alexa," he muttered against her insistent lips, "squeeze me."

She responded with a one-armed bear hug. He swallowed a burble of laughter. For all her natural sensuality, she was sexually inexperienced. And he loved it; he'd teach her.

"Not like that," he said, moving his hand across her bare bottom and pressing her to him.

"Oh," she mumbled, catching on and gently gripping him.

"Harder," he instructed as she flexed her muscles, keeping him inside her.

She squeezed and released and squeezed again.

A smoldering warmth flared anew as he said, "I want you to tell me exactly what you like about our lovemaking." His body still facing her and joined with hers, he turned his head so she could whisper in his ear. "I need to know."

While she whispered things in his ear he knew she'd never have had the courage to say out loud, she continued clenching down on him and then letting go. All the while she traced erotic patterns with her fingertips across his back. The combination of hearing her explain her most private feelings and the exquisite vise she was using on him aroused him more than had any of the lovemaking he'd enjoyed with more expert women. Swollen to full size once more, he whispered, "See what you've done?"

"I can feel it," she said and giggled. "I didn't know I could do that."

He rolled her onto her back. "You'd better be prepared to take the consequences. This may take the rest of the night."

"I hope so," she said, pulling his face to hers for a kiss.

Slowly he drew himself out and then eased forward. Repeating this dozens of times, he reveled in her uninhibited response. Each time she arched her body to meet his, encouraging him to apply more pressure and increase his speed. Every so often he'd stop and, just to tease her, he'd rub his chest against her sensitive nipples, raking the taut peaks through the rasp of hair. She moaned softly, begging for more and digging her nails into his back.

Mark found that insistent cadence men had used to love women since the beginning of time. Her soft moans and constant heaving told him she was right with him. When he came, it was a long, slow climax followed by a curious combination of utter exhaustion and exhilaration. His entire body collapsed into her welcoming arms. He remained there some minutes before he gained the strength to prop himself up on his forearms. Her hair lay hopelessly tangled across the pillow and her eyes were bright beneath heavy lids. He rolled off her and came to rest on his back staring at the ceiling. She wriggled closer, snuggling into the crook of his arm, her head resting against his chest.

Jesus! He thought he'd known everything there was to know about feelings a man could have for a woman. How wrong he'd been.

"Two weeks isn't such a long time," he said, cradling her in his arms. "Keep working on your book. That way, when I come back we can spend the holidays together at Wyndham Hill without you having to write the entire time."

"All right," she said with an unmistakable note of joy in her voice. "Christmas at Wyndham Hill."

Mark kissed the top of her head. He knew exactly what to get her for Christmas.

He must have drifted off to sleep because some inner alarm jolted him from a contented dream. He eased his arm from around Alexa and tilted his wrist to catch the available light. He had twenty minutes to shower, dress, and be downstairs to meet the taxi he'd arranged to take him to his helicopter. He reluctantly eased himself from between the sheets and tiptoed to the window. Out of the east a pearl-gray dawn was giving way to a sky streaked with the blue and mauve of the oncoming day. The sun, a halo on the horizon, was evaporating the shifting banks of fog that hung in a soft, purplish haze over the bay. Disappointment filled him. There could be no postponing this trip because of the weather. It was clear enough for his helicopter to land.

Silently he slipped into the bathroom. Alexa had given her word not to mention this to anyone. But would that be enough to protect her? Since he'd forced the network of illegitimate travel agents out of business, the threats and incidents at Triad had soared. Someone had defaced the Hogarth and his security men had intercepted two letter bombs.

After he emerged from the bathroom ready to go, he jammed his things into his suitcase without turning on the light. Unwilling to awaken Alexa but unable to leave without kissing her good-bye, he gently sat on the bed. Partially covered, she lay curled like a contented kitten, breathing evenly through seductively parted lips. With the pad of his thumb he circled her nipple, and it corrugated to a neat point as she rolled onto her back. He drew the covers up over her shoulders. He gave her a leisurely kiss and her eyes fluttered open.

"Good-bye," she whispered, half-awake.

"Good-bye, Alexa. Take care . . . and be careful."

# Chapter 27

"Who died?" Alexa joked, staring at the enormous floral arrangement standing on her desk. Dozens of miniature, baby-pink rosebuds preened from between clusters of Queen Anne's lace.

"Died?" Renata giggled and waved a beringed hand at the porcelain vase. "I'd say someone's gone to heaven."

"Is there a card?" Alexa asked Bob Wickson, seated at the desk Mark had once used. He shook his head.

"Card?" Renata gave a rich throaty laugh. "No one sends something this expensive unless he's sure the woman will at least suspect who sent it. Come on. What gives? Who would send you this?"

"I have no idea," Alexa hedged, pretending to search the masses of roses for a card. Mark! Of course he'd sent them. He hadn't sent a card because he'd asked her to keep their relationship private.

"Wel-l-l," Renata said, obviously skeptical, "You've certainly impressed someone. Got to run. Twick's waiting for me. If you find out who sent them, let me know."

"Uh-huh," Alexa mumbled as she bent to sniff the delicate buds. Impressed someone? No, Mark had impressed her, and not just physically. Once she'd decided to chase him, he'd been absolutely adorable. He'd let her make every move. She could still see the look of utter shock on his face when she waltzed into his room in that sexy black negligee. Tongue-tied. The man had been positively tongue-tied. He wanted her. That had been obvious all evening, but he needed her to come to him just as she'd needed him to come to her when they'd been in Mexico. She paused, caressing a dainty bud. Love. Could it have been only a year ago when she'd thought she'd never love again?

All weekend she'd driven Mark's Jaguar through the preserve at Dartmoor, thinking about him. The wild, lonely stretches of windswept land seemed unusually beautiful. She could hardly wait to see Mark to tell him how much she'd enjoyed it. The only thing that would have made it better would have been having him there to share it with her. He'd be proud of her. She'd driven his car with extreme caution. After all, his last words to her had been to be careful with his Jaguar. She'd even had it hand washed and waxed before returning it to the Triad garage.

The happiness she'd felt all weekend still burbled inside her. Even this morning's usual Monday drug test ritual hadn't dissolved the bubble of pure joy. *Alexa, get to work.* She couldn't possibly do any work with Mark's magnificent flower arrangement overwhelming her small desk. She moved the tall vase to the top of the file cabinet where she could look at it and be reminded of Mark.

She drove herself all morning, forcing herself to concentrate on the myriad of details concerning the play. When the phone rang early that afternoon, Alexa didn't bother to answer it. One of the jobs Bob had taken over was screening her calls. Since the play had received a tremendous amount of publicity and the soundtrack was selling better than anyone could have predicted, she received innumerable phone calls.

"Jason Talbott's on the line," Bob said from across the small office.

"Tell him I'm busy," Alexa said without looking up. She heard Bob talking with Jason and paused. The man was a pest. Why on earth had he developed a sudden interest in her? She'd been here months and he'd barely spoken to her.

"He wants to know if you like the flowers."

She bit the tip of the eraser off the pencil that she had been using and stared wordlessly at the bouquet. "Put him on," she mumbled and picked up the receiver. "Jason," she said, trying to sound pleased to hear his voice.

Still gazing in disbelief at the roses, she listened to Jason explaining he was giving a party tomorrow night and wanted her to act as hostess.

"Really, Jason, I couldn't," she said. "I know it'll be quite a bash, but I have to work the next day. I couldn't possibly act as hostess. I'll try to come though."

Her answer seemed to mollify him, and they hung up after she'd agreed to try to drop by his party. Alexa knew it would be inconceivable to Jason that she might not attend his party, but she'd purposely emphasized the word "try" without ever intending to do so. She needed to spend her evenings writing, not socializing with Jason's friends.

Tuesday afternoon a large silver box tied with a scarlet ribbon was delivered to her office. "Take it back," Alexa said. She refused to accept another thing from Jason Talbott. Taking his gifts only encouraged the man and would commit her to attending his party that evening.

"Back?" asked the young man holding the box. His face had become as red as the ribbon on the package.

"To whichever store it came from."

"I-I'm not—that is, Mr. Coombs told me to personally give this to you."

"Oh?" Alexa said, recognizing Mark's secretary's name. "Come here," Alexa cried, extending her hands for the gift. "Is there a card?"

The young man shook his head and backed out of her office while she gazed at the silver box. Tied with a five-inch-wide scarlet ribbon edged in silver, the package was about the size of an overnight case. She played with the ribbon for a moment, trying to guess what might be inside. The silver foil seals holding the box closed read: Smythson. Well known to Alexa, the Bond Street stationers to the Queen had some of the finest leather goods in Great Britain. And trust Mark to patronize a British company rather than one of their foreign competitors. She untied the ribbon, careful not to break it. She lifted the lid and peeled back several layers of tissue to find a leather attaché. Made of camel-colored doeskin, it was sleekly tailored yet utterly feminine. Above the digital lock, her initials had been embossed in discreet gold script. Inside, it had several compartments so she could carry her notes and papers.

Removing the packing tissue, she found a second box. Wrapped in white paper sprigged with violets, the small box contained a bottle of perfume from Floris. The internationally acclaimed perfume shop in St. James's sold exotic scents to some of the most famous women in Europe. Alexa removed the crystal stopper and inhaled the sweet fragrance. A delicate mixture of wild flowers with a trace of spice, the perfume was a unique blend of the scent she usually wore. Leave it to Mark to think of something special. How had he managed to describe the fragrance she wore so accurately? She'd never suspected he'd even noticed. She glanced up at the flowers, thinking he'd never take the easy way out. Anyone could pick up the phone and order flowers. Only someone who really cared would take the time to send such special gifts.

That night she went home and worked until well after two before going to bed. She remembered Jason's party but never once considered going. She frequently got up and walked over to the chair where she stored things from the play and ran her hands over the soft leather attaché.

On Wednesday morning when she arrived at the Regency, Alexa stood in her office aghast at the sight of a dozen woven birch baskets filled with lacy fern and baby-pink rosebuds.

"This is ridiculous!" she told Bob, who'd managed to move enough baskets aside to do some work. Beside him, T.S. sat on his plump rump, batting at a rosebud with an extended paw.

"I put the card on the desk," Bob said over his shoulder.

She didn't have to read the card to know they were from Jason Talbott, but she opened it anyway. The unsigned message said: It wasn't a party without you.

"Get rid of them," she said, tearing the card in half and tossing it in the wastepaper basket.

She didn't bother to call Jason to thank him. She knew that would be exactly what he expected her to do. She planned on waiting a few days and then calling him and setting him straight. Maybe by that time someone else would have captured his interest.

The remainder of the week passed without Jason calling or sending any more flowers. Alexa counted each day, knowing Mark would be home in another week. When she came home

Friday night, Alexa found Mrs. Raj, the daily char, sobbing hysterically.

"What's the matter?" Alexa asked.

It took a few minutes for the older woman to calm down enough so that Alexa could understand her broken English. "Ruin . . . ruin," she said. Above large almond eyes, her forehead creased, highlighting the ever-present red dot between her brows.

"Don't be upset," Alexa said. "Tell me what is ruined and I'll help you."

Still crying, she led Alexa up the stairs. Since Alexa had presented Mrs. Raj with the basket of roses earlier in the week, the woman who'd seemed so sullen all these months had become quite friendly. Alexa regretted not having made an overture toward her earlier, but she'd expected one of those spunky domestics made famous by *Upstairs, Downstairs,* not a woman who barely spoke English. In modern-day England staff positions had been taken over by new arrivals from former British colonies. They took jobs at low wages that Britons were reluctant to take. Frequently women like Mrs. Raj supported their extended families on their meager earnings. If she'd broken one of Steven's outrageously expensive accessories, it would probably take the char a year to pay for it.

Mrs. Raj took Alexa into Steven's room and pointed to the round bed. One of the wings of the egret in flight, which formed the curved headboard of his black lacquer bed, lay flopped to one side.

"Dusting," Mrs. Raj explained, "just dusting."

Alexa expelled her breath in an aggravated sigh. The Spurlucci bed had been custom ordered. It would take months —and a king's ransom—to replace it. But when she came closer, she realized the headboard wasn't broken. Somehow, while she dusted it, Mrs. Raj had triggered a concealed latch that dropped the egret's wing, revealing a hidden compartment. Alexa peered into it and discovered a plastic bag filled with white powder and a glass straw. Strange, Alexa thought. She realized Steven had a drinking problem, but she hadn't suspected he was into coke.

"It's not broken," Alexa assured Mrs. Raj. "See?" Alexa reached under the rim of the headboard and pressed a cleverly concealed button. The wing slid back into place, and the delighted Mrs. Raj clapped her hands.

"Thanky. Thanky." Mrs. Raj beamed.

"Run along home now," Alexa said, knowing it was late and undoubtedly her family was waiting.

Mrs. Raj left and Alexa again pressed the button, curious to see what else was in the compartment. Beside the bag was a Smythson specialty: a black, pocket-sized address book of delicate ostrich skin trimmed in gold. Alexa opened it and recognized Steven's neat handwriting. She thumbed through it, noticing most of the names were of people in foreign countries. No doubt they were movie contacts. Knowing Steven's penchant for detail—he always made detailed notes and kept innumerable lists—she wasn't surprised.

She leafed through the address book again. There was only one name that she recognized: Jason Talbott. Four numbers were listed for him. One was his villa in Marbella, another was his place in Hampshire, while the other two numbers were London exchanges. Of the two London numbers, one was his home on Eaton Square, but the other had no address. Only the initials M.T. were written in the address space. M.T.? Melanie Tarenholt? Obviously, Jason spent enough time with Melanie that Steven had her number recorded along with his other residences. If Jason and Melanie were so cozy, why was Jason calling her? Alexa wondered.

Monday morning, as usual, she met Renata at Sompers Café for breakfast before going to the lab for their weekly drug test. Immediately Alexa noticed Renata seemed depressed.

"How's Giles?" Alexa asked.

"Fine," Renata answered without looking at Alexa. Preoccupied with realigning the quartet of rings on each hand, a few moments passed before Renata spoke again. "Alexa, I know I've made a mess of my life . . ."

God almighty! She hadn't succumbed to temptation and returned to drugs, had she? Alexa put her hand on Renata's arm. "What happened? Are you all right?"

Renata gazed at her with clear blue eyes. "Nothing. Not to me anyway. I know I'm a fine one to criticize anyone, especially you, after all you've done for me. But I can see you're making the same mistake I made years ago. I know where it all will lead. It'll be a roller coaster ride through hell, and you may not ever recover."

"*What* are you talking about?"

"Jason Talbott. That whole crowd. They're not your type, Alexa. Once you start running with them—it's over."

"Running with them? I'm not running with anyone."

"But your picture with Jason Talbott—"

"What picture?" A cold sinking feeling gripped Alexa.

"Yesterday's edition of the *Evening Review* had a picture of you and Jason together. You were wearing that green dress Linda designed for you."

"Impossible. I've only worn that dress one time other than at the opening, and I wasn't with Jason. Are you certain it was me? Newspaper photos are fuzzy sometimes."

"No. This picture was remarkably clear. It was you. Anyway, they identified you by name, saying you'd been with him at a party Saturday night."

"This past Saturday?" Alexa asked, and Renata nodded. "That's simply not true. I was home writing all weekend. I never saw anyone. I can't imagine where they'd get a photo of me in that dress." Alexa paused, reviewing the wedding. No one had even thought to take a picture.

"That's not all." Renata hesitated and reached across the small table to touch Alexa's hand with her sparkling fingers. "The caption said you were Jason's latest flame and described you as a porn queen."

The shock of Renata's statement momentarily immobilized her. "I have to see the picture," she finally said.

The time at the lab and the Underground ride to the Regency seemed agonizingly slow. Renata had assured her that Addie Coniston, one of the kids in the street scene, was an avid reader and collector of the tabloids. As predicted, Addie did have the previous day's edition.

"I don't believe it," Alexa groaned as she looked at the photo. Even she couldn't deny the picture was of her. Standing next to Jason Talbott, she was indeed wearing the green dress. Just as shocking was the article heralding a party she'd never attended and revealing the fact that she was an American actress famous for her nude scenes. Nowhere did it mention her status as a writer or producer. The titillating column made her sound like some cheap starlet whose only claim to fame was appearing in the buff in sleazy movies.

"Do you want to see last week's articles on you?" Addie asked.

"Last week?" Alexa looked to Renata for an answer, but she shrugged. Evidently Renata hadn't seen those.

"Here one is." Addie triumphantly produced Wednesday's issue.

This time there was no picture, but it described Jason's party the previous evening. The article claimed Alexa had acted as his hostess.

"I never—" Alexa threw her hands, palms up, into the air.

"Here's Friday's paper," Addie said, handing her another article.

This time the column claimed that Jason and Alexa had been seen dining out at the chic new restaurant, Troubadour.

"Is this it?" Alexa asked from between clenched teeth.

"Yes," Addie replied.

"May I keep these?" she asked, and Addie nodded. "Thanks, if you see anything else, please come to me at once," Alexa said and turned to Renata. "Come into my office." She briskly left the dressing room with Renata following behind. "This is insane! I've never been out with that man. Why would anyone—?"

"Alexa, don't worry about it. No one reads those tabloids."

"Really?" Alexa came to a dead halt. "Then why are there more of them in London than first-rate papers like the *Times?*"

"Well, some people must."

"I can understand them thinking I'd been his hostess. He had asked me, but I refused. Someone could have mistakenly told the press I was to hostess. He could have been out at that restaurant with some blonde who looked like me, but there's no explaining away this picture."

She took another look at the picture. Suddenly it all came back to her. "Renata, see these earrings I'm wearing in this photo?" She pointed to the high-style, ultra-modern emeralds. "Linda arranged for Elizabeth Gage's shop to loan them to her to show with her designs, on the night her boutique opened. I loved them, but it would take me two lifetimes to pay for one!"

"Right," Renata said, "and the security men returned them along with the rest of the jewels Linda had borrowed."

Alexa started for her office once more. This time her pace was deliberate, purposeful. "Now I remember. There was a picture taken of me that night."

By late that evening it became clear to Alexa this puzzle wouldn't easily be solved. She'd reached Melanie Tarenholt's agent, who'd informed her Melanie was on leave from her television series and out of the country working on a film. The agent had no idea who might have taken the picture and all but said he couldn't care less. Alexa's efforts to reach a responsible person at the *Evening Review* were equally futile. No one seemed to know who'd written the article or who'd supplied the information.

The next morning Alexa camped outside the editor-in-chief's door and waited until he saw her. His tone condescending, the man informed her that his paper worked on tips from reliable sources. There was no way his small crew of reporters could attend every social event. Apparently someone had phoned in the information, and there was no way of tracking down the source. When she threatened to sue, the man laughed, but he did manage to find the photo.

Evidently the picture had been expertly spliced together from two separate negatives. Just by looking at the glossy black-and-white photo, no one could have identified it as fraudulent. The editor insisted it looked real. She left the paper and went directly to the one person who could explain this mess.

Seething, she waited for hours in Jason's foyer as his houseboy hovered around. It was well after dark before he appeared.

"Alexa," he said as he smoothed his windblown auburn hair and fixed his black eyes on her, "how nice of you to drop by." There was more than a hint of sarcasm to his voice.

"Jason, the photo in the Sunday paper—"

"Let's go in here and have a drink, shall we?"

Jason turned and walked into an adjacent room, forcing Alexa to follow him.

"Do you have any idea where that photo came from?" she asked.

"What photo?" Jason's tone was all innocence as he moved behind a pub-style bar and poured himself a drink.

"The one in the *Evening Review*," Alexa hissed.

"I'm afraid I never read that smut." He held up a bottle. "Wine? Vodka tonic?"

"A spritzer," Alexa said and produced the photograph.

Jason gave the photo a brief glance. "Nice dress," he said, his mouth twisting into a smile. He bent down beneath the bar, searching for something.

"Jason, we were never together in a picture except that evening when we were at Legends. Then there were four of us, not two."

Jason rose slowly, one eyebrow arched sardonically as he handed her a tumbler. "Alexa, my picture is taken so often that I don't even bother trying to remember who it was taken with."

Striving to calm her nerves, Alexa took two big gulps. "But this is important. It says we were together on Saturday night. Where were you? How could they have come up with this photo?"

An undisguised look of smug amusement crossed his handsome face. "I was with a married lady . . . who would prefer if her husband didn't know about us. As for the photo, you and I must have been together at some time."

"No, this photo was taken the night Changes opened. I was with Melanie when the picture was taken. Someone deliberately altered this photo."

Jason came around from behind the bar and led her to a leather sofa. "Have a seat and finish your drink while I explain a few things to you."

He took a seat on the far end of the couch and sipped his drink thoughtfully. Discouraged, Alexa took another sip. The soda water was flat, giving the spritzer a slightly bitter taste.

"Tabloids are part of the English scene. They do exaggerate and frequently misprint or misconstrue information they receive. You can tell what type of paper you're dealing with by their headlines: 'Woman raped by aliens on UFO.'" He paused, smiling benignly. "Now who believes that? No one, but people read it because they want to be entertained."

Alexa nodded and took another small drink. What he said made sense.

"I've been mentioned in those scandal sheets for years. Most of what they say has little truth to it. I simply never read them anymore. I suggest you do the same."

"But . . . why don't people sue?"

He shrugged, the glow of the lamp highlighting the red tones in his hair. "They do and sometimes they even win. Koo Stark was granted a settlement, and Jeffrey Archer received the highest award to date. But at what price? You'd have to prove intent and that the paper knew the information was false. Most people don't bother because it only makes the barristers richer. And it further publicizes the erroneous story. You'd go through all of that over one or two minor columns in a third-rate tabloid?" He shook his head in disgust. "Of course not. Now finish your drink. I'll drive you home."

Alexa emptied the glass. "They called me a porn queen. That's not minor to me."

Jason chortled and then said, "You did appear in a film without your clothes on. To many that is pornographic. Forget it. This is probably someone's idea of a joke."

Alexa had to agree. There didn't seem to be anything she could do about this. Getting overwrought about it was senseless. Forget the whole thing and get on with life. She opened her mouth to thank Jason for the flowers, but when she looked up she saw three of him. She blinked hard, thinking she'd had too much wine on an empty stomach. Three images seesawed before her and a loud whine droned in her ears.

"Alexa, are you all right?" Jason asked. His voice sounded as if it were being filtered from far away.

"Yes," she mumbled, lurching to a standing position. "I'd better get home."

She clutched her purse and headed for the door. She squinted and tried to make the multiple doors merge into one. She caught her foot and pitched forward. Jason grabbed her beneath her arms, keeping her from falling.

"In the bag, huh? Where were you drinking before you arrived here?"

Alexa struggled to answer but gagged on the words.

"I'll send for the car," Jason said. "Can't let you go off in this condition."

By the time Jason loaded her into his chauffeured Rolls, Alexa was seeing eerie blue and purple lights and sudden starbursts of color. She tried to tell Jason she wasn't drunk, but her words came out in a disjointed jumble. She closed her eyes, trying to block out the disturbing visions, but this in no way diminished the iridescent lights. It just made them whirl nauseatingly around her. Suddenly she felt an icy cold chill clutching her breast. She looked down and saw several hands reaching up under her sweater, squeezing her bare breast. Dimly she realized it could only be one hand—Jason's.

"Don't," she heard herself cry. Her voice sounded unusually high pitched and frenzied.

His answer was a hollow laugh. "Is this what Kimbrough likes—your tits?"

He pinched her nipple and she screamed, kicking and flailing while starbursts of light obstructed her vision and an angry hornet buzzed in her head. Groggily she realized nothing she was doing was deterring him. She looked down to see octopus hands lifting her skirt and crawling up her thigh. She thrashed mindlessly, flinging herself from side to side.

"Stop!" she screamed, trying to get the chauffeur's attention through the glass partition. "Let me out! Let me go!"

"Out?" Jason plunged his hand between her thighs. "You want out?"

Alexa sank her teeth into his shoulder and he pulled away. "Yes," she shrieked.

His hot, black eyes had a diabolical glint and his mouth twisted into a smile as he reached for the phone connecting the passenger compartment with the chauffeur. "Miss MacKenzie would like you to stop right here."

The Rolls slammed to a halt, throwing Alexa against the front seat. Jason reached across her and opened the door and she staggered out. The Rolls sped away, leaving a trail of rubber on the wet pavement. Alexa tried to focus on the dilapidated buildings. Nothing looked the least bit familiar. She staggered to the curb just as the brownstone buildings cycloned around her and the ground came up to greet her.

# Chapter 28

When Alexa opened her eyes—it could have been minutes or hours later—a group of faces loomed above her. Like images in a carnival mirror, their faces were grotesquely distorted. *I'm going crazy*, she thought. Still seeing fireworks lighting the dark night, she struggled to stand but someone held her down. Someone else grabbed her ankles and dragged her across the sidewalk. Her head clunking on the uneven surface, Alexa summoned the strength to scream. Her shrieks brought a large, angry hand slamming down on her mouth. Through the loud whine threatening to split her brain, she understood one word—"kill." If she didn't shut up, she'd be killed.

They stopped pulling her and several voices began talking all at once. Alexa tried to focus. She kept the rainbows of light at bay long enough to determine she was in a deserted alley. Dozens of hands reached for her, clawing at her clothes. A jab of pain sliced across her throat and she realized someone had yanked her gold chain from her neck. Two quick jerks removed her gold hoops and left her ears throbbing. A shrill whistle split the night, forcing Alexa to clap her hands over her ears. Head between her hands, she barely heard the thundering sound of retreating footsteps. She curled into the fetal position and prepared for the worst.

"Miss?" said a distant voice. "Are you all right?"

Squinting, Alexa looked up. Beyond the tunnel of light coming from a flashlight were the familiar blue uniforms and domed hats of the London bobbies. She concentrated, trying to focus, and decided it was just one policeman. She tried to speak but only harsh, guttural sounds came from her lips.

"You'd better come with me, miss," the bobby said, helping her to her feet.

She pitched forward, tottering, threatening to fall.

"A bit tipsy, hey? Seeing pink Beefeaters, are you?" He put a strong arm around her waist and supported her. "I heard you scream. Those blokes got your purse?"

Alexa nodded, concentrating on walking and ignoring the bright lights exploding around her.

He took Alexa to the station, where she was questioned and then left on a cot in a dark room. Half-unconscious, she lay there battling the demons and monsters coming at her from all sides. Hundreds of thoughts spun through her mind but vanished before she could capture them. There wasn't any question about it—she *had* gone crazy.

"Alexa . . . Alexa."

Someone was calling her name and shaking her. She opened her eyes and then slammed them shut again. The light from the single bulb illuminating the small room was so bright it hurt.

"Renata," Alexa said, her voice a sandpapery whisper. For a moment she wondered where she was and then remembered being brought to the station. She must have finally fallen asleep.

"Yes, Alexa. What happened?"

"The light," Alexa said, "it's too bright. Turn it off."

"The light isn't—"

"It hurts," Alexa insisted, closing her eyes. When she heard the click of the switch she eased her eyes open.

"Now," Renata said, sitting down beside Alexa. "Tell me what happened. I've never known you to get drunk."

"I wasn't drunk."

"But they said—"

"Are they charging me with anything?"

"No, they're not," Renata said. "They called me to come take you home. You're not the first tourist to spend too much time in a pub. What are you doing in this neighborhood? What happened?"

"Let's get out of here and I'll tell you the whole story."

By the time they reached Renata's flat, Alexa had explained her suspicions that Jason had drugged her.

"I don't think there's any doubt about it," Renata agreed. "The psychedelic lights, distorted images, and unusual sounds probably means he put acid in the drink. I wish Giles were here. He'd know what to do, but he's in Edinburgh for a film festival." Renata unlocked the door to her flat and let Alexa in. "Why didn't you tell this to the police? They could have arrested Jason."

"The only clear thought I had when I was brought to the station was that Jason is very wealthy, very powerful. Who would they believe—me or him? If they decided to bring drug charges against me, I'd be deported." Shielding her eyes from the small lamp Renata had lit, Alexa sat on the sofa. "Remember what happened to Stacy Keach."

"You're right," Renata said. "Jason would have been a fool not to immediately get rid of any evidence and establish an alibi. But why would he do this to you?"

"I don't know," Alexa said. "He could have raped me if he'd wanted to, but he didn't really try."

"He didn't have to. He dumped you in the sooty slums of south London. The Peckham Street Station where I picked you up is the worst in London. You were lucky the bobby heard your screams," Renata said. "Those men might not have been satisfied with merely robbing you."

"I can't believe Jason did this because I didn't go out with him," Alexa said. Groggily she remembered Jason saying something about Mark, but she couldn't recall just what.

"I wouldn't be surprised," Renata said, walking into the adjacent kitchenette and filling a teapot with water. "I remember Annette Spencer, an ingenue in a production I starred in years ago. Not only was she pretty, but she was uniquely talented. Had it not been for Jason Talbott, she'd have gone on to become one of England's greatest stars."

"What happened?"

"Jason seduced her, using his usual tactics, armadas of pink roses and dinners in swank restaurants. I warned her to stay away from him, but Annie was sweet—too sweet. She thought he loved her and would divorce his wife. The minute he found out Annie was pregnant, the tabloids trumpeted her numerous affairs. Of course she'd never had another lover."

"That bastard!"

"Rather than risk a paternity suit, he ruined her reputation."

"What did she do?"

"Called the papers. Tried to reach Jason, who'd conveniently gone to Marbella. Any fool could have seen what he was doing, but not Annette. She still loved him." A high-pitched whistle interrupted Renata and she turned to fill the teapot with the boiling water. "Annie drifted around England, floating from one provincial production to another. She'd begun drinking heavily right after the baby was born and relatives adopted it. Finally, she killed herself with an overdose of pills and booze."

"Why didn't you tell me this earlier?" Alexa asked.

"I'm sorry. I should have warned you, but I was afraid you might try to retaliate. I had no idea Jason would pull something like this," Renata said as she handed Alexa a cup of tea. "But Jason got his, after a fashion. During that same time when Annette and Jason were having their affair, a flat-chested, dishwater blonde with a weak chin and a long nose joined the cast. When she disappeared for weeks, no one missed her. Then she returned and replaced an actress with a one-line walk-on part. No longer flat chested, she had a pair of triple Ds no one could miss. Her nose had been pruned and her chin tucked—and her hair bleached platinum. The surgically enhanced phenomenon proceeded to strut and shimmy through her part."

"Melanie Tarenholt?"

"Exactly. But when she pushed and asked to understudy other roles, it became apparent gyrating her hips and heaving her breasts was the extent of her talent. When Jason returned from Marbella, he began dating Melanie 'No-Talent' Tarenholt."

Alexa tucked her feet under her skirt. "I always wondered what Jason sees in her. She's blatantly cheap and he's so sophisticated, worldly."

"Opposites attract. I don't question what a conservative businessman sees in an unconventional blond whirlwind."

"That's different," Alexa answered, wondering just how much Renata had guessed about her relationship with Mark.

"It could have been Jason merely took up with Melanie in order to defuse the situation with Annette. Who knows?" Renata said, waving her ring-spangled hand dismissively. "But in Melanie Tarenholt he'd met his match. Dozens of articles appeared proclaiming Melanie as the theatrical discovery of the decade. We learned that she'd gotten her first part by tricking the actress originally cast in the role into leaving town by sending her a phony message that her mother was dying."

"That's disgusting."

"To Melanie, her career is everything. She dumped Jason for a prominent television producer, who later gave her a part in a series. Jason sent dozens of pink roses and gifts, but Melanie never looked back," Renata said.

"Somewhere along the line she and Jason have gotten together again. They still see each other, and Steven tells me they have for years." Alexa drained the last bit of tea from her cup and set it down.

"Who cares?" Renata answered. "They deserve each other. My point is: Jason's capable of anything. He could have done this just because you embarrassed him by not hostessing his party."

Alexa thought for a moment and remembered the drug test. "Renata," she said, anxiety surging through her, "the drug test. I won't be able to pass it."

"I know. I have a plan."

"You do?" Alexa said, reluctant to involve Renata in her troubles. All the play would need would be for something to happen to Renata.

When she explained how they could substitute urine specimens at the lab, Alexa agreed. It was a bold plan, but Alexa had an even wilder scheme in mind. "I'm going to screw Jason Talbott—and royally. Really screw him. For myself, for Annette, and for every other woman he's used."

When Saturday evening came, Alexa stood before her mirror splashing "Wicked Vixen" perfume over her naked body. Lordy, if this stuff didn't attract Jason it would surely asphyxiate him. Waving her hand in front of her nose, she gave her-

self a minute to become used to the tawdry aroma before she
heavily kohled and shadowed her eyes to enhance their green
color. She slipped into the lacy black bra with push-up pads
that exaggerated her ample chest, thrusting her breasts out
like drawn six-shooters. The fabric covering the nipple area
had deliberately been omitted to expose the wearer's nipples.
She fastened the satin garters, smoothing the black stockings
into place and stepping into a clingy black satin gown. Checking her image in the full-length mirror, she saw that every
curve, every hollow, even the indentation of her naval was
revealed beneath the cheap satin. But her pert nipples, protruding through the holes in the bra, stole the show. She
groaned out loud at her reflection. This had better work, she
thought as she shrugged into her raincoat.

By the time she'd reached the flat in Soho where she'd arranged to meet Jason, she was a knot of nerves. Was Jason
really convinced he'd piqued her sexual interest with his
heavy-handed treatment of her? Could she carry this off
without muffing it? *Of course, you can!* All she had to do was act,
just as she'd done during the nude scene.

Unaccustomed to wearing gloves, it took her a few minutes
to unlock the door to the bed-sitter. Ignoring the peeling paint
on the doorjamb and the scuttling sounds of mice foraging in
a sack of garbage down the hall, she tiptoed into the room and
switched on the solitary light. The grimy bed-sitter was just
as she'd rented it except for the enormous fake plant she'd
brought in earlier. Purchased in a second-hand store, it
blended perfectly with the faded floral wallpaper. The lumpy
double bed, a wobbly chair, and the small table holding the
lamp were the only pieces of furniture in the room.

Alexa tossed her raincoat over the chair before she drew a
black satin sheet from her Harrods shopping bag and covered
the stained mattress with it. She positioned a black satin pillow at the head of the bed. On the water-ringed nightstand,
she placed the bag and the pills.

She went into the bathroom, running her still-gloved hand
up the wall in search of the light switch. The strong odor of
mildew hit her as she flicked on the light. Trying not to
breathe too deeply, she withdrew the black whip from the
shopping bag and hung it from the wobbly hook on the back
of the bathroom door. Next she lifted the black thigh-high

boots from the bag and placed them against the mildewed shower curtain that hid the moldy tub. After making certain the shopping bag was left open so she could easily throw things into it, Alexa placed her gloves on top of the sink, flipped off the light and left the bathroom.

Rubbing her bare arms briskly to counter the cold air of the unheated room, Alexa paced back and forth until a sharp rap on the door stopped her. Gulping back a rush of nerves, she plastered a seductive smile across her face and swung open the door.

Jason's jaw dropped a full three inches before he recovered and said, "Well . . . I am surprised. I thought this was some sort of joke."

Alexa gyrated her satin-encased hips as she extended her hand to pull him into the room, and purred, "Come in. The party starts here." She gestured to the bed and the amyl nitrite capsules beside the bag and glass straw.

"My." Jason's eyes lit appreciatively. "Maybe it will be worth staying. My chauffeur—"

"Get rid of him," Alexa whispered, rubbing her body suggestively against his.

While he went out to give his driver instructions, she lay across the bed, assuming a seductive pose.

Jason returned and tossed his camel's hair topcoat on top of her coat. He dropped down onto the bed beside her. "Want some blow?" he asked, reaching for the bag on the nightstand.

Alexa shook her head and ran her hand up his arm. "No, I'm way ahead of you. I've been here awhile."

She looked at the phony plant in the corner as she listened to Jason inhaling deeply. This was going according to plan— so far. Don't rush it, she reminded herself. Don't make him suspicious.

"A-a-a-h" Jason expelled his indrawn breath with a hedonistic sigh. "Now tell me why we're in this dive." He eyed the room lazily, sounding ridiculously happy.

Alexa brought herself upright, moving closer to Jason and looking directly into his eyes. "I'm from California, remember," she said as she peeled back his sport jacket, indicating he should remove it.

"You think you can show me something I haven't already seen?" Jason twisted out of the jacket.

"I can guarantee it," Alexa said, loosening his tie. "I can *absolutely* guarantee it." She unbuttoned his shirt and yanked it from his trousers. When she reached for his belt buckle, he grabbed her. His dilated eyes, obsidian-black, loomed before her face and he kissed her. *Respond,* she commanded herself, and she looped her arms around him.

He rammed his tongue into her mouth, gagging her, but she forced herself to pretend to be excited. She fluttered her fingers across his chest. With a start she realized his chest was almost totally hairless. Unbidden, an image of Mark's sturdy chest and its dense hair came to her. She pulled away, breaking the kiss. Could she really go through with this?

Jason didn't notice her hesitation. He slipped the straps of her dress from her shoulders, revealing the black bra and her exposed nipples. "I've seen it before," he said, "but I like it." He lowered his head and kissed the crest of her breast, then fastened hot, greedy lips on her bare nipple. He slid his hand up her back and started to unhook the bra.

"Not so fast," she said, jerking away and swinging her legs to the floor. "Help yourself." She gestured toward the amyl nitrite capsules sitting beside the bag of coke. She wasn't sure if Jason always used them or not. Renata hadn't been able to find out, but Alexa didn't want to take any chances. "I'll be right back," she flung over her shoulder as she sashayed into the bathroom.

Inside, she discarded her stiletto heels, tossing them into the bag before stripping off the sleazy dress and dropping it into the bag. She thrust first one leg and then the other into the black, thigh-high, military-style boots. The cloudy full-length mirror on the back of the bathroom door revealed the most disgusting sight Alexa had ever seen. Through the open centers of the black bra her bare nipples protruded. The satin garter belt rode down on her hips, almost obscuring the fact that she wore lacy black panties split at the crotch. Alexa reached down and slid her fingers between the lace panels, bringing out a cluster of dark blond curls so the black panties emphasized them. She took a quick step back and checked herself in the mirror. There, Jason couldn't miss the split panties, she thought as she took the whip off the hook and opened the door.

When she entered the small room, she couldn't keep the

grin off her face. Jason had removed his trousers and was lounging, fully erect on the bed.

"I've seen it," he said, when she moved up to the bed and dangled the tasseled tip of the whip across his lower abdomen.

"No, you haven't," she snarled, snapping the whip. "Get up. Put on your coat. We're going outside."

"S and M ?" Jason sneered. "It doesn't suit you. Somehow I can't see you—" He ran his cold hand up her bare inner thigh, squeezing it so hard she winced. "But I'd like to see this a lot closer," he said, sliding his probing fingers between the split panels of the panties.

Alexa's courage threatened to desert her. This wasn't going the way she'd planned. Jason was supposed to be into sadomasochism. Renata had confirmed it with several sources. Alexa realized she must be the problem; she wasn't being aggressive enough. He didn't believe her. She cracked the whip, bringing it down hard across his thighs. "Get up—now!"

With a swift, feline motion Jason grabbed her arms and brought her down on the bed beside him. "You like to play rough?" He buried his face in her bosom, alternately sucking wildly at one of her erect nipples and biting it. The flash of pain this caused preceded a moment of blind panic. Before she could think of what to do, he had the bra off and flung it over his shoulder. *This was a mistake. She couldn't trick Jason. She had to get out of here.* "No," she gasped, playing her trump card, "not here. I have something special waiting for you outside."

Jason's head snapped up; his hot black eyes bore into her unsteady green ones. "Outside? You're crazy. It's freezing." He pumped his hips, his stiff erection demanding she unlock her thighs.

"I-I promised you something different," she stammered. "You've never seen anything like this." She swiveled beneath him, blessing the satin sheets that allowed her to slip from his grasp. She stood up and raced to the chair and tossed him his coat. "There's a van parked at the curb. The rear door is open. Just climb in and wait for me. I'll be there in a few minutes."

Jason didn't budge. "Come back here."

Alexa moved just close enough to use the whip. She brought it down hard against his bare thigh, praying this wouldn't deflate his erection. It didn't; instead he seemed to become even harder. "This will be like nothing you've ever experienced."

He made a lunge for her, but she sidestepped his hands. She turned and slashed the whip across his bare back with all her might. He jerked away, a cruel look in his eyes. "All right," he said tightly, "let's see what kinky ploy you have in mind."

Clutching the whip with both hands to keep them from trembling, Alexa watched him put on his coat over his naked body, not buttoning it but cinching it closed with the belt.

Obviously disgusted, Jason shook his head. "This better be special."

Alexa bit the inside of her cheeks to keep from smiling. If she could just get him outside, her plan would be back on track again.

"Aren't you coming?" Jason asked, opening the door.

She grabbed her raincoat, too rushed to button it, just securing it with the sash. "In a minute. I've a surprise for you. Go on. I'll be right there."

As soon as the door clicked shut, Alexa dashed into the bathroom and put on the gloves and grabbed the bag before returning to the bedroom. She flew around the room gathering his things and hers and dumping them into the shopping bag. She was wiping her prints from the bathroom doorknob when the screaming began.

She shot back into the bedroom and found the other shopping bag she'd hidden beneath the bed yesterday. With two quick jerks, she had the sheet off the bed and into the bag. The hysterical screams had stopped, but now she heard the deeper shouts of men. Pillow under her arm, she raced over to the phony philodendron. Out of the corner of her eye, her discarded bra caught her attention. *Dammit!* She'd almost forgotten it. She jammed it into her raincoat pocket before parting the plant's dusty leaves.

Alexa was still laughing even after she'd dropped off one shopping bag and arrived at Warren's town house. Yesterday, when she'd moved her things here, she'd forgotten to leave the back light on. With the servants on Christmas holiday, no one was home, leaving the place pitch-black. Still naked beneath her raincoat except for the panties and boots, Alexa stood there shivering and fumbling with the unfamiliar lock.

Finally she opened the door and was in the kitchen when she heard the faraway double ring of the telephone. Renata! Alexa dropped the remaining shopping bag in the hall and raced into the library. A brass table lamp that must have been on a timer lit the L-shaped room.

"H-hello," she said, breathing heavily.

"Alexa? Everything all right?" Renata sounded worried.

"Perfect. And you?"

"You heard me screaming?" Renata didn't wait for an answer. "It went off just as we planned."

"You were wonderful. Super . . . really . . . there's nobody like you. I mean it, nobody does it better. Nobody. I love you. You're . . ." Alexa's voice trailed off. Something was wrong. Not only was the lamp lit when no one was supposed to be in the house, but the glass picture behind the desk acted like a mirror, revealing a fire burning in the fireplace around the corner in the section of the room she couldn't see from where she stood.

"Alexa? Is something the matter?"

"No," she said, not wanting to alarm Renata. "I'll call you tomorrow. Love you. Good-night."

Frissons of fear hackled the hair across the back of her neck. Someone was standing behind her.

# Chapter 29

Alexa whirled around. "Mark," she cried, welcome and relief sparkling in her voice. "What are you doing here?" Then she saw he had the whip in his hand. Her smile froze on her lips. He must have found the bag.

He confronted her, hostile and defiant, a glacial glint in his gray eyes. He crossed the room, snapping the whip across his open palm. Dismayed, she stood there staring helplessly at him.

"More to the point, what are you *doing* here?"

"Linda said—" She stopped, realizing he was staring at her raincoat. Without looking, she knew the ridiculous bra must be dangling out of her coat pocket. In all the excitement she'd forgotten it.

"I think this explains enough." He slipped the tip of the whip through one of the bra's straps and jerked it from her pocket.

"Mark, it's not—"

"Isn't it?" He tossed the bra aside. The vein that ran up the side of his neck pulsed rapidly. "I found your playmate's gear up the hall."

"I can explain," Alexa said, backing up. "Let's sit by the fire and—" She sidestepped around the corner toward the green

plaid sofa standing before the fire. How much of this did she
want to tell Mark? He'd never approve, and he'd be furious if
he knew she'd involved Renata. But she loved him, and if she
lied to him again, he'd never forgive her.

"Don't bother," he said, following her.

"I want to tell you," she said, coming to a halt behind the
sofa. She had to make him listen. "There's a reasonable explanation for my getup. Let's sit down"—she gestured to the sofa
—"and discuss this."

"There's nothing to discuss."

Before she realized what he was doing, he yanked on the
raincoat's sash. As the unbuttoned panels parted, revealing
her bare bosom and split panties, the cool draft raised goosebumps across her breasts.

"Mark, listen—"

His angry kiss smothered her explanation. He grabbed her
arms, pinning them against her sides. His arms were locked
around her, squeezing the air from her lungs and making it
difficult to breathe. Yet it felt unbelievably good to have him
hold her again. Mentally she scrambled for a way to make
him listen. Linda's words rushed through her head, reminding
Alexa it was impossible for a man to remain angry after he'd
made love to a woman. It had worked before, she decided,
giving up the idea of trying to talk to him. The unrelenting
pressure of his hungry mouth released her pent-up longing.
She wound her arms around his neck, returning his devouring
kisses with unrestrained ardor.

He had her so tightly pressed against the back of the sofa
that the metal buckle on his belt dug into her soft flesh. She
felt curiously light-headed as she frantically returned his
kisses and a warm glow built steadily between her thighs.
With his free hand, she could feel him working her raincoat
off. He let it drop across the back of the sofa. He broke the
kiss and took half a step back.

Alexa reached for the buttons on his shirt and undid the
first three before she realized he was staring at her. Her hand
froze on the third button, and her stomach knotted under his
withering gaze. His gray eyes explored every inch of her, lingering on the crude panties. Naked to the waist, her breasts
rose and fell with her labored breathing. Shame swept
through her at having him see her like this. She didn't blame

him for jumping to the obvious conclusion. "M-Mark," she said. His name came out a broken whisper.

He tried to jerk her hand from his shirt, but she was holding on so tightly that the remaining two buttons ripped off, tearing the fabric beneath.

"Is this what you wanted?" He yanked the tails of his shirt from his trousers, exposing his chest. He flung the shirt aside. When she didn't reply and turned her head away, he slid one cold hand across her flushed skin and circled her breast. He squeezed, crushing the tender flesh. Trembling, she looked up at him. This couldn't be Mark, not *her* Mark. A flash of pain as he tweaked her nipple between icy fingers brought an image of Jason to her mind. It must have been in a dream, she decided, because Jason had had the same cruel expression on his face and he'd been hurting her.

"Stop it," she screamed, clawing at his hand.

"Oh, but you like to play rough," he said, grabbing her and imprisoning her against his chest.

"No," she cried, pummeling him with clenched fists, but he refused to release her. "Talk to me," she mumbled into the mat of hair on his chest. This was a side of Mark she'd never suspected he had, and she had absolutely no idea of how to deal with it. "Please," she said, the word coming out in a muffled sob.

With a disgusted huff he released her, pushing her and sending her unprepared body toppling over the back of the sofa onto the plush cushions. He hurled the whip into the fire and turned to leave, throwing her a disgusted look over his shoulder.

"Don't go," she cried, sitting up.

Eyes narrowed, Mark gazed at her body with undisguised fury. "Why? What do—" His voice twisted angrily in midsentence when she snatched the raincoat from where it had fallen on the sofa and clutched to it her bare breasts. "Modest? In that outfit?" He came around the sofa and hauled her to her feet. "You asked me to stay," he said, jerking the raincoat from her. "Now make it worth my while."

It was a nonnegotiable order, but she tried anyway. "Mark, listen—"

She drew in her breath as he ran his hands across her bare breasts. This time his touch was a gentle caress that belied the savage gleam in his eyes. Without touching her nipple, he circled it until it ached for his touch. Finally he slid the roughened ball of his thumb across the tight peak. Suppressing an anguished moan, she tried to ignore the moist heat building between her thighs. She needed time to think, to explain, but with him fondling her, she couldn't think clearly. He slipped his hand down the flat plane of her stomach across the satin garter belt until his probing fingers found the cluster of curls she'd earlier pulled forth to emphasize the split panties. The heated primitiveness of his actions fired her blood in a way she'd never experienced. An almost barbaric urge to feel him deep within her coursed through her when his fingers parted the panties' lace panels and slipped between the damp curls.

"Wet," he murmured into her ear. "Already? You never get enough, do you?"

"No," she admitted, thinking he meant enough of him. "Never."

Wordlessly he stroked the hot tip of his tongue across her ear as his fingers slowly slid beneath the moist curls. She shuddered when he applied gentle pressure, caressing her with his fingertip. With a slow, undulating motion, she moved against his fingers until he slid one finger up inside her. She heard herself let out a soft gasp as she melted against him. She clung to him, rotating her hips, encouraging him until she could no longer stand it.

"Now . . ." she whispered, "please."

His response was a flurry of bruising kisses that left her breathless, but he made no move to give her what she needed. Instead he said, "You really can't wait, can you?" He languidly stroked his hand back and forth, making sure the tight curls were thoroughly wet.

"No," she said, loving him, loving what he was doing to her.

He responded with another harsh kiss. There was something about the urgent way he plunged his tongue into her mouth, matching the exquisite rhythm of his hand, that made her feel giddy and reckless. Barely conscious of what she was doing, she clawed at his back, raking her nails across his skin. For an instant he froze, withdrawing his hand from between her thighs, and she dug her nails in deeper. He nipped at the full pout of her lower lip, drawing blood.

"So you do want to play rough?" he said as she gave a startled cry. "Pain heightens the pleasure. Isn't that the idea?"

He didn't wait for her answer. His lips found hers and his roving tongue brought the taste of the cheap perfume she'd slathered on earlier into her mouth. But rather than struggling to free herself, Alexa urged him on by kissing him and tugging at his dark hair with her clenched fists. Panting, Mark broke the kiss and reached down to release his buckle. As he unzipped his trousers, Alexa slid her hand into his shorts. Thick and hard and as silky as she remembered, his hot erection filled her hand.

"Take them off," Mark demanded and she peeled his trousers and briefs down over his slim hips. He dropped onto one of the chairs beside the sofa and kicked his clothing aside. "Come here."

Alexa tugged on her heel, trying to remove the tight-fitting boot.

"Don't," he commanded, gesturing for her to come to him.

Feeling foolish because she was standing there naked except for the panties, garter belt, and black stockings that disappeared into the military boots, Alexa took a tentative step forward. He reached for her hand and hauled her to him, bringing her down, her legs straddling his, her breasts inches from his face.

"Now," she whispered, positioning herself above him.

But he wasn't paying any attention to what she wanted. He lifted one throbbing breast, bringing the taut nipple into his hot mouth, sucking and nipping. Frissons of passion shot down her stomach and centered in the moist area between her thighs. Almost as if he knew what she was feeling, he moved one hand up between her splayed thighs. Without warning he brought his free hand down across her raised bottom, giving her a stinging slap. She gasped as he plunged his hand under her panties. With long, soothing strokes, he massaged her tingling skin until she was no longer conscious that her bottom stung from the slap. The delicious sucking on her breast and the enticing movements of his hands were breath-stoppingly delightful. She kept telling herself everything would be all right. Once they'd made love, she could talk to Mark, explain everything, but right now all she could think about was how wonderful she felt. Unexpectedly Mark jerked her to her feet.

"Now . . . now," she said, clinging to him.

He tugged on her hair, forcing her to arch her neck. Kissing her exposed neck savagely, he jabbed his pulsing erection against her tender skin. Alexa dug her nails into his back, vaguely aware she might be hurting him but needing to tell him to hurry. He responded with a sucking bite to the sensitive curve of her neck and another stinging slap to her buttocks. Dimly aware this was going beyond tender lovemaking, Alexa sank her teeth into his shoulder. She knew she hadn't drawn blood, but the fact she wanted to hurt him startled her. What surprised her even more was the way she enjoyed it. Feeling him wince and react with another slap followed by gentle massaging fired her blood in a way she'd never dreamed possible. With their passion evenly matched, they'd gone over the edge. It was too late to turn back.

Mark whirled her around, pushing her face first down onto the sofa. Before she could right herself, he was on top of her. She whimpered, trying to tell him to let her up, but one strong hand held her down, her face buried in the cushions. The other rough hand hauled her into position as the tip of his shaft probed her from behind. With a guttural moan, he pushed forward, filling her with white-hot hardness. She wiggled beneath him, but his powerful body held her in place.

Tossing her head to one side and gasping for air, Alexa reveled in these completely new sensations, which brought on a flood tide of hedonistic delight. She bit down on the pillow to keep from crying out with pleasure. He lunged forward for the final time and she actually saw stars as the impact of his climax coincided with hers. With a tortured moan he slid down on top of her, pressing her into the soft cushions. In short bursts, his heated breath came across the back of her neck. Exhausted, Alexa lay there under his weight, wanting to tell him how much she loved him, loved his lovemaking, but she was unable to summon the strength.

Mark vaulted to his feet, leaving her face down on the sofa. Unlike the previous times they'd made love, he didn't take her into his arms, cuddling her and talking to her. She turned on her side. The room was almost dark with the only light coming from the smoldering coals in the fireplace and the small desk lamp around the corner. But it didn't take much light to see the scowl knitting Mark's brows. Unbelievably, he was still angry.

"Mark, about tonight. I can explain—"

"Don't bother," he said, buckling his trousers and reaching for his torn shirt. "You're a slut. You'll fuck anyone. I knew it the moment I saw you. Your hair always looks like you've been in bed because you have been. You parade around with your tits dangling, hoping to entice men."

"No." Alexa came to her feet, clutching her raincoat. A hot rush of tears stung her eyes. Is that what he thought of her? In an agony of embarrassment she scrambled into her raincoat and headed to the door.

"I don't know why I love you."

Alexa bounded up the stairs to the guest room, where she'd moved all her belongings in anticipation of living here until Warren and Linda returned. Hot tears trickled down her cheeks; she brushed them off with the back of her hand. She hated him. She loved him. She didn't know what the hell to do about him. Now that she was thinking coherently, she realized he hadn't been making love to her, he'd been humiliating her. She just loved him too much, wanted him too much, to realize that in time. But what had set him off like that? If there was one thing Mark Kimbrough was it was controlled and rational—to a fault.

She shed the raincoat and looked in the mirror and saw the answer. Of course there was a reasonable explanation for the getup—not that he'd wanted to listen to it. She paused, taking a closer look at her hair. Did it really give her a bedroom look?

She tugged awkwardly on the tight boots, finally removing them. She ripped off the offensive undergarments and stood before the mirror examining her breasts. They were larger than average, but not overly so. It was true she preferred not to wear a bra, but she could honestly say she never used her chest, as Melanie did, to entice anyone. Did he really think that she did?

*"You'll fuck anyone."* The words echoed in her ears. Well, there certainly wasn't a grain of truth to that accusation. A fresh batch of tears gathered in her eyes.

She turned to pull out a pair of jeans and a sweater from the drawer, preparing to pack her things and leave. She headed toward the bureau and stopped in midstride. What the hell

was she doing? Linda had told her to use the town house, and
they'd called her from Hong Kong to renew the offer. So why
was she leaving? She had every right to be here. She didn't
have any place to hide where Jason couldn't find her. Let
Mark go. He hadn't even said what he was doing here or how
long he planned to stay. To hell with him. She tossed the
clothing aside and walked into the adjacent bathroom and
turned on the shower.

Still seething with frustration at Mark, she stood there until
the water warmed. The fillip of excitement she'd ridden on
since outwitting Jason deserted her. She felt tired, drained,
heartsick.

Taking care not to wet her freshly washed hair, she stepped
under the steady stream. As the water sluiced over her, she
tried to decide what to do about Mark. She put herself in his
shoes. He'd found the bag with the clothing and the whip. He
couldn't have known those were Jason's things. Then she remembered Jason's shirts always had a monogrammed cuff—
JLT, for Jason Langsford Talbott. Mark might have seen the
initials and then overheard her conversation and thought she
was talking to Jason. The fact that it had enraged him so made
her think he might be jealous. His actions might have been a
reaction to what he thought was the truth. She could see his
point—she had appeared to be a slut.

Her kaleidoscoping emotions crystallized into anger directed at herself. "Can't you do anything right?" she shouted
to the tiled wall. She turned off the taps, deciding if Mark was
still in the house, she'd find a way to make him listen.

She vigorously toweled off and was reaching for the hair-
brush when she thought she heard Mark calling her name.
She scampered into the bedroom and opened the door to the
hall a crack.

"Alexa . . . Alexa?"

"Y-yes?"

"Darling, come down here, straight away," Mark called, his
voice no longer sounded angry.

"C-coming." *Darling? Darling?* He sounded conciliatory,
ready to apologize. What on earth had changed his mind? It
didn't matter; she was prepared to forgive him. She dashed to
the closet and grabbed the skimpy black robe, another Janet
Reger creation she'd bought to surprise Mark. The jet-black

silk was severely tailored except for the festoons of lace spilling from the belled cuffs and cascading down the neck, stopping just shy of her navel. It was sexy as hell. He'd love it. She slipped into the cool gown without stopping to button it. Instead she wound the silk sash around her waist and cinched the robe shut.

Barefoot, she half-skipped down the carpeted stairs to the main floor. She rounded the curve in the staircase and came to a dead halt. At the bottom of the stairs Mark stood beside two frowning strangers.

# Chapter 30

Alexa took two steps back, clutching at the robe's revealing neckline. "Just a minute. I'll change into—"

"It's all right," Mark called. "These gentlemen are from Scotland Yard. They want to speak to you for a moment. Come here."

Scotland Yard? What had gone wrong? How had they found her? Were they going to arrest her? She supposed stealing Jason's clothing could be considered a crime if he wanted to press charges. She'd counted on having time to put phase two into operation before anyone found her. Then, when Jason discovered what else she had in store for him, he'd never dare implicate her. A wave of apprehension swept through her. The raincoat. She'd tossed it onto the bed. It was still there in plain sight with the bag of coke inside its pocket. She'd intended to dispose of it as soon as she'd come into the town house, but Mark had found her first.

Alexa kept a composed face as she slowly came down the stairs toward Mark's extended hand. He stood there barefoot with his shirt gaping open where she'd torn the buttons off. He seemed relaxed, poised, as he stood waiting for her. When she reached for his hand, he pulled her close, hugging her.

"Alexa, this is Sergeant Caffrey and Inspector Morse.

They've just told me Jason Talbott's in jail and he's blaming you. Gentlemen, shall we go into the library and discuss this?" Mark said, guiding them down the short hall and into the library.

A thin, fragile-looking man with sprigs of white hair and creased brow, Inspector Morse had an odd expression on his face that reminded her of a worried beaver. Sergeant Caffrey had a shock of chestnut hair and quick, darting eyes that told Alexa he didn't miss a trick.

They entered the room and she felt her already-flushed face redden even more. Evidently Mark had left the library as hastily as she had. Her risqué black bra was still flung across a chair, his shoes and socks were scattered about, the sofa's cushions were hopelessly disheveled, and the Tabriz rug gracing the hearth was askew.

While Mark kept up a light conversation and they all took seats, Alexa's thoughts scrambled to make sense of this. Only an idiot could miss what had happened in the library. Alexa ran her tongue over her swollen lip. Then she remembered Mark biting her neck. With an effort at casualness, she inched her hand along the robe's collar. There wasn't any way it covered the angry welt at the base of her neck. She realized both men were staring at her; the heat in her face became unbearable. What a mess! She'd been a fool to think she could get away with this. She prayed they didn't have a search warrant. If they found the coke, she'd be jailed or deported. The revenge that had seemed so sweet earlier now seemed foolish. No, just plain stupid.

Mark kept up a light banter as he added two more logs to the glowing embers in the fireplace. Alexa noticed the shaft of the whip had not completely burned, but the fresh logs hid it. He sat down beside Alexa, draping one long leg encased in hopelessly wrinkled trousers over the other. He tucked his arm around her shoulders and gave her a reassuring squeeze.

Inspector Morse cleared his throat. "This is a rather convoluted tale, Miss MacKenzie . . . Mr. Kimbrough." There was a deferential tone to his voice, indicating he knew and respected Mark. "Earlier this evening Talbott left a bed-sitter in Soho clad in his raincoat and shoes but nothing else. He's accused of trying to expose himself to a young girl who was passing by. Her mother wasn't too far away and began screaming. The patrons of the Mucky Duck Pub, as well as those of Rio Hotz, the nightclub across the street, were on the scene immediately. Talbott attempted to retreat into the building, but the door had somehow locked behind him. The crowd detained him until we arrived."

"My word," Alexa gasped, trying to give her words just the right touch of concern without appearing melodramatic, "that poor little girl. She could be scarred for life. Is she all right?"

"We're still trying to locate her to be sure. Reporters and photographers were everywhere. It seemed that they'd had a reliable tip Princess Diana would be at the nightclub." Inspector Morse arched one thick eyebrow skeptically and barked a disbelieving half-laugh. "When someone yelled Jason Talbott was exposing himself, the press hopped on it like a pack of frenzied pit bulls. In the confusion the girl and her mother slipped away. Without them he can't be charged."

Alexa swallowed a laugh at the thought of Jason shielding his face from the cameras. *That bastard. Served him right.* Even if her entire plot had gone awry, Jason had to have been completely humiliated, and no matter how he defended himself, the tabloids would have a heyday.

"When he was arrested, he claimed you lured him to the bed-sitter, tricked him into taking drugs, and got him to remove his clothes before you sent him outside," Inspector Morse said.

"Outside? Whatever for?" Alexa asked.

The inspector colored slightly. "He insisted you two were to engage in some kinky sex. He said you had a whip and—"

"No!" cried Alexa. She felt like a skier trying to keep ahead of an avalanche. "I'd never . . . and even if I had been there—"

"Believe me," Mark interrupted, "I've been quite . . . close with Alexa for some time now. She's playful at times"— he rumpled her hair with his hand— "but definitely not sado-masochistic. Besides, she'd never have anything to do with Jason Talbott."

"Of course not," Alexa said, looking Mark straight in the eye. "I despise him."

She kept a composed face, her mind scrambling for a way out, a way to protect Renata. These men had the facts, but it was still Jason's word against hers. They'd have to prove she had been there. She'd been careful not to leave fingerprints. Anyway, would they even bother to thoroughly investigate a lewd conduct or indecent exposure charge? She doubted it.

"I suppose," Inspector Morse asked, "you can account for your whereabouts this evening Miss MacKenzie?"

"Of course," Alexa said, opting for gutting it out and making Jason prove she'd been responsible. "I was—"

"Here," Mark interjected, "all evening. Discussing . . . business."

The inspector kept a straight face but any fool could see he knew "discussing" didn't cover what had gone on this evening. Alexa felt a fresh wave of heat move up from her neck, coloring her cheeks scarlet to the roots of her hair. She reached up for a strand of tangled hair. That Mark was willing to lie for her took her totally by surprise. He couldn't know what he'd be getting himself into by giving her an alibi. Blackmail. She couldn't let him do it. "Mark, I—"

"It's all right, darling. Just answer their questions. They need to verify a few facts. They know you've been here all evening. I explained that to them when they asked to speak with you."

Alexa hesitated, but the subtle pressure of Mark's hand on her shoulder and the fact he'd already committed himself made her agree.

"Just what time did you arrive?" Sergeant Caffrey asked. A dour man who obviously wasted little time on pleasantries, he'd taken out a small notepad and was making notes.

Alexa started to give a definite time, but changed her mind. How many people could ever say exactly when they'd arrived somewhere?

"I-I'm not certain." She kept her voice level and stared off thoughtfully. "I left the theater between six and six-thirty. I must have arrived here about seven."

"I see," Inspector Morse answered with extreme politeness. "Miss MacKenzie, have you ever been out with Jason Talbott?"

Alexa didn't hesitate. The fewer lies she told, the less the chance she'd be caught. "Yes . . . once . . . sort of."

"Sort of?" A flare of suspicion ignited Sergeant Caffrey's hazel eyes. She'd been aware of his intent gaze since they'd entered the library. It was clear he believed Jason Talbott's story.

Calmly Alexa explained the entire sequence of events from the roses and the phony articles to the incident with the psychedelic drug. Throughout her explanation, Alexa never looked at Mark, but every word was directed to him. Come what may, she wanted him to know the truth.

When she stopped with the bobby finding her in the alley and taking her to the station, Sergeant Caffrey asked, "Why didn't you mention Mr. Talbott's involvement?"

"I'm a foreigner and Jason Talbott is a powerful man. I was afraid that somehow I'd be blamed and deported or even jailed. Everyone knows what happened to Stacy Keach. I decided to let them believe I'd been drinking."

"I see," was Sergeant Caffrey's curt reply. "May I use the telephone? I'd like to call Peckham Station and verify your story straight away."

Mark made small talk with the inspector while Sergeant Caffrey used the phone. Alexa snuggled closer to Mark and he responded with a hug he didn't try to hide from Inspector Morse. Alexa felt an immense sense of elation. Mark cared enough to help her no matter how brutal his earlier criticism had been. And now he knew enough of the truth about this evening to be willing to discuss it in depth later.

"They remember you," Sergeant Caffrey admitted when he hung up. "Why didn't you tell us you'd been released to Renata Tremaine?"

"I-I didn't think it mattered," Alexa stammered. She'd deliberately left Renata out of it, fearing they'd contact her and she'd provide Alexa with a second alibi for tonight. Having no alibi would be less incriminating than having two for the same evening. And nothing would be worse than implicating two people she cared about.

Inspector Morse stood up and Sergeant Caffrey slowly followed, saying, "I believe that's all for now. Where can you be reached? Are you staying here?"

"I'll give you a number," Mark said. "It's my office. Call it and they'll contact Alexa immediately."

"Fine," Inspector Morse said as he and Sergeant Caffrey took turns shaking Mark's hand. "Sorry to have bothered you two, but we had to check out Mr. Talbott's story. We won't be contacting you unless he can provide us with something more substantial than this yarn to prove you were involved."

I can't believe I'm getting away with this, Alexa thought as they walked the two men to the door and said good-night. When the heavy door shut, Alexa couldn't control her burst of triumphant laughter.

Mark clamped his hand over her mouth. "What the hell will you think of next?" His words were harsh, but the grin on his face told a different story.

She threw her arms around his neck, hugging him tightly. "I'm sorry I got you involved. Are you still angry with me?"

"How could I be? Being around you is one crazy gambit after another." He brushed a gentle kiss across her lips.

"Did you lie to help me or because you hate Jason Talbott?"

Mark took her face in both his hands. "I lied because I'd been a jerk not to let you explain." His voice was low, almost a whisper, and brutal in its self-condemnation "I lied because I'd said such cruel things to you to hurt you. I never meant them. Surely you know that." Alexa nodded, realizing what he'd said earlier had hurt him more than it had her. "But most of all I did it because you said you loved me, and I thought I'd been so rough with you that I'd lost you."

"Impossible," Alexa said, coming up on her tiptoes and looping her arms around his neck. "I'm tough; I don't give up easily."

His lips slowly descended to meet hers. The passionate turbulence of their earlier lovemaking was gone and she quivered at the tender sweetness of his kiss. He lifted his head and whispered, "I'm sorry for the unforgivable things I said. When I found that bag with Jason's things and heard you telling him no one did it better, the very words you said to me, I went crazy. Forgive me?"

"Of course, darling." She tilted her head, offering her lips for another kiss.

"Did I hurt you?" he asked.

"No, not at all. You were rough, but not too rough. No one's ever made love to me like that. I . . . never knew I could be that . . . passionate," she said, running her hand through the open panel of his shirt and finding the row of raised welts where she'd scratched him. She buried her head in the curve of his neck. "I didn't mean to hurt you either. I can't explain what came over me. And I never intended to involve you in this thing with Jason either. If they discover the truth, you could be charged."

"Hush." Mark kissed her forehead. "You'd better tell me the whole story. Then we can decide how to proceed—together."

As he led her back into the library, she told him that essentially everything she'd told the detectives had been true. They sank down onto the sofa in front of the now-blazing fire. Mark tucked an afghan around her bare legs.

"I came home early from my trip to see you, you know. At my house there was an envelope marked 'personal.' Inside were clippings of the articles about you and Jason and the picture. I couldn't believe it, but the photo looked real. I did a slow burn for the next few days, and when I saw you tonight I went crazy."

"The photo was a fake, but it had been expertly altered. After that and the drug incident, I decided to give Jason some of his own medicine."

"The screaming woman?" Mark asked. "Renata?"

Alexa nodded. "She was the one on the phone. And believe me nobody does it better. Her screams sent the bedbugs in that dive scurrying. But it wasn't a child with her; it was a midget she knows. Of course, I tipped the press that Princess Di would appear. It just goes to show you they'll believe anything. Can you imagine her in Rio Hotz? You've probably never seen it, but take my word for it, the place is as sleazy a joint as Soho has to offer."

"Christ! What will you think of next?" Mark paused and gazed at her thoughtfully. "How did you manage to pass your weekly drug test?"

"Renata went in first and left me a bit of her untainted pee in a plastic baggie behind the toilet tank. I merely poured it into my jar and gave it to them."

"Okay," he said, gathering her into his arms and holding her snugly, "you're clever, maybe too clever. You've just made a powerful enemy. If he can't prove you were involved in this, he'll—"

"I thought of that. When he was in the room, I had a camera hidden. As we speak, a friend of Twick's is altering the photos to show Jason molesting a young boy."

Mark frowned. "Where did you get the boy?"

"We didn't; we used some photos from Denmark. Tomorrow I'm sending Jason three dozen pink roses and copies of the doctored photos. My note will make it clear that if he ever bothers me again, I'll release copies to the papers."

"They'll never print them."

"Of course not, but they'll write about them. Coupled with this incident, he'll be ruined. Do you think Inspector Morse and Sergeant Caffrey believed us?"

"Certainly. With that love bite on your neck, that gown, and your nonstop blushing, they believed us. Why wouldn't they? It's a far more logical tale than the one Jason told. Besides, I have a reputation for being a conservative businessman while Jason's antics are well known to the police. I'm still concerned," he said, pulling her to her feet. "You don't know Jason Talbott the way I do. He won't be satisfied until he destroys you. We're getting you out of here."

"Where are we going?" she asked, following him up the stairs.

"To Wyndham Hill. We'll spend Christmas there. By then we should have this straightened out."

The rain had turned to a thick, mushy sleet as Mark maneuvered his Jaguar along the road toward Kent. He gazed over at Alexa. Bundled up in her wool coat, its collar turned up and hiding her chin, her eyes seemed larger than usual. Her pupils, enlarged by the dim light, were encircled by soft green rings. She smiled at him and his chest tightened in response. Warm and loving, she was exactly what he needed. What an unreasonable bastard he'd been. He'd all but raped her, and she'd forgiven him, saying she loved it. Well, he could believe that, considering the way she'd responded to him. The magnitude of his passion dismayed him, but the way he'd lost control with her alarmed him. Had he fallen so far under her spell that he'd hurt her—or destroy her—rather than lose her?

"Did Jason ever mention me?" he asked.

"N-no, I don't think so . . . but I'm not sure. I can't remember everything he said that night he dumped me in south London. Why?"

Mark hesitated, reluctant to bring up the old bones of the

past when he was striving to build their future. "I wondered if Jason knew anything about us."

"You asked me not to mention it to anyone and I didn't." She sounded defensive.

"I didn't think you had." He gave her a quick smile before he turned his attention back to the road and the oncoming headlights. "Jason and I have always disliked each other. It goes back to my days at school. Jason tried his best to make my life miserable. I wasn't the only one. He and Steven picked on all the boys he considered his social inferiors. I received more of the attention because I challenged Jason." There was more he could have added, but he left it at that.

"But Steven doesn't have a title. Why'd he act so superior?"

"Nigel Hunter's name, even then, packed the punch of success and glamour. Movie stars, especially to horny teen-age boys, may easily be substituted for a listing in *Debrett's Peerage.*"

Mark slowed the car as they drove through Pildowne Crossing and turned onto the side road leading to Wyndham Hill. A few minutes went by before he realized Alexa hadn't said anything. He looked over at her and found her giving him a troubled stare. "What's the matter?"

"I'm wondering when you're going to tell me the whole story about Jason."

# Chapter 31

Mark saw he didn't have any other choice. "I met my wife, Caroline, at a party, and even though she flirted openly with me, I didn't call her. At that point I still wasn't comfortable with anyone who could trace their ancestors back to the Norman Conquest. A week or so later she showed up at the flat I shared with Warren. Misty-eyed, she wanted to know why I didn't like her. She took me by surprise; I didn't know what to say. When she burst into tears, I explained it wasn't personal and I told her about my background. She said she already knew all about my family and didn't care. We began dating and before I knew it, I had fallen in love with her and asked her to marry me. Of course her parents objected; her father tried to reason with me, pointing out how he'd spoiled Caroline. She was used to having the best and she was easily bored. Although I knew everything he said was true, I was young enough to believe love conquers all. Finally, Caroline persuaded her parents to accept me and we were married. I didn't find out until several years later how she managed to change their minds."

"How?"

Mark took a deep breath. "She threw a tantrum and told them she couldn't live without me. That night she took an overdose of sleeping pills. Her father found her in time. I didn't find out any of this until years later. But her sulking and crying were techniques she'd found effective in manipulating her father. She perfected those techniques on me. When she didn't get her way, she'd pout. If I didn't bend—and usually I didn't—she gave up unless it was terribly important to her. Then she'd threaten to kill herself."

"Did she ever . . . try?"

"Twice. The first time was when I wouldn't let her go to Marbella with her friends. We couldn't afford it. She wanted to ask her father for the money or use her trust funds, but I wouldn't let her. She cried and sulked for days and days, but I didn't consent. When she saw I couldn't be convinced, she took an overdose of sleeping pills. Naturally I relented and she went off without me. When she returned, I tried to take her to a counselor, but she refused to go. Fortunately my investments had begun to pay off and money was no longer a problem, because Caroline needed constant diversion—holidays in exotic spots, parties, new clothes. I suggested starting a family, but she thought it would tie her down. We'd become married singles. When I realized this, I knew it wasn't what I needed to make me happy and I told Caroline I wanted a divorce. She became hysterical, accusing me of having affairs, of not loving her, of being cold . . . of being more interested in making money than in her. I didn't want to argue with her while she was in that state, so I went for a walk. When I returned, I found her unconscious. Again she'd taken an overdose, but this time the alcohol she'd consumed earlier in the evening complicated matters. You can imagine how I felt when she didn't regain consciousness for two days."

Alexa made no response but slipped her small hand into his.

"I was at the hospital with Caroline when I received word my parents had been killed in a motorcar crash."

"Oh, no." Alexa moved closer. "It couldn't have come at a worse time, could it?"

"The loss of my father"—he paused and hastily added—"and mother was traumatic. Surprisingly, Caroline couldn't have been more supportive. For the next few months we were closer and happier than we ever had been. But gradually we slipped into our old patterns. I have to say it was mostly my fault. My business took a quantum leap forward when I began investing in foreign real estate. During the last year of our marriage she was seldom at home. I'd become tired of fighting with her. Whenever she asked to do something, I just let her. Consequently, she spent most of the time with her friends in the country, in Gstaad, in Cap D'Antibes, in Marbella. Still, I didn't realize the marriage was over until I discovered she'd been having an affair."

He hesitated, thinking even now, all these years later, he vividly recalled that evening when he learned the person he loved and trusted most in the world had betrayed him.

"What the hell is he doing here?" Mark asked Caroline when Robert Talbott, Jason's brother, came to the surprise party she'd given for Mark.

"Darling," she crooned, running her lacquered nails up the lapels of his dinner jacket, "he's between postings. He'll be leaving for Angola in a few days. Be a good boy; don't make a scene."

He didn't give a damn where the diplomatic service sent Jason's younger brother. Mark swallowed his pride and covertly observed Caroline, wondering where he'd gone wrong when he'd given her everything she wanted. When she slipped away with Robert Talbott, Mark followed them. He'd suspected for some time that Caroline had been having an affair. He came up to the library door, pausing where they couldn't see him, expecting to catch them in a lovers' embrace.

"Jason says he wants you in Marbella for the party next week."

"I can't. Mark will suspect something," she replied.

"Jason says it's time to make a choice. If you really love him, you'll leave Kimbrough."

The floor seemed to drop from beneath Mark's feet. Caroline couldn't possibly be having an affair with Jason. Of all the men in England, how could she pick him?

Mark stopped recounting the story to Alexa as the car pulled into Wyndham Hill's drive.

"What did you do?" Alexa asked as they dashed from the car into the dark house.

"The next thing I knew, a gang of my friends was pulling me off Talbott. Caroline was standing there crying, and blood —his blood—was everywhere. I went upstairs and packed my bag. Six months later Caroline came to me and begged me to take her back. It seems Jason no longer wanted her. As much as I thought I loved her, I refused to reconcile. I knew if I did, it would be more of the same for the rest of my life."

They lugged their things up the stairs to the master suite. While Mark built a fire, Alexa made the bed and asked, "How did Caroline die?"

Mark cleared his throat and turned to face her. He hated going over this, but Alexa deserved the truth. "She killed herself. When she came to me pleading to be forgiven, she threatened to kill herself. Caroline had said this so many times over the years, first with her father and then with me, I doubted she'd do anything. But I called her father and warned him anyway. Several months went by and I didn't hear from her. I thought everything was all right. Late one night her father called. Caroline had driven her car over a cliff and been killed. She'd left a note saying she couldn't live without . . . Jason. Her father asked me not to mention her suicide attempts or the note. The family wished to explain her death as an accident and I agreed. Apparently she'd been chasing Jason for months, but he wanted no part of her. I blamed myself for her death. I should have insisted she get professional help."

"Darling, it wasn't your fault," Alexa said, moving toward him. "You couldn't have known."

"Let's put the past where it belongs—behind us," he said, turning away, reluctant to keep discussing this. "Get in bed. I'll bring up more wood."

When he returned, she was snuggled under the eiderdown comforter. "Hurry," she called as he shed his clothing, "it's freezing."

He hopped into bed and pulled her into his arms, kissing first her forehead and then the tip of her upturned nose before meeting her parted lips. He had a burning, aching need to make love to her, to possess her again. This time they made love slowly and with an incredible tenderness that hadn't seemed possible after the primitive coupling earlier.

Afterward Alexa gave a sleepy yawn and stretched. She slid farther beneath the covers, resting her head on his chest. Moments later her even breathing told him she was asleep. But sleep didn't come that easily to Mark. He ran his hand over Alexa's silky hair, fanning it across his chest. He raised a tangled curl to his lips. It smelled like a spring bouquet, he thought as he kissed it. Alexa had a knack for getting herself into trouble. But what bothered him most was a suspicion that this mess with Jason was somehow his fault. As Alexa had told the police, she'd known Jason for some time, but only recently had he shown any interest in her. Mark had the niggling feeling that somehow Jason had learned he was in love with Alexa and that was the root of his unexplained conduct. Jason had deliberately pursued Caroline and then ruthlessly destroyed an emotionally unbalanced woman just to get even with Mark.

Beside him Alexa turned, adjusting her position until her head found the pillow and she burrowed into it. Earlier he'd told her about his security problems and that he had been staying at Warren's while a security system was being installed in his home, but he couldn't keep her down here forever. He'd merely bought three or four weeks' time when they could be together. Perhaps by the first of the year the private investigators he'd hired would have uncovered something, or Interpol might have arrested the black-market ringleader. Whoever he was he'd been careful not to let any of the agents receiving the tickets know his identity. In Mark's opinion the arrest of the agents had been a temporary setback for the ringleader. Given enough time, the culprit would organize another network of greedy agents. But by then the new computer tracking system for tickets should be in place at Windsor Air, leaving it less vulnerable.

Tomorrow—no, make that today, he thought as he realized the gray light of predawn had stolen the amber glow the fire had earlier given the room— he'd go into the village and ring up Axel Marley at Interpol and ask him if anything had come of the tip Mark had given them. Using a friend in the Foreign Office, he'd taken Alexa's suggestion and cross-checked by computer the countries where black-market tickets had originated against the names of embassy personnel who'd ever been assigned to that country. His hunch was that the ringleader had to have been in a country long enough to make contacts there. A person couldn't just walk into a country and find a black-market agent willing to participate in the scheme. Governments, especially in the less-sophisticated Third World nations, had laws about how much currency could be exchanged and the amount that could be brought in or taken out. The ringleader would have to make contacts with shady government officials who could be bribed. The list the computer generated had been surprisingly long. One name had jumped out: Robert Talbott. Alexa moved in her sleep, her arms unconsciously searching for him. He bent to kiss her just as her roving hands found him. With eyes half-open and velvety soft from sleep, she whispered, "I love you." She gave him a nuzzling, puppydog kiss and closed her eyes again. He eased out of bed, making certain not to disturb her, and went downstairs.

The thin blanket of snow that had fallen the previous night melted beneath his tires as he drove into Pildowne Crossing. Not being able to get a telephone installed until after Christmas would be damned inconvenient, he thought as he made his way into the Heart in Hand Tavern to use the public telephone.

When he reached Vincent Ferrier, the investigator he'd hired, Mark said, "Pull out all the stops, Vincent. Do a real in-depth study on Jason Talbott."

"Since you picked up Robert Talbott's name on the cross-check, I've been looking into his activities. Yesterday he flew home from his post in Gabon."

"Really?" Mark's interest perked. "If my suspicions are correct Windsor Air should be hit with a rash of black-market tickets from there. Put our agents on alert."

After Mark hung up he purchased three tabloids and the *Times.* Jason was front-page news on all three papers, but Alexa wasn't mentioned at all. Mark didn't bother to check the *Times;* they wouldn't print anything unless formal charges were filed. Since the police had been unable to locate the girl and her mother, no actual charges had been made. Naturally that hadn't stopped the scandal sheets from printing the story.

Two days later Vincent Ferrier had some interesting news. It seemed Robert Talbott had one minor blemish on his diplomatic record. Years ago while posted in Hong Kong, he'd invested in a company that made phony Rolex and Piaget watches. Talbott had claimed not to have known what the company was doing, and since nothing could be proven, no action was taken against him.

By the end of the week Interpol had intercepted a batch of

tickets being rewritten in Denmark by a shady travel agency. They'd originated in Gabon.

The information on Jason Talbott proved to be more elusive. There wasn't anything Mark hadn't known except that Jason had purchased a home for Melanie Tarenholt in the fashionable Chelsea area of London. Mark hadn't realized Jason was so involved with Melanie. What about Jason's wife? Short and mousy, Mary Emerson wasn't the type of woman Mark had pictured Jason marrying. But then he'd told Mark he'd been forced to marry her. The Talbott fortunes, like many of the titled elite's, had succumbed to twentieth-century realities and were on the wane. For an infusion of cash Jason had married a plain woman, leaving her in the country with her horses while he lived alone in London, leading a lavish life with his wife's money. Mark stopped and rethought that one. He'd had several business dealings with Cranston Emerson, Mary's father. Like most men who'd made their fortunes in postwar England, the man was shrewd. Somehow Mark couldn't see Emerson putting up with a bloodsucker like Jason Talbott. Mark gave Vincent Ferrier instructions to research the Emerson fortune as well as Jason's sources of income.

"Well," Alexa demanded when Mark returned from the private screening of *Last Chance,* "how was it? How was I?"

"Wait," Mark said. "May I come in and take my coat off?" Teasing her, he took an exaggeratedly long time removing his topcoat and hanging it in the closet. He turned to her and gave her a big hug. "It was terrific. A smash. And *you* stole the show. There isn't any question about it; *The Last Chance* will be an unprecedented success."

"How was I?" Alexa asked, unable to hide the quiver in her voice.

"Angel, don't worry. You were fabulous! Giles edited your scene brilliantly. There was no doubt you were naked, but the focus of the scene was on the emotion, not on the nudity. The majority of your shots were close-ups. The emotion you conveyed would make even the most accomplished actress envious." Mark kept his tone upbeat, disguising the displeasure he felt at seeing the woman he loved naked, looking sexy as hell for the whole world to see. "They'll be begging you to accept other roles."

"Not interested." Alexa tugged on his arm. "Come into the kitchen. It's warmer in there and I have coffee made."

Mark followed her, thinking how easily Alexa fit into his life. Since coming to Wyndham Hill, they'd spent long days making the place habitable. Alexa never complained that the antiquated furnace refused to work and that their only heat came from the kitchen stove or one of the fireplaces. He hadn't minded either. Days at Alexa's side restoring Wyndham Hill and nights snuggled with her under the eiderdown comforter were his idea of how he'd like to spend the rest of his life.

"I wish I could have been there," Alexa said, handing him a mug of coffee.

Not wanting to reopen this argument, Mark took a sip of coffee. He'd had to take a strong stand to convince her not to come to the opening. She assumed her little stunt with the pictures of Jason would protect her. Mark knew better. "I'm glad you weren't there. Jason came with Kelly Holmes. Remember her? One of the bit players in *The Last Chance.* I've got to hand it to him. Even after all the adverse publicity, he just brazens it out by acting as if nothing happened."

"Did he mention me? Or us?"

"I didn't speak with him, but I doubt he knows anything about my verifying your alibi. Scotland Yard wouldn't release that information unless it came to trial, which it won't, since the charges were dropped. If Jason asked anyone about you, he would have been told you'd returned to the States to await the opening there."

"What did Nigel say? He should have a better feel for this. He's produced dozens of blockbusters."

"He wasn't there." Mark kept his voice matter-of-fact. "Apparently he's in Los Angeles preparing for the screenings." He quickly drained the remainder of his coffee and handed the cup to Alexa for a refill.

Where the hell was Nigel these days? Over the last few months Mark had tried to reach Nigel to verify that Alexa's outtakes had been destroyed, but he had never returned his calls. Mark couldn't imagine any reason Nigel would be avoiding him, but that's the way it had looked until Mark spoke with Giles. He mentioned he'd hardly seen Nigel since they'd returned to England. Nigel hadn't been involved in the editing process. Of course, Giles had the final cut, but Nigel hadn't even overseen the director's work. According to Giles, who had worked frequently with Nigel, this was highly unusual. Something about the whole situation didn't sit well with Mark.

"Let's go upstairs; I'm knackered. I guess I'm getting used to this country life. One night in the big city and I'm exhausted."

"Hurry," Alexa called after they'd closed down the kitchen and moved upstairs, "these sheets are freezing."

Mark banked two logs on the fire before quickly stripping and climbing in beside her. He took her into his arms, holding her snugly. He'd assumed he'd get over his constant need to make love to her when he'd spent this much time alone with her. He hadn't. She nuzzled his neck and kissed his ear, flicking her tongue lightly across it. Even before his lips found hers, he had a hard-on.

When they finished making love, Mark held Alexa and they talked until he heard her rhythmic breathing and realized she'd fallen asleep. He stared at the dancing shadows the firelight threw across the ceiling. With the movie's success would come tremendous pressure on Alexa—on their relationship. He swiveled his head to look at her. A stray moonbeam sparked a golden curl as it lay across her cheek. In person she was every bit as sexy as she appeared on screen, but she didn't realize that. Once the picture was released, it wouldn't take the world long to recognize her appeal. It was selfish, he knew, but he wanted to keep her to himself. But soon he'd be living with a celebrity. The book, the movie, and the play showed the breadth of her unique talent. She'd be in demand, and with her ambition there'd be no way of telling where this would lead. He couldn't keep her to himself forever. He'd have to conquer the ungovernable jealousy he'd felt at seeing her naked on the screen. He pulled her closer. Restlessly she moved one silky leg between his and snuggled against him.

Just before Christmas, Vincent Ferrier reported that Emerson gave Jason a monthly stipend to remain married to Mary. It seemed she'd developed what Vincent described as an "unnatural attachment" to another horse breeder—a woman. Her family didn't wish this to become public knowledge; hence the payments to Jason. But this money couldn't begin to support his lavish lifestyle. His additional stream of income was unclear since he did his banking in Switzerland.

"You wait in the pub while I make a few calls," Alexa said as they came into the Heart in Hand Tavern. "I want to wish my friends Merry Christmas."

He ordered a pint of Goose Eye Bitter and sipped it while he waited. When she returned, Alexa slumped into her seat giggling.

"What's so funny?"

"You'll never guess what T.S. did on your desk."

Mark hadn't thought of the feisty feline in months. It hadn't been his desk in months either. Bob had taken his place, but Mark was touched that she still thought of it as his. "What?"

"Had kittens—five of them."

Suddenly Mark couldn't stop laughing either. There was absolutely nothing motherly about that cantankerous cat. "I thought you said he was a male."

"So I was told by the little kid who gave him to me. He was standing outside a greengrocer in Shepherd's Market in the pouring rain, trying to give T.S. away." Mark shook his head and she responded, "Have you ever tried to verify a cat's sex?" Alexa gave him a winsome smile. Her eyes had darkened to emerald in the dim light. "Mark could we . . . do you think we could keep one kitten? Don't you think we need a cat at Wyndham Hill?"

There wasn't any way he could say no to her. He didn't particularly care for cats, but when she said "we" that way he couldn't deny her anything. "Sure," he said, "just make certain this one's a male."

On Christmas Eve they finished the library and brought down a dusty old sofa from the attic to use until the room could be properly furnished. They sat in front of the fire sipping a bottle of 1966 Lafite-Rothschild.

"Do you think we—" Alexa began. "I mean maybe you—"

"Start over. I liked the 'we' part better."

Alexa lowered her luxurious lashes and stared at the top button on his shirt. "Do you think we could get a partners' desk for this room? That way we both could work at the same time. We could put the desk over there by the window. During the day we could look out across our meadow and at night we wouldn't be too far from the fire."

With one finger under her chin, he tilted her head back until she looked him in the eyes. "Do you know how many times you've said 'we' lately?" She shook her head. "Not nearly as many times as I've thought it." He slipped his hand into his pocket and then handed her the small box. "Let's make 'we' official."

Her smile vanished when she saw the box: Tessiers Jewelers. The gold logo embossed on the maroon velvet lid named the Bond Street jeweler who dealt in precious estate jewels. She'd passed by the store many times, pausing to look at jewels that had once belonged to princes or dukes or maharajas. Some of the most sought-after stones in the world, these gems came with papers of authentication detailing their history, which often added significantly to their value. With trembling fingers she lifted the lid. A flawless pear-shaped emerald flanked by rows of channel-set diamonds formed the most astounding ring she'd ever seen. Alexa's expressive eyes misted over and she whispered, "Does this mean . . ."

"It means I love you and I want to marry you."

"Oh, Mark." She slid the ring onto her finger. "You do love me."

"Sometimes words don't come easily to me. That doesn't mean I don't love you. I do."

Alexa drew back; her expression grew serious. "Last year, this very night, do you know where I was?" When he shook his head, she continued, "Alone . . . crying over Paul. In one short year, so much has happened. The movie, the play, the soundtrack, Linda and Renata . . . and you. I need—"

Mark held up his hand, indicating she should stop. Any woman who had to think about a marriage proposal couldn't possibly be in love. "Think about it," he said, his voice full of sarcasm.

"I have thought about it. For hours," was Alexa's quiet reply. "And I know how I feel. I love you, but we need to settle a few things so that we don't make a second mistake."

Mark let out a relieved sigh. "You're right. I never intended to marry again. This time's forever."

Alexa gazed down at the ring and then back at him. "When I married Paul, I never thought about what I wanted, where I was going, or what I would be doing in three, five, or even ten years. I clung to him. He was the comet; I was the tail."

"I realize you have a career. You and I can work here and commute into London when necessary. You may want to return to the United States to work on a film or whatever. It may not always be possible for us to be together. We'll have to deal with those situations as they arise."

Mark expected her to embrace his broad-minded view of their situation. His willingness to compromise, to accommodate her and her career, was something that even surprised him. He hated thinking of her trekking off anywhere without him, but he had to be realistic. As soon as this film hit the mass market, she'd be a hot property. No matter what he wanted, he couldn't keep her to himself. But as he sat there waiting for her response, he knew his words hadn't had the desired effect.

"You expect to be out of England a lot?" she asked.

Mark didn't know what she wanted him to say. "I don't know," he answered truthfully. "I have to leave in two weeks to go to Australia to conclude a deal there. But after that I can structure my life the way I want it."

She peered down at the ring, twisting it back and forth. An uncomfortable minute passed before she said, "Once my obligation to the play is over, I can restructure mine."

"Alexa, I'll have that contract rewritten. You won't be obligated for two years. You'll be free to do whatever you like."

Alexa continued looking down, seemingly more interested in the Tessiers logo scripted onto the ring's velvet box than in what he was saying. "I-I don't want to be an actress." She looked up at him. There weren't any visible tears in her eyes, but her lashes were moist. "I don't want to live out of a suitcase, flitting from one place to another, and I don't want you to be gone all the time. I want to put down roots, to stay here near my friends. I need to complete my book, but after that I . . . I want to stay here and have a baby—your baby."

# Chapter 32

"What gives?" Alexa asked Giles after she settled into his cramped Morris Minor for the ride to the Cotswolds to visit Nigel. "There isn't a problem with *The Last Chance*, is there?"

"No, definitely not. The Christmas screenings went better than we ever expected. We'll get two or more Academy Award nominations." Giles hesitated. "I wanted to speak to you privately."

"Oh? Why?" Alexa shifted uncomfortably. "Renata . . . is everything . . . all right?"

Giles smiled, creasing his forehead right up to his woolly cap of gray curls. "Couldn't be better. She lives for the play, you know. I don't even worry about the drugs anymore. Nothing could tempt her. I can't thank you enough, but I didn't ask you to come with me to talk about Renata. I have a proposition for you. How would you like to work with me?"

"I'd love it," Alexa exclaimed. "But what would you want me to do? I don't have a screenplay ready at the moment."

"I'm talking about something much bigger than a single project. I mean long-term—five years."

Seeing her shocked look, Giles quickly added, "Nigel is reorganizing Hunter Films. I'll have twenty percent of the stock in the new company and I'll be directing exclusively for

Hunter Films. You could come on board right at the inception."

"But I'm not a screenwriter. And I don't intend to become one. Selling a screenplay is like throwing a rabbit into a pack of wolves. Everyone bites off—or I should say rewrites—a piece. Several screenwriters have at your work. Then the director has his say and it's again rewritten. And don't forget the stars; they'll have their own ideas. When it's finally filmed, it hardly resembles the original product. The only reason *The Last Chance* survived was because everyone knew the plot. If it hadn't been such a popular book, no telling what would have happened."

"I can't say you aren't right," Giles admitted. "Why do you think so many credits read 'Written and Directed by'? Directing is a way writers have found to protect and enhance their work. I'm not asking you to write anything . . . unless you want to. What I have in mind is a position as creative director of special projects. You and I would work together and discuss your ideas. Then we'd select a team to implement them. There are plenty of writers who could do the actual writing. Does this sound interesting to you?"

"Yes, it does." More than interesting, she thought. How many people would ever have the chance to work with a unique talent like Giles Acton?

"I thought it might. You have a wealth of talent. The play will prove that."

"But many of those ideas were Twick's," Alexa protested.

"You work well with people. That combined with your ideas is what I'm trying to find. I want you on my team." He turned the tiny car up the M4 toward the Cotswolds. "This could give us both what we want—to remain in England. The success of *The Last Chance* has already begun to generate innumerable offers for me to direct. Most of them are from America, but I want to remain here close to Renata. Her work is on the stage." He turned and gave Alexa a warm smile. "The problem with finding the perfect partner is staying with that person. Being separated for months at a time isn't conducive to a happy relationship. If this Hunter Films deal develops properly, neither of us will be forced to work in Hollywood."

"Aren't you forgetting the British production companies like Lord Grade's and Cubby Broccoli's?" Alexa asked, thinking of Grade's successful films and Broccoli's James Bond series. "You could work for them."

"Hollywood casts a long shadow. Neither of them have been able to get out from under it. No one will be able to compete with what Nigel has in mind. The money he'll be able to raise by taking the company public will provide monumental amounts of cash." He maneuvered the sluggish car aside to let the lorry hanging on their bumper go around them. "I think you have as compelling a reason to remain here as I do, right?"

Alexa nodded, not bothering to tell him she'd already worked things out with Mark. Before he left for Australia they'd decided she'd remain with the play until April, when it opened. By that time she would feel comfortable turning the management of the play over to Bob. Then she and Mark would be married and move to the country with T.S. and her adorable marmalade kitten, B.S. Mark didn't like putting off their wedding. He'd made that clear as soon as she told him she wanted a family. She'd been shocked at how much he wanted one as well, but finally they'd agreed it might be better to wait until after the play opened before being married.

"I've been planning to take some time off," Alexa said to Giles.

"That's the beauty of this. You could work at your own pace. All I'd need from you is a commitment to develop four projects over five years."

"I see." Alexa had to admit working with Twick and Quint as well as the seasoned professionals Renata had found had been tremendously stimulating. What Giles was proposing could be the most exciting opportunity ever to come her way. She could have the life she and Mark had planned and expand her career. The proposition became even more enticing when Giles specified the money involved.

They drove up to a half-timbered Elizabethan-style cottage with a thatched roof that hung over the leaded-glass windows. Draped in ivy, the cottage had a storybook look about it.

With a military bearing, a housekeeper clad in an institutional-white uniform, white nylons, and white shoes escorted them into a small conservatory overlooking a terraced garden.

"Thirty minutes," she said, checking her watch. "That is as long as I'll allow you to stay."

. "Hello, Alexa, Giles," Nigel said. "Pardon me if I don't get up."

Alexa flashed him an overbright smile but knew her face must have registered her shock. Nigel Hunter had to have lost more than a hundred pounds. Even sitting in a chair, his lap covered with a plaid blanket, he looked emaciated, skeletal. "Hello," she managed, throwing a questioning glance at Giles.

"Sit, sit," Nigel said. His once-brusque voice was grainy, barely above a whisper.

She and Giles took seats on the sofa as a maid appeared with the tea trolly.

"Help yourselves," Nigel said.

When he swung his chair to the side and rolled closer, Alexa realized he was in a wheelchair.

"I see Giles didn't tell you," Nigel croaked. "Let's get it out in the open. I'm dying."

Alexa gasped and set aside the cup of tea she'd been handed.

Nigel raised his thin hand. Around the IV shunt was a yellow-violet bruise. "I don't want sympathy. That's not why I asked Giles to bring you here. I want you to promise me word of my illness won't leave this room."

"I promise," Alexa mumbled.

"Giles explained to you about my new production company?" When she nodded, he continued, "And you agree to join us?" Again she nodded. "Did he explain my reasons for going public?"

"No." Alexa's hand shook as she picked up her teacup and took a sip.

"My entire life has been Hunter Films. I've built it into the best damned film company in the U.K. Except for a brief five years when I had Louisa . . ." He stared off toward the terraced garden, his faded blue eyes wistful. "She was Steven's mother, you know. She died of cancer shortly before she was thirty." He stopped talking and gazed out the window, apparently lost in thought.

Alexa looked at Giles and saw Nigel's condition hadn't come as a shock to him. She twisted a sleek lock of hair around her finger. An uncomfortable minute passed before Nigel continued.

"Except for her, Hunter Films has been my life." He paused and Alexa thought she saw him blink back a tear before he again looked at her. "Don't mind me. Get damned sentimental these days. I want you to know how important it is for me to leave a legacy, something of value. Hunter Films has to be that legacy. Shortly after I bought the rights to your book, I discovered I had lymphocytic leukemia. All my life I've been a fighter. While Giles filmed *The Last Chance,* I stayed in Los Angeles getting treatments at the City of Hope. Wasn't worth a damn. When I returned to London, I continued to seek a cure. Now I'm just waiting for the inevitable."

Nigel stopped, out of breath. Evidently, just speaking weakened him. Alexa swallowed hard, her throat constricting as a hot sting of tears burned her eyes. Beneath his gruff exterior Nigel was a genuinely nice man. He'd understood it when she wanted to be made a story consultant. And he'd come to her rescue with funds for the play. It wasn't fair; he didn't deserve this.

When Nigel resumed, his voice was even weaker. "This fall when I finally accepted there would be no cure, I began planning this. By selling shares of Hunter Films and getting you and Giles to join the team, I'm assured of attracting investors and raising more cash than any production company in this damned business has ever seen. Then, after I'm gone, I'll know Hunter Films has the talent and the money to continue into the next century."

Self-consciously Alexa nodded and reached for a finger sandwich she didn't want. "Who'll be doing the producing?"

"Don't worry about Steven. Under the new arrangement he'll have a third of the stock and Giles will have twenty percent. The rest will be sold through the public offering. I'm confident Steven will be able to produce these films. If he can't, the board will have to replace him."

Alexa took a bite of the watercress sandwich. So that was it. This had sounded too good to be true. Steven would be the fly in the soup on this one. She was surprised Giles didn't think so. Then she recalled all the people with the title producer who had worked on her film. She supposed assistant producers could be hired to handle things. Evidently Nigel had

handed the reins of *The Last Chance* to others, and it still became a hit.

"Of course, I wouldn't want to see Steven ousted. He's my
only child. Louisa wouldn't want that." Nigel shook his head,
his eyes weepy once more. "When I learned of my illness, I
cut Steven off."

Involuntarily Alexa's eyebrows lifted.

"I know, you think that's cruel. But I should have done it
years ago. Hell, I gave him everything he ever asked for. I felt
guilty because I never spent time with him. I couldn't. He
reminded me too much of his mother. Satiny blond hair . . .
those blue, blue eyes. Did I tell you how we met?"

Alexa shook her head. As he gave the details, it became
evident Nigel's overpowering love for his wife and his subse-
quent devastation at her loss meant there was no love left for
his son. Alexa realized why Steven was an emotionally under-
nourished boy who'd grown into an insecure man.

"Ten minutes," the grim-faced woman who'd escorted
them in warned. Alexa realized she must be Nigel's nurse.

"I cut Steven off for his own good. Earning a salary and
living on it makes a person appreciate hard work. I took him
from my television subsidiary, where'd spent his time seducing starlets and entertaining his worthless friends, and gave
him *The Last Chance* to produce. I saw to it he had a generous
salary and enough support to sink a friggin' battleship. What
the hell does he do? Not a damned thing. He couldn't make a
decision because he'd never had to before. Giles bailed him
out; the assistant producers bailed him out. Hell, even Mark
Kimbrough had to help him. I saw then and there he'd have to
do it alone. Make his own film—start to finish—before he'd
be ready to take over Hunter Films. I refused to give him a
shilling, but he managed to put the whole thing together. He
horsetraded for your script"—Nigel nodded at Alexa—"and
he found his own location and studio space. He was doing
great"—Nigel tried to smile—"until they went on location."

Alexa wondered if that was true. Steven had seemed to be
struggling when he'd come to her and asked for the money.
That was *before* he'd gone on location.

"I blame his problems on that Italian faggot he hired to
direct. Asante Anselmo. Sounds like a goddamned drink. I
want him to finish this film," Nigel said. "I don't care that it's

a B movie. Hell, when I began, I'd have been happy to have
my movies called B's. Damn happy. There's a market even for
B movies, particularly in poor countries. Just dub them and
redub them and distribute the hell out of them. That's how I
began Hunter Films. And that's what I told Steven—just finish the goddamned film and we'll decide how good it is and
where to market it." A raspy cough interrupted his sermon.
Nigel directed his gaze at Alexa. "I need you to help him."

"Me?" Alexa glanced at Giles and saw this wasn't the first
time he'd heard this.

"Yes, I told Steven I was taking Hunter Films public and
unless he completed this film, there'd be no place for him. He
knows I'll make good on my word. You see, he doesn't know
how ill I am. He thinks I have an intestinal disorder."

"But you wanted him to do this on his own," Alexa said.

"That's why I'm not sending Giles," Nigel said. "He knows
too much. He'd overpower Steven. But you could help him
without threatening him."

"I suppose I could offer to rewrite the script." Alexa tried to
keep her reluctance from her voice.

"The script, hell, that's not the problem. That fag . . .
Delmo—"

"Anselmo," Giles corrected. "What Nigel is trying to say,
Alexa, is the director seems to be having a problem communi-
cating. You could help."

"The only Italian I speak is menu Italian! I couldn't translate." She frowned at Giles. Language barriers had never been
a problem for directors. Some of the best in the business were
French or Italian. She could understand Nigel, in his weakened condition, thinking of this idea, but not Giles.

"We want you to help direct if necessary." Giles voice was
quiet. After he spoke, he waited a minute for his words to
register.

"What?" Alexa muttered.

"I saw you work with Melanie in Mexico. You knew the
material, your material, and you were wonderful. It wasn't
your fault she couldn't follow your instructions." Giles put
his teacup down and looked at her intently. "I think you have
great possibilities as a director. There are plenty of women in
the business now. Start here; help Steven. After all, this is

your screenplay. Just discuss it with Anselmo and pretend to translate."

Alexa stared out the window. Snowflakes had begun to fall. "I can't walk away from the play."

"You aren't going to the provinces on trials with them," Giles reminded her. "Go with Steven for a week or so. He can't have much more than that to go. They've been there six weeks already. He's only shooting half of it on location."

Alexa shook her head. Not only did she not want to go, but she knew Mark wouldn't want her to help Steven. In the two weeks since they'd returned to London, Mark had kept her well away from Jason's crowd. "I'd like to help you, but I can't."

"You're concerned about the checks you think Steven took, aren't you?" Nigel asked. "I spoke to him. He didn't know anything about them. They've never been cashed. It's possible someone else took them, or that the printing company omitted a page. It's happened before."

"It's possible," Alexa conceded, although she didn't think it was likely.

"I'd consider it a personal favor if you helped him out," Nigel said. Now his voice was so low Alexa had to lean forward to hear him. "Blame me for whatever faults he has. I didn't take the care with him I should have. When I join Louisa, I'd like to think of you three, Steven and Giles and you, running Hunter Films."

The nurse appeared and without saying a word came over to Nigel's chair. She wheeled him to the door saying, "That's all for today."

"What do you say, Alexa?" Giles asked. "Will you help Steven?"

Watching the old man, his earnest blue eyes on her, Alexa couldn't say no. "Yes," she said, "I'll try." She walked over to Nigel and kissed him on the cheek. "Don't worry about Hunter Films."

"Thank you," he said in a grainy whisper.

All the way home Giles tried to encourage Alexa, telling her Steven was still in town and convincing her to talk to him. Evidently, this new film company mattered more to Giles than she'd originally thought.

"Look, I know you don't want to do this, but will you really be missed if you take off two weeks now? Isn't most of your work done and can't Bob do whatever is left during your absence?"

"Yes, I can be spared, I guess," she said. "I simply don't want to work with Steven. I adore Nigel, and you, but Steven . . ."

Yet as she thought about it, the more attractive the idea Giles had given her earlier became. She could write something and possibly direct it herself. Directing was an art; watching Twick and Giles had convinced her of that. It wasn't just working with actors. It was equipment and sound systems and lighting and camera angles and God knows what else. But if she spent the time learning from Giles, she might want to try it herself one day. The only real stumbling block to all of this would be Mark. He'd object to her helping Steven in any way. Mark would be certain Jason Talbott would somehow get to her through Steven. In her note to Jason she'd made it clear if anything happened to her, a close friend would release the pictures. Alexa knew Renata would do just that. She smiled to herself; Mark was incredibly protective of her, obsessively so. If he'd had his way she'd still be secreted at Wyndham Hill instead of living in his London town house.

By the time Giles dropped Alexa off, she'd decided how she'd tell Mark that she was helping Steven.

# FINAL CUT:
## *Khartoum*

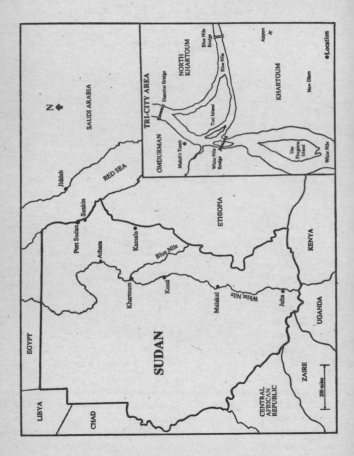

# Chapter 33

On its final approach the plane swooped low over the Bayuda Desert, providing Alexa with an excellent view of the merging of the White Nile with the Blue Nile leaving the curious little Tuti Island stranded in the center. The two rivers hooked together to form one Nile that flowed on toward Egypt, making it easy for Alexa to see why, even before Christ was born, Arabs plying the trade route through the Sudan called it Khartoum: the elephant's trunk.

To the west the sun's narrow crescent slipped below the horizon, casting a coral glow over the thousands of mud huts lining the rivers' banks while a silver dome rose above the earthen buildings and caught the fading light. The city below was Omdurman, Alexa realized as she stared at the glistening roof of the Mahdi's tomb. The plane dipped one wing and she saw the wide, tree-lined boulevards of Khartoum that lay on the opposite bank of the White Nile. The plane descended even lower now, coming perilously close to the rooftops. She craned her neck and tried to see North Khartoum, the third of the tri-city group populating the confluence of the Niles, but the Windsor jet touched down before she could sight it.

"Finally," Steven huffed, rising before the fasten-seatbelt sign flicked off and grabbing their carry-on luggage from the overhead compartment. "Let's get the hell out of here. Brad will be waiting."

"Are you sure?" Alexa asked. There had been a five-hour delay in Cairo on the flight from London to the Sudan.

"He'll be here, luv," Steven smiled down at her.

At his joking tone Alexa squeezed out a smile. Ever since she'd volunteered to help him, Steven had been unbelievably accommodating. The mercurial mood swings she'd noticed when he'd been home before seemed to have vanished, she thought as she followed him from the first-class section to the waiting ramp. Except for a persistent allergy that kept him sniffling, he seemed inexplicably happy, too happy, considering the snarl his movie was in. Only one thing seemed able to darken Steven's mood, and that was Jason Talbott. When Alexa had mentioned him, hoping to determine if Jason had told Steven anything about the stunt she'd pulled, Steven had become depressed. Alexa had been surprised to learn Steven hadn't spoken to Jason since early December. Of course, Steven had heard Jason had been accused of lewd conduct, but he didn't take it seriously.

Steven confided in her that this was the first year that he hadn't been invited to spend Christmas in Marbella. Jason had gone there with his brother, Robert, and Melanie Tarenholt. But he hadn't even bothered to call Steven to wish him a Merry Christmas. Alexa had wanted to scream: *What about your father?* But she hadn't. The less said about Nigel, the better. It was evident Steven had no idea his father was dying, and if Nigel had his reasons for not telling him, Alexa had to respect them.

Inside the terminal she followed Steven through the mob of Sudanese waiting to clear Customs to the visitors' line, where few people stood. She reached into her purse and brought out her passport and the visa she'd hastily obtained from the Sudanese embassy in London. She smiled inwardly, remembering the shocked looks on the officials' faces. Since the embassy was located directly across from St. James's Palace on Cleveland Row, she'd assumed they would be used to Westerners requesting visas. They weren't. Not high on the list of desirable tourist destinations, Khartoum seldom attracted young, single women traveling alone.

"There's Brad," Steven said, waving to a man standing in the waiting area beyond the Customs checkpoint.

Shorter than average and thickly built, Brad Willingham, a Vietnam vet turned property manager, had the well-honed, muscular body of a football player. His chestnut-brown hair, worn longer than currently fashionable, tumbled across his forehead, emphasizing his oft-broken nose and electric-blue eyes. Clad in well-worn jeans with a khaki shirt unbuttoned to the navel to reveal a wealth of chest hair and a fifty-pound gold chain, Brad had a mercilessly arrogant expression on his face. Even at this distance she sensed this pit bull of a man lived on the wild side—and loved it.

He waved back and moved closer to the spot where they'd exit from Customs. The distance of several yards and a dirty glass partition made conversation impossible. With one shoulder braced against the wall, Brad lit a cigarette, took a long drag, and gave Alexa an obvious once-over. Twice. She looked away, pretending not to notice while she waited for the people ahead of them to move through the inspection. When she glanced up again, he was scouring her with a rude, animal-like stare. Determined to set him straight even before she met him, Alexa gave him a singeing, drop-dead look. He responded with a carnivorous smile and an exaggerated wink.

She turned her back on him and said to Steven, "You didn't tell me your friend Brad was such a jerk."

"He's harmless, luv. Remember, we need him."

All the way here, Steven had told her how indispensable Brad was, but already Alexa had her doubts. "What's taking so long?" she whispered, trying to forget Brad. The first person in line had yet to clear the checkpoint.

"They're checking passports for an Israeli stamp or an Egyptian border stamp, indicating you've been to Israel. This could take a while. A transaction that takes two minutes in London, ten in Rome, forty-five in Cairo, takes two hours in Khartoum. Now do you see why I insisted we carry on our luggage? If we'd checked it, we'd be here all night."

When her passport and visa had finally been stamped, she walked up to where Steven was standing with Brad discussing something in lowered voices.

"Hullo," Brad said, forcing Steven to stop talking and introduce her. "Been looking forward to this, babe. Steven's told me *all* about you."

Seeing that Steven looked vaguely uncomfortable at the comment, Alexa wondered just what *all* meant. But before she could inquire, he moved off in the direction of the exit.

"Swing by the People's Palace," Steven said once they were inside the rusty Rover.

"What the hell for?" Brad asked.

"Alexa would like to see where Gordon died," Steven answered, smiling at Alexa.

"I'd love it." She smiled back. Steven could be charming and considerate when he chose. He'd remembered what a history buff she was.

"Who?" Brad asked.

"Colonel Gordon, a British officer, was besieged in Khartoum by the Mahdi," Steven explained. "He kept pleading with London to send reinforcements. The Mahdist forces besieged the palace, and when Gordon came out, they beheaded him and hacked his body to bits."

"He showed exceptional courage," Alexa said. "Although surrounded and without enough food to withstand a prolonged siege, he refused to let the civilians in Khartoum starve. Had he not fed them as well as his troops, he might have been able to hold out the three additional days until reinforcements arrived."

"Jesus!" Brad turned down Nile Avenue that ran along the waterfront of the White Nile. "That was stupid. He shoulda' let 'em starve."

"I agree," Steven said. "As it turned out, the Mahdi razed the city, killing most of them anyway."

Alexa disagreed; Gordon had done the right thing. It crossed her mind for a moment that had Mark been in the same situation, he'd have behaved as honorably. But she didn't voice her opinion; she wasn't in the mood to argue.

So this is Khartoum, she thought, looking out the window at the architectural hodgepodge of arcaded colonial buildings and fifties-style concrete-and-glass structures dominated by the lighted minarets of mosques.

"Then the Mahdi built his capital, Omdurman, across the river," Steven continued. "When Khartoum was finally liberated Winston Churchill was serving under Kitchener."

"When was all this?" Brad asked.

"Khartoum fell in eighteen eighty-five," Alexa answered, "but the Battle of Omdurman that Churchill participated in came much later—eighteen ninety-eight." She stopped there; it would be futile to ask Brad if he'd read Churchill's book *The River War.* Undoubtedly Mark had read it; they could spend an evening in front of the fire with the kitten, B.S., in her lap discussing the book just as soon as she returned.

"Ancient history," Brad snorted and then paused. "Just like Nam, though. Too often the Gooks had us backed into corners." He brought the Rover to a halt in front of a decaying structure built in the British Raj style of architecture.

Alexa climbed the steps of the palace and stood there alone, gazing down at the tree-lined banks of the Nile and then across the river at the lights of Omdurman. She inhaled deeply, letting the desert air fill her lungs. It had cooled considerably since the sun had set, but it was still much warmer than London and without England's ever present humidity.

How had Gordon felt? she wondered, looking around her. He'd been alone. Completely alone.

When she returned to the Rover, Steven said, "I'm staying at the Sudan Club. You have to be a member of the Commonwealth Club to get a room there, luv. Brad has booked you a room at the Oasis Hotel where he and the rest of the group is staying. He'll take you out to the location in the morning."

They left Steven at the Sudan Club and then drove to their hotel in silence. It was so like Steven not to mention a little detail like this. Clearly he felt justified staying elsewhere—in deluxe accommodations, no doubt. Brad insisted on carrying her one suitcase and tote into the dimly lit lobby where the sweet, cloying scent of jasmine incense filled the air. The hotel had been built thirty years earlier, and it had been almost that long since it had been cleaned.

She glanced around at the curious assortment of characters —all men—staring at her. She felt the color soar up her neck to her cheeks, but she couldn't look away. Straight from the pages of a spy novel, an Indian pipe salesman hawked his wares and a balding Englishman with a walleye read a tattered copy of the London *Times.* Several Arabs in flowing robes and an Italian in a suit that looked as if he'd slept in it for a month sat watching a black-and-white television playing *Popeye* in Arabic.

It took some time for the clerk to find her reservation, but finally he did. The hotel had no porters, Brad informed her as he carried her things past the broken elevator and up the stairs to the second floor. He stood so close behind her while she unlocked the door that she could feel his breath ruffling her hair.

"Thanks for helping me with my bags. I can manage from here."

Brad ignored her comment and pushed the door open and deposited her bags inside. He came in and flopped down onto the concave double bed. "Not bad. Not the Sudan Club, but not bad. We'll have to try it out."

"Let's get something straight. I'm here for two weeks to help Steven. I'm a professional and I'm assuming you are as well. We have to work together. Let's keep this *professional*, not personal." She held the door open for him.

"Sure, babe, whatever you say," Brad answered, hopping up from the bed. "Let me know when you change your mind." He gave her a playful whack on the fanny as he left. "Be ready tomorrow at eight."

Alexa slammed the door behind him and locked it. *What a jerk!* She yanked on the frayed cord on the ceiling fan and shook her head as it slowly rotated, wobbling precariously and emitting a tortured whine.

By the time she'd unpacked her newly purchased tropical outfits from the Monsoon shop near Linda's boutique, she was exhausted, but she felt too dirty to go to bed without a bath. It took a full twenty minutes to raise two inches of amber-colored, tepid water in the tub. She dipped her hand into the water and then sniffed it. Nothing. It was probably just the rusty pipes, but she shook a generous portion of Gilbert and Soames bath salts into the tub before climbing in.

She was toweling off when the twenty-five-watt bulb went out and the fan screeched to a halt. Power outage. Steven had warned her about the fitful electricity. Tonight it didn't matter; she wanted to sleep. She needed her energy to be able to work quickly and finish what Steven had begun. She wanted to get back to London—to Mark. He wasn't there, of course; he was still in Australia. He wouldn't be back for another two weeks, but he'd call before then and discover she'd left. She hadn't told anyone where she was going; only Renata and Giles knew. Mark would find out as soon as he returned and read her note. With any luck she could finish here and return before he did. She disliked deceiving him, but had opted not to tell him about this trip the last time she'd spoken with him. His hatred of Jason and his suspicion of Steven would only have provoked a long-distance fight. She counted on being back and explaining the situation to him in person.

She climbed into bed, thinking Steven said he was close to wrapping. He'd filmed here for over six weeks. It had been monetary madness, unparalleled even in the film industry, to release the cast and crew for the Christmas holiday. How much longer could it take? Not long, he'd promised her with that same wide-eyed candor he'd had when he told her he hadn't taken those checks. It had been impossible not to believe him, but there had to be some explanation for their disappearance. As she slipped off to sleep, she tried to think of what it might be.

At first light a high-pitched Arabic litany wailing from a loudspeaker awakened her. The muezzin, she realized, when she stumbled to the window and saw the crowd, carrying prayer mats, heading toward a nearby mosque. Sleepy-eyed, she climbed back in bed and fell asleep again. When she awakened, the poison-green light on her digital travel alarm read 8:30.

She scrambled into her clothes and rushed downstairs. Lolling in a chair, Brad was reading *Sports Illustrated*. He did a silent double-take before vaulting to his feet. He whistled as he inspected her with diamond-bright blue eyes.

Alexa frowned at him and fought the urge to smack him. There wasn't anything the least bit suggestive about her blue safari-style camp shirt, wrap skirt, and matching neck scarf. "I'm sorry I'm late. Let's go. I'm in a hurry."

"Sure, babe," he replied, following her out to the Rover.

"Where are we going?" she asked when she realized they were heading into the city rather than to the location.

"The Alien Registration Office. Didn't they tell you that you have to register within three days of arrival? We might as well do it today before the cast and crew return from Italy and we begin shooting."

She looked out the window at the fractured sidewalks where men in business suits hurried beside other men dressed in ankle-length white tunics and wearing loosely wrapped white turbans rather than the checkered headpieces she'd grown accustomed to seeing Palestinians on television wearing.

When Alexa presented her documents to the man in the Alien Registration Office, his look told her she was about as welcome as last year's locusts. Minutes later he disappeared along with the cadre of workers while she stood waiting at the counter. "Where are they going? My papers are in order."

"At nine the Sudanese take time off for breakfast," Brad said before lighting a cigarette. "They were up at dawn, remember? Everything will close at two, and then the traffic jam getting out of Khartoum equals any L.A. freeway. Things reopen again from six to eight." He blew a series of smoke rings in her direction. "Their week runs Sunday to Thursday; Friday's the Muslim holy day. *Nothing* happens on Friday, babe, *nothing.*"

Sudan had no rivals when it came to plodding bureaucracy. It was another three hours before she had the single stamp necessary to authorize her visit. In an officious tone the man told her she couldn't go to another city without reporting to authorities here first and obtaining a permit. He warned her, as had the Sudanese embassy in London, the south was unsafe due to the civil war and therefore closed to foreign visitors.

"Lunch?" Brad asked when they were back in the Rover. "There isn't a commissary at the location, ya' know. This is a bare-bones operation."

Alexa agreed and they went to Maxim's Burgers, a café popular with Western expatriates living in the city. She followed Brad through the noisy diner to a table in the rear. They ordered burgers and Pepsis, but when the food arrived Alexa eyed hers distastefully.

"Hello," a clipped British voice said, and Alexa looked up to find a tall, lanky man in his late fifties standing beside their table.

"H'lo," Brad said.

"I'm Austin Reeder," the man said, gazing down at them with quick, intelligent brown eyes. After they'd introduced themselves and asked him to join them, Austin continued,

"I'm an independent reporter doing a piece on the Sudan. One of the stringers for the BBC said you were making a movie. Do you have any video equipment I might use?"

"What for?" Brad's eyes narrowed; his tone seemed guarded.

"I need to play back some of my film," Austin said, raking his fingers through his thinning gray hair. "I'd like to see just what I have before I go back to London. When you don't have a big network behind you, its too expensive to return without double-checking what you've got."

"No problem," Brad said. "We were just about to go out there."

"Will you need the equipment long?" Alexa asked. "All our rushes are on tape and I'd like to review them before the cast arrives from Rome tomorrow."

"Not on the Alitalia flight?" Austin said. "There's an airport service workers strike in Rome. The BBC boys just told me."

"Shit!" Brad ground out his cigarette. "We'll be stuck here forever with the sand and the flies and the goddamned Arabs."

"They'll get here," Austin said. "All they need to do is take a train to a neighboring country and leave from there."

"Guess so, but it'll take days for all of them to make it here." He turned to Alexa. "I'm going to find Steven. He's with Abdulla over in Omdurman, checking on things. Wait'll he hears this. Christ!" Brad tossed several Sudanese pound notes on the table. "C'mon, Alexa."

She'd slumped against the back of her chair. Just what she didn't need—a delay. "I want to get that script. Maybe Austin would take me out there, and he could use the equipment."

"Yeah, sure," Brad said and turned to give Austin directions.

On the ride through the New Diem, the southern extension of Khartoum, to the location, Alexa silently noted the hordes of people crammed into shanties. The war in the south had forced them north where they hoped the government would feed them. From the looks of things, nothing much had been done.

"I'm helping a friend with a film he's making," Alexa replied when Austin asked her why she'd come to Khartoum. "I wrote the original script, but it's been rewritten. I need to see what changes have been made. What kind of project are you working on?"

He hesitated briefly, tightening his grip on the steering wheel. "I'd rather you didn't mention my project to anyone. The authorities think I'm here doing a documentary on the locust plague. I wouldn't want my footage confiscated." He hesitated again, this time for even longer. "Alexa, Muslim countries are extremely repressive with their women. I've seen the rising tide of fundamentalist Muslim beliefs sweep across North Africa from the East."

"I know," she said, "I purchased a more conservative wardrobe just to come here." She didn't mention she was wearing a bra for the first time in months. "Steven, my friend who's making the film, told me women aren't allowed to use hotel swimming pools while men are present and some restaurants insist on the sexes dining separately."

"It's more than just that. The religious fervor here has become quite strong now that the fundamentalist party controls the government. To many, you, an independent woman, represent all that's decadent, and threatening, about our culture."

"What can I do?" she asked.

"In all Muslim countries, women take the veil or cover their heads in deference to Allah."

"But I'm a Christian."

"In Japan would you take your shoes off before entering someone's house?" he asked. "It's the same thing," he said when she nodded. You're showing respect for their culture, that's all."

She untied the scarf she wore around her neck and retied it babushka-style over her head. "Better?"

"Much. And you should try to be accompanied by a man when you're in public."

Alexa reviewed Austin's information thoughtfully as the camp came into view. She liked the reporter, sensing in him a wise, fatherly figure. She'd probably do well to heed his advice even though it grated on her image of herself as an independent woman. Alexa's thoughts vanished into the desert heat when the jeep came to a stop outside the cluster of tents comprising the location. The security men were snoozing in the shade of a tent as they walked up. One opened a sleepy eye and peered at them for a moment before closing it again.

They tried the first tent, thinking it was the production tent, and discovered the combined properties and wardrobe department. Props were haphazardly stacked and left uncovered while costumes were heaped on portable racks or left tossed over chairs. White dust, like a fine talcum powder, covered everything. The other tents were in even worse condition. It was difficult to believe even a home video could come from this chaos.

When they found the production tent, she saw someone had had the foresight to wrap the ultra-sensitive camera and sound equipment in a plastic tarp to protect it from the dust. While Austin set up the equipment, Alexa went to the far corner of the tent to the single desk to find the script.

She couldn't believe this was Steven's desk. A jumble of papers, empty coffee cups, and candy wrappers cluttered the top. This really wasn't like Steven. His well-ordered town house had to be kept religiously clean. His personal things were in perfect order, and he kept detailed notes on everything. She glanced at the memos scrawled in a bold, uneven handwriting and realized Brad must also be using the desk. That would certainly account for the mess.

She reached down and slid open the desk's bottom drawer. At least Brad knew exactly where he'd put the master script, which was more than she could say for Steven. It rankled her that he'd come home without even bringing a copy with him. Where was his head these days? The script had been thoroughly worked over half a dozen times in Italian. She couldn't make any sense of it and dropped it onto the chair.

She checked the files, expecting to find production information such as daily footage counts, budgets, cost sheets, and payroll ledgers. Instead, she found a cache of Playboys, and even raunchier European magazines and a series of file folders labeled in Brad's handwriting. They appeared to be property inventories. What on earth were they going to do with so much rice? Then she remembered bagged rice was often used on sets to weigh down cables and hold canvas tarps in place. Still, it seemed silly to buy it when they were literally sitting on a sand dune which could easily be bagged. But she wasn't surprised; movie companies were notorious for their excesses.

"I'm up and running," Austin called from across the room. "Would you like to review my footage with me?"

"Sure," Alexa said, picking up the script. She'd get Brad to explain the changes to her or she'd snag the first Italian to arrive and get him to translate. She couldn't do anything more now.

She sat down beside Austin, expecting to spend the next few hours bored witless. It didn't take two minutes before tears, like silent raindrops, rolled down her cheeks, plopping onto her camp shirt.

# Chapter 34

In his Sidney hotel suite, Mark dropped the receiver into the cradle. Mrs. Cumberbatch had just told him that Alexa had left. She hadn't told his housekeeper where she was going, but Mark knew that she'd ignored his warnings and had joined Renata in Liverpool, where the play was previewing. He'd known she would, just as he'd realized she hadn't believed him about how dangerous Jason was. He thought of trying to call her but decided against it. He had no idea how to reach her, and even if he did, they'd only argue. She'd said she wanted him—wanted a family—but she'd refused to marry him until after the play opened. She had some misguided notion that if her last name became Kimbrough, people would assume she'd ridden his coattails to success. Believing her attitude was a remnant of her relationship with her ex-husband, Mark had reluctantly agreed.

The phone rang and he grabbed it, hoping it was Alexa. "Kimbrough here."

The fractional pause and blip on the line indicated a satellite-transmitted call. "Axel Marley, returning your call."

"Thanks for getting back to me. Did anything come of your leads on the tickets from Gabon?"

Another pause, which had nothing to do with the satellite,

followed. "All I'm at liberty to tell you is that we're widening the investigation, using undercover agents. This appears to be more than a simple scheme to defraud Windsor Air. There may be a tie-in with a circle of international black marketeers. I can't discuss any more than that."

"I see," Mark answered, wondering if Jason and his brother were capable of masterminding anything this extensive.

"But we haven't forgotten your problems. Today we received information about tickets *before* they were marketed. It was a sloppy job and probably not related to the previous schemes."

"Really? Did the tickets originate in Gabon?"

"No. The Sudan."

"Feeling better?" Austin asked Alexa when she met him the next morning to go to the *souk* in Omdurman. "You had me worried yesterday."

"I'm sorry I cried. I never expected to see footage like that. What are you going to do with your film?"

"Getting it out of the Sudan will be a bit dicey," he said as they climbed into his jeep. "The government has imposed censorship on all foreign journalists. We have to submit our work to the Information Minister for approval before it can be sent overseas. They're very sensitive about charges that they've mishandled the relief effort in the south. The cover-up of mass starvation in Ethiopia brought down Haile Selassie's government, remember?"

The scene from his film replayed, vividly clear in her mind's eye. Lines of people waited for the meager quarter-cup of rice while those behind the barricades would go without. Her thoughts focused on the one image that had obsessed her thoughts: A skeletal woman, her eyes filled with tearless sorrow, extended her arms, holding her baby out to the camera. She hadn't uttered a word, but her poignant plea any mother anywhere would understand: Save my baby.

"Your film will generate an international food drive, correct?"

"Perhaps," Austin said. "But there's a bigger story here that I want to tell. Will you help me?" When she eagerly nodded, he continued, "You must know someone in London who would let me use their facilities to edit this material. I'm rather short of funds."

While they followed a *bokassi* ("boxes"), a Toyota pickup whose bed had been modified to contain a dozen seats, along the dusty road to Omdurman, she referred him to Giles. "Just what is the bigger story?"

"Part of the film showed the southern rebels, the Sudan People's Liberation Army, receiving weapons. Normally, this wouldn't be particularly newsworthy, since southerners have been fighting the government for years. But as my footage showed, they now have the latest in American arms—black-market weapons."

"You've lost me," she confessed. "I'm not up to date on Sudanese politics."

"In nineteen eighty-three the Sudan adopted Islamic law." Austin pointed to the dark blue waters of the Nile. "It's a day Nile perch will long remember, because all the liquor in Khartoum was emptied into the water, and the absolute hand of Islam descended on the country. With the imposition of *sharia,* Islamic law, the Christian south rebelled. Since then, Colonel John Garang, the Christian rebel leader—a graduate of your Iowa State University—has been fighting for repeal of *sharia.*"

"It's hard to imagine an Iowa State graduate leading anything but a tailgating party."

"He's not just any graduate," Austin said. "He's a Dinka, the largest single tribe in the Sudan. Tenacious and intelligent, Garang has fought for years, and despite the fact he's been minimally armed, he's slowly moved north. The government refuses to admit how far he's advanced, or how tight his hold on the south is. That's why foreigners aren't given permits to go there."

"How'd you get into the south then?"

"I drove in at night. Garang's radio broadcasts piqued my curiosity. Have you ever heard one?" When she shook her head, he continued, "He broadcasts in English daily, listing the serial numbers of the weapons he's taken and announcing the names of government soldiers he's killed or captured. I did a little checking and discovered Garang's northernmost position is four hundred miles south of here in Malakal. Soon the rebels will be knocking on Khartoum's back door."

"But what does this have to do with black-market arms?"

"I found Unity International relief trucks, the ones with the symbol of the blue dove encircled by laurel leaves, making weapons deliveries to the rebels. My footage also shows bags of Unity International supplies being sold in *souks* throughout the country."

"Relief supplies are being black-marketed?" Alexa asked as the jeep shuddered to a halt to allow a herd of goats to cross the road. "That's horrible."

"The same thieves who are stealing relief supplies are funneling black-market weapons to the south using the Unity International trucks. Now mind you, I'm not taking sides. I respect Garang, but I want to see the fighting stop now, before the millions trapped in the south by the fighting die. Exposing this scandal would force the Sudanese government to negotiate with Garang so relief supplies can be brought south again."

The jeep lurched forward, following the *bokassi* bound for the *souk.* "I love this country. I want to make a difference here, the way Frederick Forsyth did when he brought Biafra to world attention."

"And found himself blackballed by the BBC as I recall. Of course, he went on to become a multimillionaire by writing spy novels."

"My point is—he made a difference. When the BBC refused to fund his reports from Biafra, he used his own money. He believed in what he reported just as I believe in this. You see, a cup of rice is merely a stopgap measure. The people need to quit fighting and go back to their villages. They need help, not just with food, but with planting and combating drought and controlling the damn locusts. Escalating this war with modern weapons is dangerous. It'll drag on for years, just as it has in Afghanistan, and those cut off in the south will die."

The jeep rolled into a rutted field that served as a parking lot. "Enough politics for now. Let me show you the Mahdi's Tomb and then the *souk.*"

Alexa noted Omdurman had no Western pretensions. From a warren of dusty streets and back alleys came the jingling of bells on the camels' bridles and the braying of donkeys pulling overloaded carts. "Boxes" tooted incessantly, trying to bully aside the goats who roamed free, clearing the streets of garbage. She drew in her breath, inhaling the spicy scent of cumin, turmeric, and saffron combined with an unfamiliar but sweet odor. "What's that sweet smell?"

"Molasses-dipped tobacco," he said, nodding toward the groups of men squatting in corners and puffing on what appeared to be water pipes. "Smoking a *hooka* is a daily ritual in the bazaar."

Here all the men wore *jellabas,* and the long tunics fell loosely to the ground, allowing for a comfortable circulation of air. *Imamah's,* the white turbans she'd noticed before, covered their heads. The women were garbed in short sheaths overwrapped by *taubs,* which were nothing more than several yards of sheer fabric, swaddling their heads, then wrapping around their bodies.

At the tomb, with its dome glistening in the bright sunshine, a long queue of people waited to enter. "Let's get in line," Alexa suggested.

Austin shook his head. "Foreigners aren't allowed inside. I just wanted to show it to you. You see, when Kitchener recaptured Khartoum in eighteen ninety-eight, the British razed the monument and burned the Mahdi's body before throwing his ashes into the river. It wasn't until after the Second World War that they erected this building. The tomb represents a sacred shrine to the Sudanese Muslims. A visit here is second only to a pilgrimage to Mecca."

"I see," Alexa said. "No wonder they have little use for Westerners."

After walking around the impressive building, they went on to the center of the city, *Souk el Kebir.* Semipermanent stalls, set up by draping lengths of fabric or rugs around small areas, formed the marketplace. Poles supported woven-reed shade awnings. The cloud of smoke emitted by the *hookas* hung in the hot air, enhancing the feeling Alexa had of having stepped back in time.

"Everything is available here," Austin reminded her when they'd walked for a good two hours, checking out the backstreet operations, which sold everything from bottles of kat oil and jars of concoctions for every imaginable ailment to thirty-year-old used car parts.

At the edge of the *souk,* they came upon a cluster of women with paraffin tins in their hands, waiting for sesame oil. Six blindfolded camels, one with blood dripping from his bit, were tethered to poles. Goaded by an old man with a vicious hippo-hide whip, they stumbled in endless circles, their movement rotating a large wooden mortar that ground sesame seeds, extracting the oil. Beneath the wheel, a fly-ridden drip pan caught the precious liquid.

Tugging on Austin's arm, Alexa moved away, thinking not only of the Western technology she took for granted, but also of the poor beasts sentenced to a life of trudging in endless circles. With a start she remembered the people living in shanties within shouting distance of the location and the starving children in Austin's film. For many, life here was just one step from death. She was incredibly lucky.

"What's happening over there?" she asked, anxious to think of something else. Ahead, a crowd gathered around a small booth, frantically waving pound notes in the air as they vied for the owner's attention. Coming closer, she saw the items for sale were pouches with several nubby points and long, long straps.

"Udder snoods," Austin explained. "They put them on female camels so the babies can't nurse when the mothers should be working."

They wandered along a series of booths where heaps of silver and gold earrings and bangles and rings filled baskets and hung by strings from the awnings. Here the pitch of the haggling increased several octaves, and a new scent filled the air: the smell of money.

"Silver's the best buy," Austin informed her. "The filagree is all done by hand. Excellent craftsmanship."

Alexa haggled until she purchased a three-inch-wide silver bracelet for herself and similar ones for Renata and Linda.

"What's that?" she asked, nodding toward a tiny booth with no visible wares except a small jeweler's scale.

"That's Abdulla; stay away from him. He's the biggest black-market currency exchanger. See the lineup of small leather pouches? Gold. He's able to arrange a trade for anything, anywhere in this country, and pay for it in gold because the Sudanese pound is virtually worthless. Hotels demand their bills be paid for with hard currency. American Express has been burned so many times that they no longer change money at the Khartoum office." Austin nodded toward the swarthy man tinkering with the scale. "Unless I miss my bet, the black-market weapons Garang gets comes through Abdulla. He has a stranglehold on this country."

"Really? How?" Alexa asked, wondering why the name Abdulla sounded familiar.

"It's easy. Three-quarters of the goods come in through Port Sudan, this country's only port. Despite being the largest country in Africa, it has but one port, and Abdulla has a lock on the activities there. When you combine that with his control of the country's two major *souks*, Omdurman and Kassala, you have an impregnable network of black-market operators. Of course, proving that he's involved with the Unity International fraud is another matter."

"But would a Muslim betray his countrymen and supply Garang, a Christian?" Alexa asked.

"For the right price, Abdulla will do anything."

They'd moved on to inspect the ivory and animal-skin stalls opposite the gold market. It took Alexa less than two minutes to realize that the skins were from endangered species—rare lizards and reptiles. The intricately carved ivory, filling stall after stall, brought to mind the continual slaughter of elephants that now threatened their once-numerous herds.

"Let's go," Austin said quietly, and they went back, returning along their previous route through the jewelry market.

Alexa spotted a man with ash-blond hair entering Abdulla's stall and recognized Steven. She started to call out to him but stopped when she noticed Brad with him. She came to an abrupt halt, letting the shoppers school around her as she watched Steven pocket one of the small bags of gold and turn, grinning at Brad.

"Isn't that your friend?"

"Yes." Alexa suddenly remembered why Abdulla's name was familiar. Yesterday at the restaurant when they'd met Austin, Brad had mentioned Steven was with Abdulla.

Brad and Steven came toward them, laughing and talking, but without seeing Alexa and Austin until they were within a few feet of them.

"Hiya," Brad grinned. He seemed completely relaxed except for the hard gleam in his watchful eyes.

"We're picking up a few props," Steven said. His voice had

a forced note to it, and his opaque eyes kept darting from side to side as Alexa introduced Austin.

"We're on our way to see the whirling dervishes," Austin said.

"Swell. I'll come along," Brad said. "I've been meaning to do the tourist bit. Steven has a bash at the British embassy tonight, so I'm free to have dinner with you two."

Steven said a hasty good-bye and left. Alexa didn't listen to the conversation as they went to see the dervishes; her own thoughts centered on Steven. Could he be black-marketing tickets? Maybe she should have Mark check into it. Then she remembered the rice listed on the property inventory. As soon as she got the chance, she'd read those files more carefully.

By the time they reached the mosque, a crowd was milling around, waiting. Moments later a band of men beat huge drums and clanged cymbals, while from across a nearby field marched the dervishes, clad in bright patchwork gowns. Chanting and twirling green banners, the men danced into the crowd and circled a pole. The drum beat faster and the tempo of the chant increased with it. Round and round they danced, whirling and swirling at a frenzied pace.

"When do they stop?" Alexa asked.

"Not until they fall down or sunset, whichever comes first," Austin said. "The real whirling dervishes are in Turkey. These men are members of the Ansar cult. Their dance confirms their belief in the coming of another Mahdi—a religious and secular leader."

They watched for another twenty minutes until the sun set and the men, most still standing, stopped dancing. As they made their way back to their cars, Brad told Alexa that the Italians were expected on tomorrow's flight from Frankfurt.

"But you can start working on your script tonight. That is, if Her Highness remembered to return with it."

"I thought you just said the Italians wouldn't be here until tomorrow," Alexa said.

"Melanie's flight wasn't delayed. She flew in this afternoon as scheduled from Spain."

"Melanie Tarenholt?" Alexa gasped.

"Right, babe. Who else?"

# Chapter 35

Alexa waited in the lobby of the Sudan Club until well after midnight, when Steven came sauntering into the hotel. Her anger had gone from hot to cold to hot again more times than she'd ever thought possible until now a white-hot rage simmered beneath her cool exterior.

"Alexa, what are you doing here?"

"You know why I'm here." There was no edge to her voice; it was completely level.

"Yes," Steven said, collapsing onto the overstuffed chair beside her.

"I want to know why you hid the fact Melanie Tarenholt is playing the part that's causing a problem."

"I didn't mention Melanie; her work here is secret. After what happened in Mexico she can't afford another movie failure."

"I refuse to believe you risked your money on her." Alexa waited a moment, and when he didn't reply, she walked away.

Steven caught up with her, saying, "There's more to it. Come sit down."

They went out onto the veranda overlooking the pool and sat on a wicker settee.

"When I was a child—"

"I don't want your life story!"

"I'll keep it brief. Try to put yourself in my place. My father never did anything with me or took me anywhere—not once. By the time I went to Bilbrough Hall, I thought no one cared about me until I met Jason." At the mention of Jason's name an unusual glint came to Steven's eyes. "As the years passed, Jason and I became closer. . . . I can't tell you how much he means to me."

Alexa nodded, unwillingly softening. She could very well imagine Steven's loneliness and the deep hurt a father's rejection could cause. She wondered for a moment what her life would have been like if her mother hadn't overcompensated with time and love for Alexa after her parents divorced. Her sympathy, enhanced by the fact Nigel had told her the same story, went out to Steven.

"Jason and I dated, but women were a game—nothing more —until Melanie. Jason thought some twit he'd gotten pregnant might cause a scandal, so he used Melanie as a cover, paying for her plastic surgery. She thanked him by dumping him for the first guy who could further her career." Steven shook his head. "Jason never got over it. It made him want her all the more. He was—is—crazy about her."

"Really?" Alexa asked, more shocked at the deep hurt in Steven's voice than at the fact Jason loved Melanie.

"Jason found the only way he could interest her was by helping her with her career."

"That's why you cast her in *The Last Chance* and now in *Revenge?*"

"I didn't have any choice. I hate her"—he hesitated— "but I love him more. He didn't speak to me after Melanie and the director had problems and she left in a huff at Christmas. It's the first time in twenty years that I haven't spent Christmas with him. I . . ." his voice trailed away.

"Oh," she mumbled, the light dawning. "But Melanie?"

"Jason goes both ways; he's bisexual." When Steven spoke again, his voice was barely above a whisper. "Forgive me for not telling you all this in London. I've never discussed it with anyone." Tears in his eyes, he gazed out across the deserted pool. "There's more . . . my father is dying. He doesn't think I know. How stupid does he think I am? He gave me some crap about having an intestinal problem. Even now, when he's close to death, we can't talk. I want to complete this film and prove to him I can run Hunter Films. Please say you'll stay with me and help."

Alexa had never had any indication before that Steven knew—or cared—about his father's condition. "I'll do what I can under one condition."

"Name it."

"After you wrap, you'll go see your father. No matter what you think, he loves you."

"Alexa," Melanie gushed, sashaying into the production tent the next day. "I'm so-o-o glad to see you. I know you'll be able to rewrite this so that jerk, Anselmo, can direct me."

"I hope so," Alexa said, wondering if deciding to stay had been the right choice after all. By the time she and Steven had reviewed the mess the film was in, he'd convinced her that they could salvage the project by reworking Melanie's part and editing carefully.

"Alexa," Brad called to her.

Leaving Melanie, Alexa walked to the desk where Brad sat reading an old issue of *Playboy*. She'd been waiting all day for Brad to get off his duff and do something so she could check the files. "What is it?"

"Wanna get outa' the Sudan in a hurry?"

"You know I do." Since Melanie had no idea what version of the script the director planned on using, there was nothing they could do until he returned.

"Don't wait for Anselmo. Start rewriting Melanie's part. Make it the same character she plays on television."

Alexa started to protest, but shut her mouth, deciding that maybe this was the answer. She needed to show Nigel that Steven could finish this film. A man who'd devoted his entire life to building a first-rate studio deserved to die in peace. Let him die believing his son could run Hunter Films. Undoubtedly that job would fall to Giles, but Nigel didn't have to know that. And there was no reason for Nigel to learn about Steven's homosexuality.

Alexa hung around until late afternoon without being able to check the files. It appeared that Brad was going to stay at the desk until the Italian technicians rewired one of the transmitter cables. She couldn't wait; she'd promised Austin that she'd meet him.

Alexa joined the reporter at a waterfront café overlooking the Blue Nile. "I'm leaving tomorrow," Austin said after they'd been seated. "I'm catching a lorry to Port Sudan; from there I'll get a freighter to England. Port security is extremely lax. I shouldn't have any trouble hiding my film."

"I see," Alexa said, accepting the menu from the waiter. She hated to see Austin go, but she'd been expecting it.

"I think you'll like the Nile perch. It'll be fresh and fried in a batter with red peppers. I'm having *Gammonia,* stewed sheep's stomach. I won't be able to get it until I return—if I'm ever granted another visa."

After they were served, Alexa looked around for a fork, but noticed Austin had torn a piece off a piece of bread and was scooping his stew up with it, Moroccan style. "I feel silly in this," she touched her head, indicating the double-wide headband she'd tied as fashionably as possible with an off-side bow. "I'm the only woman in here with her hair covered."

"That's because they're prostitutes."

She flicked a sidelong glance around the room. "They look like nice young girls to me."

"The war between Ethiopia and Eritrea has forced thousands of people into the Sudan. Many of them are in refugee camps along the border, but those that can, come north to Khartoum, hoping to find work. These girls have turned to prostitution, the only job they can get. They're extremely popular because they're uncircumcised."

Alexa leaned forward, her bread arrested midway to her mouth. "Un-what?"

"Uncircumcised. Sudanese Muslim girls are circumcised at about age ten."

"How . . . I mean . . . why?"

"An old woman in the village does it. She clips the clitoris, and removes most of the labia major and minor. Women in this country exist solely for the pleasure of their men."

"That's barbaric!"

"It's been practiced here for centuries. There's been some attempt to eradicate it, but it's difficult. Foreign women, then, are considered pleasure seekers."

"It must be extremely painful. The girls must have to be dragged kicking and screaming—"

"Not at all," Austin interrupted. "It's tradition. The girls are delighted at being the center of attention. It's a rite marking the coming of age; afterward they have a big party."

Stunned by what she'd learned, Alexa silently finished her dinner. Over *shai-saada,* sweetened tea laced with goat's milk, Alexa told Austin about the film's latest delay—the director refused to return. Steven had stormed into the production tent just as she was leaving and told Brad what had happened.

"He's smart," Austin said. "Get out as quickly as possible. The anti-American sentiment is escalating."

"I want to get home," she said, then told him all about Mark.

"Don't take any chances, Alexa. Forget the film. Get out of the Sudan before it's too late."

On top of the silver inkstand, Mark found Alexa's note. He read it twice before sinking into his chair and rereading it. A primitive stab of jealousy hit him at the image of Alexa dashing to Steven's aid. She had what she described as "compelling reasons," which she'd discuss with him later. For safety she'd left her ring in the vault in his office. Jesus Christ! He wadded the note into a ball and tossed it aside. How stupid could she be? Hadn't she believed a thing he'd told her? Evidently not. She did what she pleased regardless of the consequences.

He knew where she was staying but didn't attempt to contact her. She'd be home soon, and when she was, he'd set her straight. Letting her dictate the terms of their relationship had been a mistake. He'd made the same error in dealing with Caroline. This time he intended to let Alexa know exactly where he stood and how he felt.

Late at night three days later, his private line rang. He was at his desk, trying to catch up on the business reports that had accumulated during his absence. Despite the phone being within easy reach, he let it ring half a dozen times before answering. "Kimbrough here."

The crackle on the line, as if someone was playing with tissue paper, assured him this call came from a Third World country where communications were frozen at a pre–nineteen thirties level.

"Hi, darling," Alexa said, seconded by a hollow echo, "How are you? How's the B.S.?"

"He's fine." He forced his voice not to reveal his anger.

"Darling, I know you're upset with me. You won't be when you hear this story. I had to come. You see . . . hold on a minute." When she returned to the line, Alexa said, "I want to explain this in person. When I return—"

"There's a Windsor Air flight tomorrow. Be on it; I'll meet you." He slammed down the telephone.

When the phone rang several hours later, he was awake. He'd been unable to sleep; he couldn't dismiss the feeling someone else had been in the room with Alexa when he'd spoken with her. He didn't answer the phone; this time he might say something he'd regret. The best plan was to let her come home and discuss this with him face to face.

The following evening's flight from Nairobi via Khartoum arrived at Heathrow without Alexa. At his office the next day there was a message she'd been trying to reach him. Instead of calling her he rang his solicitor. For the next several days his private line rang late at night and Alexa called his office. He refused to speak to her. Any woman who declared her love and desire for a family one day and then flitted off to help a world-class flake, ignoring her duties to the play, was unstable. When she came home, he'd give her an ultimatum. She'd have to make a choice; he wouldn't be yanked around by a woman again.

"Melanie isn't having any trouble now," Alexa grudgingly admitted. Rewriting the role so Melanie played herself had been divine inspiration. She'd found her niche in television because she played herself. Once Brad pointed this out to Alexa, it hadn't been difficult to rewrite the part. At the time it had seemed the easiest, quickest way of getting out of Khartoum and back to Mark. With the play due to return to London for its final two months of preparation before opening, she needed to return immediately. Then Mark's solicitor sent a letter stating that unless she returned by Friday, she'd be replaced as producer by Bob Wickson. She'd tried to phone Mark innumerable times since their only telephone conversation. She wanted to explain that Brad had come to her room, and she'd been unable to tell Mark why she'd come to Khartoum, entrusting him with Nigel's secret. She'd known he'd be angry at her, but she'd never expected this.

Alexa fought with herself for several days but decided not to return to London. Bob could easily handle the play. If she went home now, it would set a precedent for her relationship with Mark. Her life, her career would be at his direction. As much as she loved him, she couldn't let that happen again. Thankfully she'd discovered this now. Alexa decided not to marry Mark until she knew him better. Much better.

Alexa agreed to rewrite other scenes that weren't working now that Melanie's character had changed. Determined to gather some knowledge from this experience, she spent hours watching the new director, learning how to develop projects with Giles. Renata had told her the stock offering for Hunter Films would take place the following week. Alexa intended to have several ideas ready for Giles when she returned to London.

"Why the hell wasn't I told?" Mark asked. "What am I paying you for?"

"It's in our report," Vincent Ferrier answered.

When Vince mentioned the date, Mark knew he'd been out of the country. He'd skimmed the voluminous back reports, but somehow he'd missed it. He took a deep breath, striving to bank his temper, which had had a hair trigger the last few weeks. It wasn't their fault; they couldn't have known how important Alexa was to him and how significant this development might be. Axel Marley had known, of course, and had brought to Mark's attention Robert Talbott's appointment as ambassador to the Sudan.

On the eighteenth page of the next morning's *Times*, a single-column article reported an anti-American demonstration at the U.S. embassy by the fundamentalist group, the Muslim Brotherhood. The President of the United States had issued an advisory requesting all non-embassy personnel holding U.S. passports to leave the country. Apparently the endemic guerrilla war in the south had escalated and Americans were being blamed.

Late that night Mark called Alexa's hotel and the reception=

ist told him Alexa was out with Mr. Willingham. The next morning Mark called Haifa and spoke with an old friend from his days at the London School of Economics.

"Avram, could you do me a favor?" Mark asked. "Do you know anyone in Israeli Intelligence?"

"Certainly. Why? What do you need?"

"Something is wrong in Khartoum. I know Israeli Intelligence will be abreast of the situation."

"I'll check on it and get back to you."

Late that evening Avram called. As soon as they hung up, Mark made another call. "I know this is illegal, but I need a tremendous favor. I don't care what it costs."

# Chapter 36

"Let's have you practice by shooting off the rest of this film, babe."

"Steven, do you need us?" Alexa called, looking across the production tent to where he stood packing the canisters of film.

"No. You go with Brad."

"We'll only be gone an hour or so," she tossed over her shoulder as she followed Brad out of the tent, wondering if Brad or Steven had put the file folders in the locked drawer of the desk. When she'd finally been able to get into the file cabinet, the folders hadn't been there.

In the jeep heading south, Alexa decided things had worked out quite well—considering. Steven had been euphoric since they'd wrapped two days ago. And Melanie was already writing her Academy Award acceptance speech. When they'd phoned Nigel with the news, he'd wept with joy. So, Alexa thought, why was she miserable? Mark. She hated having their relationship in limbo like this. Things would be better tomorrow. She had a seat on the evening flight to London; she'd call him as soon as she landed.

Brad waved his hand in front of her face and she realized she hadn't heard a thing he'd said. "Are you still worried because you couldn't leave the second the President issued that warning?"

"I didn't expect it to take almost a week before I could get a flight out of Khartoum," Alexa answered, still stunned that the unanticipated surge in requests for seats and the fact no American airlines serviced the city had caused a backlog in bookings.

"So, we've had to stay a few days longer. What's happened? Just what I told you—nothing. Look at Libya. The President forced everyone to leave. Those that stayed have been perfectly safe. It's just a bunch of scare tactics. A few demonstrations and the State Department panics."

"What about Beirut?" Alexa reminded him. "Americans haven't been safe there."

Brad brought the jeep to a halt on a hill overlooking a shallow valley, Belly of the Stones. The *jebels* around the location were picturesque hills, softly rounded and gently piled as if some child at the beach had formed them from wet sand.

"Focus on Jebel Aulia," Brad said as she took the camera. "Take your best shots; we'll look at them in London and see how you did."

She felt his breath on her cheek and the heat of his body. As usual, he stood closer to her than necessary. "I can't concentrate with you so close."

He didn't move. Instead he clamped his arms around her, encircling her from behind and kissing the back of her neck. She elbowed him in the gut.

"C'mon, babe, you've played hard to get long enough."

Alexa spun around. "I'm in love; I'm going to be married as soon as I return to England."

"No shit! Not to one of those limp-wristed Englishmen with a double-barreled last name?"

"He's not gay, and he has a beautiful single last name."

"So where's the ring?"

She turned her attention to the camera again, saying, "One doesn't wear a nine-carat emerald ring to an impoverished country."

A talisman, the word *ring* cooled Brad's ardor. They shot footage and discussed the intricacies of the camera.

"Pan across Jebel Aulia, babe. Zoom in on something interesting. This is the last of our film. Whadda ya see?"

"Smoke," Alexa said, "thick black smoke."

"Lemme see." Brad grabbed the camera, looking through the lens that brought the distant hills as close as looking through high-powered binoculars. "Holy shit! C'mon, we've gotta get outta here."

As Brad lugged the camera back to the jeep, she asked, "What is it?"

"Bahar Dar," he said, "the oil-storage facility. It's burning."

"How can you tell?" As she hopped into the jeep, Brad carelessly tossed the camera into the back. "They could be burning the cotton fields south of here."

With a whip-lashing jerk the jeep shot forward. "Nope. Not after Nam. Only one thing burns that way. Oil. My guess is that the rebels have hit the oil-storage facility at Bahar Dar."

"Then the reports that they're advancing on the capital must be true," Alexa said, remembering Austin's warning and cursing herself for believing the government's assurances that the city was safe.

Minutes later the jeep slammed to a stop in front of the deserted location.

"Sonofabitch!" Brad banged his fist against the desk in the production tent. "I'll get that little fag. Not only did he leave without me"—Brad rifled through the center drawer, which had always been locked—"he took my notebook."

"What notebook?" she asked, looking into the drawer. There lay the missing page from the play's checkbook.

As the jet taxied to a halt, Mark mentally reviewed his plans and calculated he had about forty-eight hours to get Alexa out of the city. If Israeli intelligence was correct, and it usually was, the Sudanese would move against Americans by week's end, refusing them permission to leave the country.

As Mark waited in the line to clear Customs, he looked around the airport. Desperate to leave the country, people jammed the terminal, crowding the ticket counters. He noted numerous young soldiers armed with World War Two-vintage machine guns. As in most poor countries the civil airports were also military facilities, but this was an unusually high concentration of soldiers.

His passport and visa stamped, he was waiting for a taxi

when he heard someone calling his name and turned to find a short, blond man walking toward him.

"Herb Russell," the younger man said. "I'm from the embassy."

"Oh?" Mark said, unable to disguise the wariness in his voice. Almost no one knew Mark was in Khartoum. He'd phoned Axel Marley at Interpol to try to get the name of the undercover agent. Mark thought it might be a good idea to have someone, other than Robert Talbott, to turn to in case the situation deteriorated more quickly than he anticipated. As he expected, the agent's name was classified; Mark didn't have time to waste going through channels to get it.

Herb lowered his voice, "Axel Marley said you wanted to meet me."

"Yes, of course," Mark said, shocked Marley had gone against regulations. "Thank you for coming. What's going on here?"

On the way into the city Herb explained the government was blaming Americans for the sophisticated weapons the rebels were now using. With them, they'd destroyed the nation's primary oil storage unit at Bahar Dar, just south of the city. In retaliation the government was now refusing to let Americans leave. Mark groaned; all this had come together much faster than he'd expected. He patted his breast pocket, assuring himself both passports were still there. As long as British subjects were allowed to leave, he could get her out.

"You understand everything I say is confidential?" Herb asked and Mark nodded. "Talbott's disappeared. Yesterday he went into Omdurman alone and never returned. I've documented his involvement in the ticket scheme—contacts here, abroad, everything. He ran one of the smoothest operations we've ever encountered. He and his brother, Jason, dealt in numerous black-market items, not just airline tickets. We suspect they've been selling contraband weapons to the rebels here, but I haven't been able to document it yet."

"Do you have enough evidence to convict the Talbott brothers on ticket fraud? Are you authorized to show me?" When Herb nodded, Mark grinned. Twelve years. It had taken twelve long years, but he finally had Jason Talbott.

"Her Majesty's government has a request of you," Herb said as he drove into the embassy's side gate. "We'd like you to divert three Windsor jets from their normal routes to Khartoum. We want to get every subject out as quickly was possible. We'd call in the Royal Air Force, but foreign military aircraft landing here could create an international incident. Your planes are authorized to evacuate British subjects. No Americans are to be on board."

"I need to contact my fiancée immediately."

"I've been instructed to keep you with me. We'll send someone to find her."

While Mark waited for an attaché to find Alexa, he did what he could to help Herb, who was responsible for the embassy until Talbott reappeared. The small, inexperienced staff, assigned to a backwater nation where nothing had happened for almost a century, struggled to cope with hundreds of frightened people.

Well after midnight the attaché sent to locate Alexa returned without her. He hadn't been able to find her anywhere, not even among the hundreds of frightened Americans huddled at the American embassy.

In fractured English the night clerk attempted to read Alexa a confusing message. Apparently Mark had heard of the trouble and wanted her to go to the British embassy. Wearily she climbed the stairs and went to her room, thinking she was reluctant to put herself at Robert Talbott's mercy. She flopped across her bed and tried to decide what to do, reviewing the confusing events of the day.

After they'd found the deserted location, they'd sped back into Khartoum, where they'd learned Americans couldn't leave the country. Naturally their first thought had been to get help from the American embassy. Brad had shoved his way to the front of the mob gathered there only to be told not to panic and to return to his hotel until the embassy worked something out with the authorities.

"Shit! I'm not waitin'," Brad announced as they left the embassy. "They'll shut down Khartoum Airport anytime now and use it as a military field. With the weapons the rebels have, the government will have to make the most of its air power. The only weapon Garang doesn't have is planes. The limey planes are still being allowed to leave. If Abdulla can get us phony British passports, we can get outta here."

For hours they futilely searched for Abdulla. Although the *souk* was still operating, the gold and silver merchants had disappeared, as had the purveyors of carved ivory.

"Figures," Brad said. "Take anything of value and hide it—just in case. Wait 'til you see the price of food go sky high if Garang gets any closer."

With nowhere to turn, they'd come back to their hotel, agreeing to get some sleep before searching for Abdulla in the morning. After tossing fitfully Alexa drifted off into an uneasy sleep, haunted by the knowledge Steven had deceived her. She'd been a naive fool to listen to his smiling lies. What else had he done?

Without warning a staccato burst of machine-gun fire split the morning air. Alexa tried to run, but the dense crowd kept her from moving. Rivulets of perspiration ran down her spine and collected on the small of her back. She elbowed her way off the sidewalk and leaned against a whitewashed building, gasping for breath. What should she do? This morning Brad had left without her. She'd have to go to the British embassy; there was no other choice.

Another round of shots echoed in the distance, sending a fresh surge of panic through her. *Get going.* Time had become her enemy. Time and her U.S. passport carefully hidden in the lining of her handbag.

Dodging camels, donkey-drawn carts, and *taub*-garbed women, Alexa pushed her way toward the street. Unperturbed by the gunfire, overanxious merchants, their hands covered with a patina of dirt and grease, grabbed at her. She jerked away, quickening her pace and struggling to catch her breath. An unpleasant taste filled her mouth. Khartoum, an island in a sea of sand, tasted brown. All she had to do was breathe the air and she could taste the city.

There were no taxis in sight, nor were there any "boxes" going their usual routes. *Don't panic.* Go to the British embassy; perhaps Mark's used his influence and can help you.

Pacing herself for the long walk, she started up the street. She kept turning and checking the road behind her. Half a mile later, a "box" so loaded it could barely move drove up behind her. Frantically signaling for it to stop, Alexa jumped into the street. The driver rolled past her shaking his head.

She exhaled sharply when she saw the pickup's bed, which normally held twelve, had at least fifty people piled into it. She jammed her hand into her purse, came up with a fistful of British pound notes, and waved them at the driver, knowing that in a crisis, hard currency would be more in demand than ever. Snatching the wad from her hand, he flashed her a wide, toothless grin and motioned for her to take a place on the hood. After gesturing for the passengers on the already crowded hood to make room for her, she vaulted up beside several men. Feeling the crush of bodies and sensing the staring brown eyes, Alexa had never been more aware she was a woman. A woman alone.

When she reached the corner of Palace and Barlaman Avenue, she got off and saw the Union Jack hanging limp in the still air. She presented herself at the embassy's gate; her taut muscles relaxed slightly. The panicked mob atmosphere prevailing at the American embassy yesterday was absent here. Dozens of people filled the courtyard, but they formed a neat queue that was typically British. She blessed the inbred sense of calm and order that never seemed to desert the English, even in an emergency.

"Mark Kimbrough asked me to report here," she told the guard at the gate in what she hoped would pass for a British accent.

"Are you a subject of the United Kingdom?" When she nodded, he said, "Queue up over there."

Alexa waited in line well over two hours before speaking with a staff member. "I have a message from Mr. Mark Kimbrough to report here."

"I'm sorry, Mr. Kimbrough is busy. I'll get someone else to help you."

Alexa's thoughts reeled. She'd misunderstood the message. Mark was here. Why? Why would he be here? The ticket fraud. That must be it.

"This is personal," Alexa said. "I must see him."

Again Mark counted the passports. He hadn't made a mistake; when it came to numbers, he seldom did. There were far more British subjects desperate to leave Khartoum than his planes could accommodate.

A sharp rap on the office door interrupted him. "There's a Miss Alexa MacKenzie here to see you. Shall I show her in?"

"No, let her wait." Mark returned to the passenger list, adding one more name. Thank God she'd turned up at last.

Time passed slowly as Mark read Russell's confidential report on the Talbotts. The extent of their operation and the number of years it had been in existence were incredible. There was no question about it—Mark would have his revenge. As heartening as this knowledge should have been, Mark found it difficult to find much satisfaction in it. He checked his watch. How much longer should he make her suffer? Longer, he decided, recalling his own sleepless nights.

Time moved in slow motion, frame by frame, as Alexa tried to concentrate on script ideas for Giles while she waited. She refused to look at her watch again; it had been over three hours.

"Alexa MacKenzie," called the clerk and she dashed across the room, cramming her notes into the attaché Mark had given her.

The clerk closed the door behind her and Alexa looked across the walnut-paneled room. At a desk strewn with piles of papers and innumerable passports bearing the insignia of the lion sat Mark. Her stomach contracted; a sinking feeling chilled her despite the warm air. Flat gray, his eyes had an abstracted look that was completely unfamiliar to her. Her heart thundered, each beat sending despair through her entire body.

"Yes, Alexa? You wished to see me?"

"Mark . . . I need your help."

"Why didn't you leave when Washington issued the advisory?"

"I tried," she said, "but no seats were available. I suppose I could have taken the train to Cairo. But I—"

"Why didn't you leave with Steven?"

She felt a telltale flush rise to her cheeks. Why didn't he simply say "I told you so."

"Did you know he'd left?"

She forced her gaze to meet his. "No."

"I see." A derisive smile tugged at the corners of his mouth, but vanished almost before she'd seen it.

Mark looked at the passports, searching through them. "I don't have time to talk with you. I—"

A short blond man appeared from an inner office and added another stack of documents to the avalanche on the desk.

"Any word on Talbott?" Mark asked, but the man shook his head and disappeared into the adjacent room.

Alexa drew the remnants of her pride around her and continued looking directly at him. She couldn't believe he was acting like this, then she remembered that he'd dismissed her from the play. His hatred for the Talbotts ran deep. By helping Steven she'd allied herself with his enemies. Mark wouldn't help her now. But somehow she'd get out of Khartoum even without his help.

"If you want my assistance, Alexa, you must do exactly as I say. No questions asked."

"Of course," she whispered, filled with a joyous surge of relief.

He motioned to the antechamber. "Go in there and have Mr. Russell shred your passport, credit cards, and anything else you may have that indicates your nationality. You're to remain here in the embassy."

Alexa slowly walked into the next room. "Shred my passport?"

# Chapter 37

Alexa had surrendered her passport and had been escorted to a waiting room when she heard a familiar voice.

"What are you doing here?" Melanie eyed her suspiciously.

"I'm seeing if the embassy can help me get out. After all, I am living and working in London." It was a weak explanation, but it seemed to satisfy Melanie.

"Mark Kimbrough's here, you know. He has three planes coming to pick us up. I told him I'm a *personal* friend of Ambassador Talbott's and he'd better make certain I'm on the first plane."

"Hey, babe, how'd you get in here?" Brad said, coming up to them from across the crowded room. "Abdulla got me a passport."

Alexa repeated her explanation, adding, "Thanks for leaving me."

"Every man for himself," he said, shrugging. "But if they let you in here, they must be planning to take care of you. I had a bitch of a time trying to get in—even with the passport. That prick, Kimbrough, worked me over, checking my passport. Couldn't find a thing wrong with it. Gotta hand it to Abdulla, he comes through. He finagled Steven a seat on yesterday's SAS flight."

A loud commotion on the far side of the room, where people were gathered looking out the window, captured their attention. Alexa followed Brad over to the group, edging in beside him and looking out the window. Plumes of black smoke rose above the El Kabir Mosque.

"The American embassy," someone said, and Alexa remembered how close it was to Khartoum's main mosque.

"It's not burning," Brad informed the crowd with a bogus British accent. "The Muslim Brotherhood is just scaring them with a little fire outside the gates."

Alexa gulped. Scaring them? She could imagine how terrified those inside must be. Tehran. The American Embassy. It had been years ago, but the memory of the hostages was still clear. A few lucky people had managed to get to the Canadian embassy, where they were hidden until they could be given phony passports and taken out of the country. They had escaped—thanks to the Canadians? Would she be as lucky?

After dinner they were instructed to assemble in the auditorium so the vice-consul could discuss tomorrow's plans with them. When Alexa took her seat with Brad at her side, she saw the man who'd shredded her passport behind the podium with Mark beside him.

"For those of you who don't know me," the short blond man began, "I'm Herbert J. Russell. I want to let you all know the Sudanese government assures us this is a temporary problem which they anticipate resolving shortly. The United Kingdom's relations with the Sudanese people, despite any difficulties any other nation may be experiencing, remain cordial. Nevertheless, Her Majesty's government has instructed us to assist her subjects, in any way we can, to leave the Sudan." He took a deep breath and flashed a quick glance at Mark before continuing. "As some of you know, Ambassador Talbott has been missing. Late this afternoon the police located his body in Omdurman."

A buzz broke what had been dead silence. From the front row Melanie let out a frenzied sob. Alexa looked at Brad, who whispered, "His throat was slit."

Alexa wondered how Brad knew this. He was a ruthless man; he'd left her this morning without so much as a second thought. He'd been obsessed with punishing Steven for taking his notebook. She hadn't a clue as to what was in it; he'd avoided her questions. But recalling the files, she wondered if it had anything to do with the black-marketing. Could it be that he was the one behind it?

"We're certain Talbott's death came, not as a result of this disturbance, but as an outgrowth of personal difficulties," Russell continued. "His untimely demise leaves me in charge of this embassy. It is vital that you follow my instructions." Again he paused and looked at Mark. "We're fortunate Mark Kimbrough is in the Sudan." At the mention of his name, many who knew of him but didn't recognize him began whispering. "He's arranged for three of his planes to evacuate you. With Ambassador Talbott's death, I've had to see to a great many matters, so I've left working out a priority list for passengers to Mr. Kimbrough. I'm turning the meeting over to him now. He'll tell you what he's decided."

Russell stepped aside and Mark moved up to the podium saying, "There isn't any way I can seat all of you on just three planes." He paused and let his words take effect. "Unless you agree to my plan." He went on to explain that passengers would have to share the larger first-class seats and some men would have to sit on the floor in the galley in order to get everyone out.

"Naturally this overcrowding violates international safety regulations. If anyone wishes to make their own arrangements, I'll understand. In a moment we'll be giving you a seat assignment and flight number. I've prepared charts of the planes; I want you to memorize *exactly* where your seat is. When you board, we want to do it as swiftly as possible. They may close the airport at any moment. That's why we'll be loading the planes from back to front—it's faster. Also, you'll be limited to one carry-on piece of luggage. Take what you absolutely cannot do without and leave the rest of your things here. The embassy will forward them as soon as this trouble is resolved. I believe that's it except for a final word from Minister Russell."

Herbert Russell cleared his throat. "We have reason to believe that some of you are United States citizens in possession of fraudulent U.K. passports. This won't work and could jeopardize everyone's safety. During the rash of terrorist activities in recent months, Khartoum installed a new computer with terminals linked to Interpol. When the Sudanese key in

the number on your passport, it must agree with British security numbers stored in the data bank. A first-class cover, a
great photo, and official looking stamps may fool me, but it
won't deceive the computer. You must come to us after this
meeting. We can help you."

Hours later Mark stood at the window in the ambassador's
office. The glow in the distance had gone out; perhaps the
demonstrators had gone home. For the Americans' sake he
hoped so.

He thought of joining Herb in the communications center
but decided against it. They didn't need him to cable London
with the names of those Americans using ersatz passports. By
working all night, programmers could alter information, so
any reasonable-looking passport could be given a computer
blessing.

But who would bless Robert Talbott? Certainly not his
murderers. Mark had been surprised to learn his death came
as no shock to Herb Russell. Apparently Talbott had run a
first-rate operation until recently, when a woman tried to get
in on the action. When she was discovered, she bandied
Talbott's name about Khartoum. Evidently this had frightened his local connections into killing him.

Mark turned and caught the watchful eyes of Queen Elizabeth's portrait, staring at him from the far wall. Her portrait
graced every ambassador's office. Her Majesty's justice would
soon find Jason Talbott when Russell sent the evidence back
to London with Mark tomorrow. Funny, Mark thought, revenge so long in coming shouldn't be quite this empty. But it
wasn't revenge that was bothering him; it was Alexa. He'd
been hard on her—far too hard. He should go to her and tell
her about the passport. He'd let her suffer long enough. This
was ridiculous. They were both behaving immaturely.

Mark checked dozens of places where clusters of people had
gathered to try to sleep before finding her. Curled up in an
armchair, she was asleep. He stood there gazing down at her,
wanting to gather her into his arms and carry her away, but
the embassy was so crowded that he couldn't walk down a
hall without stepping on someone. Anyway, what would he
say? He needed to take her to Wyndham Hill and sit down
with her to discuss their problems. He bent down and lifted

the ruff of golden hair off her neck before kissing her on his favorite spot just behind her ear.

With a stiff neck and a mouth that felt as if a camel had died in it, Alexa wandered into the dining room for breakfast. She quickly took a seat before Brad could spot her. She didn't want to be seen with him. Last night he and Melanie had been unbelievable. She'd pitched a fit because she wasn't on the first flight but had been assigned to the third plane with Brad and Alexa. Mark stood firm. Then Brad had refused to tell Herb Russell about the fake passport. Nothing Alexa did could convince him.

"They're just covering their asses," Brad had said. "They'll leave me behind if I tell."

"If you don't tell Mr. Russell, I will," Alexa said. "You could be jeopardizing everyone's safety."

The hard gleam in Brad's eyes intensified. "Open your mouth and I'll fix Kimbrough. I'll tell everyone he's harboring an American actress—a porn queen at that."

"You wouldn't dare!"

Brad chuckled, then said, "I watched you while he was giving his little speech. You were drooling. He's the man you're going to marry, isn't he?"

"That isn't any of your business."

"No? I'll tell you what is. Gettin' out of this hellhole alive. If you say *anything,* I'll kick up a ruckus about Kimbrough that they'll hear all the way back to Buckingham Palace. Think they'll like Mr. Goody Two-Shoes lying to get his fiancée outta here? Top that off with him gettin' you a black-market passport—he's done."

"You wouldn't."

"Bet on it. Anyway, I'm not worried about my passport checking. Abdulla said it was encoded with the security numbers already. It'll pass muster, you'll see."

Shortly after noon they were called into the auditorium, where Mark and Herb Russell were at the podium again. Alexa noticed Mark had shaven and changed shirts, but his face had a drawn, pinched look. He drummed his fingers on the podium while he waited for everyone to take a seat. They explained the first flight had been delayed four hours. Apparently the brigade of soldiers assigned to guarding the airport were members of the Muslim Brotherhood. They conducted diligent searches of luggage and double-checked passports, trying to find anyone who might have collaborated with the rebels. The next two flights would be delayed, but they hoped to make the midnight deadline when the government would take over the airport, turning it into a military facility.

It was ten o'clock before the third group went to the airport. Everyone kept checking their watches, knowing the airport would close precisely at midnight. Inside the international terminal, a military officer informed them they'd be the next-to-the-last flight out.

The uneasiness Alexa had kept at bay edged through her as she waited at the rear of the line with Stacy, the young girl she would share a first-class seat with. Behind them were Brad and several other men assigned to the forward galley, while ahead of them stood Melanie. A crowd of Frenchmen hovered at the luggage inspection station, preparing to follow the Windsor Air group up to the passport checkpoint. This Air France flight would be the last out.

Herb Russell came down the line handing out passports. When Alexa got hers, she flipped it open and stared down at her picture. The tears welled up in her eyes and she looked up, trying to find Mark, but he stood at the passport station with his back to her. She gazed down again, smiling in disbelief and swiping at her tears with the back of her hand. Obviously Mark had gone to an incredible amount of trouble in bringing this from London. Somehow, he'd gotten hold of her pictures from that night in Soho, because her photo showed her in that sleazy black gown, wearing a lifetime supply of make-up and mascara-embalmed eyelashes. He had even lifted her signature from some document. The passport stated she'd been born in Pildowne Crossing, Kent, but other than that the vital statistics were her own. She knew the computer wouldn't reject this passport. Even so, the cold, metallic finger of fear that had been prodding her gave her another nudge.

Finally their turn came, and Alexa pushed Stacy forward. Behind them the only ones left to check in were Brad and the others assigned to the first-class galley. The Air France group stood nervously in the rear, staring at their watches.

Cleared to board, Stacy stepped aside and Alexa moved up beside Mark and Herb, who were overseeing the check-in.

She didn't venture a look at Mark; if she did the tears might start again. As soon as they were airborne, she'd go to him. Alexa handed the passport and attached visa to the agent at the computer terminal, giving him a bright smile. He nodded, then keyed her number into the computer. It took a full ten seconds—an entire lifetime—for her file to come up on the screen. The agent scanned the monitor, stamped her passport, and started to hand it to her. One of the soldiers moved up beside the agent, saying something in guttural Arabic. The agent gave her passport to the officer in charge. Her stomach cinched into a tight knot as he leveled the most merciless eyes she'd ever seen upon her and motioned her inside.

"Stacy," she said, realizing the child was waiting for her, "get on the plane. I'll be right there."

Alexa stood aside, allowing the others to continue checking in. She couldn't imagine what had gone wrong, but the soldiers kept looking at her picture and then at her. Whatever it was, it had nothing to do with the computer.

Mark moved over beside Alexa, letting the men assigned to the galley check in on their own. He gave her an encouraging smile, but the tense set of his shoulders didn't reassure her.

"Is there a problem?" Herb asked the officer in charge and, when he didn't respond, repeated the question in Arabic.

"American actress!"

Cold pincers of fear gripped her. How could they have seen her movie? It had only recently been released in America and had never been screened abroad.

Herb whispered something to Mark and he paled visibly. His arm went around Alexa as he said, "Miss MacKenzie is my fiancée." His calm voice had an edge to it she'd never heard before. "I own Windsor Airlines. It's important to your government that my planes continue to fly between here and the continent. I'll personally vouch for Miss MacKenzie. I'm taking her with me."

The officer nodded, apparently convinced, but just then the agent at the computer shot a volley of Arabic at the officer. Alexa saw Brad Willingham standing alone at the counter. He'd been last in line; the others had checked in and were standing to the side waiting for him. A frenzied exchange in Arabic followed before the officer flung the passport at Brad. "No good! No good!"

Out of nowhere Melanie appeared. "What's the matter? Why aren't we leaving?" Her voice had an hysterical quiver to it. "You aren't going to keep us all here because of them, are you? They're both Americans."

Mark left Alexa and strode up to Melanie, grabbing her by the arm and pulling her aside before the officer, who clearly hadn't understood her, could ask questions. But it was too late; one of the soldiers knew enough English and informed his superior.

"Let her go," Herb said, his fair face scarlet, after a scathing exchange in Arabic with the officer. "He wants to hear what she has to say."

Alexa's stomach plummeted.

Melanie grabbed the officer's sleeve. "Have you seen her picture? She takes all her clothes off and says: 'I can't do it.' Don't punish us all because they're Americans."

Stunned, Alexa froze. How well she remembered those words.

The soldiers standing nearby nodded. Despite their minimal English, they recognized those words. The officer snapped his fingers and a phalanx of soldiers surrounded Alexa and Brad. Mark pushed toward Alexa, but they leveled their guns at him.

"I demand you stop this—" Mark began, but one of the soldiers, responding to an order in Arabic, slammed the butt of his rifle, catching Mark on the underside of his jaw. Another soldier drove his rifle into Mark's stomach while a third hit him squarely on the back of the head, sending him crumpling to the ground. His attaché flew out from under his arm and skidded across the floor. Alexa screamed and tried to go to him, but the soldiers held her back. The officer issued an order in Arabic to Herb.

"Put him on the plane," Herb said, motioning to the men assigned to the galley, who had been cleared and were standing there watching. "Get out of here, all of you. Tell the pilot to take off. I'll take care of these two."

Alexa stood there praying Mark would be all right. The last she saw of the group was the men carrying out Mark, unconscious and bleeding.

And Melanie smiling.

* * *

Two men were carrying him up the ramp when Mark opened his eyes. At first he couldn't imagine where he was; his head felt as if someone had buried an anchor in it, and he could taste his own blood. They had him inside the jet on the galley floor before he managed to say anything.

"Alexa," he mumbled. A white-hot pain seared along his jaw and met the thrumming ache in his head. "Don't leave without her."

It was too late; the plane trundled forward, gathering speed. The world went black on him again as a single vision affixed itself before him: Alexa's terrified face. His muddled thoughts focused on Steven Hunter. He'd shown Alexa's outtakes all over Khartoum. The moment Herb had whispered that to Mark, he'd cursed himself. Why hadn't he double-checked with Nigel?

Mark opened his eyes; the galley spun nauseatingly around him. At his side someone had deposited his attaché, with the evidence that would convict Jason. It didn't matter. Revenge wouldn't be worth a damn if anything happened to Alexa.

The passengers, completely silent before, cheered raucously when the jet lifted off the runway. Mark struggled to his feet, clutching at the galley's counter, while the plane climbed heavenward at a thirty-five-degree angle. He knew it wouldn't level off for another few minutes, but Mark couldn't wait. He staggered into the first-class compartment.

Blood ran down the back of his neck and dripped from his cut lip. He felt everyone's eyes on him, but he didn't give a damn. Ahead he saw Melanie, watching him coming. Yesterday's mascara was smudged beneath her eyes and one false eyelash was askew, emphasizing her panic-brightened eyes.

"You bitch," he said, ignoring the cabin full of curious eyes and the shooting pain each movement of his jaw caused him. "You selfish bitch. How dare you? How dare you call yourself British?" He waved his arm in an unsteady gesture, indicating the people in the cabin. "We . . . we're the people who stood alone against Hitler. We're the people who are at our best in a crisis. We stick together; we don't give up. What you pulled back there proves one thing—you care for no one but yourself. I can promise you this. If anything happens to Alexa because of what you've done—I'll get you."

He turned, oblivious to the cheering and clapping following his tirade. Somehow he managed not to pass out again as he staggered forward and found his assigned seat opposite the flight engineer in the cockpit.

The jet swerved abruptly, banging Mark's throbbing head against the bulkhead. He knew the plane had been assigned a runway facing south and had planned to veer east immediately after takeoff rather than fly over rebel-held positions. The pilot had discussed this with Mark, reminding him that the previous year the rebels, using a SAM missile, had shot down a civilian airliner, killing everyone. No telling what weapons they might have now. Mark slumped in his seat, praying Herb could help Alexa.

"Sonofabitch!" yelled the pilot.

"Jesus!" seconded the copilot.

"What?" Mark asked, leaning forward, straining to see what was wrong. Below orange-red flames leapt hundreds of feet in the air, blistering the moonless sky.

"The friggin' rebels have blown up the airport!"

# Chapter 38

"I'm going to kill Jason Talbott," Mark said, ignoring the shocked looks on Linda and Warren's faces. In the two weeks since Alexa had died when the rebels destroyed the Khartoum airport, he'd stopped caring if people thought he was crazy.

"You'll have to find him first." Warren tried to make light of the situation despite knowing his friend was serious. Dead serious.

"I wonder how he knew to get out of town so quickly," Linda said as she nodded to the maid to serve dessert. They all suspected Steven had somehow gotten wind of the under- cover investigation and warned Jason—they'd rehashed this numerous times. But Mark still needed to talk about it. She and Warren had invited him to dinner tonight to give him some happy news for a change.

"Steven told Jason," Mark said as he was served a piece of white chocolate mousse. "He managed to bribe his way out of Khartoum before the rebels struck. Evidently Robert Talbott warned him that their black-marketing operation had been uncovered."

"Who do you think killed Robert?" Warren asked.

"One of the Sudanese he'd been working with. At least that was Herb Russell's information. With his death in the airport, there's no way to verify it." Mark ate his dessert out of sheer politeness; he'd permanently lost his appetite.

"Speaking of death," Linda said, trying to change the subject, "how's Steven Hunter doing since Nigel died?"

"He's happy heading Hunter Films," Mark said, feeling a fresh wave of guilt. Nigel had called Mark to his deathbed and told him how he'd coerced Alexa into going to Steven's aid. The old man had cried, genuinely remorseful at what had befallen her. Mark didn't have the heart to wound the old man any further by telling him about the outtakes. It was too late for Nigel to do anything. Revenge was for the living. Mark intended to see Steven got just what he deserved. And Melanie. But first he needed to find Jason.

Linda nodded to Warren, giving him the signal to leave the table. "Let's have coffee in the drawing room."

As Linda stood, Mark decided marriage agreed with her. Always a beauty, her skin had taken on a rosy glow and she'd gained a few pounds. Warren looked relaxed and totally in love. So, Mark thought, I was wrong. Their marriage is working out nicely. A stab of longing and loneliness surged through him as he followed Warren into the drawing room.

"We have something to tell you," Warren said after coffee had been served. "We're going to have a baby—"

"We'd like you to be the godfather," Linda finished.

"Great," Mark said, bringing the coffee cup to his lips. A baby. His insides twisted. While they rattled on about possible names, Mark thought about revenge. He had to—it was all he had left. "Linda," he said when they paused, "did you know a reporter friend of Alexa's by the name of Austin Reeder?"

"No. She never mentioned him."

"He's probably just one of the press snooping for a new angle on the story," Warren said as he walked over to the bar and poured them cognacs. "I'd stay away from him."

"Mark," Linda said, her eyes wide with concern. "Try to put this behind you. Nothing is going to bring Alexa back."

Mark took the snifter of cognac from Warren and committed the ultimate sacrilege of downing it in one gulp. "If I'd just leveled with her . . . told her the whole truth, she might not have gone to Khartoum."

"What do you mean?" Linda asked, a tight frown wrinkling her brow.

"Haven't you ever wondered why Jason and I hate each other?" Mark directed his question to Warren.

"Well, I assumed the old school grudges—"

"Before I was born, Jason's father and my mother had been lovers. She'd expected Gilbert Talbott to marry her."

Noticing the shocked expression on Warren's face, Mark got up and helped himself to more cognac. "What peer would wed a poor shop clerk—even a beautiful one? He married someone else and my mother moved to Manchester where she met my father and quickly married him. She never loved him; all she thought about was Gilbert Talbott. When I was born, she decided I needed to go to Bilbrough Hall where the Talbott boys went. When I did, she saw Gilbert again and they resumed their affair."

Disgusted, Mark shook his head. All these years later, he still hadn't forgiven his mother for not having loved his father. He hadn't told Alexa the entire story because he felt the parallel between his parents' lives and his marriage to Caroline was too close. Two generations cuckolded by Talbotts. Pathetic. Now Mark saw his mistake. He'd overreacted to Alexa's misguided attempt to help Steven, thinking he was again making the same error he had with Caroline by giving Alexa too much freedom.

"Jason found out about the affair," Warren guessed.

"Yes. He let me know my mother was a whore. All through the following years, Jason took every opportunity to make my life miserable. I had already started my business, staked by ten thousand pounds my mother said came from the insurance policy of a relative who'd been killed in an auto accident, when Gilbert died. I'd parlayed it into a small fortune when Jason came to see me. The Talbotts were virtually bankrupt and a check of Gilbert's financial activities before his death revealed the money he'd given mother. Jason wanted it back. I gave it to him on the spot—plus triple interest. I never would have taken it had I known whose it was. Jason exploded when I handed him the check, blaming my mother for their financial ruin."

"Nonsense," Warren said, "that sum wouldn't have paid the

upkeep on their cars alone. He was probably jealous that you'd run it into a fortune."

"Jason swore he'd get even with me. He accused me of keeping Talbott money that could have prevented him from having to marry his wife. He said I'd as good as stolen the woman he loved."

"Who?" Linda asked. "It's hard for me to imagine Jason loving anyone—but himself."

"He didn't say. He was too busy telling me he'd see me in hell."

"That was a long time ago," Warren said. "Surely you don't imagine he was somehow responsible for what happened to Alexa."

Mark recounted the entire story of Caroline, and how he suspected Jason had put Steven up to showing those outtakes around London and Khartoum. "Jason may be my half-brother, but I'm going to get him. No matter how long it takes."

"Mark, just a minute," Giles called, his face grave beneath the cluster of kinky gray curls. "Have you heard the news? Melanie Tarenholt is dead."

"Really? What happened?"

Giles walked up the stairs to the theater office with Mark. "I guess after the press crucified her for costing Alexa, Brad Willingham, and Herb Russell their lives, her devoted fans deserted her. The producers of her show fired her; she began to drink and take pills. She overdosed. Suicide or accident? Who can say?"

*One down. Two to go,* Mark said to himself.

Giles stood there, shifting from foot to foot. "I want to tell you in person how deeply I regret my part in convincing Alexa to go with Steven. I—"

"I don't blame you; I don't blame anyone." *Except myself.*

"There's no possibility she survived even by some wild chance?"

"No, none. A French woman who miraculously escaped told us she saw Alexa just moments before the blast, standing where I'd left her." Mark didn't add he'd spent the past two weeks checking numerous sources, praying she'd somehow managed to get out. She hadn't.

"I'm sorry," Giles said. "Next week her play opens. You'll be here?"

"No. I'll be in Australia." Mark didn't add that he'd deliberately scheduled the trip so he couldn't attend the opening. Seeing the play Alexa had devoted herself to would be more than he could stand.

Mark said good-bye to Giles and walked into the theater office. He shut the door behind him without switching on the light. He stood there a moment, his back braced against the door, thinking he could almost feel her in the room with him. Of all the places they'd been together, he always pictured her here. He'd flash on the light and she'd be there, bending over the desk. She'd look up and give him that slow, slow smile he loved so well. The finality of her death overwhelmed him; he'd never be able to see her or touch her again. *Stop it—don't torture yourself.*

The snick of the switch revealed the deserted office. Almost deserted. T.S., curled up in a tight ball, slept on Bob's chair. Mark crossed the room to the box he'd left earlier on Alexa's desk. He'd been putting off cleaning out her things for too long. Asleep, sprawled across the bottom of the box, was T.S.'s kitten. Apparently he'd played war earlier because the inside of the box had been clawed, leaving shreds of cardboard scattered about the bottom of the box. Mark picked up the kitten; it mewed once and settled in for a snooze as Mark nestled it against his chest.

He recalled that day in early January when he and Alexa had moved back to London from Wyndham Hill and had come to the theater to check on the kittens. The night watchman had told them all the kittens lived in the office except the orange runt of the litter, who kept trying to go backstage. They'd nicknamed him B.S. for backstage. Naturally, Alexa had insisted on keeping him.

Mark put B.S. down on the floor and set about cleaning out the desk. Other than the computer terminal, which stayed, the desktop had a day calendar and a small snapshot in a Lucite frame. The picture of Linda and Renata flanking Alexa had been taken in front of Daiquiri Dick's. He took another look at the three bikini-clad women, laughing like school girls. With an unanticipated rush of emotion, he relived that afternoon on the deserted beach. Alexa had been standing there in the same red bikini she wore in the photo. Her hands had been on her hips and the soft breeze off the Sea of Cortéz lifted her golden hair. At that moment he'd made up his mind she'd be worth waiting for, worth spending time to get to know. It hadn't been easy; she'd been defensive and difficult, but he didn't regret it.

Casting his memories aside, he placed the calendar and photo at the bottom of the box before opening a drawer and finding her stash of junk food. He removed seven Yorkie Bars, one half-eaten, and placed the unwrapped ones on Bob's desk and tossed the partial into the trash. Mark pulled out an empty blue and white box and chuckled out loud when he read the label: Boston Tea Party—Revolutionary Cookies—Made with Swiss Chocolate. So she'd fallen for Harrods edible tourist trap and purchased a box of chocolate chip cookies. But why had she kept the empty box? She probably thought it was clever. He carefully flattened it and placed it in the box.

Crushed in the back of the drawer was a receipt. He smoothed it out and read it. Had she really paid *that* much for those bookends she'd given him?

The next drawer was empty except for a blue spiral notebook. Another idea book, he decided as he thumbed the pages. She always kept one with her; whenever she had a thought about a book or play, or anything she wanted to remember, she'd write it down. Undoubtedly one had been with her in the attaché he'd given her.

That thought stopped him cold. He told himself for the thousandth time it was better this way. She'd died quickly without knowing what hit her. It would have been much worse had she lived and suffered God-knows-what fate at the hands of those militant soldiers. He hated to think what they might have done to Alexa. Still, he found it difficult to believe she wasn't going to walk into the office, laughing and talking and spouting a dozen new ideas at once. Face it, she wasn't coming back—there hadn't been enough of her left to send home in an envelope.

He flipped through the idea book again, this time from back to front, and a dog-eared page caught his eye. On it was a double-columned list with the name Kimbrough at the top. One side read: Allison, Pamela, Julia, Lauren, Sherry. Opposite those names were: Jeffrey, Ross, Blake, Vincent, Timothy.

Lauren and Ross had been circled in red. What? The light
dawned; these were possible children's names. He fought back
the lump in his throat as he ran his finger over the names:
Lauren and Ross. A boy and a girl. They'd both agreed two
would be a minimum; neither of them had enjoyed being only
children. Lauren and Ross.

He dropped the notebook into the box, knowing he
couldn't afford to think about this much longer. He forced
himself to get on with it and checked the hatstand in the
corner where he found three forgotten umbrellas and a navy
wool sweater. Folding the sweater, the scent of jasmine and
wild flowers, Floris No. 9135—her special fragrance—filled his
nostrils. He recalled ordering it custom-blended for Alexa and
having it sent with the attaché to her after that night in Torquay. What a night! *Thank you for a lifetime of memories.*

The sweater tucked in neatly on top, Mark glanced around
the room, wondering if there was anything else he should
take. There wasn't.

"Come on, T.S.," he said, picking up the sleeping mother
cat and placing her in the box. "You're going to love Wyndham Hill."

Deciding this was a new game, B.S. proved all but impossible to capture. Mark finally cornered him by the Omni mini-
kitchenette built into the closet. "Now stay in there, you ras-
cal," he told the kitten as he put B.S. in beside his mother.

Mark picked up the box and walked to the door. Balancing
it on one hip, he turned around for one final look before turning out the lights and standing there in the dark.

*Loving you has been the sweetest thing that ever happened to me.*

# Chapter 39

Silent as a pharaoh's tomb, lit only by pinpricks of light shooting through the holes in the roof, the warehouse formed a large L. From outside the building Alexa heard shuffling footsteps coming to a stop at the door. It couldn't be Brad; he'd just left. Had they been discovered? With food in the tri-city area at a premium, someone might have decided to check out the abandoned warehouse.

She tiptoed over to where they'd made a small camp and picked up the rifle. Whoever was at the door was now trying the latch. It was locked, of course; she'd secured it herself when Brad left. Slowly the footsteps retreated and Alexa let out a long sigh before propping the heavy rifle against a bag of rice. It wouldn't be long before they were discovered, she thought, sitting down once more. They were lucky they hadn't perished when the rebels had destroyed the airport.

For the hundredth time in the past five days, imaginary cameras rolled, replaying the whole ordeal again with sickening clarity. As always, a cold, tight knot formed in her chest when she remembered Mark being carried to the plane.

"Move, move," a soldier commanded, jabbing Alexa in the ribs with the barrel of his rifle.

She followed Brad, who had three guns trained on him,

across the terminal. She looked for Herb, but he stood at the counter, still arguing with the officer. Without warning an ear-shattering boom rocked the building, blowing out the windows and sending shards of glass hurtling like spears through the air. Instinct sent her to the floor. As she went down, her purse over her head, she saw the domestic terminal across the street was ablaze. The force of the blast had knocked out the windows in the international terminal where they were, allowing smoke to fill the building. Above the hysterical screams of the panicked passengers awaiting the last flight, she heard the masculine shouts of the soldiers, barking orders in abrasive Arabic. The soldiers guarding them had rushed back to where their commanding officer stood with Herb Russell. Alexa checked for Brad; he was crawling toward one of the blown-out doors. Spurred by panic and adrenaline, she shimmied on her hands and knees across the glass-strewn floor. When Brad ducked through the space in the door, which had moments before been glass, she catapulted herself through the same opening, ignoring the pieces of glass still in the frame.

Outside, confused soldiers dashed in every direction; frenzied Arabic ricocheted back and forth, but no one paid any attention to her. She was running, terror prompting her to keep up with Brad, when the international terminal behind her exploded. Knocked flat by the force of the blast, she lay there stunned, struggling to regain her breath, watching the building become a crematorium as chunks of flaming debris peppered the ground around her. With a whoosh the roof collapsed, sending a scorching, suffocating wall of flame at her. *How did it feel to die?* It hurt—just listen to the screams from the hell of those trapped inside. *Oh, Lord, please don't let me die.*

Searing smoke clogged her nostrils; she gagged and coughed, her lungs heaving as she gasped for air. *Get up! Run!* She struggled to her feet with every instinct for self-preservation spurring her forward. Blindly charging through the billowing smoke, she caught a glimpse of Brad before another wave of smoke obscured her view. She ordered her legs to run full-speed in the direction he had taken. "Brad . . . Brad," she heard herself shrieking.

He kept running, never looking back. Suddenly he slammed to a halt and crouched against the side of the freight building.

Unable to take herself off automatic pilot, she raced past him. He grabbed her arm, bringing her to a wrenching stop. A sharp pain knifed through her shoulder as he slammed her up against the building and clamped his hand over her mouth.

"Shut up! Look over there."

The inferno behind them clearly illuminated a World War Two-vintage jeep and a single soldier guarding it.

"Don't leave me," she whispered when he removed his hand from her mouth.

"Stay here."

Brad inched his way along the building. Naturally the soldier's attention was on the firestorm to his right. Unless he turned around, he wouldn't see Brad. In a lightning sprint Brad raced across the open space and tackled the soldier from behind. A swift punch rendered him unconscious. Brad retrieved the man's knife, rifle, and holstered pistol. Brad was putting on the man's uniform when Alexa ran up.

"That's my ticket outta here." Brad motioned to the jeep. "If you're comin' with me, you'll have to stay on the floor outta sight. Understand? I want them to see a soldier on official business, not a ditsy blonde."

She jumped into the jeep and sat on the floor, wedging herself between the passenger seat and the dashboard. Brad stood over the still-unconscious, partially clothed soldier, drawing out the knife he'd just taken from the man and placing it under one of the soldier's ears. With a quick flip of his wrist, Brad sliced across to the other ear. Blood spurted from the gash, flowing in scarlet waves as the soldier's life soaked into the thirsty African sand. At the liquid gurgling and sucking sounds coming from his severed windpipe, Alexa's stomach roiled spasmodically, contracting and sending waves of nausea through her. *That wasn't necessary.* Brad wiped the blood from the knife on the soldier's bare torso, vaulted into the jeep, and drove away.

Suddenly she recalled Brad telling her how Robert Talbott died. Brad had killed him; she was certain of it. Why?

Her head banged and slammed into the dash as she struggled to brace herself against the raucous bucking and pitching of the jeep as it sped across the open terrain. It took a few minutes for her to realize they weren't heading into Khartoum. "Where are we going?" she shouted above the noisy engine, trying to forget the soldier they'd left behind. And the fact that she was with a murderer.

"Remember Gordon? I'm not gettin' trapped in Khartoum with both Niles hemmin' me in and the rebels advancing from the south. No, sir."

His words startled Alexa; she hadn't thought he'd given the discussion of Gordon another thought.

"You saw how fast they blew the airport. They've planted bombs—highly sophisticated incendiary devices. They'll hit the bridges next."

Head between her knees, Alexa hung on as the jeep clambered over the railroad tracks en route to the Blue Nile Bridge. They were on the bridge, accelerator floored, when Brad shouted, "Holy shit!"

The White Nile Bridge over Wad Dakin Island to Omdurman exploded, lighting the Western sky with thousands of pyrotechnic lights.

"Start praying," Brad screamed. "We could be history. This bridge should be next."

Fear, the third passenger in the jeep, commanded her to pray. She put her head to her knees and asked the Lord to let Mark live and to make him forgive her for being such an idiot.

"Yaaahooo," Brad screamed as he patted her on her bent head. "We made it, babe. Keep prayin' we get across North Khartoum and the Shambat Bridge into Omdurman. I know a place to hide there."

Two thirds of the way across North Khartoum, the Blue Nile Bridge behind them went sky high. They were on borrowed time now. But in sight of the Shambat Bridge, the jeep pinged and knocked to a halt.

"Sonofabitch!" Brad shouted. "Outta gas. Let's go. I figure this bridge will blow in four minutes."

He streaked forward, running for all he was worth across the bridge. She had a split second to make a decision: Staying with Brad was the only thing that made any sense. Alexa ran, panting and gasping for breath and trying to forget the pain in her side caused by her overexertion and erratic breathing. She had to get off the bridge. She wasn't ready to die—not yet.

Her brain chose that moment to replay the scene at the airport. She hadn't understood all the soldiers had said, but she knew one thing: Steven had used the outtakes and had made them into a porno flick. He'd also taken the checks and lied to her about them. What else had he lied about? She intended to live—to pay the bastard back. And Melanie—selfish, ambitious Melanie.

They made it off the bridge; it didn't blow for another twenty minutes. By then they were well inside Omdurman. For what seemed like hours, they ran, twisting and turning, darting and dodging through the narrow labyrinth of streets and down back alleys. Finally they found the dilapidated building and rushed inside. Alexa, so exhausted she could no longer think clearly, collapsed, curling up on the dirt floor. Her confused thoughts whirled faster than the dervishes, blending into terrifying half-dream images of Mark and soldiers and fire, before vanishing into oblivion.

When she awakened, every muscle in her body ached; her legs and arms were stiff and spattered with scratches from crawling across broken glass. She eased herself to a standing position and looked around for Brad. Had he deserted her? Very possibly. If she hadn't followed him, she'd have been left at the airport. Pondering his whereabouts, she noticed the burlap sacks, piled ten feet high throughout the entire warehouse. The logo, a blue dove encircled by laurel leaves, caught her attention. Unity International. Alexa ripped open a bag and found it filled with rice. She checked a few others and found they contained grain.

White gold, she thought as she returned to the area where she'd spent the night and sat down beside the shoulder bag she'd somehow managed to keep with her throughout the desperate flight. Brad would be back, not for her, but for the cache of supplies. With the rebels besieging Khartoum and the bridges across the Nile gone, food would become scarce. This would be his—their—ticket out. She stared up at the porous ceiling, recalling her conversations with Austin. Undoubtedly Brad and Steven were part of the group black-marketing the relief supplies. And it could very well be they were supplying the rebels. It was entirely possible she'd stumbled upon the missing link in Austin's story. If so, she'd chanced on something potentially more deadly than anything she'd yet encountered.

The lock on the warehouse door clicked, and as it rumbled open she hid behind a stack of bags. Even in daylight deep shadows cloaked the building; the only light came from the holes in the roof. In walked a man clad in a *jellaba*, his head wrapped in an *imamah*, carrying a heavy sack over his shoulder.

"Alexa . . . Alexa, where are you?" a familiar voice called.

"Brad?" she said, coming out.

He dropped the canvas bag and jerked off the *imamah*, flinging the turban to the ground. "Anarchy . . . pure anarchy. No one knows anything. The rebels destroyed the television station as well as the radio station. Luckily I had enough rice with me to trade for these clothes. I don't think it's too smart to run around in a military uniform. Someone might wonder why I'm not out looking for the rebels."

From the sack he produced a handful of charcoal and a small brazier for cooking as well as a shriveled carrot and an onion that had sprouted days earlier. "Do the best you can," he told Alexa, handing her a jug of water. "God knows we have plenty of rice. First, change into this, babe." He tossed her a man's tunic.

She looked down at her once-white linen suit, now a mottled gray. Besides the smoke, smudges of grease and dirt from the floor of the jeep had stained it. The sleeve had been ripped when she'd jumped through the broken glass door. She'd been cut too, she realized when she saw the dried blood plastering her blouse to her skin. Heaven only knew what she looked like. Alexa ran her hand across her face, feeling the soot from the fire and the gritty sand kicked up by the jeep. After taking a tissue from her purse, she wiped off her face and then found her comb and gave her hair a quick once-over. What she wouldn't give for a hot bath, she thought as she looked up and caught Brad watching her. Their eyes locked; her heart thumped uncomfortably. She grabbed her purse, pretending to be searching through its contents. There could be no mistaking what he wanted, just as there was no denying the fact she didn't have any options. He represented her best hope of getting out of here alive, and he could provide information that would hang Steven. Despite her plans to use him, she had to remember he was a dangerous man.

"Whadda ya lookin' for?" he asked, moving closer.

"Perfume," she lied, clearly remembering she'd left the bottle from Floris at Mark's house.

"Come here."

Taking a deep, unsteady breath, she walked up to him, stopping just beyond his reach.

"Strip."

"What?" she gasped.

"You heard me."

Give him what he wants, her inner voice warned. After kicking off her shoes, she slowly unbuttoned her jacket and tossed it aside. The silk blouse was difficult to remove because the dried blood had glued it to her arm. When she eased the fabric from her skin, the two-inch gash oozed fresh blood. "I'm bleeding."

"Give it a minute. It'll clot."

She hesitated, standing there in the sexy lingerie set she'd bought at Janet Reger's. Splurging on lacy undies, she'd never intended for anyone but Mark to see them.

"Hurry up."

She slithered out of her slip, letting it drop onto her blistered feet. The white demi-bra lifted her breasts, and the sheer silk panties clung provocatively to her hips. She took a fortifying breath, unhooked the bra, and then slid off the panties.

Brad's eyes boldly assessed her, scanning her critically. He stepped up to her and grabbed a handful of hair at the nape of her neck, jerking her head backward. "Don't you ever . . . ever say no to me again. Understand? I've had all the shit from you I'm gonna take. Not good enough for you, huh? We'll see."

With his free hand he ran calloused fingers across her bare breasts. Lingering on a nipple, he rotated his thumb across it over and over. His fingers were still twined through her hair, holding her head back at an unnatural angle.

"You're hurting me."

"Wanna know what hurts—really hurts?" He released her hair and grabbed her hand, jamming it between his thighs. His turgid penis probed at the confining tunic. Brad squeezed her fingers around his short, thick shaft. His face went rigid and he sucked in a gulp of air. "Having a hard-on for a woman for weeks hurts. When that woman treats you like shit, something else hurts. Now it's my turn."

Brad's hands came up, caught her shoulders, flipping her

backward onto the dirt floor with such force her breath was knocked from her. Effortlessly he slipped out of his tunic and stood over her, his feet still booted. He lowered himself onto her until his heated body crushed her against the hard earth, his insistent penis poking her soft flesh. His lips found hers and he thrust his tongue into her mouth.

I should have run, she thought, deciding she couldn't go through with this, but knowing it was now too late to change her mind. She took a calming breath and found the sweaty smell of his skin made her stomach heave. She had to get control of herself. Pretend he's someone else, she thought as his lips sought her breasts. Mark. She slid her hands through his hair, but the scent of smoke and the straight, lank hair, so unlike Mark's, brought tears to her eyes. She couldn't cry now; if she didn't cooperate, he might leave her or even kill her.

Suddenly she realized his marauding mouth had deserted her breasts and was moving lower across her taut abdomen while his sweaty hand parted her legs. Hair-roughened arms circled her buttocks, bringing her up to his face. He fluttered his tongue along the smooth skin of her inner thighs. Alternately nipping and then gliding his tongue over her flesh, he stopped short of the nest of tight curls. Then he nuzzled the cluster of tendrils for a moment before sending his hot tongue into her tender flesh, seeking the pert nubbin beneath the folds of skin. His mouth clamped over her, sucking, relentlessly sucking. Involuntarily Alexa gasped.

"You like that, don't you? The ole Willingham magic."

He fastened his mouth on her again, his lips seeking the swollen nub, finding it, and taking it between his greedy lips. She wanted to tell him she hated him, but was too afraid.

A low growl came from deep within his throat and he pushed himself to his knees. Poised between her parted thighs, his engorged penis in one hand, Brad's look of unadulterated lust shocked her. With one savage thrust, he drove himself into her. His arms clamped her to him as he jerked back and forth a half-dozen times before collapsing in a sweaty heap on top of her. She lay there a moment, fighting the almost irresistible urge to reach for the pistol he'd discarded along with his tunic.

The revulsion she felt must have shown in her eyes because

as she sat up and turned away, he grabbed her hair, yanking her back down to the ground. With the lightning quickness she'd noted when he'd attacked the soldier guarding the jeep, he sprang onto her, straddling her and pinning her to the ground. "Don't pull any of your bitch shit with me. You loved every minute. Don't pretend you didn't."

Beads of sweat peppered his forehead; he caught them in a long swipe with the back of his forearm. Then he ran his hands over her breasts, cupping them and squeezing until she winced. His eyes narrowed as he sneered down at her, and slid his flaccid penis between her breasts. Mounding them around it with his hands, he rhythmically moved back and forth until his short shaft stiffened a bit. Moving forward slightly, he hunkered over her. "Take it," he said, poking at her closed lips. "Make it hard."

She tried to turn away, but she couldn't move with the bulk of his weight crushing her and his vicelike legs cinched to her sides. She parted her lips and closed her eyes against the hot tears forming as he slid his penis into her mouth. She gagged and tried to cough but couldn't. He kept thrusting in and out and groaning. Mercifully, he came fully erect quickly. He withdrew and fondled himself with a satisfied sigh. Scooting down her chest to her hips, he thrust one hairy knee between her thighs, forcing her legs apart and nosing his way inside her again.

"All right," he moaned, "you're so tight. I love it, babe. I was gonna wait 'til later, but you gave me an idea. It'll be a while before I come again. But that shouldn't keep me from enjoying your tight little pussy."

She wasn't sure how long it actually was—it seemed as if she'd been caught in a holding pattern over hell—before he climaxed. But while he churned and writhed, seeking release and assuming, with his usual misguided macho, she loved this, he whispered to her. She gathered from his passion-induced ramblings he'd seen the outtakes last fall just after Steven had returned to London and stolen the checks. She was surprised to learn Jason had seen the clips and that had been the reason he'd called her.

"We had a good laugh over that one," Brad panted into her ear. "Melanie shit when she found out you were seeing Jason. 'Course Steven did it on purpose. He saved those outtakes just to titillate Jason. He'd try anything to break up Melanie and Jason. When I saw Steven's little film, I had a hard-on in two seconds. But I won't anymore, will I?" he grunted.

After Brad finally came, he sprawled deadweight across her and said, "I'm hungry. Get cookin'."

She stared at his hairy body and made herself a promise: *I'll get even.*

From that first day nearly a week ago, the pattern had been set. Brad went out trading for what they needed while she remained hidden. Uppermost in Brad's search was a way out of Khartoum. He wanted a ride to Port Sudan, but with the rebels having mined the highway south through Wad Medani, the only route to the coast remaining open was along the dirt road to Atbara.

Two quick taps on the door broke into her thoughts. She came back to the present as she waited for the pause and then the third tap. Brad was back; he'd be hungry and horny.

She unlocked the door and eased it open, squinting against the bright sunlight. Brad dashed inside, dropping the canvas bag he took with him on his daily foraging. "We're leavin' tonight."

# Chapter 40

The rising moon gave a half-light to the road, not more than a faint ribbon in the sand, stretching endlessly before them. A handful of pyramids, bathed a ghostly gray, stood their deathwatch over the ruins of the ancient Kingdom of Meroe. Alexa craned her neck, looking around Brad, out of the truck's cab, trying to get a better view of the Nile downstream from the Sixth Cataract.

Oil and water, she thought, looking at the pyramids and remembering what Austin had told her about the Sudan. Divided in the last century by the colonial powers, the northern third of the country belonged, geographically and sociologically, to Egypt. The desert terrain with its Muslim people differed radically from the film Austin had shown her of the natives in the equatorial rain forest of the south. Those Christian tribes had far more in common with neighboring Zaire and Kenya than they did with the Muslim government in Khartoum. Now she was caught in the struggle the southerners had been waging for years.

Wondering if Brad cared about the outcome of the conflict, she looked at him; but he didn't notice her, nor did the driver. They were both on the lookout for government troops. Since they'd fled Omdurman, they'd been forced to travel by night

with their lights out in order to avoid the convoys of trucks
and soldiers bringing supplies from Port Sudan along the back
road through Atbara. If they were stopped going east with a
full truckload of rice and grain, the phony permits and docu-
mentation Abdulla had obtained for them might not be
enough to fool the soldiers.

Alexa reached up to take a strand of hair and twist it
around her finger, but met instead the brim of the bush hat
Brad insisted she wear at all times. Beneath the hat was a head
of hair cut ruthlessly short in a mannish cut that comple-
mented the men's camouflage trousers and shirt she wore. She
looked ridiculous and absolutely nothing like the woman
whose French passport and visa she carried. Of course Brad
maintained Abdulla's documents were foolproof, but then
he'd said the same thing about the false passport that had
been easily detected at the airport. He'd countered her argument, saying Abdulla hadn't realized the computer codes had
been changed.

Alexa remained unconvinced, but she had no alternative.
Brad had managed to exchange enough rice in Omdurman to
bribe Haziz, one of Abdulla's many relatives, to take them and
the remaining rice to Port Sudan. There they'd barter the rice
for passage on a freighter bound for Egypt.

"What the hell happened to those pyramids?" Brad asked,
bringing an unexpected end to her private thoughts.

Alexa looked out across the moonlit sand and saw a cluster
of pyramids missing their pointed tops. "An Italian named
Ferlini knocked them off. He was looking for treasure, and
didn't want to take the time to find the hidden entrances."

"Really? What did he get?"

"Not much, a little gold. Certainly nothing worth destroy-
ing archaeological treasures over."

Alexa didn't continue; she could see he wasn't interested.
Any further discussion of history and politics would have to
wait for England. And Mark. How was he? she again wondered. Brad thought Mark's wound had been superficial. She
hoped he was right. And what did Mark think had happened
to her? He probably thought she'd been killed. From what
they'd gathered from the BBC broadcasts they'd picked up on
the transistor radio Brad acquired, few survived the explo-
sions that destroyed the airport. She hadn't been able to tell

Mark how much she appreciated what he'd tried to do for her, nor had she had the chance to tell him how much she loved him. She'd been a complete fool to try to help Steven. Did Mark realize that? Had he forgiven her?

Her thoughts drifted to Melanie. Alexa had been an idiot to have anything to do with her. The drug raid and Renata's story should have warned her. But no, Alexa had wanted the golden ring Giles offered. She'd been greedy and almost paid with her life. She still might be killed, but she didn't blame Melanie for her predicament as much as she did Steven. He'd used her from the moment he'd met her, piling lie upon lie. Selfish Melanie had merely reacted hysterically; it wouldn't have mattered if the soldiers hadn't seen the outtakes. As soon as she got out of this mess, she'd take care of them both. Steven first—*número uno.*

They drove into Atbara a scant hour before dawn and found a *lakonda.* This hostel had one shower off the central courtyard where most guests slept during the warm evenings. Alexa washed her hair in the trickle of cold water with a bar of homemade soap. Heaven, she decided. One of life's simplest pleasures was being clean. For days now they'd scrubbed, as so many Arabs did, using sand. Surprisingly, it worked in removing grease from cooking and sweat, but she never felt really clean.

"No shit!" Brad smiled, holding the transistor radio to his ear as she came into their tiny room. "Your picture was nominated for seven Academy Awards."

"Really? Which ones?" When he told her that Giles and Colin had both been nominated and *The Last Chance* had been named for best picture, she couldn't help feeling proud. Now if only she could get back to London before the play opened. She wanted to be there to see Renata's triumphant return and to share it with Mark.

"Sonofabitch!" Brad jumped as a howling wind peppered them with sand through the open window. "A *haboob!*"

Alexa drew the burlap curtain across the glassless opening, remembering the fierce desert sandstorms called *haboobs* could reach gale proportions within a matter of minutes. They were forced to wait it out, sitting on the bed talking. As usual, she steered the conversation to Steven. She needed to covertly find out as much as possible about his involvement in the black-market operation. She planned on going to the authorities as soon as she returned to London, but she realized she didn't have enough hard evidence. She hoped, by playing to Brad's ego, his insatiable need to brag would reveal something more concrete.

"Steven's got shit for brains, babe. Without me he'd never have finished this movie."

She listened to Brad brag about the same things he'd told her earlier. He'd been involved with black-marketing since his days in Viet Nam, when he'd stolen supplies from the military and sold them in Saigon's black market. From there he'd kicked around the world, dealing mostly in stolen or contraband arms from the U.S. Working through a series of middlemen and his contacts in the army, Brad saw nothing wrong with supplying the strife-ridden Middle East and Africa with weapons. He'd served in Viet Nam, he'd told her. And what did he get? Nothing, not even a thanks. Now it was his turn. He was entitled.

Brad didn't see anything wrong with selling supplies intended for relief. But the memories of the girls forced to prostitute themselves and the homeless living in makeshift camps around Khartoum haunted Alexa. Even more disturbing was her recollection of Austin's film showing the starving children trapped in the south by this senseless war. When she asked Brad how he could live with himself, his glib answer startled her.

"They're gonna die anyway. Starvation is a fact of life in Africa. It's been around since biblical times. Save 'em now and they'll be back in camps in another year or two."

From there he launched into a detailed explanation of how he'd met Steven. Steven was short of cash because Nigel had cut him off and was thinking of horning in on an airline ticket scam he'd found out about from the Talbotts. Brad declared the whole Talbott operation penny-ante stuff and showed Steven how to make some really big money by raising cash from selling relief supplies and then buying arms and reselling them at a tremendous profit to the rebels.

Alexa knew then she owed Mark still another apology. Somehow she thought he had been paranoid in thinking Jason Talbott was behind the ticket fraud. But once again Mark had been right.

A sharp rap on the door brought in the owner of the *lakonda*
with a lantern and a bottle of homemade brew, which he
brought to make up for the inconvenience of the *haboob*. Apparently the Muslim ban on alcohol wasn't taken as seriously
in Atbara as it was in Khartoum. Brad poured her a small glass
of the *Anagi* and served himself a generous portion. She took a
sip. It hit the roof of her mouth, ignited, and flared down to
her intestines. Gasping, she handed Brad her glass.

"Tastes like rum," he said, after slamming back half a glass,
"but packs ten times the wallop." Instantly pinpricks of sweat
riddled his brow.

By the time he finished three glasses, the *Anagi* had loosened Brad's tongue, giving Alexa more insight into the man
than she'd previously had. Although he'd tried to make it
sound as if he were a big-time trader, she gathered he'd spent
most of the last decade roaming around making small deals in
regional bush wars. He had some money stashed in a Swiss
account, but Brad wasn't rich. He was tired of kicking around
the world making arms deals.

A sudden thought hit her, jarring her with its perfection.
She quelled an insane desire to laugh, deciding that staying
close to both Brad and Steven was her best chance for revenge.

"You're not listenin' " Brad muttered, slack-jawed, his eyes
fighting to focus in the hazy lamplight.

"I have an idea. Steven owes you. Where would he be if
you hadn't helped him find the money for this film? He
should make you a producer. Wouldn't you like that?"

"Hey, thatsa good idea," he said, then belched. "I'm gonna
fuck him. He took my notebook. He'll copy it the way he did
the Talbotts' source book."

At the mention of the notebook Alexa remembered the hidden compartment in the headboard. The ostrich-skin address
book with the names of people in various countries hadn't
had anything to do with film making. It must have been Steven's black market connections. Now that she thought about
it, she remembered there'd been a series of numbers written
on the Z page. Swiss bank account numbers? Steven's? The
Talbotts'? Both? She took a good look at Brad. His eyelids
were at half-mast and his eyes kept crossing. There might
never be a better time to ask him.

"What was in your notebook?"

"Contacts. Years of information about third parties who can arrange illegal arms sales. Steven had better not use 'em or I'll slit his throat," Brad said, running his index finger under his chin from ear to ear.

Tarred and feathered with government troops, Port Sudan had so many soldiers roaming the streets and patrolling the wharf that, in order to sell the rice without being discovered, Brad had to take less money than he'd expected.

"Jesus!" Brad said as he stood gazing out at the freighters anchored offshore in the Red Sea. "How the hell are we supposed to get on one of those tubs with all these assholes standing around watching?"

As Alexa had suspected back in Khartoum, the government was frantically guarding its sole port with its adjacent oil refinery, the only one left in the Sudan since the destruction of the facility at Bahar Dar. It would be impossible to get on a ship with all these soldiers around.

"I have an idea," Alexa said. "An hour south of here is the old port, Suakin. It was used before boats became too big to get in through the coral reefs."

"How do ya' know?" he asked suspiciously.

"From Churchill's book. He was with Kitchener when he returned to rout the Mahdists. Plenty of ships came in then. We could hire a *felucca* to sail us across to Saudi Arabia—to Jiddah. There are so many local fishermen out in the Red Sea that the troops won't be searching them the way they'll be checking freighters."

Brad fingered the thick gold chain he kept hidden beneath his shirt. "You know, babe, you might be onto something."

It took the rest of the day to arrange for a *felucca* to pick them up in Suakin and to find a "box" to take them down the coast to the abandoned port. The moon guided them as they drove across the short causeway to Suakin. Deserted except for thousands of howling cats, the island, with its buildings made of coral from the nearby reef, had an eerie, ghostlike quality.

They paid the driver and sat on the broken-down pier to wait for the *felucca*. Brad brought out a bottle of *Tedj* and offered it to Alexa. She took one sip of the date wine and decided it was far too sweet for her taste.

Brad knocked back his wine in a single gulp. "No one ever comes out here anymore?"

"Divers come from all over the world to explore the reef. I'm sure they do night dives, but with all the trouble in the Sudan, I doubt any divers are coming out here now. We should be quite safe."

Her answer satisfied Brad and he leaned against a piling and stared out toward the east and the Saudi coastline. She let him consume all the wine, hoping it would make him more receptive to her plan. She had to make herself indispensable to him, or she might find herself with a knife to her throat before she reached Jiddah.

"We're sitting on a gold mine, you know that don't you?"

"No. Whadda' ya talkin' about?" he said, slurring every word.

"The number-one story of the decade—our escape. It would make a perfect movie. Betrayed by a jealous actress, we're trapped in the Khartoum airport. You carry me out only moments before the terminal itself blows. You shield me as we rush through the streets, narrowly escaping the hordes of soldiers chasing us. You hot-wire a jeep and we take off across the open plain for Omdurman. Bridges blowing; bombs exploding. We hide in a warehouse until you can make arrangements to get us to Port Sudan." She paused and smiled at Brad, who was grinning from ear to ear. "There the hostile government troops nearly nab us at every turn, but you find us a way out."

"Ya' know, babe, you've got quite a 'magination."

"Don't you agree this has all the makings of a hit movie? Action, adventure, intrigue . . ." She stopped and gave him a sly smile that she hoped he'd consider seductive. ". . . and sex. You and I fall madly in love. I'm going to write the script myself."

"Fantastic!" Brad hugged her.

"You'll produce it with Steven's backing at Hunter Films. An action adventure like this could make the money *Rambo* earned look like small potatoes."

She stopped there, letting him make the mental link between himself, Rambo, and hero. He loved it. Brad went on and on, inventing chase scenes and tussles, with soldiers and fights enough for ten movies.

"We'll need to decide on a single version of this," Alexa said. "Let's work out the kinks in the story as we sail. Then I'll begin writing the script. I want to have a rough draft finished when we return to London."

Brad poured himself the remainder of the *Tedj* and slammed it back with a jerk of his head before saying, "About this love bit."

"Yes?" Alexa disguised the concern in her voice. So far he'd taken the bait nicely. She wanted to make herself indispensable to him for as long as possible so he wouldn't kill her.

He leveled diamond-bright eyes at her and leaned forward, kissing her with wine-soured breath. "If we're so in love, we'd better get married."

"Married?"

"What'sa matter? I thought you liked me. Aren't I better in bed than Kimbrough?"

"Of course," Alexa said, struggling to keep her voice level. "Face it, without his money—he's nothing. Once we make this movie, I won't have money problems again, will I?"

"Right," Brad said, his eyes darkening as he held her gaze, "you won't need that whussy. We'll get hitched in Jiddah."

Alexa smiled brightly, pondering his suggestion. She thought his offer of marriage was a test, but she wasn't sure. Too often she'd assumed his brains were below his belt, but with frightening, animal-like cunning, Brad frequently targeted subtle things other men might miss. Anything she said now would have to be logical and eradicate any suspicions he might be harboring.

"Let's do it with a big splash in London. When we appear in Jiddah, we'll grab headlines worldwide. We'll keep the media focused on us. It'll be good hype for our movie. We'll let Steven foot the bill for the wedding. He owes you."

# Chapter 41

Mark answered the door and was surprised to find Linda and Warren standing there with grave expressions on their faces. "What's the matter?"

"Alexa's alive—in Jiddah," Warren said solemnly.

For a moment Mark stood there, stunned. "Thank God!" He hugged Warren and gave Linda as big a squeeze as her protruding tummy allowed. "How did she get out?"

Warren put a hand on Mark's shoulder to keep him earthbound. Sick at heart, he wondered how to break the news. Mark had vowed to trade everything he had, or ever hoped to have, if she'd somehow be spared. Now what would his friend do?

"Let's catch it on BBC One," Warren said. It might be better to let Mark hear Alexa say it himself. "We saw the interview with her this morning. They should be repeating it."

"How did she escape?" Mark's prayers had been answered. Nothing could match the sense of elation he felt. Soon she'd be home, here.

Linda hesitated. "Brad Willingham got her out."

That bastard, Mark thought. He'd been too selfish to own up to the phony passport. When it came right down to it, that, as much as the outtakes, had sealed Alexa's fate. Mark had already talked the soldiers into letting her go when Willingham's passport failed to check. Don't curse him, he told himself as he clicked on the television in the study. He got her out; be grateful for that.

"Hey, what's the matter with you two?" Mark asked. With the most forbidding expressions he'd ever seen on either one of them, they'd taken seats on the sofa. He barely noticed that neither answered because Alexa's face dominated the screen.

Except for her enormous green eyes, he hardly recognized her. Painfully thin with her honey-blond hair clipped into a sawtoothed bob barely covering her ears, she looked exhausted and dead serious. One glance at her and he knew she'd been through hell. He wanted to hold her, love her, make everything all right again.

The taped interview had already begun and Mark listened carefully, not wanting to miss any detail. She told the wildest tale of being chased, of hiding and fighting, that he'd ever heard. If it had been anyone but Alexa, he might never have believed all of it. But anyone could see her sincerity as she looked directly into the camera, tears limning her eyes as she spoke.

Why hadn't she tried to reach him? Mark wondered. She could easily have called him from Saudi Arabia.

Alexa went on to give Willingham full credit for their escape. By the time she'd finished, she'd painted a picture of a hero rivaling Rambo. "Some good comes of anything, no matter how bad it may seem. We've found each other and a long and lasting love. As soon as we return to London, we're going to be married."

Mark stared at the screen, her picture already gone, her words emblazoned in his mind. He'd lost her to something more difficult to comprehend than death, but every bit as final.

As Steven's chauffeured Bentley sped them into elegant Belgravia, Brad was impressed by the embassies on Eaton Square. He nodded approvingly at the mansions on Chester Row as Steven filled them in on all that had happened while they'd been gone.

So Melanie was dead, thought Alexa. Fate had taken care of her. Now it was up to Alexa to expose Steven Hunter, bringing Jason and Brad down with him. She cast a sidelong glance at Steven as he chatted with Brad. She'd managed to convince him that she blamed Melanie for what happened at the airport, dismissing the outtakes as if she thought they were merely excess footage, not a deliberately cut erotic scene. She never mentioned the checks.

They turned off the boulevard and down Minera Mews, driving past the rows of narrow houses standing side by side like cigars lined up in a box. The last house, white accented with Delft blue, was the one Steven had leased for them.

Since they'd called him from Jiddah, Steven couldn't do enough for them. Not only had he leased them a house, he'd arranged for credit at a bank and major stores. But Alexa wasn't deceived. She'd trusted him for the last time. She would let him think she was the same old naive Alexa until she had the goods on him. Her sixth sense told her she'd need to act quickly. Even though Steven readily embraced the idea of filming their escape, Alexa wondered just how long he'd want them around. They knew too much.

"Just what does mews mean?" Brad asked Steven.

"The alley behind town houses leading to their stable area was called mews. When London moved into the era of automobiles, the mews were no longer needed. Over the years, they were split off from the original houses and made into elegant homes."

"They get a million pounds for these joints?" Brad asked skeptically when Steven told him how expensive they were.

"Yes. They want more than that for this one." Steven pointed to the mews house just across the narrow lane from the one he'd leased for them. "I would have bought it, but it wasn't for lease, while yours was."

"Christ," Brad cursed as they stepped from the limo. "I wouldn't pay that much for it. It's so close to ours we can see in the windows without binoculars." He nudged Steven and winked. "Hope a babe with a set of double-D knockers moves in."

As they entered the furnished house, Alexa tried not to think of the double mews house Mark had converted to one of the most elegant mansions in Mayfair. She'd been tempted —so tempted—to call him as soon as she'd landed in Saudi Arabia, but she hadn't. Sometime during her ordeal, she'd seen herself clearly. Too clearly. She'd let Mark bail her out too often. The last time he'd come to her rescue it had almost cost him his life. This was a dangerous game she was playing. She had no right to risk his life again.

They stood in the living room of the narrow three-story house, and Alexa noted how different this was from Mark's authentically restored Lees Place mews. Here the high-tech decor in gray accented the chrome and leather furniture. One wall of the living room was a tropical fish aquarium filled with glittering exotic fish lit by dozens of cleverly concealed lights.

"Don't worry about cleaning it or feeding the fish," Steven said as he led them upstairs for a tour of the house. "A service comes three times a week."

After Steven left, Alexa considered how she'd get the notebooks from him. She couldn't put her plan into operation unless she got away from Brad. "I've got to see the caterer, the florist, and pick out a dress. You know, a week doesn't give me much time to plan our wedding."

"I was ready to get hitched in Jiddah," Brad said peevishly, making Alexa again wonder if he really did want to marry her, or if he was playing some bizarre game.

"And miss all this publicity? When we're done with this film, it'll show that you're not only a hero but a first-rate producer as well."

Brad grinned. "You're right. I'm going to go test-drive an Aston-Martin. Meet you back here for dinner."

Half an hour later Alexa arrived at a modest brownstone in Maida Vale. She took the steps two at a time, but Austin opened the door before she could knock. He swept her into his arms, hugging her enthusiastically.

"I'm so glad you made it out of the Sudan, kid." Austin guided her inside. "Now what's so hush-hush that you can't even talk about it on the phone?"

Alexa looked around the comfortable parlor as she took a seat on the sofa. "Is anyone at home?" When he shook his head, she said, "I can get you all the information you need to expose the black-marketing in the Sudan."

"Really?" Austin arched one eyebrow.

"There are two notebooks. One details all the international arms connections and the Unity International people involved in the scheme. The other notebook contains information on the international group black-marketing airline tickets—the Talbott group."

"I believe the authorities already have that information. Numerous warrants are out for Jason Talbott."

"I know. When we arrived in Jiddah, we learned Talbott was on the run. Even if there isn't anything new in that notebook, the Swiss bank account numbers are there. But it's the other notebook that I want. The kind of black-marketing the Talbotts did was petty compared to stealing contraband U.S. government weapons and selling relief supplies."

"How do you know all this?"

She spent the next hour relating the entire story, from the Sea of Cortéz to their meeting with Steven that morning.

"My God, you mean to tell me that Brad believed Steven when Steven said Brad's notebook with the international arms connections listed in it had been confiscated by the authorities in Khartoum?" Austin asked when she'd finished.

"Steven can be very convincing—I should know. And it *was* a mad scramble to get out of Khartoum. But I don't buy it. Brad's so enamored with his new career in show business, he doesn't care. My theory is that Steven will let Jason Talbott use the information to set up another black-market network. How else can he raise enough cash to support his lifestyle and keep himself beyond the reach of the law? Apparently Robert Talbott was the brains behind the operation. Without the sources listed in the notebooks, it'll take years to rebuild a viable network."

Austin considered the situation as he lit his pipe. "What makes you think that Jason doesn't have his own set of records?"

"Because Steven told Brad that Robert insisted there be but one copy; he kept it because he was setting up the deals. Steven came across it when he was staying at the Talbott villa in Marbella one Christmas. He didn't have a way of getting it out of the house to be duplicated, so he copied all the sources into a Smythson address book he'd received as a present."

"Some friend." Austin shook his head, disgusted.

"In his own misguided way he is a friend—to Jason. He called him from Khartoum and warned him to leave London. Jason fled before Steven returned, so he hasn't had a chance to get the notebooks yet. I'm certain that just as soon as the investigation cools down, Steven will get those notebooks to Jason. But I intend to get them first."

Austin took a long draw on his pipe, held it for a moment before releasing it with a sigh. "Do you have any idea of what you're getting involved in?"

"Yes, I'm journalistic gold right now. But has it done any good for those starving children you filmed or the girls forced to prostitute themselves? No. Soon something else will grab the public's attention. But with your footage and the evidence in those notebooks, the international pressure to negotiate with the rebels will be tremendous. Do you have your footage edited? Would it be ready to go the moment I get the notebooks?"

"Hold on a minute. You'd be killed in an instant if anyone knew what you planned to do. What about Mark Kimbrough? In Khartoum you told me you loved him. Is he willing to let you risk your life?"

"He doesn't know about the notebooks, and I don't want him to find out. Promise." When Austin nodded, she continued. "This is *my* fight. He's helped me enough. Believe me, I wouldn't come—even to you—if you didn't have the footage. The public heard how terrible the famine was, but it didn't touch them because they couldn't see it. When your film airs on television, backed by hard evidence, no one will be able to ignore it."

Austin shook his head. "All right, let's contact the authorities and have them search Steven's—"

"No." Alexa jumped up and walked over to the window and saw dusk was falling. She should return to the town house. Brad had become quite possessive since their return. She'd been surprised he'd been so easy to shake today. Undoubtedly thoughts of the snazzy Aston-Martin diverted him, but he'd expect her to account for every minute of her time. Alexa couldn't afford to make him suspicious now.

"I think I know where those notebooks are." She turned to face Austin. "But if I'm wrong and we tip him by sending in the police, Steven will hide them where no one will ever find them. I have to do this on my own. Steven's throwing an engagement party for us Friday night. At the party there'll be so many people traipsing around no one will notice me looking for the notebooks." She sat down again, asking, "Will you help me?"

Austin put his pipe in the ashtray and stared at her intently. "On one condition. Once we have those notebooks, the authorities will be notified. It's irresponsible journalism to air a story such as this merely for our own ends—however altruistic they may be. The authorities need advance notice so they can make arrests. Otherwise we'll merely be giving some of these men time to go underground."

"Of course. I don't want a single one of them to get away. I just want to make certain Steven and Brad know I'm responsible."

After they worked out a plan to conceal the notebooks once she had them, Austin said, "I want you to promise me you'll get rid of the notebooks immediately after you get them. That way, if anything goes wrong, you could deny taking them. Whatever you do, get away quickly."

# Chapter 42

Brad flopped back across the bed. "Come here." He patted the space beside him.

She swallowed a grimace and collapsed onto the bed, smiling seductively. She'd been late in getting back from Austin's, but Brad had been so busy with the Aston-Martin he'd purchased that he hadn't noticed.

Closing her eyes, Alexa let Brad make love to her. She blocked out his grunting, concentrating on her play. Were all the last-minute details in order? How had the costumes turned out? She wished she could go to the theater and check on everything herself instead of relying on clandestine calls to Renata. But she couldn't. Brad and Steven had to believe the film was the center of her life now.

"Ready for tonight?" Brad asked as he collapsed on top of her.

She nodded, although Steven's party at Hunter Films' new studio promised to be another boring night when Steven and Brad would certainly be bent on impressing everyone. "Tomorrow night is Chauncey's party," she said, not adding that the following day would be the last day she ever had to spend with Brad Willingham.

"Isn't he a duke or something? Have you ever been out with him?" Brad's eyes narrowed.

"Yes, he and Charmaine Crowne will be getting married soon." She didn't mention that this news had been a surprise until Linda had told her that Charmaine had begun making a play for Chauncey on the night she'd given the surprise party for Mark and he'd left early.

"Did you fuck him?"

"No," Alexa said, wondering if he was jealous or merely curious. She should alleviate the judicial system's overload and smother Brad in his sleep.

"Hope Chauncey isn't as snotty as your other highfalutin friends."

"Warren and Linda like you," Alexa said, although she knew nothing could be further from the truth. "They were just surprised I'm not returning to Mark. Anyway, they won't be coming tonight, but Renata and Giles will be." Alexa smiled, hoping her explanation for the cool reception Warren and Linda had given Brad when they'd welcomed Alexa home satisfied him. She wanted him relaxed and happy so he wouldn't watch her too closely.

"Great," Brad said as he grinned, pleased at her words. "I like the redheaded broad."

Alexa doubted the feeling was mutual. Renata was an accomplished actress and wouldn't want to hurt Alexa's feelings by being rude to Brad. But Giles couldn't hide his dislike; only his guilt over persuading her to go to the Sudan and pressure from Steven convinced him to direct their film.

Alexa was slipping back into her lavender jumpsuit when the doorbell rang. More reporters? She couldn't answer another question, tell another lie.

"I'll get it," Brad said, jumping off the bed and hitching up his jeans. He didn't bother to put on a shirt as he went downstairs.

Content to let Brad handle the reporter, Alexa went into the bathroom and ran a comb through her hair.

"It's Mark Kimbrough." Brad propped his shoulder against the doorjamb and glared at her. "He wants to see you."

For a heart-stopping second, Alexa thought she'd burst into tears. "Really?" she said, inwardly pleased she sounded so disinterested.

"Make it quick. We've got a party."

Alexa had sensed Brad's possessiveness before, but not to this degree. She doubted he truly cared for her, but he was the type of a man who jealously guarded what was his. And right now she was his. Alexa looped her arms around his neck and gave him a long kiss.

"I'll be right back."

Alexa slowly walked down the stairs. She'd been back almost three days. With all the interviews she'd given, she was surprised Mark would come to see her. If she'd made one thing clear, it was her newfound love for Brad. Her stomach churned with anticipation. More than anyone else in the world, she wanted to see Mark. Yet she knew she had to get rid of him.

Mark watched her coming toward him, thinking how much sweeter reality was than memories. Nothing could compare with seeing her in person. She wore a pale shade of violet that offset her matchless green eyes. Her hair had been professionally styled into a short, ultra-chic cut he considered too severe for her face.

"Hello, Mark," she said in a friendly yet impersonal voice that still managed to be softer and sexier than he'd recalled.

Mark stepped forward and pulled her into his arms as a thousand forgotten feelings swept over him. He couldn't resist kissing her although her arms didn't welcome him and her back was rigid. She pulled away and moved toward the front door.

"I see you've brought me T.S.," she said, opening the cat carrier Mark had left there. "Where's your kitten?" she asked the yowling feline.

"I couldn't catch him," Mark said. Her back was to him, and she kissed and nuzzled the cat, cradling him in her arms. "He was in the fields chasing mice. He's happy at Wyndham Hill. I'd like to keep him if that's all right with you." He jammed his hands into his pockets to quell the almost irresistible urge to embrace her again.

"Of course," she said, turning to face him. The cat was tucked into the curve of her neck, licking the tip of her earlobe. "Come sit and tell me what's new with you."

*Is she kidding?* He followed her into the living room, and when she sat down on the leather sofa, he sat beside her.

While she kept kissing the damned cat, he took a closer look at her. A telltale flush warmed her cheeks and her pupils were slightly dilated. She always looked that way after making love. Remembering Brad answering the door shirtless, clad in just his jeans, a sickening feeling plummeted through Mark. And the urge to kill.

"I meant to come see you," Alexa said, releasing the cat. "But . . ." She shrugged and smiled that slow smile that never failed to tug at the corners of his heart. "I've been so busy."

*That busy? Come on.* Aware that she was waiting for some reply, Mark nodded.

"You know Hunter Films is going to make a movie of our adventure?"

*Who didn't?* It would be a Kleenex classic guaranteed to score big at the box office. He listened, watching her closely as she launched into an animated explanation of the cinematic tour de force she planned. She'd become a stranger, a beloved stranger, but a stranger nonetheless. She'd stopped playing with her hair and she no longer blushed. Her eyes had a hard gleam to them, and there was a new sense of coldness, an uncharacteristic remoteness, about her. Since he'd met her, he'd hated her and loved her, but had he ever understood her? Never. Especially now.

"What about *you?*" he asked when she finished. "How are *you?*"

"Fine," she smiled. "As you can see Brad got me out in one piece."

At the mention of Brad's name, Mark merely nodded. She was in one piece all right. He should leave now, he thought, before he told her things she didn't want to hear.

"I want to thank you for what you tried to do for me in Khartoum," she said. Her eyes had softened a bit and her voice was earnest. "You tried to help. I appreciate it."

*Then why didn't you call me as soon as you were free and tell me so?* "I talked to Nigel before he died," Mark said. "He told me why you'd gone. If I'd known, I wouldn't have been so hard on you. I'm sorry."

"It doesn't matter. Things have changed."

"I wanted to talk to you about that. Don't you think you're rushing this marriage?" She shook her head, but he continued, not giving her time to respond. "You know, when someone's been through an ordeal like this, they often lose their perspective. Somehow you may be feeling what they call 'survivor guilt' because you lived. You could be projecting these feelings as love for Brad."

"Mark," Alexa said, a peculiar, concerned expression in her eyes, "it's nothing like that. Brad—"

"I'm suggesting if you gave this time, you might reevaluate your relationship. I'm willing to wait for as long as it takes."

"I know Brad better than I've ever known any man . . . and he knows me. Our relationship has undergone a trial by fire and overcome it. You see, he was there when I needed him."

The implication he'd failed her by being hauled aboard the jet cut to the quick. Still, he couldn't refute what she said. No matter what happened, they shared a common bond that would never include him.

"I understand," he said, even though he didn't and doubted he ever would. He reached into his pocket for the engagement ring he'd given her. That Christmas Eve seemed as if it had happened a lifetime ago—to another person. He handed her the box, saying, "Keep this—for old times' sake."

"Mark, I can't accept this ring." She started to hand it back to him but Mark stood up.

"I insist. I want you to have it—no matter how you feel about me."

"I'm marrying Brad," she said, staring down at the ring.

"I love you. Surely you know that. I'm just asking you to wait to be certain—"

She shook her head, her soft cluster of short curls fluttering and then settling back into place.

Mark swallowed hard. "Tell me you love him and I won't bother you again."

She didn't hesitate; her gaze was level. "I love Brad. I always will."

# Chapter 43

"Here, kitty, kitty . . . here, kitty, kitty," Alexa called. Where was the dratted cat? Probably across the street pestering the elderly gentleman who'd just moved into the mews cottage opposite theirs. Well, T.S. would come home when she was hungry. If she didn't hurry, they'd be late for Chauncey's party. She stood there a moment anyway, waiting for the cat to appear, thinking about Mark.

When he'd left yesterday, she'd sat there, hating herself for what she'd done. She'd almost burst into tears as she heard his Jag roar down Minera Mews, taking him out of her life. It had taken all her courage, even more than she'd had in the Sudan, to jettison their relationship with a lie. Just then Brad had called to her and she heard him clomping down the stairs. If he saw the ring, he'd think she still cared for Mark. He'd never believe a man would give something this valuable without expecting something in return. Before Brad came into the room, she'd hidden it in the bag of kitty litter Mark had brought.

Today she'd planned on retrieving the emerald and putting it in a safe deposit box, but Brad hadn't given her a chance to go to the bank. He'd spent so much time with her, even doing all the little errands necessary for the wedding, that she wondered if he suspected anything. Brad's booming voice interrupted her thoughts.

"C'mon, Alexa, we're gonna be late. Leave the fuckin' cat alone."

Alexa wearily climbed the stairs, hating the thought of still another party. If she could just get through tonight, not just the party but Brad's bestial rutting later, she'd be down to her last day. Tomorrow Steven's party would give her the opportunity of checking the headboard for the notebooks.

"We're gonna be late," Brad huffed when he saw she hadn't begun to dress.

"We'll make an entrance."

"Wear the green dress," Brad said as she stood at the closet trying to decide what to wear.

"I'm wearing that tomorrow night," she said, yanking a red gown she'd never worn off the hanger to end the discussion. Her plans would be ruined if she wore the green dress tonight. She couldn't possibly wear it two nights in a row without Brad suspecting something, and she didn't have the time to alter another gown to accommodate the notebooks. It had been difficult enough to fix this one without Brad seeing her.

"Something special about that green number?"

"Linda designed it for me. I've been saving it for something special—Steven's party."

She'd slipped on her dress and was applying a trace of blusher to her pale complexion when she heard T.S. at the front door. As usual she was pummeling the door with her front paws and meowing in double time. Alexa started to call to Brad to have him let her in, but he was in the study on the telephone with one of his newfound movie industry hangers-on, so she decided to do it herself. If Brad went down, he'd probably kick the poor cat again.

She hurried downstairs and opened the door just in time to catch the tangerine devil scampering across the street into the old man's side yard. On spiked heels Alexa gingerly crossed the cobbled lane and peeked into her new neighbor's tiny garden. T.S. was nowhere in sight.

"Kitty, kitty," she called softly. She hadn't met the old man yet, but she'd heard him speaking with a German accent to the paper boy. Perhaps he went to bed early; she didn't want to wake him. "Kitty, kitty," she called again, louder this time.

"Alexa, what the hell are you doing?" she heard Brad bellowing.

Forget the cat, she told herself; she'd come home when she was ready. Alexa returned to the house and found Brad in the garage warming his new toy's engine. She lowered herself into the low-slung red Aston-Martin's seat.

"Shit! Why are you so hung up on that cat?" Brad put the Volante in reverse, backed ten feet, and then pivoted it so sharply the tires squealed. It went from zero to fifty miles per hour in a matter of seconds, but not before Alexa caught a glimpse of T.S. peering out at her from the neighbor's window.

When they returned from what had to be the longest, most boring party of the century, Brad was drunk. He refused to let her drive, but it was only a matter of blocks from the Chauncey's posh Belgravia mansion where the party had been held to their mews cottage. In his drunken state Brad drove slowly, taking each turn with exaggerated caution. Alexa stared out the window, thinking how very much he enjoyed being the center of attention. The fact that Chauncey Beddington, a duke no less, had insisted Brad be invited impressed him. He had an almost childlike awe of anyone with a title.

Alexa had held her breath all night, hoping Mark wouldn't come in with some stunning woman. Toward the end of the evening Charmaine came up to Alexa.

"It's too bad Mark couldn't come," Charmaine said, shaking her head so that her new hairstyle, a tousled, casual look, fluttered across her shoulders. "He'll be in Australia for a month. That means he won't be in town for the opening of your play," she said, her voice clearly indicating that she couldn't care less.

"Renata will miss him," Alexa said, eyeing Charmaine's crimson gown with yellow ruffles that made her look like a British edition of Carmen Miranda. Although Alexa was grateful she wouldn't have to face Mark tonight, she'd hoped that he would attend the play's opening. By then, she prayed, she'd have the goods on Steven and could explain everything to Mark.

When Brad pulled up in front of the house, T.S. was curled up on the small porch. So she'd driven the elderly gentleman nuts. Brad kicked her aside and staggered in before Alexa could grab the cat. Howling as if mortally wounded, she raced off across the street. Alexa snagged her as T.S. crouched giving a blood-curling, five-alarm yowl at the old man's door.

"I'm sorry he kicked you, but quit digging your nails into me," she said, wincing and holding her tightly. She settled down, purring riotously and snuggling against her. Alexa kissed the top of her head, silently promising her that they'd both be home soon. As she switched off the porch light, she noticed the drapes flutter in the cottage across the street. They'd awakened the old man. She'd have to go over there tomorrow and apologize for T.S. being such a pest.

Stalling for time, hoping Brad would fall asleep so she could avoid making love to him, Alexa treated T.S. to an oversized bowl of cream. Lapping greedily, her tongue going a hundred miles an hour, she slip-sloshed cream onto the floor as Alexa double-checked the bag of cat litter. The ring was still there.

Upstairs she found Brad, spread-eagle, fully clothed across the bed, emitting a foghorn snore. She tossed her clothes aside and crawled between the sheets. A good night's sleep was imperative; tomorrow would be a long day. Her body refused to cooperate. She lay there thinking she hadn't had a good night's sleep since she'd last slept with Mark. She still longed for that comfortable, secure feeling of falling asleep next to someone she loved.

Alexa tried not to let it appear that she was prowling Steven's living room, but she was. It was late; the place was crowded, with the overflow filling the library and the study as well as the foyer. All the plans she and Austin had made were in place. No one would possibly suspect the slinky green dress concealed a hidden panel in the ten-gallon froth of lace fish-tailing from the kickpleat behind her knees. If things went according to plan, she'd only have the notebooks in her possession a matter of minutes. She'd dispose of them, call Austin, then she'd retrieve the ring and T.S. and go into hiding until the authorities completed their arrests.

"Here, honey, have another glass of champagne," Brad said. "I just heard Kimbrough's in Australia. Did you know that?"

"Yes. He won't be back for the opening either." Alexa kept her tone matter-of-fact. Brad was inordinately interested in her relationship with Mark. She couldn't risk making him suspicious.

"Whatsa matter. You keep looking at the door. Expecting someone?"

"Yes," she said, pretending to sip the champagne. She'd managed to water a silk flower arrangement with her last drink. Where could she inconspicuously get rid of this one? "I'm expecting Gina Gerrard, Renata's cousin. You remember, she wants a part in the movie. I thought it would give you a chance to chat with her informally. If you don't think she's right to play Melanie in our movie, we won't accept Giles's suggestion. After all, we want total creative control, don't we?"

Apparently believing her story, Brad nodded. "Some party, huh?"

"Yes," she said, noting the steady flow of people up and down the stairs. Evidently, the candy noses were getting their treats on the second—make that the first—floor. This played right into her hand. No one would be suspicious when she wandered upstairs. Now if only Renata's "cousin" would appear.

Right on cue at ten-thirty, Gina arrived, dressed in electric pink. A leonine mane of cotton-candy hair framed her Nordic features, accenting her sky-blue eyes and spilling over her bare shoulders in a lush, wanton mass. A navel-skimming decolletage revealed her impressive bosom.

"Holy shit! Get a load of those hooters."

With an alluring smile Gina sidled up to Alexa and Brad. "Hello, I'm so pleased to meet you. 'Specially you, Mr. Willingham. I just think you're so wonderful," she said in a breathy voice, which had to be the worst imitation of Marilyn Monroe that Alexa had ever heard.

"I'm glad to meet you," Alexa said. "Giles has tremendous faith in your talent, and I can see why. Can't you Brad?"

"Yeah," Brad said, gazing at the twin peaks Gina had positioned directly under his nose.

Alexa took a huge gulp of champagne to drown her laugh. Without asking any questions, Renata had outdone herself. Where had she found her "cousin"? Alexa wondered. This bait would keep Brad busy while she checked the headboard.

"I'm going to let you two chat a moment while I trot off to the powder room."

Alexa placed her glass on a table in the foyer and drew a long, head-clearing breath before starting up the stairs. *Please, God, let them be there. Don't make me have to go through any more of this madness.* Heart pounding in her ears, she casually walked up the stairs. She paused outside the door to Steven's room, listening to the strange noises coming from across the hall. After she decided it was a couple screwing in the upstairs study, Alexa cautiously opened Steven's door. A frisson of alarm prickled her nerves, heightening her awareness. No one was inside the bedroom, but there was a strange medicinal smell hanging in the air. She checked the adjacent bathroom to be certain she was alone. No one was in there, but she saw what was causing the odor. Ether. Steven and his friends were freebasing in the bathroom. Great, with her luck, he'd probably blow himself to kingdom come before she had a chance to get him.

Alexa closed the bedroom door and walked over to the bed. The black lacquer was highly polished and revealed no fingerprints, indicating it hadn't been opened recently. There were no wires to the bed or the wall that she could see. Too small to hold much, the compartment probably hadn't been included in the house's alarm system. She slid open the compartment.

There were several plastic bags filled with cocaine. She quickly fumbled through the stash and found first the black ostrich address book and then Brad's small spiral-bound notebook. Unable to resist temptation she quickly flipped through them both. *Thank you, God,* she silently whispered. They contained exactly what she'd hoped—enough to kill dozens of birds with one stone. After slipping them both into the narrow panel in her fishtail flounce, she reached up to close the headboard.

"Hello, luv."

She turned slowly, trying to decide what to do. How long had he been standing there? "Steven, great party. I was just helping myself."

"So I see." He came in and closed the door again. "How'd you know about the compartment?"

"Mrs. Raj showed me," she said, knowing he'd fired the woman and telling this couldn't get her in trouble.

"That's why I canned her. She was always stealing from my supply."

Alexa doubted that, but she nodded sympathetically. It was more likely cocaine-induced paranoia had made him suspicious of his daily.

"You could have asked me," he said, walking over and snapping the headboard shut. "I have a setup in the bathroom."

"Well, I'd rather . . ." She lowered her eyes dramatically, trying for a guilty look. "Brad doesn't know."

"So that's how it is, luv," Steven smirked.

Alexa shrugged; she'd decided he hadn't suspected she'd lifted the notebooks. She needed to leave as quickly as possible. If Brad came looking for her, she might not be able to get away in time.

"Come talk to me," Steven said as he walked into the bathroom. "I need a quick hit."

Alexa covertly took a peek at her watch. Eleven o'clock. She had to be there by eleven-twenty at the latest.

Every inch the parasitic, pampered rich kid, Steven took several puffs, inhaling right down to his Lobb's custom-made patent-leather dress shoes before she said, "I'd better get back to Brad."

"Sure, luv," he said, but she doubted he knew she'd left.

Alexa dashed down the narrow servants' stairs to the kitchen, past the caterers and out the back door.

She shivered, wishing she'd had a coat. A bone-chilling mist descended, gilding Mayfair's streets with moisture as the enshrouding fog rolled in off the Thames. Alexa walked as quickly as she dared; she couldn't afford to call attention to herself by running. When she reached St. George's Primary School at the end of Waverton Street, she took another look over her shoulder. A vaporous curtain of mist obscured everything beyond ten feet or so, but no one had followed her. Fog wreathed the Gothic building, deepening its shadows while a stealthy wind rustled through the leaves on the trees in the garden behind the building. Alexa ran along the barely visible trail until she reached Mount Street.

Even after she'd disposed of the notebooks and had reached the phone booth at the corner of Mount and South Audley, her heart still pounded lawlessly. She kicked off her shoe and retrieved her phone card from under the innersole and jammed it into the slot and dialed Austin's number.

He answered before the first ring finished.

"I made it," she said, trying to breathe normally. "They were right where I thought—under enough coke to give all of London a two-day high."

"You got rid of them," he asked, "and you're sure no one followed you?"

Alexa tried to appear nonchalant as she glanced around. The specterlike fog cloaked the street, haloing the street lights in swirling mist, making it impossible to see much. There was the normal amount of traffic heading down South Audley to Park Lane. The only people in sight were two couples and an old man with a cane. "No, no one's followed me."

"Then get out of there. Come here immediately. Just make certain you aren't being followed."

"I'm on my way."

"Be careful."

Alexa rushed around the corner to where she'd parked the car she'd rented earlier. As she used the single key she'd hidden in her other shoe, she glanced over her shoulder. In the murky light silvering the mist-dampened streets, she thought she saw someone duck into the shadows, but when she took a closer look he'd disappeared. *Stop it. You're imagining things. If they were onto you, they'd have snagged you before you unloaded the notebooks.* Alexa floored the accelerator and raced down the street into the fog-slowed Saturday night flow of traffic along Park Lane.

Alexa knew she should have gone the opposite direction, toward Maida Vale, but she couldn't leave T.S. behind—or the ring. Austin would be irate; he'd specifically instructed her not to return to the mews house. But Brad would most certainly kill the cat when he discovered what she'd done. And she'd have no way of getting the ring. Earlier she'd locked the protesting T.S. in her office on the third floor, bribing her silence with a special platter of her favorite, Fortnum and Mason's minced quail.

The minute she turned down Minera Mews, she groaned. There were cars everywhere; someone was having a party. She waved the valet parking attendant aside and inched her car up the lane. She looked over her shoulder again. Through a patch of fog-blurred light, she saw another car had come in behind her, but he was evidently a guest because the attendant took the car. Alexa parked in front of her house and left the keys in the ignition, the car running while she ran in for T.S.

She flicked on the lights in the entry and rushed toward the stairs, intending to get the cat first, when her peripheral vision caught the innovatively lit aquarium. She turned, a tendril of horror unfurling deep inside her. Floating on top, a fish nibbling on her ear, was T.S. No! She couldn't have fallen in; the tank had a tight lid. She stepped closer, the tears slipping from her eyes, and saw the cat hadn't drowned. Someone had wrung her neck, turning it completely backward on her small frame. Her jade-green eyes were frozen open, fixed on Alexa. "Poor baby," she said, ripping the lid off and grabbing the sodden body.

Clutching the dripping corpse to her breast, a sudden sweat broke out under her arms and across her back. An explosive charge detonated in her brain: *Run! Get out of here!!* She whirled to find a thirty-eight automatic with a shiny chrome silencer leveled at her.

"Hello, Alexa."

# Chapter 44

Jason Talbott's jet-black eyes stared at her over the top of the gun, gleaming with a triumph so intense, so terrifying, all Alexa's instincts for self-preservation fired at once. She flung the dead cat in his face, ducked, and then sprinted to the front door. She jerked it open, shrieking her loudest raise-the-dead scream, as she bolted toward her car. Jason jumped on her, yanking her backward by her hair, pinioning her in a hammerlock, and dragging her into the house. The fog muffled her screams and shrouded the scuffle in a damp mist, making it unlikely she'd attracted the attention of any of the partygoers.

With explosive force Jason spun her around and jammed the pistol against her temple. "I'd kill you right now if I hadn't promised Brad I'd wait for him." He prodded her with the gun, moving her over to the sofa. "You thought you fooled us, didn't you?"

"I-I don't know what you mean," she said, eking the words out from between clenched teeth as she collapsed onto the leather cushions.

"Our source books. They're out in the car aren't they?"

"I don't—"

"Faking isn't going to get you anywhere," Jason said, sitting beside her with the gun still trained on her. "You tripped a filament alarm the second you touched them. You're as good as dead. I'd love to do it myself, but Brad wants to take care of you personally." Jason eased back into the cushions, making an obvious show of getting comfortable while she sat ramrod straight. "You didn't know Brad was with us, did you?" It was a rhetorical question; he didn't wait for an answer. "He didn't buy Steven's story about losing his notebook. We had to let him in on the action."

Alexa had no illusions as to what her fate might be. She wondered momentarily if there was a heaven—Melanie knew by now. But she would be damned if she'd let them kill her without causing as much havoc as possible.

"Brad will slit my throat," Alexa said calmly, watching for Jason's reaction. Something flickered behind his eyes. "The way he did your brother's—from ear to ear, up high just under the jawbone."

"You don't know what you're talking about," he said, anger thinning his lips.

"Don't I?" she asked. "He told me he killed Robert; they'd had a falling out over black-marketing. I saw Brad kill another man the same way. Do you know how slowly a man dies? Slit throat—sounds quick. It isn't. There's a liquid gurgling as the severed windpipe gasps for air. As long as they get oxygen they live—until they bleed to death."

"Shut up. You're making this up."

"Am I?" Despite his outward appearance of bored disdain, she sensed she had him. "How long do you think it'll be before Brad turns on you?"

"Never. He wouldn't have turned on you either, except you tipped your hand."

She refused to give him the satisfaction of asking how, but she wondered. After all the weeks of pretending, what had gone wrong?

"That little scene with Kimbrough gave you away." She must have looked as shocked as she felt because a low, diabolical chuckle came from deep in his throat. "You never told Brad about the ring, but he knew Mark had given it to you. He'd been eavesdropping. What a sucker! You had him fooled until then. Brad really believed you'd fallen in love with him, especially when you told Kimbrough you loved him. Too bad you weren't smart enough to simply tell him about the ring. Then you might have deceived him."

"You won't get away with this. The notebooks are already in the authorities' hands."

"So far they haven't been too successful in catching me."

"This time they'll cut off your funds. They're planning an international dragnet to pick up all the criminals involved in your schemes. And you won't be able to rely on Steven much longer. The rate he's putting his inheritance up his nose, he'll be broke soon. With Melanie gone you have—"

He jabbed her with the long barrel of the silencer, sending her back against the cushions. "Don't you ever, ever mention her name, or I'll not bother waiting for Brad."

"Why not?" Alexa mumbled, knowing her only chance now was for Austin to realize she was overdue and call Scotland Yard. But would he think to send them here? "Melanie tried to get me killed. What did I ever do to her?"

"She overreacted, but she didn't deliberately try to get you killed," Jason said. For an unguarded moment agony flared in his eyes.

"She tried to frame me in Cabo," Alexa insisted, playing for time.

"No, she didn't," Jason said. "Steven did that. They both told me so."

Alexa considered that for a moment and knew Jason was telling the truth. "She got your brother killed by trying to pull off a ticket scam in Khartoum. She muffed it, of course, and bandied his name all over town. That's when Brad had to take care of him." This was pure speculation based on some comments Brad had made, but she saw she'd guessed correctly.

"You bitch—"

A sudden banging on the door cut him off. "If you even breathe, I'll shoot," he whispered.

A lot more loud knocking followed by shouts in German came through the door.

"The old man across the street," she said, making it up as she went. "He's saying something about my car. I left the lights on, the motor running."

Jason looked confused, but said, "Go to the door and talk to him. Get rid of him."

On shaky legs she stood up and went to the door, trying to

decide if there was any way of escaping. She called out, "Yes, who is it?"

A garbled stream of German too rapid to decipher came at her.

"What'd he say?" Jason asked.

Obviously he knew German about as well as she did. "He says my car's leaking gasoline and he's afraid of a fire."

"Shit! You'd better turn off the engine. But I swear, if you pull anything, I'll shoot you *and* the old man."

She reached for the doorknob.

"Remember," Jason said, stepping up beside her, "I don't have anything to lose."

Just as Alexa swung the door open, a teak cane sliced through the air and someone shoved her to the ground. Mark! She saw it was Mark and that he'd knocked the gun from Jason's hand and was down on the floor on top of him. She grabbed for the gun but Jason kicked it away. Mark and Jason scrambled across the floor, arms flying, delivering blow after blow. Alexa jackknifed to her feet and dashed to where the gun had slid under an end table. She snatched it up with trembling hands, trying to remember the one lesson she'd had years ago. She checked; the safety was off. All she would have to do would be to pull the trigger. She assumed a police stance and pointed the gun. It was futile. They were tumbling around the floor so rapidly even an expert marksman wouldn't have had a clean shot. "Mark, get away from him. I've got the gun."

"He's got a knife," Mark called.

Until that moment, Alexa hadn't seen the switchblade Mark had trapped in his opponent's hand. It was clear he couldn't hold Jason off forever. They skirmished across the floor, knocking things off tables and cursing each other. Although she'd calmly faced Jason, she now verged a hair's breadth from utter panic at seeing how easily he could kill Mark. Alexa's mind scrambled; there had to be something she could do. She waited until they'd rolled back across the room and were directly under the aquarium. Then, she squeezed the trigger, slowly, excruciatingly slowly, until a loud zip came from the gun. She'd forgotten about the silencer, she realized as the bullet silently hit the tank and it burst, sending an avalanche of water, fish and aquarium pebbles onto the men.

They broke apart, sputtering and gasping. Alexa didn't hesitate. Hanging on as tight as she could, she aimed at Jason and
pulled the trigger. She kept firing at him even though each
shot wrenched her shoulder painfully. When the gun emptied, she dropped it and sank to her knees.

A sudden commotion at the door was followed by shouts.
"The police," she moaned. "Finally."

Austin walked in behind the contingent of officers. "Are
you all right?" he asked, seeing the several inches of water
standing in the living room and the bullet-riddled walls splat-
tered with blood.

"I've never killed a man before," she said, shaken.

"He's not dead," Austin said, "just wounded."

While the officers examined the unconscious Jason and
questioned Mark, Alexa asked Austin, "You told Mark, didn't
you?"

"Of course. I contacted him when I learned you'd died. Any
fool could see how much the man loves you. I refused to allow
you to go through this alone. I knew Mark had the funds to
hire the necessary private detectives to watch you. You're not
angry?"

"No, I'm not. But Brad, he'll be here any—"

"He's in custody. When you told me about that cocaine
stash, I tipped the police and they raided the party. The entire
group's in jail. That will hold them until the authorities have
time to sift through the Royal Mail for the package you addressed to me. When they find it, they can file more substantial charges against Brad and Steven."

"And the television special? Is everything all set?" she
asked, wondering if the authorities would allow him to ex-
amine the notebooks. When they'd decided the safest place
for them was in the Mount Street mail drop because it would
be picked up at eleven-thirty, they'd assumed the package
would be delivered on Monday. Then Austin would have had
time to work with the information before turning it over to
the authorities.

"I have my connections. I'll be going over the notebooks
tonight. The film will air tomorrow night on the early news
just before your play opens." Austin smiled, his brown eyes
twinkling. "You did it, kid."

# Chapter 45

Alexa peeked through the curtain at the Regency's full house. Men attired in dinner jackets and ladies dressed in evening gowns filled the refurbished theater. The first bell had sounded; late arrivals hurried to their seats. Sold out for months, *No Chance* was the hottest ticket in town. In a moment every seat would be taken. All but one.

"Mark still isn't here?" Renata whispered from behind her.

Alexa shook her head. "He's not coming. Perhaps he went off to Australia on business after all." She couldn't keep the somber tone from her voice.

"He'll be here, you'll see," Renata whispered.

Alexa nodded but remained unconvinced. Last night, after the police had questioned her, detectives from Scotland Yard had taken an extensive statement, and American embassy officials had debriefed her, she'd emerged from the interrogation room to find that Mark had left without her. She'd tried to reach him, leaving messages all over London, but he never returned her calls. She wondered what he'd think of the inserts she'd placed in the playbills, saying profits from the play would go to a relief fund for the Sudan. She was certain he wouldn't care, but she'd wanted to tell him about it. More than that, she wanted him here—with her—tonight.

Dejected, Alexa joined Twick in the wings as the house-lights dimmed, the footlights came up, and Quinton Malmsby's score lilted out from the stereo speakers artfully hidden in the old-world decor of the theater. Alexa looked at Renata, checking her costume for the hundredth time. Linda had out-done herself. Alexa had no idea what to call the muted shade of tangerine Renata wore, but it contrasted beautifully with her red hair, enhancing its vibrant color.

As the curtains parted, Alexa checked her own gown, again touched by Linda's account of Mark buying it for her. Last night it had been torn in the fracas, but Linda had managed to mend it. Alexa had always seen herself wearing this gown as Renata made a triumphant return, but she'd always pictured Mark at her side. She twisted the emerald ring Mark had given her around her finger. Why would he have left without saying a word to her?

When the houselights came up at intermission, Alexa caught glimpses of Linda and Warren, Giles, Chauncey with Charmaine, and even Austin, looking out of place in a dinner jacket. Mark's seat was still unoccupied.

At the final curtain the audience vaulted to its feet clapping enthusiastically. There wasn't any question about it: Renata Tremaine, the titian-haired goddess of the London stage, had regained her crown. Through all eleven curtain calls, Alexa craned her neck, peeking from the wings, praying Mark had come. The seat remained empty.

The twelfth time the curtains parted, Renata, her arms filled with a bouquet of five dozen peach-colored roses handed to her during the first curtain call, emerged alone. She waited a moment, her rings refracting the light from the footlights until the audience stopped clapping and sat down.

"Thank you. Thank you all. I can't tell you what it means for you to welcome me back this way." Renata paused to take a deep breath. Alexa could tell by the way her usually perfect stage voice trembled, she wasn't acting. "This night doesn't belong to me. I'd never be here if it weren't for the faith and love of my dear friend Alexa MacKenzie."

Beaming, Renata turned and waved to Alexa to come on-stage. She blushed furiously, feeling terribly awkward as she came up beside Renata. The clamorous applause of a standing ovation shook Alexa to the core. Her eyes misted over with unshed tears. When the noise died down, she said, "Thank you all for giving us a chance." She squeezed Renata's hand. "We appreciate your buying tickets months in advance. I'm sure you're not sorry. Renata's back—better than ever."

Again Alexa waited for the applause to die down before continuing. "This night belongs to the cast and crew, but even more it belongs to one man whose vision, not just for us but for this country, makes us all proud to know him. He can't—"

Renata tugged on her arm and whispered, "There he is."

"Mark Kimbrough," Alexa said, squinting into the bright lights, trying to make out the tall form coming down the aisle. "Our producer and our friend."

Alexa barely heard the round of applause as Mark joined them onstage and the cast and crew came out behind them for one final bow. "Where have you been?" she whispered, blinking back the tears.

"Thinking," he said. "Did you miss me?"

"Yes. Please take me home to Wyndham Hill."

The leaden sky of early dawn rising behind a storm front contrasted sharply with the yellow, green, and pink of Kent's spring landscape as they drove across the downs. After the cast party at Le Caprice and the reading of the theater critics' verdicts in the early morning editions of the papers, Mark and Alexa had driven out of London in silence, ignoring the tension between them, neither knowing what to say, where to begin. During all this time they'd been together, hand in hand, but they hadn't had a chance for a private discussion.

"You didn't believe me when I said I loved Brad, did you?"

"No," Mark said, his voice low. Although she'd only said it once, her words had echoed through Mark's mind a thousand times. "I believed you when you said it. You're a damn convincing actress, but after I left, I began thinking. I knew you wouldn't take the ring unless you still cared for me. And your story was too pat yet too wild. It smacked of your schemes for the play and your caper with Jason. Then Austin called and I knew what you were up to. He was terribly concerned about you stealing the notebooks. The moment I knew the truth, I arranged to use the place across the street."

"You did?" Alexa asked in amazement. "Then why didn't you knock on the door earlier?"

"I wasn't across the street all evening. I'd been following you. You weren't supposed to go back to Minera Mews. I had men stationed downstairs at Steven's party posing as guests and on the street, but we lost you in that damned fog. I knew you planned to make the eleven-thirty drop at the Mount Street post office, but I had no idea where you'd parked the car. My agents followed you and alerted me that you were heading home. I stopped at the party up the street and called Austin to tell him. That's when he told me that Interpol had called him saying Jason had slipped back into the country. I rushed up the lane. You can imagine how frantic I was when I saw your car idling in front of the house."

It began to rain as Mark brought the Jaguar down the lane and she saw Wyndham Hill in the distance. Out of the corner of his eye, he saw Alexa take a quick swipe with the back of her hand at the lone tear zig-zagging down her cheek.

"Let's run for it," he said, bringing the car to a halt as close to the front door as possible.

"Go upstairs, get out of your wet clothes," Mark said after they'd dashed through the downpour into the house.

She nodded, her eyes slowly moving around the room and looking into the hall beyond, taking in the rich woods, over-stuffed furniture, and brass lamps. "It's beautiful," she said, but he caught the sound of the lump in her throat.

"At least the heat works," he replied, striving to lighten the moment for both of them. "Get upstairs."

Mark went into the kitchen to check on B.S. He wanted to give Alexa time alone in the bedroom. As much as he wanted to make love to her, he sensed this ordeal with Brad might have changed her attitude toward sex, toward him. He flicked on the light in the butler's pantry. B.S. opened a sleepy eye briefly before closing it again and curling tighter in his basket. Satisfied the villager paid to feed him had done his job, Mark took the back stairs to his room.

Beneath the mile-high eiderdown comforter, Alexa's cropped curls captured the hazy light of the new day. He stood beside the bed for a long moment before determining she'd fallen asleep. He drew the heavy drapes against the faint light finding its way through the rain-bloated clouds. Wearily he placed his damp clothes over a chair and crawled in beside her. Unable to crush his smoldering longing, he eased her into his arms, and her whole body relaxed against his. They'd both been running on nervous energy for days, he told himself, listening to her contented breathing. He inhaled the sweet, flowery traces of perfume on her skin, thinking he, too, should get some sleep. His body refused to cooperate. Mark was afraid that if he closed his eyes, he'd awaken to find it had merely been another dream.

At first he didn't know he'd dozed off. He stretched, trying to relax, and then groaned, realizing he had a world-class hard-on. With that sweet, sweet magic of a midnight dream, he let her come to him as she had dozens of times over the past weeks. He arched his back, enjoying the deep, deep drawing of her mouth on him, sucking relentlessly. He reached down to grab his prick and found Alexa's head on his stomach.

"I thought I was dreaming," he muttered, jerking up from the pillow and peering at her.

"About what?" she asked with an impish smile while fondling his cock with one hand before running the liquid tip of her tongue up his rigid shaft. "I thought you were going to wake me," she said between moist caresses.

"You need your sleep," he said, moving his hands over her bare bottom. Her skin had a delicacy he hadn't remembered for all his dreams.

"I need you to love me," she said. Her wide green eyes flecked with gold were suddenly serious.

Mark pulled her up to straddle him and she bent low offering him her breasts. Taking one hot nubbin between his lips, he applied gentle suction while he probed her with the tip of his penis, teasing her.

"Now," she whispered, "now."

She forced herself down on him, and he drove upward, filling her with one swift motion. Wet and tight, she felt exactly the way he remembered her. She shimmied down on him, taking his length deep inside her. With her face in the hollow of his neck, her breathing hot against his skin, she moved up and down. Drawing herself up, up, up until he barely remained inside her, Alexa then plunged downward and wiggled. Over and over she wantonly repeated her movements, until he bit an imaginary bullet to keep from coming. Inwardly he smiled. Whatever had happened with Brad hadn't affected her desire for him. Craving release, he flipped her onto her back and thrust into her again and again.

She was home; she was his.

As Alexa climaxed, she felt herself clawing at Mark's back and heard herself calling his name and telling him she loved him. After weeks of pretending, nothing was sweeter, more satisfying than making love to the one man she adored. Satiated, she snuggled into the crook of his arm. The heavy, rapid-fire thud of his heart under her head had to be the most secure, comforting sound she'd ever heard, she decided.

"Where were you last night?" she whispered. "All day?"

"Walking around thinking about us."

"Thinking what?"

"What I should have told you in Khartoum." Mark kissed her gently and looked directly into her eyes. "I love you and I want to marry you."

Alexa held up her hand. The enormous emerald winked at them. "I'm wearing your ring. The minute I put it on I became yours." She kissed him, her lips lingering on his as she whispered, "Nothing will change that."

"You know, when I thought you'd died my world went with you. Nothing in my life would have been the same without you. As I walked around London today, I decided the only way to love someone is to think of what you'd do if you lost them."

"Darling, you won't lose me. This is forever."

## AUTHOR'S NOTE

On December 7, 1988, the International Committee of the Red Cross carried supplies to starving refugees in southern Sudan, torn by a famine caused by a five-year-old civil war. This was the first time since the Sudan People's Liberation Army rebelled in early 1983 that planes were allowed to fly into the area with guarantees from both sides that they wouldn't be shot down. The airlift, slated to continue indefinitely to help the more than six million refugees in the south, came after Sudanese Prime Minister Sadek Mahdi accepted a preliminary peace plan agreed upon by the rebels and the members of Sudan's ruling coalition. As part of the agreement, Islamic law was suspended until a national constitutional conference can be held.

Following the accord, British Midland Bank forgave Sudan's debt, donating the money to UNICEF for health services and crop development in the southern Sudan. In pioneering this new form of debt relief to Third World countries, the bank hopes that other institutions will follow its example. UNICEF officials stated that this type of relief represents the most effective way that nations with severe internal problems can overcome the debilitating effects of debt to Western nations while building a better future for their people.